About the Author

When **Virginia Heath** was a little girl it took her ages to fall asleep, so she made up stories in her head to pass the time while she was staring at the ceiling. As she got older, the stories became more complicated, sometimes taking weeks to get to the happy ending. Then one day, she decided to embrace the insomnia and start writing them down. Over twenty books and three Romantic Novel of the Year Award nominations later, it still takes her forever to fall asleep.

Regency Rebels

Regency Rebels:

Wild Attraction

VIRGINIA HEATH

MILLS & BOON

First Published in Great Britain 2023
By Mills & Boon, an imprint of HarperCollins*Publishers* Ltd,
1 London Bridge Street, London, SE1 9GF

www.harpercollins.co.uk

HarperCollins*Publishers*
Macken House, 39/40 Mayor Street Upper,
Dublin 1, D01 C9W8, Ireland

ISBN: 978-0-263-32121-0

MIX
Paper | Supporting
responsible forestry
FSC™ C007454

A WARRINER
TO TEMPT HER

For all my former students at the Hathaway Academy. Believe you are good enough and always follow your dreams.

Chapter One

July 1818

Dr Joseph Warriner sat down behind his desk with an air of resignation. Despite today's genuine attempt at resolve, he realised such efforts were ultimately futile. His situation was pathetic. Worse—he was pathetic. He flicked out the dented gold pocket watch he always wore secured to his sensible dark waistcoat and knew, before even looking at the dial, it was almost eight o'clock. The fact he had checked the stupid thing every two minutes for the last half an hour irritated him, as did the sorry realisation he had also been drawn to participate in this ridiculous ritual for almost a month now. Drawn like a sailor to the sirens.

And for what? One transient dance exactly twenty-eight days ago. A few exchanged, meaningless pleasantries whilst he had stood with her other eager admirers, tossed randomly like discarded breadcrumbs to a yard full of chickens. Or like today, for a surreptitious glimpse of the cause of his torment, guiltily stolen through the heavy lace that covered the windows,

when he knew, deep down, his foolish heart was once again chasing a shadow.

The whole sorry situation was pathetic.

Angrily, he snapped the watch closed and turned his chair towards the window and waited. Just like he had every Tuesday or Friday morning in the last few weeks, at precisely eight o'clock, the glossy black carriage turned into the square exactly on time. It was market day in Retford and she always came to shop on market day. And the fact she was always so punctual also irritated him. Just for once he wished she would be late and he would be forced to attend to his first patient of the day, whose appointment was now timed for five past the hour on market days instead of on the dot of eight as usual. Another sign of how lamentable this folly was. It would be much better to do something worthwhile rather than waste his time engaging in this pointless ritual, especially as he already had a mountain of tasks to complete today. But, no—this carriage was a creature of habit, much like its vexing occupant, and it slowed to a stop just past the window of Joe's surgery as it always did. To torture him.

Carefully, he moved the very edge of the curtain so that he could get a better view and watched as the footman opened the carriage door. After a few seconds, one surprisingly sensibly shod foot, with an intriguingly shapely ankle, appeared. His breath hitched.

He had never seen her ankles before and was staggered a common formation of bones would affect him so. How many ankles had he seen in his career? Hundreds? Thousands, probably, yet the sight of hers made his heart beat faster.

The glorious ankles was closely followed by a bonnet-

covered head. Without even seeing it, he knew her golden hair would be arranged in a becoming and fashionable style, but that already several of the silky strands, the colour of which he had often considered to be the exact shade of wheat freshly harvested and kissed by the sun, would have resent being tamed and begun escaping its pins. True to form, these would frame her bewitching face in tiny spiral curls he yearned to wind around his fingers.

Of course, he could never do that. If he did—well, then he would probably have to remove every single pin so he could enjoy watching that mass of curls tumble over her shoulders and down her back. Especially now he had seen those ankles. He closed his eyes and savoured the fantasy for a moment.

Lady Clarissa Beaumont.

Joe exhaled slowly and watched her gather herself together. For a fleeting moment she turned and he saw just her cheek—perfect peaches and cream skin—but was cruelly denied the sight of her wide, almond-shaped blue eyes in a shade so glorious that it would have made even the Caribbean Sea jealous. He caught a fleeting glimpse of her plump pink lips as she smiled at the footman and a bolt of ridiculous jealousy surged through him at the innocent exchange.

Because the delectable Clarissa, fêted society beauty, was largely ignorant of the fact he even existed. Thank heavens the ethereal Clarissa was also blissfully unaware the man currently hidden behind the curtain of his office was suffering from a terminal case of unrequited love. More painful this morning, for some reason, than it had ever been before. Probably because of those ankles, he realised. A few

inches of silk-covered leg and he was already burning with lust. The lust was a new sensation. Up until today his love had been pure, the courtly kind of old and not sullied with that base, human emotion. But up until today he had been denied the sight of those magnificent ankles, so he supposed his sudden physical reaction was to be expected. What was love without passion anyway?

She turned and his heart soared—then promptly plummeted to his toes. She was quite the wrong sister. Not Lady Clarissa Beaumont at all, charming, blonde and effervescent. But Lady Isabella Beaumont. Pretty, yes, and clearly in possession of a damn fine pair of legs, but rather a serious, unsociable individual. And very definitely a brunette. Her ruler-straight dark locks suited her dour personality. She took the basket the footman offered her, stood and regarded the marketplace with obvious disdain and strode away purposefully. Hardly a surprise when Lady Isabella did everything with purpose, whether that be blatantly reading a book during an assembly when every other girl was dancing or doing good deeds.

Whilst she always accompanied the beautiful Clarissa on market days, until this week Joe and the scary Lady Isabella had collided only briefly. Once at the monthly assembly held in the village hall, where she was stood next to her lovely sister. For the duration of the festivities, as far as Joe could ascertain, she had worn what he suspected was a permanent expression of complete disgust, as if the provincial society of dankest Nottinghamshire was quite beneath her. Fortunately, she tended to fade into the background stood next to her sparkling sister, so Joe rarely noticed her.

That wasn't completely true. He always noticed her; he just wished he hadn't. Why would he waste time staring at the darkness when he could gaze at sunshine? Yet something about those dark, serious eyes always drew him, nevertheless, and he found himself frowning. A little bewildered. A little irritated, yet oddly curious. Goodness knew why. It was almost as irritating as yearning for her unobtainable sister.

However, since last week, he had seen Lady Isabella twice at the foundling home run by his sister-in-law Letty, so he had no choice in the matter. She was volunteering in the infirmary and watched him like a hawk whenever he visited and while he examined the young patients with such determined concentration, and such a sour expression, it made him feel as though he was not a particularly good doctor at all. It was most disconcerting. Yet she never said a word. Not one! Preferring to loiter in the doorway as he worked and then bolt the moment he turned. It was all very curious. All very odd. Much like Lady Isabella.

If anything, Isabella was vinegar to her sister's honey. Always so stand-offish. Devoid of any discernible sense of humour as far as he could make out. Dour. Certainly rude. Perhaps even a little intimidating. He felt his lip curl at the thought.

He waited with bated breath for the appearance of the other Beaumont. The one his poor heart yearned to see, but alas, the footman smartly closed the carriage door and took his place at the back, forcing Joe to accept the disappointing fact he would not see the object of his unrequited affections today after all. A crushing blow when he had been so looking forward to it, even though he knew it was an exercise in futility and

one which rendered him utterly pathetic. Lady Clarissa would never consider him.

Aside from his unfortunate Warriner ancestors and the dreadful family reputation which still lingered in Retford like a bad smell, he was merely the brother to an earl with no hope of ever getting a title, what with another brother and already two robust nephews in the way. Not that Joe had ever coveted any title other than Dr, but women like Lady Clarissa were raised to care about such things. She was the daughter of the Earl of Braxton and would one day, no doubt, marry another title and live in a grand stately pile surrounded by miles and miles of her rich husband's land. Such ladies did not marry third sons nor did they marry doctors. His job was as gruesome as it was rewarding. Sometimes he came home with his clothing covered in all manner of unmentionable things—none of which was suitable for the tender sensibilities of a lovely, well-bred woman like her.

If he was lucky, he was able to sleep for a whole night uninterrupted. More often than not, his sleep would be disturbed by a frantic knock on the door and he would be summoned to the bedside of another patient. He got called away from social functions and dinners. He could not even guarantee he would be left in peace on Christmas Day. Not that he minded those things either. It was who he was. His vocation and he would not have it any other way, but it was a big leap of faith to expect another person to be so forgiving of the demands his career placed upon him. Especially if that person was so exquisite she could have her pick from a crop of suitors much more impressive than him.

Mrs Patterson, his formidable housekeeper, rapped

her knuckles swiftly on the other side of his consulting room door, bringing Joe unceremoniously, and blessedly, back to the present.

'Dr Warriner, Mr Simmons is here for his appointment.'

'Send him in, Mrs Patterson.' Joe sat up smartly and put on the wire-rimmed spectacles he needed to read his notes. The allotted time for self-indulgent dreams was over.

Bella stared at the already crowded marketplace and immediately felt nauseous. Usually she made the short walk across the square with Clarissa, which meant it was not as daunting, but her sister had claimed to be ill to get out of the chore of holding Bella's hand, so drastic times called for drastic measures. Bella could have stayed at home. But at home she would soon become bored because she found no purpose in embroidery. Filling her day with purpose took her mind off the fear and allowed her to leave the house. Purpose was making her better, or so she fervently hoped, and she had to be brave. She would conquer this fear logically. Scientifically.

It was just a short walk to the foundling home.

It was broad daylight.

And nobody here meant her any harm.

She could and *would* do this!

In less than five minutes she would be safely ensconced in the infirmary. The place she had only just discovered she preferred above all others in the world.

It was rare that she ever felt truly comfortable enough to be herself any more. Ever since *the incident*, as her family whisperingly called it behind her

back, a huge chunk of her character had crawled deep
inside her body and was too terrified to come out.
Being well meaning and good-natured had been the
cause of it, after all, so it was hardly any wonder Bella
was reluctant to be so trusting again around a man. Or
feel comfortable in crowds. Or go outside alone, for that
matter, where danger lurked. Perhaps coming here un-
accompanied had been foolhardy. Hasty. She should
turn around and get back in the carriage...

You are pathetic! the real her screamed. *You man-
aged to live twenty years without coming to any harm
at all. You cannot let one incident dictate the way you
live your life.*

The voice of the real her had been becoming louder
and louder for months now. A constant voice in her
head which emboldened her to remain hopeful and de-
termined. From its cave inside her soul, it parried with
pithy retorts, tackled problems with a level, logical and
practical head, revelled in irony, argued against idiocy
whilst constantly issuing witty and sometimes hilari-
ous comments about the world around her. That voice
might not yet be strong enough to make its way up her
vocal chords and out of her once-tart mouth, but it was
there. Somewhere. Chivvying her on.

*Those foundlings need you. And think of all the won-
derful things you are learning.*

Bella set her jaw and stared across the crowded
square. Those sick foundlings *did* need her—she was
discovering so much about medicine in the infirmary
that the hours flew by. For the first time in her life she
was doing something she had always yearned to do,
something which would have been frowned upon in
London, so she had never been able to pursue it. But

sleepy Retford wasn't London and as it was unlikely any of her parents' society acquaintances would ever hear of it, and because her mama and papa had been delighted Bella had finally found some interest in life again, they had allowed her to volunteer.

Gently bred young ladies were not supposed to find the study of anatomy or healing interesting, yet spending time with those children, learning about what ailed them and the best way to treat it, was one of the most rewarding things Bella had ever done. She had a sneaking suspicion it was her calling, her vocation, and that she had always been meant to be a nurse. Finally, she was putting into practice all the things she had read in the scientific journals she had always devoured like biscuits. It also gave her enough purpose that she quite forgot to be petrified for huge chunks of the day. What was that, if it was not progress? Frankly, she was counting the minutes until she could be back there, roll up her sleeves and help those poor cherubs get better.

All she had to do was walk across this market square alone. Because Bella was tired of always being frightened and the real her was right. Living in fear smacked of surrender and she was determined never to let that bad man win.

She forced herself to smile politely at one of the market traders who greeted her, ignoring the irrational panic which occurred whenever she was close to a man. If she had been a little more observant and a little less terrified, she would have noticed the precarious basket of potatoes on his stall. But because she was feeling exposed and her tenuous grasp on logic was slipping, she did not see the laden basket topple, nor did she see a surge of muddy potatoes as they cascaded from the

table like a waterfall and rolled haphazardly across the ground towards her. Too late, Bella turned, allowing a couple of the careening vegetables the opportunity to disappear, like mice in a haystack, beneath her trailing skirts and tangle hopelessly beneath her feet.

Her body lunged sideways when she stepped on one. Her heavy basket tilted, aiding gravity to pull her towards the floor at an alarming rate. Bella landed awkwardly on her front with enough force to knock all her breath from her lungs. The subsequent sharp pain in her ankle brought tears to her eyes. The palms of her hands, now muddied, burned angrily in protest. The puddles floating on the hard cobblestones were already seeping through her clothing whilst humiliation relentlessly seeped into her soul. If there was one thing Bella now hated above all others, it was being the centre of attention when invisible was safe.

Several market traders and locals rushed to her aid, but she assured them that she was quite all right and tried to stand. White-hot pain shot up her leg and forced her to remain exactly where she was. To make matters worse, she helplessly watched the back of the Braxton carriage turn out of the market square as it headed home and her only means of escaping this dreadful spectacle leaving with it. She smiled weakly at the growing crowd of onlookers and tried to pull together the tattered shreds of her dignity whilst fighting the panic of being at the mercy of others. Most of them male.

'My lady—I am *so* sorry.' The stallholder twisted his felt cap in his hands nervously. 'Are you seriously hurt? Shall I fetch Dr Warriner? His office is just across the square.'

Mortified by the prospect of even greater humiliation in front of the brilliant Dr Warriner, Bella shook her head. The very last person she wanted to witness her clumsy stupidity was the handsome doctor. The man who, despite being a man, made her silly heart flutter every single time he spoke to her, thus rendering her mostly mute. Probably because of his brilliance, rather than his handsomeness, but it was difficult to be sure. 'That will not be necessary—I think I will be able to stand in a moment or two.' She would crawl home if she had to.

Two things soon became apparent. Firstly, standing was an impossibility. Bella tried three times and each time fresh, blinding pain shot up her leg and brought tears to her eyes. Secondly, despite her protests to the contrary, somebody had called the good doctor after all. The crowd of onlookers were parting like the Red Sea and he was suddenly striding purposefully towards her.

'It's just my ankle… I would prefer you not to waste your time on such a triviality.' Bella tried to push herself up once again using her hands and failed miserably. The poor man had genuine sick people to heal and certainly far more important things to deal with than a clumsy, irrational girl's superficial injury. 'I shall put some ice on it when I get home and keep it elevated.' She turned her head away and silently willed him to disappear.

'Please do not try to stand, my lady.' He knelt beside her. 'I will need to take a look to properly assess the damage first.' One arm slipped beneath her legs, making her flinch.

He was touching her!

Instinctively, she stiffened and tried to shuffle away. Undeterred, he continued. 'Place your arms around my shoulders. I promise I won't drop you.'

Good gracious! He intended to carry her and create even more of a spectacle. 'I am sure I can manage to hobble to your surgery, Dr Warriner.' Perhaps then everyone would stop gawping at her when nowadays she preferred to blend in. Except she wouldn't hobble towards his surgery. She would drag herself back up the lane to the safety of home and never leave it again. Logic could go to hell in a hand cart. She never should have listened to the voice. She never should have come out all alone, but staying home after her sister had claimed a sniffle and remained in bed had felt like defeat. Clarissa had made no secret of the fact she was beyond tired of being her sister's keeper. Not when it had been over a year and it wasn't Clarissa's fault Bella had suffered *the incident*. Bella had to get over it because it could have been *worse*.

Worse didn't bear thinking about. Unfortunately, she thought about it all the time.

The doctor slanted her a superior glance. 'Hobble, will you? And create more damage for me to fix in the process, no doubt? No, my lady—I will carry you if you don't mind.'

But she did mind. He was a man and she was now a spectacle. A spectacle who was on the cusp of bursting into tears and apprising everyone of the fact that she was no longer capable of being rational, not quite right in the head any more, yet so desperate to be right again.

Chapter Two

You are being ridiculous! Bella scrunched her eyes tightly closed, gripped his shoulders and willed herself lighter in the faint hope it would all be over soon. He hoisted her into the air and began to walk across the square. Less than half a minute later, he gripped her harder still and his breathing became more laboured with exertion. It was then she decided that willing herself lighter was not working in the slightest and began to wish herself invisible instead. Mercifully, he covered the distance to the surgery quickly, and once inside, he deposited her gently on an examination table.

'I need to fetch some things. I will only be a moment.'

He returned with his housekeeper in tow, no doubt for propriety's sake. Bella was ridiculously grateful for the woman's presence and tried to relax.

'Where does it hurt?'

She touched her left leg in response. 'My ankle. I was sabotaged by a potato.' She smiled weakly, praying the fear did not show in her face. *Think logically!* He was simply doing his job. He had no intention of

hurting her. Perhaps if she repeated that mantra, her heartbeat would begin to slow and the tight bands of fear constricting her ribs would loosen.

Bella bit the inside of her cheek as he matter-of-factly lifted the hem of her ruined dress and carefully pushed it to her knee.

He has no intention of hurting you. He is simply doing his job.

To her own ears her breathing was laboured. Dr Warriner appeared to sense her rising panic, although he thought it was caused by pain rather than the acute reminder of another time when a man had lifted her skirts...one filthy hand clasped over her mouth while the other was fumbling with the buttons on his breeches. Touching her.

The unwanted memory made her whimper.

'Breathe slowly and deeply. That will help.'

She did as he suggested, her eyes never leaving his hands.

He has no intention of hurting you.

His gentle touch around the bones of her ankle did not feel like the worst sort of violation.

He is simply doing his job.

He was a doctor. A man of science. He had the deepest blue eyes Bella had ever seen. Bluer even than Clarissa's. They were kind eyes, she realised.

Patient.

The voice deep inside of her soothed that she could trust him and she forced herself to believe it.

Slowly, and with surprising tenderness, he removed her half-boot and gently examined the swelling around her ankle. His dark brows were drawn together slightly. He had a good nose, Bella mused to avoid thinking

about the past, neither too small nor too large, and a strong chin that was already showing evidence of a very dark beard, even though he had clearly shaved it this morning. His black hair curled slightly at the snowy-white collar of his shirt and fell softly forward over one side of his brow in a slightly boyish manner. The natural style reminded her that the good doctor was not one for pomades or unnecessary frills like the dandies in town. She liked that about him.

Not that he needed them. He was incredibly hand-some. Bella had surprised herself by thinking it the first time she had seen him at the local assembly, be-cause it had been over a year since she had thought such things about a man. She had never seen him wear anything other than stark, dark black or navy blue, and although he was always smartly turned out, his attire gave off the air of a man both comfortable in his own skin and far too busy with important things to pay much attention to his wardrobe. He was a true man of science and it showed.

He had handsome hands, too, if indeed hands could be described as such. Clean, sensibly trimmed finger-nails, but capable. So very different to the hands of that scoundrel. Healer's hands. Just like hers.

She found herself scrutinising his technique as the panic began to wane. After all, he had been properly schooled in the precise art of medicine whilst all her knowledge had come from whatever books she could find. Those books were no substitute for practical experience.

'Mrs Patterson, would you mind…' His words trailed off and he wore an odd expression as he gestured to his housekeeper to remove the stocking on Bella's left

leg. Feeling horribly exposed and conscious she had been intently staring at him, she lay back on the bed and fixed her gaze on the ceiling as his large hands meticulously prodded and probed her foot, calf and ankle.

He is simply doing his job. Stop being a pathetic coward. It's irritating. You're irritating. Be logical.

Once she had succumbed to the inevitability of her situation, and repeated her new mantra another dozen times silently in her head, it turned out not to be such an unpleasant experience. He had lovely warm palms and his deft touch left a trail of tingles on her skin which caused havoc with her pulse. Bizarrely, it had nothing to do with fear or panic. Bella knew those emotions too well and this was nothing like them. How peculiar.

His fingers suddenly left her skin and the real her willed them back. In fact, the real her was positively swooning. 'The good news is that it is not broken.' Bella watched those capable hands as he absently returned her skirts to order. He had obviously touched a significant number of ladies' legs on a regular basis, she concluded, because he looked decidedly nonplussed with hers. 'But it *is* badly sprained and bruised, so you will have to keep your weight off it for a few days.' He smiled his detached doctor smile and spoke quickly to his housekeeper.

'Mrs Patterson—could you fetch some ice and some towels, please?'

They would be alone! She missed the end of the conversation due to the hammering panic in her head and the older woman left to do his bidding. Bella levered herself to sit, just in case she needed to run, wincing as cuts on her hands protested at being used to lever her.

'Let me see.' He said this in a reassuringly detached

and professional way as he took both her hands in his. Instantly, her silly pulse leapt even as she froze, then continued to bounce around frenetically as he turned them palms up to examine the filthy grazes caused by her fall. Strangely, there was no urge to run at being so intimately close to him. She hoped that was more evidence of progress. 'These need cleaning.'

He dropped her hands dispassionately and went across the room to a large washstand. After pouring water into the bowl, he added a generous dash of clear liquid from a bottle next to the jug, and after tossing a clean towel over his shoulder, he carried the basin towards her.

'Put them in here, please.'

Bella plunged her hands into the water and immediately snatched them out again as it stung so very badly.

'What is in there—acid?' She eyed the water warily.

'Gin. I have noticed that wounds regularly cleaned with alcohol are less susceptible to infection. Besides, it is also very cheap. And I would prefer not to waste good brandy.'

He was attempting to put her at her ease as he did the children in the infirmary. He had such a lovely voice. Deep. Kind. Yet Bella blinked back at him rather than smile at the little joke and saw his own smile slide off his face within seconds. He did not like her and who could blame him when she could not stand her new self either?

A blush of shame bloomed instantly. Here he was, being nothing but nice, and all she could do was blink? Once upon a time she would have responded with something appropriate. Friendly. Usually funny. She missed that girl and willed her back every single day.

But the old Bella was missing, presumed dead, and the new one was not quite right in the head.

For the only time in living memory, she fleetingly wished she was her sister. Clarissa would have replied with something witty and charming, happy to talk. Bella remained mute. Even her real self could think of nothing to say, so the silence was quite deafening. Once again the atmosphere became uncomfortable, something she was painfully aware was brought about at her doing, and she wondered if she could drown herself quickly in the shallow basin of water—putting them both out of their misery—while he continued to dab at her hands with the towel.

Satisfied that they were thoroughly clean, he then patted them dry and went to the wall of shelves at the back of the consulting room and rummaged for a pot of salve. He opened it and gently applied the ointment to the worst of the grazes.

'That smells like honey.' She willed the words out. It was a desperate and feeble attempt at normal conversation, but at that moment it was all that she had. At least she was conversing with him. A man. Surely she could take heart it signalled progress?

He resealed the pot and put it to one side. 'That's because it mostly is honey. We waste it on bread, but the Ancient Egyptians realised that it has exceptional healing powers. Like the gin, I have found honey acts as a barrier against infection. And is perfect on bread, of course.'

He smiled briefly and it did funny things to Bella's insides. She tried to ignore it and forced herself to stop biting her lip and reply. 'The Egyptians had metal scalpels, bone saws…' This comment earned her another

odd look, as if she were the most peculiar of females, and made her voice trail off. 'Or so I have read…'

'You pass the time by reading about surgical instruments?'

'I am not an empty-headed ornament.' And now she sounded snippy and defensive. Clarissa would certainly never try to engage a gentleman in discourse about bone saws! She would smile and compliment him on his superior knowledge. But then Clarissa had been born charming and Bella had lost that part of herself, and her current circumstances were *particularly* trying.

He was saved from having to respond by Mrs Patterson returning with the ice. It had already been smashed into small chips, which he wrapped in a thin square of linen and placed over her swollen ankle. 'Your curricle will be five minutes, Dr Warriner.'

He intended to take her home!

Just her and him. The lane to her house was long and deserted. There were trees and bushes on either side. Trees and bushes would hide her from the world if he had a mind to drag her behind them… Fresh fear began to claw in her gut.

'No! Send a message so that my father's carriage can collect me directly.'

He straightened, frowned and pinned her with his deep blue stare. 'Suit yourself. Mrs Patterson will show you to the parlour, *my lady*. I have other patients to attend.'

Good lord, she was rude! Joe was still smarting from her peculiar behaviour hours later as he walked towards her front door. She hadn't even thanked him

for his time. Just glared at him as if he was offensive, her face wrinkling in disgust every time he had touched her, and she spoke to him worse than to a misbehaving servant. Whilst he knew full well some folk dealt better with pain than others, he had never seen anyone behave quite so badly over a sprained ankle in his life. Or perhaps it was not the injury at all which had made her so curt and obnoxious. Perhaps that was exactly how she always was? It was a pity. She was lovely. If she learned some manners and smiled occasionally, she would be as dazzling as her sister. Perhaps more so. Those dark almond eyes, framed with even darker lashes, were quite beautiful. When they weren't narrowed suspiciously at him.

Maybe it was his surname which elicited her hostility? Despite the best efforts of all four Warriner brothers, the memory of their infamous father and grandfather still left a sour taste in the mouths of the locals. Nobody trusted a Warriner. It made no difference to some that his eldest brother, Jack, and his wife, Letty, were now hugely philanthropic within the area. Nor that his brother Jamie and his wife, Cassie, were responsible for bringing many tourists to Retford as their readers travelled across the country to see with their own eyes the locations of the hugely successful *Orange Blossom* books. Only a few had truly thawed enough to accept the family were decent. A great many more were waiting for them to return to type.

Lady Isabella had obviously been swayed by the malicious gossip and he disliked her for that. She had lived in Retford little more than a month but had already passed judgement! If he were as nefarious as his ancestors, would he have taken time out of his

busy day to visit the most ungrateful patient he had ever attended?

However, Lady Isabella's injury did give him the perfect excuse to call at her home, something he had desperately wanted to do since dancing with the delectable Clarissa at the assembly last month. In fairness, the physician inside him needed to check on his patient more, which was the main reason he was knocking on the Earl of Braxton's door. He sincerely doubted the dour Isabella would be grateful, yet he was still compelled to do it. Sometimes his own diligence irritated him. As much as he wished he wasn't so softhearted and desperate to help people, especially those who treated him with nothing but disdain in return, Joe could never seem to help himself. He would never get to sleep if he had not first reassured himself she was feeling better. It had been a nasty sprain and occasionally a bad fall caused clots to form in the blood. Such a complication was a rarity, especially in one so young, but it was better to be safe than sorry. Another brief examination of those splendid legs was necessary, no matter how distasteful the patient was.

Truth be told, Joe was also feeling guilty for enjoying the sight of her ankles. Once that silk stocking had been removed, he had had a moment where he forgot to be a detached physician and had gazed upon her silky skin like a man. He never did that. He had sworn the Hippocratic Oath solemnly and took his responsibilities far too seriously to ever allow himself to be waylaid with inappropriate thoughts before. However, Lady Isabella's habit of regarding him as she would a Viking marauder about to pillage a village soon put paid to his temporary lapse of judgement and he was back to being

irritated by her attitude again in seconds. So irritated he almost forgot about her splendid legs.

Joe rapped the knocker smartly. This afternoon's visit was strictly professional. If he happened to collide with the adorable Lady Clarissa in the process, then it would certainly make it more tolerable. As would the sight of those legs which were unfortunately attached to the other, vexing, Beaumont.

The door opened quickly.

'Could you inform the Earl of Braxton that Dr Warriner is here to check upon his daughter? I attended her injuries this morning.'

The austere butler appeared confused. 'The physician is already in attendance, sir.'

Of course he was. No doubt the family had immediately summoned that aged old fool Dr Bentley the moment they learned their precious daughter had been treated by a Warriner. Usually Joe tried to ignore the old prejudices, but sometimes it grated. Especially when he was a far better doctor than the quack they preferred.

'Even so, I should like to see her, for my own peace of mind, you understand. I will not delay the family long. I will be in and out quicker than a ferret in a rabbit hole.'

Chapter Three

The affronted butler invited Joe to wait in the hallway. A few moments later he was ushered into the drawing room, where he was met by the Countess of Braxton. 'Dr Warriner! I cannot thank you enough for coming to Bella's aid.' She squeezed his hands effusively and appeared far too grateful, almost on the cusp of tears, which he supposed made up for her daughter's blatant disregard.

'No thanks are needed,' he said as his eyes automatically scanned the room for Clarissa. The object of his desire was sat in the far corner of the room, embroidering something on a small hoop, and did not bother looking up. Her usually smiling face contorted into a frown. A niggling voice in his head told him she was rude, but he ruthlessly blocked it out. An angel like Lady Clarissa couldn't be rude. Not like the other one. His eyes drifted to the other side of the room where the younger sister was sat on a sofa, her injured ankle raised on pillows and her eyes narrowed in hostility. Next to her, Dr Bentley was packing away his equipment, which included his ever-present bleeding

cups—the old fool's usual treatment for everything. He glanced at Joe and nodded curtly.

'Warriner.'

Always just Warriner. Never the title he had earned. The upstart. The charlatan who had the audacity to set up a rival practice in Bentley's town, taking money which should rightly be his. What did that Warriner know anyway? Joe had studied medicine only since the age of eight. Toiled at medical school in Edinburgh in order to qualify top of his class. Built up a sizeable practice despite the horrendous reputation of the Warriner family because he was damn good at what he did. And he had worked hard, honing his craft every single day since. One of these days Joe would allow himself the pleasure of saying exactly what he thought, then quashed the idea instantly. 'Good afternoon, *Dr* Bentley. How is *our* patient?'

'She is *my* patient now and as such I will not discuss her treatments with *you*.' Dr Bentley turned towards the Countess. 'Good day, your ladyship. I will await your further instructions regarding the *other* matter and hope Lady Isabella sees some sense shortly.' And off he marched out without a backwards glance. Bentley was obviously miffed. Clearly Lady Isabella had been a delight for him, too.

Because it was what he had come here for, Joe walked towards the sofa and smiled. 'How is your ankle?'

'Better now.' She appeared about to burst into tears. The tears tugged at his heartstrings. He was always too soft and prone to want to rescue. A fault he had apparently been born with and one he had long given up fighting. Without being asked, he lowered himself on

to the corner of the sofa and took her hand. He almost dropped it again when odd tingles shot up his arm and he found himself frowning at the anomaly. That had never happened before and certainly shouldn't be happening with her.

'Sprains can hurt like the devil, but in the main they heal quickly with rest.' He glanced down at her raised foot and the obvious swelling. 'You need ice.'

'Dr Bentley said hot water was best for sprains.' Lady Braxton appeared apologetic at usurping Joe's advice. 'He insisted the ice pack was removed.'

'Ah...' Tact and diplomacy were second nature, especially when it came to Dr Bentley's diagnoses. As physicians, they were always at odds. Dr Bentley was mired in tradition and Joe dared to break that mould. 'Tell me, Lady Isabella, did your ankle feel better with or without the ice?'

'With,' she said without hesitation, 'I queried it at the time.' It was clear she held Dr Bentley in little regard, so she evidently had a brain underneath all the attitude. Joe smiled in encouragement and watched her dip her eyes.

'She also refused to be bled.' Lady Braxton appeared at her wits' end at her daughter's stubbornness. 'Do you think she needs to be bled, Dr Warriner?'

'I cannot see any cause for it.' Joe could never see any cause for it as he had never seen the painful procedure achieve any beneficial effects. However, saying such things out loud tended to bother people brought up to revere the wisdom of physicians—most of whom still clung to ideas from the Dark Ages—as well as the supposed health benefits of slimy leeches. 'Ice and rest are the best treatments for sprains. If the pain is severe,

some willow bark tea would not go amiss either.' She peeked up at him through her ridiculously long, dark lashes and offered him the ghost of a smile. More tingles bounced along his nerve endings and his collar felt suddenly tight. Perhaps Clarissa was watching him. Joe ignored the desire to turn around to check. 'Do you mind if I take a quick look? Just to be certain it is nothing more than a common sprain?'

Lady Isabella nodded warily, the smile now gone, and bit down on her bottom lip, so he did a swift examination and sat back. 'Most of the swelling has already gone down. I dare say it will be gone completely by Friday and you will be dancing at the assembly with your sister... Will you *all* be attending the assembly on Saturday?'

How pathetically unsubtle he sounded to his own ears. Joe cast a glance towards his patient's sister, who was still jabbing her embroidery with a needle and had yet to acknowledge his presence. He silently willed her to look to no avail, ignoring the niggling voice of outrage in his head. Angels weren't meant to be rude. They were meant to be...well, angelic. Maybe she hadn't noticed him. A weak excuse, but she deserved it.

'Yes, of course we are going!' Lady Braxton smiled encouragingly at her daughter. 'And it is splendid news that Bella may be fit enough to dance! Would you like some tea, Dr Warriner?'

'I wouldn't want to trouble you...'

'It's no trouble at all. No trouble at all.'

She bustled off to ring the bell, leaving Joe with Lady Isabella. Bella—a very pretty name and one he was not sure suited her. It was too vivacious for the quiet, introverted woman next to him. Bella conjured

up images of a different sort of girl. One who was
witty and a pleasure to be around rather than the one
currently judging him in silence. At a loss as to what
else to do or say to her, and in view of her older sister's
blatant indifference, Joe smiled his reassuring doctor
smile. 'Is the pain very bad?'

'No.' She stared down at her hands and the cus-
tomary brittle awkwardness she always incited hung
heavily in the air. The big question was, did he bother
attempting further conversation with either sister, when
one was intent on ignoring him and the other looked
like she was disgusted by him, or did he quietly wait
for the tea? Or better yet, did he make a hasty excuse
and escape? Joe had never felt so uncomfortable in his
own skin before. He was seriously contemplating the
leaving when she finally spoke in a voice so small he
had to strain his ears to hear. 'I should have thanked
you for your help this morning. It was unforgivably
rude not to have done so at the time...but I am not very
good at... Since the... What I mean is...' She sighed
and seemed to steel herself. 'What I mean is...I wasn't
quite myself.'

Her dark eyes were troubled as they briefly locked
with his before she stared back at her clasped hands
again. A very becoming pink blush burned on her
cheeks. A blush which did not fit with the sour and
dour character he had attributed to her. Was it possible
Lady Isabella was shy, rather than rude? Or was his in-
nate good nature frantically hunting for an excuse for
her bad behaviour? He did have a tendency to attribute
better character traits to people than they actually had.
Women especially. Joe decided to probe further rather
than trust his overly benevolent instincts.

'You had just been sabotaged by a potato. I doubt I would have been particularly sociable if the tables had been turned.' Those dark eyes slowly lifted and locked with his.

'I think you are being kind.'

He was, but she didn't need to know that. Glancing at the book lying open face down next to her, he acknowledged it with a nod. 'A scientific tome?'

The blush burned even brighter at being caught reading a flagrantly romantic novel. 'Sometimes I need to be reminded the world is a good place.'

Joe would have questioned her odd response, but her mother was back, conducting servants carrying the tea things and a small table which was arranged close to the invalid. 'I hope you have a sweet tooth, Dr Warriner, as there is plenty of cake. And biscuits, too! Both my girls are extremely fond of biscuits. Come along, Clarissa! Come join us for tea!'

The object of his affection slapped down her embroidery with a huff and sauntered to the table like a surly child. Immediately, Joe stood and inclined his head. 'Lady Clarissa. I hope you are well.'

'Actually, Dr Warriner, I am *not* well. I have a cold. But my health must be ignored for the sake of dear Bella, as she is the one everyone *must* worry about. *All* of the time.'

'You have the tiniest of sniffles, Clarissa dear.' Lady Braxton was embarrassed. 'And your sister could have broken her leg!'

'I am here and can attend to you, too, my lady.' Good grief, he sounded eager. Far too eager. He pasted on a professional expression of concern. 'What are your symptoms?'

Lady Clarissa cast her sister a brittle smile and plopped her bottom on the chair just placed for her by a footman. It bothered Joe she did not thank the poor fellow for his efforts. 'My head hurts and my nose is quite blocked.'

'Congestion of the sinuses does cause headaches. Do you have a fever?' He avoided the temptation to reach out and touch her forehead.

'I am a little warm.'

'Something which might be caused by your insistence on wearing that wool frock in July.' Lady Braxton's eyes were shooting daggers at her daughter. There was an undercurrent here, a dynamic Joe didn't quite understand. Jealousy? Hostility? Palpable underlying friction between the two sisters, although mostly coming from Clarissa. Lady Isabella was the very picture of mortification and back to staring down at her hands. The mother seemed ready to strangle her eldest daughter. 'Why don't you *go* and change and stop wasting the good doctor's time, dear?'

'Oh, yes! Why don't I? Then you can go back to fussing over *poor* Bella. Why, she hasn't been fussed over enough, has she? Thanks to her, we are stuck here and I am bored senseless!'

'Have you tried a steam inhalation?' Ever the diplomat, Joe intervened and tried to diffuse the fraught atmosphere. If this was a case of sibling rivalry, perhaps Lady Clarissa would return to her sweet self if her minor ailment received some attention and he would stop feeling disloyal for feeling irritated at her. 'I would recommend a few drops of peppermint oil in boiling hot water. It's excellent for unclogging sinuses. I could send some back here directly.'

Lady Clarissa beamed at him and Joe basked in the glow. 'Why, thank you, Dr Warriner. It is so nice to know that someone cares about *my* well-being.'

The next half an hour passed without incident. Lady Braxton and he maintained the bulk of the conversation. Lady Clarissa added the odd snippet and her sister not at all. Her silence bothered him, although he couldn't say why. As he made his goodbyes, Joe made one final attempt at engaging her. Goodness only knew why. 'I am certain you will be well enough for Saturday's assembly.'

'Whether she is or she isn't, I shall be there. Retford is such a dull place, we must find our entertainments where we can.' Lady Clarissa rolled her eyes. 'I cannot wait for this summer to be over.' Which suggested their residency here was only temporary. Something that was probably for the best. A month of dreaming about the angelic, unattainable Clarissa was a month too many, as his misguided heart was doomed to be disappointed for ever.

'Then I shall look forward to seeing you there.'

'I am relying on *you* to dance with me, Dr Warriner.' His heart soared. 'There is a distinct shortage of eligible men in the area and, in the absence of any titled gentlemen, I shall have to content myself with handsome ones instead.' And his heart dropped back to his toes where it belonged.

'I am glad to be of service, my lady.' Although he wasn't. He was miffed. The butler passed him his hat and Joe started towards the door, feeling dejected and foolish. And angry at feeling guilty for being rightly peeved at Lady Clarissa's words.

'Dr Warriner...' Lady Isabella had found her voice. 'When might I go back to the infirmary to attend my duties?'

He saw her sister's obvious eye roll and felt another stab of irritation at her selfishness. At least the dour Bella wanted to help people. Her eagerness shone in her dark eyes. They almost sparkled. 'I suppose that depends on the type of duties you undertake. Racing around the ward, or standing for long periods of time, not for at least another week. But if you are doing something lighter—reading to the children or keeping a sick child company—I see no reason why you cannot resume those things in a day or two. As long as you are sitting down, of course.'

This answer pleased her immensely and for the first time he saw her proper smile. It was quite something. Quite something indeed. Dazzling, almost, and wholly responsible for a fresh wave of tingles. 'Thank you, Dr Warriner. And thank you again for this morning.'

'It was my pleasure, Lady Isabella.' And for some inexplicable reason, as he left her, it was.

Chapter Four

The next two days seemed to go far slower than days ever had before. Being stuck on the sofa with no purpose made Bella's anxiety worse. She fought it, of course, by reading or painting or sewing—anything to stop the debilitating melancholy which constantly threatened to suffocate her. Logically, she knew keeping active helped to ward off her demons. Dr Bentley's assessment of her mental state and the invasive treatment he suggested had terrified her, and whilst she was fairly certain he was a quack at best, there was only so long her family would allow her to get over it all herself. Her way. They had moved to Retford, at her insistence, to give her the summer away from London to sort herself out. If she couldn't, then the threat of more dreadful water treatments, and perhaps even Dr Bentley's cure for her blatant hysteria, loomed on the horizon because she couldn't go on like this.

She had to get better. There really was no other option and sitting around all day embroidering handkerchiefs was not helping her recovery or stopping her mind whirring. Her big brain needed proper stimuli,

something meaningful, and her big heart needed to focus on others rather than herself.

On the third day, when her father announced he was going into town, Bella insisted on accompanying him, although he did not take much persuading. Both her parents saw her desire to leave the house as a positive step forward and delighted in seeing tangible evidence of *progress*, although they never, ever discussed it.

The lack of communication about *the incident* made it harder. Her parents, or more specifically her father, had decided from the outset it was better for everyone if they pretended *it* had never happened, as if blithely ignoring that dreadful night in Vauxhall Gardens would somehow erase it from existence. Yet how could it? Bella could still see his eyes boring down into hers. Still smell the fetid odour of the man's filthy clothes and body. Still feel his hands groping her bare skin, pawing at her breasts and between her legs. Feel *that* part of him pressing against her flesh insistently. And all of it whilst pinned powerless beneath him in the dark bushes, unable to scream. Unable to run. All around her were the sounds of the laughing crowds and the fireworks and she was at the mercy of a monster.

In that dreadful instant, she had learned that the world was not the safe, cossetted place she had always believed it to be. Darkness and evil lurked, waiting for the unsuspecting. The trusting. The good-hearted. She had stopped to give a poor beggar some coins and he had wanted something else entirely. He'd almost taken it...

'Will you read to us again, Bella?'

One of the three children currently in the cosy infirmary thrust a book into her hands. She stared down

at the colourful picture book and grinned. 'But I have already read you this one, not an hour ago.'

'Yes, but we love that book, don't we?' Three pairs of angelic eyes pleaded with her. 'Especially the way you read it. We love the way you do all of the voices.'

'Very well.' At least entertaining them gave her some purpose, even though she would much prefer to be doing something more…practical and, frankly, medicinal. Although a part of her enjoyed reading this particular *Orange Blossom* book, as a certain handsome doctor made an appearance in it, delivering a newborn foal to the horses on behalf of the stork and then a baby to Captain Galahad and Miss Freckles. As the book had been illustrated by Dr Warriner's older brother Jamie, she was convinced Dr Sensible was based on the local physician. He certainly looked like him. Floppy dark hair, piercing blue eyes behind studious wire spectacles. Kind blue eyes. Eyes which she had noticed gazed longingly at her sister. Why did his obvious interest in Clarissa hurt, when every man had always preferred Clarissa and Bella no longer liked men? And whilst Dr Warriner was a brilliant scientist and she admired him for that, and whilst she might want to convince herself he was kind, trusting and noble, he was still a man. Another man who fancied her sister. No matter how many times she thought about it, it still stung. If it wasn't so ridiculous a concept, she might even have described her initial reaction as jealousy. Which was impossible when one considered Bella now couldn't bear the thought of being with a man. Any man. Even a brilliant and handsome doctor, with eyes as blue as the ocean. All in all, it was better to *not* think about it, despite her brain's inability to stop.

* * *

Bella had read the book from cover to cover. Two of the children had drifted off to sleep by the time she quietly closed the book. The third, a usually boisterous lad by the name of Tom, stared listlessly at the ceiling. His cheeks were almost scarlet. Earlier, he had complained about a bit of a sore throat and had a slight cough. Now he was glassy eyed and still. Despite promising her father and the matron she would confine herself to the chair, something about the look of the boy did not sit right. She limped towards his cot and laid a hand on his brow. His skin was on fire.

She hobbled across the ward to pour a bowl of cool water and dunked a clean square of linen into it. After placing it across Tom's fevered brow, Bella quickly found a maid and told her to summon the physician. All her reading told her the rapid onset of a high temperature did not bode well and signalled something nasty.

Back at his bedside, she sat and used the cold flannel to cool the boy's skin. 'The doctor is on his way, Tom. Are you in any pain?'

'My throat.' His voice was so hoarse he winced as he whispered and frightened tears gathered in the corners of his eyes.

'Let me see.' His mouth was so swollen that seeing was impossible. Remembering the spare medical tools Dr Warriner kept in the cabinet, Bella rummaged through them and returned with the ivory tongue depressor she had seen him use before. 'Say *ah*, Tom.'

The boy did as instructed, with some difficulty, but Bella saw the swollen and infected tonsils. To her untrained eyes they appeared very infected indeed, which suggested quinsy. The high temperature and general

malaise confirmed the diagnosis. The poor lad must be in agony and his rapid fever was a worry.

'Dr Warriner is attending a birth, my lady.' The matron, Mrs Giles, scurried in, looking flustered. 'His housekeeper says he might be gone many hours, but she will send him with all haste as soon as he returns.'

'Then send for Dr Bentley!' Bella did not want to wait hours. Hours of high fever killed children.

The matron shook her head. 'Dr Bentley won't come here.'

'If it is a matter of money, Mrs Giles, tell him I will pay him personally.'

'It's not the money, my lady…it's the *family*. Dr Bentley will not come here because it is owned by a Warriner.'

Bella had never heard anything so ridiculous in her life. 'The man is a physician, is he not? As such, his first duty is to attend to those who need him. Send for him immediately.' Petty feuds had no place in an emergency.

Just a few short minutes later, word came that Dr Bentley would not be attending the foundling home, now or at any time in the future and no amount of money would sway him. 'I'm sorry, my lady, but the old prejudices still run deep in Retford. I'm sure Dr Warriner will be here presently.'

Such an outrage beggared belief and at some point she fully intended to give the silly man a piece of her mind, but in the meantime Tom was burning up. 'Can you brew some willow bark tea, Mrs Giles?' That was known to help reduce a fever. 'And some ice.' Common sense told her cooling the boy's skin might help, just as it had her hot, swollen ankle. Then Bella remembered her conversation with the doctor in his office.

Honey fights infection… If it worked externally, then there was a chance it might work internally as well. She called at the woman's retreating back. 'And bring me a jar of honey, Mrs Giles!'

A few minutes later, she helped the boy to sit and carefully spooned the warm, hastily mixed willow bark and honey concoction into his mouth. He really didn't want to swallow, so she tilted his head back to allow the liquid to trickle over those inflamed tonsils and into his stomach.

Mrs Giles moved the other boys to another room at Bella's insistence and all the windows in the sunny infirmary were thrown open and the blankets stripped from the bed to allow the linen parcels of ice she had made to rest against his limbs, torso and head. Despite her best efforts, the boy's temperature remained dangerously high. The willow bark alone was not going to be enough. What else could she use? Feverfew—wasn't that known to have a calming effect on inflammation? And she had recently read a very enlightening paper on the benefits of echinacea flower…

'Mrs Giles, send somebody immediately to Dr Warriner's surgery and ask his housekeeper to send us the following things.' Bella listed all the herbs she could think of which might be of use: yarrow root, black elder berries, chamomile, ginger, more white willow, much more honey. In the absence of a proper physician, Bella was all little Tom had.

It was almost midnight when Joe finally made it to the infirmary. The twins he had just delivered had been most uncooperative. The first had been breech and the second baby had the cord wrapped around his

neck. It had been a difficult and dangerous birth and he was supremely grateful he had been called early enough to be able to save the mother and both of her babies. Now he was practically dead on his feet and had already called for a large pot of coffee to sharpen his wits ready for his next emergency. He only hoped the child's fever was manageable and that the hours of delay had not been catastrophic. Dealing mostly with the many poor of the parish, Joe was often spread too thin and, because of his innate need to rescue, felt personally responsible for every failure—especially the children. Today, three of them had needed him and he prayed he was not too late for the third.

The ward was dim as he walked in. A single candle burned in one corner of the room and he could just about make out the outline of a napping nurse resting in the chair beside the sleeping boy's bed, her head buried in the scrunched-up pillow which had been propped behind her and her legs tucked under her skirts. He crept to the opposite side of the bed and rested his palm on the boy's forehead. He was warm, but not burning. A good sign. Fortunately, this nurse had not closed up the room or had a roaring fire burning in the grate. No matter how many times he told Mrs Giles heat was the worst thing to use to treat a fever, the old matron was set in her ways and always reverted to it in an emergency. It was all she knew.

This nurse was obviously more intelligent. Tom was covered in only a thin cotton sheet, the fireplace was stone-cold and the lace curtains billowed in the gentle summer breeze coming through the wide-open windows. Joe placed his bag on the edge of the bed and the

movement woke up the sleeping woman with a start. Her terrified eyes were round in the darkness.

'I didn't mean to frighten you.'

'Dr Warriner!'

He knew that voice. 'Lady Isabella?' To find her still here, at a sick child's bedside so late at night, was a huge surprise. 'What are you doing here?'

'I wanted to stay with Tom…just in case his fever returned.' She had hastily stood and was in the process of lighting a lamp close to the bed. 'His temperature was so high earlier I was worried about him.' As usual, she was already backing away towards the open doorway, her posture stiff. He could see her chest rising and falling rapidly almost as if she was in the midst of a panic, but her features were composed, if slightly strained.

'Is he having any difficulty breathing?'

She took a step forward and gazed down at the sleeping child and shook her head. 'Not so far—thank goodness.' In the lamplight, he could see her hairstyle had collapsed on one side. One slippery coil of dark hair hung down against her cheek almost to her waist. The rest of that side of her head charmingly resembled a bird's nest. Rumpled and groggy with sleep, she appeared younger and much softer than usual. Instead of their usual wariness, those soulful dark eyes were now filled only with concern for the little boy. 'The fever came on so suddenly.'

'His temperature is not unduly high now.'

Almost as if she didn't believe him, her own palm brushed against the boy's brow and she exhaled in relief. 'I mixed willow bark with feverfew, echinacea and chamomile in a tea to fight the fever and have been

feeding him it every two hours since midday. I didn't know what else to do.'

Joe took in the scene, the open windows, the ice, the cool cloths draped over the boy's arms and head. The child's distinct lack of a nightgown. 'I think you did everything I would have done. You have managed the symptoms perfectly.'

'Not all of them. He's wheezing and his tonsils are badly infected and he is in a great deal of pain. I mixed a generous dollop of honey in with the tea because I recalled you said it had healing properties against infection. I have no idea if it has actually made a difference, but it seemed to help.'

She really had thought of everything. 'The warmth of the tea will have soothed them and the honey *will* help to fight the infection. As for the pain, I think you have alleviated a great deal with your quick thinking— he is sleeping very soundly. I doubt he would be so deep in the arms of Morpheus if he were still in the grip of pain. I was expecting to walk into a crisis, but thanks to you, it was deftly avoided… Well done.'

She smiled at him shyly but then brushed the compliment away. 'I can assure you, it was merely borne out of necessity. When we learned you might not return for hours, I sent for Dr Bentley and the fool refused to come.' The flash of annoyance had her scowling. 'And the man has the cheek to call himself a physician!'

'Dr Bentley is quite particular about who he treats.' People with no money to pay him for his services up front, for example, were callously ignored. Joe hated that, yet at the same time he was strangely grateful for the fellow's ambivalence. Had Bentley been a good doctor who treated first and sought payment after, then

nobody in his Retford practice would have given Joe a chance. His willingness to treat all comers and to accept whatever payment in kind the families could afford had granted him a level of acceptance he would never have enjoyed otherwise. Of course, it also meant he was given all manner of things he had no use for— like the ornate lady's hair comb which had been sent to his surgery only yesterday by an elderly patient who was as fit as a fiddle but imagined she suffered from everything. Nothing he could use to pay the wages of an assistant to help him with his growing workload.

'Doctors have no place being selective in their choice of patients. Ignoring a sick child is nothing short of cruelty. In fact, it is criminal!'

'I keep trying to appeal to his better nature.' Joe refrained from saying what he truly thought. Dr Bentley was motivated by money rather than the need to heal. Meanwhile the poverty-stricken people suffered unnecessarily from his neglect. However, knowing what he did about Dr Bentley's archaic and draconian practices, he supposed it was just as well he was not more charitable. His antiquated methods rarely worked and often made things worse. If Joe ever found himself bleeding to death in the middle of the road, the very last person he would call was Dr Bentley, as he'd probably end up dead.

'I am not sure that man has a better nature. I didn't take to him when I first met him and respect him less now. It is a wonder that he is still condoned by the locals when his attitude towards the sick is so appalling.'

'Dr Bentley has been practising medicine here for as long as I can remember. People are unwaveringly loyal to him after so many years of service.' And, of

course, it helped he did not have the unfortunate sur-
name of Warriner.

'Service?' She was so outraged she forgot to whis-
per. 'Leaving a sick child to potentially die is hardly
service!' Her fierceness amused him and reminded Joe
of the way he had seen Dr Bentley glare at her as he
left her the other day. Lady Isabella clearly hid a bit of
a temper beneath her usually silent, suspicious exte-
rior. It made her forget to be silent and it was nice not
to be on the receiving end of her disdain for once. The
noise roused their patient and he whimpered slightly.
The change in her was instantaneous. 'Oh, I'm sorry,
Tom.' Her hand brushed his hair affectionately. 'Dr
Warriner is here. He is delighted to see you getting
better. Would you like something to drink?'

The boy nodded and she began to fuss over him,
so different from the uptight and dour woman he had
always assumed her to be. To be still here because a
foundling was sick and to be treating him as if she
genuinely cared about him was…well, frankly nothing
short of admirable and not at all what he would have
expected of her. She stepped aside while Joe did his
own examination of the boy, watching with barely dis-
guised interest from her preferred spot nearest the door
as he took his stethoscope out of his bag and used it to
listen to Tom's chest. 'His lungs are clear. The wheez-
ing is in his throat, not his chest.'

'You can tell such things just from listening?'

'Yes, indeed. With this wonderful instrument I can
hear all manner of things I couldn't before.'

'Is that Laennec's stethoscope?' She took two steps
forward. At her apparent fascination with the instru-
ment he passed it to her to examine. She took another

step forward, took it eagerly and scrutinised both ends of the wooden tube whilst holding it as if it were as precious as the Holy Grail. 'I read his paper last year but have never seen one used before.'

She kept surprising him. 'You read his *Treatise on the Diagnosis of the Diseases of the Lungs and Heart*?'

'I didn't understand all of it,' she said, holding his stethoscope like a telescope and peering through the hole, 'but his claims that different diseases caused the chest cavity to sound different was intriguing.' Lady Isabella was the first person he had ever met who had read the great Dr Laennec's work, a surprising choice of reading matter for a young lady, yet one which proved she had more than a working knowledge of all things scientific if she had read that weighty academic essay.

'I had one made to Laennec's exact design as soon as he began to publish his successes. He has used it to great effect when diagnosing the treatment of consumption. I have heard of a few other physicians who have started to use a stethoscope rather than rely on just their own ears—but it is still a relatively new invention. Everyone who tries it, swears by it. It's amazing how clearly one can hear congestion in the lungs, or an irregular heartbeat—which in turn makes diagnosis and treatment of such dangerous conditions faster. When an illness affects the lungs, without swift intervention a patient can quickly develop pleurisy or pneumonia. That stethoscope you are holding has saved a few lives here in Retford in the two years I have been using it.' In fact, it was Joe's most essential piece of equipment aside from his spectacles. Without those, he couldn't read a damn thing or see anything close

up. 'I have been experimenting with it with expectant mothers. During the first stage of confinement it is also possible to hear the heartbeats of a foetus.' Was it appropriate to discuss such things with a gently bred young woman? Probably not, yet her eyes lit up and he reminded himself she *had* read Laennec.

'How can you be sure you are simply not hearing the mother's heart?'

'Because I can clearly hear both, beating in tandem. The mother's is louder, as one would expect with an adult, fully grown heart, and the babe's is softer and beats much more rapidly. I was staggered at how fast it was at first, but it is a wonderful thing to hear.'

'Rapid heartbeats? How fascinating. To hear life at such an early stage of development. Is the instrument easy to use?'

'I'm sure young Tom here won't mind you listening to his chest. Why don't you give it a go and see for yourself?'

There was no hesitation this time. No wariness. Lady Isabella placed the end on the boy's sternum, ever so slightly left without having to be told the human heart did not sit dead central, and rested her ear against the other end. Within seconds she was smiling again. 'My goodness! Why, I can hear it as clear as a bell.' Then she giggled, a delicious, warm sound which did odd things to his own heartbeat and made him feel uncharacteristically vain. Joe found himself unhooking his spectacles from his ears and stuffing them into his pocket and quashed the urge to neaten his unruly hair. 'I can also hear your tummy gurgling, young man. There are so many noises going on inside your body it is like an orchestra is playing a symphony with your organs.'

A symphony of organs. What an apt description. 'Listen again while Tom takes a deep breath. Can you hear any wheezing in his lungs?'

She bent her head again and listened intently for almost half a minute before standing up. 'You are right. There is no congestion in his lungs. The only sounds of laboured breathing I hear clearly come from the swelling in his throat.' Anticipating his next move, she handed him the tongue depressor on the nightstand so he could get a better look inside the boy's mouth at the source of the trouble, then went to fetch the candle to shine light on the right spot. Just as she had said, the offending tonsils were quite nasty, but he had seen far worse. 'Will you have to remove his tonsils, Doctor?'

Little Tom's eyes widened and Joe winked at him and shook his head. 'Only if they keep causing problems. In my experience, this is a stage many children go through and grow out of. I am of the belief, if one is born with an organ, then it serves a greater purpose remaining in the body unless it proves to be absolutely necessary to remove it. For the time being, Tom's tonsils can stay put.'

The boy yawned and she was all concern again. 'It's time for your medicine and then it's back to sleep for you, I think.'

'Indeed. A good night's sleep works wonders, young Master Tom. That and more of Lady Isabella's tonsil-taming tea.'

She stood and began to limp towards the door to fetch it and Joe remembered she had been injured. 'I can see to that. You should be at home, resting your ankle. Is your carriage waiting for you or would you

like me to send for it?' He didn't dare offer to drive her home after the last time.

'No, thank you, Dr Warriner. I shall stay till morning. I have already sent word to my family not to expect me home until then. The carriage is returning for me at six when Mrs Giles arrives.' A servant chose that exact moment to return with his pot of coffee, which she glared at with blatant disapproval. 'Coffee at midnight? Is that wise? If anyone needs rest, it is probably you, not I. You have a great many other patients to attend to tomorrow, including Tom, whilst I can sleep all day if I wish to. I believe your bed will do you more good than coffee will tonight. I can hold the fort here—as you have already plainly seen—and if the danger is passed, you might as well get some well-earned rest. A good night's sleep works wonders, after all.'

As there was no arguing with his own good advice, he did exactly as she suggested.

Chapter Five

The assembly room in Retford was small by London standards, but no less the crush. In the hour since their arrival, Bella had found a group of married ladies she felt comfortable conversing with and had deftly avoided being asked to dance by anyone by looking straight through any man who was fool enough to come close. Like sentries, her parents hovered close by, standing guard, which reassured her immensely. Clarissa, as usual, was stood some distance away surrounded by a positive battalion of men all fawning over her every word, enjoying being the adored centre of attention. As yet the handsome doctor was not one of them, but as he was still to make an appearance, his absence in Clarissa's entourage did not make her feel any better about it.

She hadn't seen him since the night he had come to call on Tom and Bella wasn't entirely certain how she felt about that either. His visits to the infirmary had not coincided with hers, despite the fact she had taken to volunteering every day since the little boy had fallen ill. She had felt somehow responsible for the child, seeing that his treatment regimen had begun with her

and the doctor had not altered it. The sense of achievement she had at being instrumental in his recovery was phenomenal. Tom was clearly on the mend now and Bella couldn't help patting herself on the back for being the cause. Having the brilliant Dr Warriner say 'well done', and without being the least bit condescending about it, had been the icing on the cake. And they had conversed about medicine! It had been so enlightening to be able to discuss the things she had only read about. Since being allowed to use his stethoscope, she now had a hundred questions about both lung and heart conditions, which the real her, deep inside, was determined to make her ask. Perhaps she would find her courage and her voice enough to ask one tonight? If he ever turned up, of course, and if he could tear himself away from her sister.

His brothers were all here. All so like him in appearance, yet none quite as handsome despite their near-identical features and physiques. It was probably the scholarly demeanour which made the good doctor stand out as the single most attractive Warriner of the bunch.

And the spectacles.

Not that he wore them often, but when he did they made her mouth strangely dry. They magnified the cobalt irises of his eyes just a little bit, rendering them bluer still and more striking, and when he peered through them they served to magnify the power of his intelligence, too. Which was probably what Bella was drawn to. It couldn't be anything else. It was only his scientific mind which drew her. His considered and reasoned logic. Even though she couldn't stop staring

at his lovely blue eyes. And perhaps the way his broad shoulders filled out his dark and sensible coat...

She was in the midst of pondering her odd thoughts concerning the good doctor when he strode in, looking quite splendid. In deference to the occasion, his normally plain black waistcoat had been replaced by one of blue silk, which did wonders for his eyes and made her gaze at the wide expanse of his chest for a second because the real her wanted to look and she couldn't muster up the strength to argue.

He paused in the doorway, scanned the crowd, and Bella watched his eyes settle on her sister before he set his jaw. He watched Clarissa flirting with her harem of vying men for a few seconds, then he seemed to exhale—in defeat, disappointment, perhaps even irritation? Bella couldn't tell but experienced the sting of it none the less, before he turned away and walked towards his family.

For over an hour she watched him surreptitiously. He had an easy way about him which she envied, clearly comfortable in his scholarly skin and enjoying the company of his boisterous family. When Bella accompanied her mother to the retiring room, she returned to see him dancing with one of his brothers' wives. Bella had briefly been introduced to Mrs Cassie Warriner and had liked her immediately. She had not been introduced to her husband but had noticed his pronounced limp the first time she had seen him, so it stood to reason that particular Warriner did not dance, so his brother was standing in for him. Justifying why the doctor was dancing with a pretty woman—a pretty

and obviously pregnant woman—made the fact he was
dancing with one more palatable, not that Bella *wanted*
to dance with him, of course. Dancing would mean
touching and the very thought of that sent her into a
panic. She never wanted to be touched again.

At the end of the dance she lost sight of him and was
scanning the crowd for his dark head when he came
up alongside. 'I see your ankle is better.'

Instinctively, she jumped and took a step back even
though he was not that close. 'Yes, it is…although it's
not up to dancing.' Why had she felt compelled to say
that when he hadn't asked her to?

Idiot. He dances so well, too. I miss dancing.

The voice inside was sighing. It was most discon-
certing.

'Tom is doing well.' A safer topic and one Bella
could manage without palpitations.

'The inflammation is almost gone and there has
been no sign of a raised temperature for a whole day
now,' she said.

'I think we should keep him in the infirmary for at
least another day. Little boys tend to pass on illnesses
in the dormitories and we don't want any more cases
of quinsy if we can help it.'

We.

He kept referring to the patient as theirs, as if they
shared the responsibility of his treatment, and that
warmed her. He recognised her part in Tom's recov-
ery and her place in the infirmary. Recognised it and
acknowledged it. 'I shall check on him on Monday, and
if he continues to make rapid progress, we can send
him back to be with his friends.'

'He's very bored.' Now that the crisis had passed,

Tom wanted constant entertaining. She had read him every book on the little bookshelf. Some of them twice.

'Excellent news. Bored is good. The very ill are rarely bored. They are too busy being ill. Only the well get bored.'

You're bored, the voice inside her reminded her. *Bored is good. He just said so. Do you remember when you were too terrified to be bored? What is that if not progress?*

'Dr Warriner!' her mother interrupted a little too casually, with her father in tow. 'You have not yet met my husband, have you?'

'Your lordship.' Joe bowed his dark head politely. 'It is a pleasure to finally make your acquaintance.'

'I was curious to meet the man behind the infirmary my daughter is wedded to.' Her father looked the doctor up and down, assessing his worthiness, and to Bella's mind he did not approve of what he saw. 'It seems I must thank you for coming to her rescue the other day. Bella speaks very highly of your skills as a physician.'

'She does?' Those fathomless blue eyes regarded her with amusement and she blushed crimson to the tips of her toes. Subtlety was never her father's strong suit and he had rather given the impression she had been waxing lyrical, which perhaps she had once or twice when she regaled her day to her family over dinner. It was splendid to be *doing* something again. Especially something as useful and important as healing.

'I've been telling my parents about Tom's tonsils and...' Perhaps it was better not to try to explain and simply brush it off, except she couldn't muster the non-chalance to brush it off when he was still smiling at her, so she clamped her mouth shut instead.

Always so benevolent, Dr Warriner finished her sentence for her. 'And I hope you have also told them how your swift intervention prevented him from going downhill. I was detained with another patient and your daughter single-handedly brought down the poor lad's fever. By the time I arrived, the crisis had passed and he was already on the path to recovery.'

Both of her parents gaped at her. 'You did?'

Once upon a time they would have expected her resourcefulness. It was a stark reminder of how far she had fallen in a year that they were both astounded and pathetically grateful to see some remnants of their old daughter return. It made Bella even more self-conscious than she was already. 'I only brewed some willow bark tea.'

'I fear I must contradict you there, my lady.' Kind blue eyes were even more amused. 'She sent to my surgery for a precise concoction of herbs to ease the child's distressing symptoms. I was mightily impressed with her knowledge of medicine.'

Her mother was now completely beside herself with joy, reading far too much into a silly potion than the thing warranted. As if being able to remember a few herbs would somehow return her to her old self. Her father was positively scowling. How she wished they would all stop staring at her. 'Bella has always had a very scientific mind. Had she been born male, I have no doubt she would have been the most dedicated and brilliant of scholars.' Her father disapproved of her 'hobby' but had allowed it in Retford while she 'convalesced', even though he had decreed that daughters of earls were not supposed to get their hands dirty. He was, however, prepared to indulge her for the duration

of the summer whilst she was out of sight in Retford to see if industry reaped better rewards than the water treatments and bloodletting.

'If you'll pardon me for saying it, sir, your daughter *is* a dedicated and brilliant scholar. Anyone who is familiar with the recent writings of Dr Laennec has a knowledge of medicine which exceeds that of the average layman.' Things her father would be mortified to hear. Dr Warriner began to rifle in his coat pocket. 'Which reminds me, I brought you this, Lady Isabella.' He handed her a wooden stethoscope. 'This was the original one I had made, but it is far too dainty for my enormous hands and I thought you might like it.'

Bella supposed most girls would melt if a man gave her flowers, but the exquisitely turned medical instrument was more beautiful to her than a bouquet of a thousand crimson roses. A funny little nerve jumped in her tummy and her heartbeat was so fast and so loud in her own head she doubted anyone would need a stethoscope to hear it. 'I don't know what to say... Thank you... I shall treasure it.'

Her parents shared a knowing look and instantly Bella wished the floor would open up and swallow her whole. Her father was clearly both concerned and horrified in equal measure. They were reading things into this innocent exchange which were not there. Dr Warriner was being nice and respected her mind. Just as she respected his mind...except there was so much more she was coming to like about him.

'There you are, Dr Warriner!' Clarissa sailed towards them and his eyes swivelled automatically. She threaded an arm through his possessively. 'You did promise to dance with me, did you not?'

'I did.' Apparently, Bella was now forgotten, which was probably just as well. She had no place having fanciful thoughts about a man when being alone with one of them terrified her and the thought of being touched by one was quite repellent. Although Dr Warriner's touch hadn't been exactly that. If at all.

'I pencilled you in for the waltz, which is the next dance. Isn't it a good job I found you in time?' As she led him away, clamped to him like a barnacle to the hull of a ship, Clarissa briefly turned back and smiled, letting Bella know the handsome doctor had been stolen away on purpose—because she could steal him, or any other man for that matter, away. Ever since she had been lauded as the Incomparable of the previous Season, Clarissa had become preoccupied with her own attractiveness. She had to be the prettiest girl in any room and all the handsome men, even the untitled ones, had to want to fall at her graceful feet. Dr Warriner was yet another willing conquest, something Bella suddenly found irritating.

Her father seemed fit to burst. 'I shall be having words with Clarissa. I do not approve of her dancing with *that* man. I've heard dreadful stories about *that* family—and we already know about his brother's antics in London. Jacob Warriner is a shocking rake and, if the locals are to be believed, the elder two are no better. Both tricked innocent girls into marriage. The Reverend Reeves lost his daughter after one of them seduced her. Father and daughter are now quite estranged as her husband cruelly keeps them apart. He told me so himself just a few minutes ago.' The stick-thin vicar was stood piously in the corner, clutching his tattered Bible, silently but obviously disapproving of

the dancing. 'There is also talk the eldest abducted his wife to get his hands on her fortune. How else would such a man come to marry the *Tea Heiress*?'

Bella glanced across the room to the group of laughing Warriners. The wives appeared very happy with their husbands. The two women and their men could not look more besotted if they tried, and after Dr Bentley's scandalous refusal to attend to Tom, Bella was inclined to be on the family's side rather than the humourless vicar's. 'There are as many people here in Retford who would tell you the Warriners are good people. Dr Warriner runs a busy practice and the Countess of Markham runs the foundling home I have been volunteering in.'

'That is as may be, but until I see tangible proof they are not as they have been reported, I should prefer it if my daughters maintained a safe distance. And that includes any and all dealings with Dr Warriner.'

Bella felt compelled to defend him, even if she was disappointed he preferred her self-absorbed sister. 'Dr Warriner is a brilliant physician, Papa.'

'Hmm.' His eyes followed his eldest daughter to the dance floor. 'I doubt you would be so foolish, Bella, but if he asks you to dance tonight, make sure you decline.'

'I do not wish to dance with him, or anyone, Papa.' The real her inside was longing to dance with the doctor. To be twirled around and to gaze up into those spectacled eyes. *Where did that thought come from?*

'But he is very handsome.' This came from her mother and it earned her a sharp look from her husband which she ignored. 'And he seemed very taken with you.'

'Are you blind, woman? The scoundrel has clearly

set his cap at Clarissa. Or perhaps, like his eldest brother, it is her dowry which appeals to him.'

'Dr Warriner is a man of science, not a fortune-hunter.' Bella was compelled to defend him.

'Then already he has lured you into his web of deceit if you believe such nonsense! Are you telling me you are also tempted by Dr Warriner?'

'The only part of Dr Warriner which interests me is his brain.' *Liar.* 'Clarissa is welcome to the rest of him.' *Lord, spare me the sight of the pair of them together.* 'When can we go home?'

Miraculously, Joe enjoyed an entire night of uninterrupted sleep at his brother's house. Jack and Letty had insisted he come home and spend a Sunday with the family because he looked tired and needed a break. Knowing they were right, he hadn't argued. Mrs Patterson knew exactly where to find him and would not hesitate to rouse him for the smallest emergency, yet thankfully no midnight messengers had come to spoil his slumber. Joe woke naturally to soft daylight and the delicious smell of a hot breakfast for the first time in months.

He was also feeling pretty pleased with himself. He had danced with the delectable Clarissa twice and one of those had been the only waltz of the evening. As he had spun her around the floor, several pairs of male eyes had watched them jealously, all coveting the rare prize in his arms. Not only had the woman of his dreams danced with him, she had favoured him with her attention throughout. They had chatted over refreshments and she had practically dragged him towards her gaggle of admirers and kept hauling him

back every time he wandered off. Clarissa might not be head over heels in love with him, or, if he was being brutally honest with himself, anywhere close, but she certainly now knew he existed. His poor heart swelled at the knowledge and he ignored the nagging voice which kept questioning why there had been no intriguing tingles when he had touched her hand or held her close.

Instead, Joe took his time shaving and dressing, intent on savouring the luxury of time passing, and sauntered into the breakfast room feeling more refreshed than he had in ages. His younger brother, Jake, was the only occupant and was sat with his feet crossed on another chair, reading a newspaper.

'Good morning.'

His brother's head popped over the newspaper and he grinned. 'I should imagine it certainly is! I never thought I'd see the day when my scholarly big brother was wooing two ladies simultaneously.'

'Two?' Joe was genuinely baffled. 'How much did you drink last night?'

'Nowhere near enough to miss the delicious *frisson* in the air. But be warned, Dr Sensible, whilst I heartily approve of wooing two ladies at the same time, the fact they are sisters will cause all manner of complications. Juggling both Beaumonts is not going to be easy. Especially with their father watching you like a hawk.'

'Very funny.' Joe began to load his plate with the bounty on the sideboard. 'But as usual you have got the wrong end of the stick.' He balanced two crisp rashers of bacon on the mountain of scrambled eggs and carried a slice of toast to the table in his teeth.

'I most certainly haven't. I have eyes.'

'Which clearly do not work if you believe I am juggling both Beaumonts.' Jake had a way with the ladies and out of the four brothers they were closest in age. Joe couldn't resist asking his opinion. 'What do you think of Lady Clarissa?'

His brother shrugged. 'Very pretty. Very highly thought of in London and considered quite the catch—and knows it, if you want my honest opinion. But I know the type too well to fall for her man-traps. Man-traps, I noted, she was using to great effect with you.'

'Man-traps?' The words came out mumbled as Joe enjoyed the first delicious mouthful of eggs. Mrs Patterson could cook, but the chef his sister-in-law Letty had brought with her from Mayfair was a culinary genius. Who knew the humble egg could taste so sublime?

'Yes, indeed. The subtle, oh-so-casual way she kept touching your arm. The tinkling laugh. The flirtatious way she kept batting her eyelashes at you.'

'She was?' Joe had enjoyed the flirting immensely but had no intention of letting on. 'I thought she had a touch of conjunctivitis.'

'That would be why you were falling all over yourself to be so attentive. It was purely medical. My mistake.' Jake snapped the paper back up in front of his face. 'Yet it still doesn't explain your fascination with the bookish Beaumont, who, by the way, I think is a much more exciting prospect.'

'Bella!' The very idea was preposterous. 'I am not fascinated by Bella.'

'*Bella*... Ah. My mistake.' Joe could tell his brother was smiling behind his newspaper wall. Jake's smugness always grated. 'I shall assume all the lingering glances I witnessed were not lingering at all.'

'Bella was *not* glancing at me in a lingering manner. The girl's nose was constantly in her book.'

Jake threw his head back and laughed. 'Not her, you idiot. The lingering glances were *yours*, else how would you know her nose was in her book? *You* were *looking*. You kept *looking*. Even whilst waltzing with the calculated Clarissa, your eyes kept wandering to her beautiful sister.'

A valid point, although his brother was quite mistaken as to why. His eyes had sought Bella out, but only out of concern. Seeing her sat amongst the wallflowers, doing her best to blend into the walls, bothered him. Nothing more. 'She hurt her ankle a few days ago and I treated her. I was merely checking she was not in pain.'

'Of course you were. I've often thought your concerned physician face mirrors your soppily pining face. And, I suppose, giving the lady a gift was also part of your medical service? I saw you give her that trumpet thing.'

'It was a stethoscope. Lady Isabella has an interest in science and is volunteering at the foundling home.'

Jake gave up his pretence of reading his paper and dropped it on his lap. 'The plot thickens. Have the pair of you been making gooey eyes over the patients?' He sighed wistfully and clutched his heart. 'How romantic…'

Joe had had quite enough. 'My relationship with Bella is…well, for want of a better word, professional. A boy has been suffering from quinsy and *we* have been treating him. Bella has a brilliant mind…' At his brother's grin he scowled. 'But if you must know, I prefer her sister.' Not strictly true. Joe was coming to like Bella, too. She was clever and resourceful, and he was

now convinced she was more shy than dour. And, of course, she had magnificent legs and then there were those tingles.

'I see. So you find Clarissa *attractive* and Bella *interesting.*'

'Clarissa is also interesting.' If he was honest, her conversation last night had been a bit dull. But mundane topics like favourite colours or flowers were to be expected when an acquaintance was so new—and Lady Clarissa was not exactly the type to find discourse about stethoscopes or bone saws riveting. The fact Joe had struggled to care about the scintillating parties she attended in London was proof he was working too hard and had simply forgotten how to have fun. As they became more familiar with one another, he was convinced they would find a great deal in common. A great deal. It did not mean anything that he might have tried to escape her company once or twice, or had found his eyes wandering to her sister in the corner. He merely felt uncomfortable in the crowd of admirers he had no desire to be part of.

His foolish brother did not need to know Joe had toyed with the idea of asking Isabella to dance as well. Then remembered she couldn't dance. She had firmly stated her ankle was still not strong enough. Although she walked with no difficulty, he noticed. Each time he saw her move, she glided effortlessly without any discernible sign of a limp and her hips undulated in a very pleasing fashion with each graceful step. Towards the end of the evening, his feet had been compelled to head in her direction again. The studious Bella might appreciate his scholarly conversation and he was tired of making small talk with those who would

deign to tolerate a Warriner. He was curious to know her thoughts on Laennec's paper, or maybe to discuss ancient Egyptian medicine some more. Even the state of Tom's tonsils was more appealing than listening to more gossip and nonsense about ribbons. He had been a few feet away when the ethereal Clarissa had appeared out of nowhere and claimed him again for a second dance and then the opportunity was gone. The Beaumont carriage had left shortly afterwards after both girls were ushered out by their father, who had obviously had quite enough provincial society for one evening. 'I thoroughly enjoyed Clarissa's company.'

'And the lovely *Bella*?'

'Frankly confuses me. One minute she is as prickly as a hawthorn and the next she is…' How to explain it? Joe frowned and pondered for a moment. 'Bella is obviously clever and her commitment to the infirmary is surprising for a woman of her upbringing. Yet she is eminently capable, very well read…yet insular. Sometimes she is downright snippy, although I suspect she is shy. And then—*bang*—she is animated and engrossed in a topic.' Like his stethoscope and Laennec's research. 'Half the time I don't know what to make of her.'

Jake had leaned forward and was listening intently. 'She's a conundrum.'

'Yes. I suppose she is.'

'You've always liked a conundrum. They excite that enormous brain of yours.' He grinned, looking every inch the rake he was. 'Admit it! You find the enigmatic Bella intriguing.'

'I find her sister *intriguing*—and Bella interesting.'

Jake pierced him with a glare, one which reminded

Joe his flippant brother was more astute than he liked
to let on. 'You're lying. I saw you trying to sneak off
when she was surrounded by her other suitors. I saw
you look at your pocket watch, the wall, *her sister...*
you were bored stiff by Clarissa!'

'I adore Clarissa. She is an angel. A diamond...'

'Good grief, you're at it again! Listen to yourself—
diamonds. Angels! Why is it whenever you set your cap
at a girl, she becomes this ethereal object to be revered
from a distance? A woman of such dazzling perfection
she is untouchable and unflawed.'

'I don't know what you mean.' But of course Joe
did. It was a familiar pattern and both brothers knew
it. Joe built an image of a woman in his mind which
rarely bore any resemblance to the real woman at all
and it usually concluded when his heart had been bro-
ken after she'd shown her true colours.

'You are so intent on the construct, the fantasy, you
fail to see the flaws. It's our mother all over again. I'm
surprised someone with such a mighty brain cannot
make the connection. You invent the perfect woman
and attribute those characteristics to whoever happens
to have caught your eye at the time. Clarissa, for in-
stance, is a practised flirt and a tease, not an angel,
big brother.'

She was also a tad self-absorbed, not that Joe would
admit such a thing to Jake when he was struggling
to come to terms with it himself. 'I know the differ-
ence between fantasy and reality. I'm a good judge of
character.'

Jake shook his head and grinned. 'You are an ap-
palling judge of character and far too soft for your
own good.'

An annoyingly accurate assessment which was best ignored. Joe popped a piece of bacon in his mouth and snatched the newspaper from his brother's lap and quickly pretended to be engrossed in it. Typically, Jake was having none of it. 'Do you remember the Widow Talbot?' How could he forget. The beautiful young widow was the first woman to break Joe's tender young heart. 'That vixen was a predator who wanted another notch on her well-used bedpost—but you believed her to be your soulmate despite the fact she was twenty years your senior and had a reputation as a man-eater. And we all warned you of it.'

'I did not believe she was my soulmate.' Yes, he had. He'd assumed her interest in him went beyond the physical, when in actuality it had been entirely physical, which with hindsight explained why he hadn't ever really known her at all. He had constructed a perfect set of characteristics and mapped them on to her, ignoring her true character until it slapped him firmly in the face. His foolish, immature dreams had come crushing down when she had suggested he bring one of his brothers along to her house next time, so they could both take turns with her. Joe was still disgusted with himself for not seeing the truth sooner.

'And then there was Miss Simkins.' Clearly Jake was going to dredge up all of Joe's mistakes. 'That chit you declared yourself in love with in medical school. Now, there was a conniving woman if ever there was one. A blind fool could see all she saw in you was Letty's money! How much of your allowance did you waste buying her gifts?'

Nearly all of it, until she'd attached herself to a

richer prospect. An heir rather than a spare. With not so much as a backwards glance.

'A good judge of character! Good grief, Joe, only *you* continue to believe there was good in our father.'

'It is possible he turned to drink because he was heartbroken over our mother.'

Jake snatched his newspaper back and thwacked Joe around the head with it. 'He was a drunkard before she threw herself in the river and you're rather missing the salient point. To be heartbroken, he would have needed a heart in the first place, when we all know he had none. But why am I bothering? You never listen. Go. Get your heart broken by Clarissa. Waste your time on the fantasy rather than the real thing.'

'You are wrong, not that it matters. At best all I can expect from her is a mild flirtation at the occasional gathering. Diamonds like Clarissa are not destined for men like us. They want titles and riches and social standing—not the younger sons of infamous earls.' Just saying it out loud was depressing and quite put Joe off his bacon.

'If she is the angel you seem to think she is, then your lack of title and riches will make no difference. Court her. Get to know her properly. Tug Lady Clarissa off the pedestal you've put her on and take her for a tumble in the hay.' He wiggled his dark eyebrows suggestively. 'In my experience, proper young ladies do love to dally with a shameless rogue. Or better yet, dally with her sister. The one you watch so intently. The conundrum. I bet she doesn't give two figs about trivialities like titles. She's far too intelligent.'

'You're an idiot.' Joe stood and tossed his napkin on the table, his appetite now spoiled completely.

'Oh, I'm the idiot?' Jake called to his retreating back. 'I'm not the one besotted with a woman who expects adoration as her due and so placid, or scared, I won't act on my feelings. If you want the girl, go get her. Stop pining after the dream and immerse yourself in the reality. Or are you scared the reality won't match up to the angelic Clarissa in your big, fat head?'

Chapter Six

'Dr Warriner is here, your lordship.'

Her mother appeared delighted at this news. Clarissa was triumphant. Bella couldn't quite put her finger on how she was feeling. Apprehensive, more than a little disappointed and ridiculously glad all at the same time. The warring emotions made her queasy.

'I think I made quite the impression on him last night. The poor man is now quite besotted. How is my hair?' After pinching her cheeks several times to give herself the perfect level of bloom and rubbing her lips together firmly, her sister patted her coiffure.

'You know there is not a strand out of place. You check the mirror often enough.' Clarissa's vanity was usually a source of amusement. Bella never understood why she put so much effort into improving her appearance and yet none into improving her mind. However, this time Bella had the urge to check her own hair, too, but didn't. It would only leave her wide open to Clarissa's mockery and confirm her father's ridiculous suspicions she had her sights set on the handsome doctor when he was obviously quite besotted with her sister. With her

hair being ruler-straight and resistant to even the most incendiary of curling irons, she always made do with a simple knot for daytime, spicing things up with some ornate plaits should the occasion call for it.

Clarissa's hair *always* complied, to the extent she was rarely seen without a few artful ringlets framing her face. The amount of rags the girl went to bed with made her resemble Medusa and couldn't be comfortable. No doubt Dr Warriner would appreciate the result. After last night, she couldn't help feeling quite belligerent towards him. A man of science shouldn't simper over a flirtatious and flighty girl like Clarissa.

He should simper over you!

'Tell him we are not at home.' Her father's tone brooked no argument.

'But, Papa!' Clarissa pouted. 'If he is at the front door, he can doubtless hear us. This silly house is so small and it is just after midday. Nobody who is anybody goes out before midday, especially on a Sunday when they have barely arrived home from church.'

'I do not care if he can hear us.' Her father turned to the butler and ushered him away with his hand. 'We are not at home.' The servant nodded and closed the door behind him. A few seconds later they heard the muffled sounds of the message being passed on and the front door being shut.

'Can't he at least come in for a cup of tea?'

'No. He cannot. After your lack of propriety last night, Clarissa, I made it my business to make more enquiries about the family, and Dr Warriner in particular, and after careful consideration of all the facts...' he glared at Bella as well '...I have decided we cannot pursue the acquaintance. His presence here today confirms

my belief he has designs on Clarissa and I will not allow him to use *your* good nature, Bella, to wheedle his way into her company. Henceforth, you are both forbidden to speak to any member of the Warriner family.'

Which meant her visits to the infirmary were now also forbidden. 'But, Papa…'

He held up his hand. 'It is my job to protect my daughters and I cannot, in all conscience, allow you to continue to fraternise with him. I know you have enjoyed your visits to the foundling home and I have been heartened to see the rapid change in you, Bella, however, such work is not appropriate for the daughter of an earl. It never was and it's time it ceased. You have been indulged long enough. I'm sure you can find some other worthy causes to support whilst we are here. Causes which are not aligned to Retford's most notorious family. The Reverend Reeves does many good works at the church and there are several ladies' groups that knit stockings and such for the poor. You may volunteer at one of those.'

'But at least allow me to finish my work. My patient…' not a good choice of word as it smacked of menial work '…Tom is expecting me…and I should like to see him discharged from the infirmary fully recovered.'

'It is out of the question.'

Seeing her upset, Clarissa could not resist one final dig. 'I suppose it is for the best. Whilst Dr Warriner *is* handsome, he lacks the social stature befitting an earl's daughter and I only danced with him to relieve the tedium of being stuck at that dreadful assembly. I shan't speak to him again, Papa. You have my word. And I'm rather glad you've finally agreed we are indulging Bella.

I was so *bored* of accompanying her to town as she always insisted on leaving so early. It was dreadfully unfair on me, yet nobody seemed to care I was being inconvenienced. At least now I can get my beauty sleep without having to play the nursemaid—which is ironic, isn't it? Seeing as that is what Bella was to Dr Warriner's patients.'

It was obvious her mother and father had had words. Angry ones if her mother's expression was anything to go by, but her mother was also concerned about Bella, too, who had left the drawing room in tears earlier and had refused to come down to dinner. It was childish and petulant, but Bella didn't care. Her father had taken away the one thing she cared about. The one thing which made her feel less like a future inmate at Bedlam and more like her old self. Thanks to the infirmary, in the month they had lived in Retford she had not only left the house alone, she had gone several hours without feeling frightened and exposed. She had felt normal. Or on the way to being normal and it was marvellous. Without that real and genuine purpose to her life, all she would be left with was nonsense which bored her and her own crippling anxieties. Neither appealed.

'He will not back down.' Her mother sat on the mattress and stroked her hair. 'I have tried to reason with him, but he won't be swayed.'

'But I've made such progress.' The tears fell again, angry, bitter tears of self-pity and frustration at the unfairness of it all. 'I am so frightened I will go backwards and then...' She couldn't bring herself to speak about the treatments which had been threatened by every physician they had consulted. Cruel, invasive,

humiliating treatments—all carried out by men while
Bella would be powerless to stop them. The one course
of water therapy she had allowed had resulted in her
being restrained to a chair with leather straps. Petri-
fied. The fear of the cure had melded with the con-
stant fear she had carried with her since *the incident*,
completely powerless, and had succeeded in turning
her into more of a wreck within a matter of weeks. It
had taken months to get back to where she had been
beforehand. To suffer through that, and worse, again
was too awful a prospect. Just thinking about it gave
Bella palpitations. Her fear must have shown on her
face, because her mother became agitated as well.

'It will not come to that. You won't go backwards. We
will find some other pursuit to occupy your time, my
darling. Your father is right—there are many charitable
endeavours hereabouts. Perhaps one of those would in-
terest you as much. The ladies' circle I attend is very
pleasant and we don't just knit stockings for the poor.
We make up baskets, visit the needy. You could come
with me. I could try to become more active.'

Her mother meant well, but they both knew she had
too many responsibilities as an earl's wife to be able to
commit to more than a few mornings a week and mak-
ing up baskets was not the sort of meaningful purpose
Bella relished. However one looked at it, her situation
had become hopeless again. 'I was learning so much
about medicine at the infirmary.' Without thinking,
Bella sought out the wooden stethoscope on her pillow
and she clamped it in her fist. 'It's been marvellous.'

'I've enjoyed watching you these past few weeks.
Every day, I've seen a little bit of my daughter return to
me. You always were so tenacious. Always so mindful

of the plight of others and keen to help them. I was so proud to hear about how you saved that boy.'

'I hardly saved him. I merely helped to control his fever.'

'Fevers kill, my darling. Who knows what might have happened to that child if you hadn't been there?'

A valid point. 'Perhaps I should tell Papa exactly that? What will happen the next time a child is in danger? Dr Warriner is run off his feet and cannot be everywhere. Does Papa really believe I would find knitting stockings more rewarding than saving a life? He wants me to get better. He keeps telling me he will do whatever it takes to help me get better—and then he does this? I've been trying so hard to be logical rather than irrational...it isn't fair.'

'It isn't fair.' Her mother stood and paced to the window, her arms folded tightly across her chest. 'Men always believe they know what is best for us.'

'Being forbidden to set foot in the infirmary is not what is best for me.'

'But he thinks it is. He thinks he is protecting you.' Her mother sighed, then turned, her eyes narrowed. 'Perhaps it is best if we allow him to continue to *think* he is protecting you? If he *thinks* you are knitting stockings or making up baskets, he will be content knowing he did the right thing.'

'And my feelings do not matter?'

A slow smile began to spread over her mother's face. 'You are so like your father. The world is so clear cut to you both. Things are either wrong or they are right and there is no in between. Fortunately, like your sister, I have a devious streak. I am not suggesting you knit stockings. I am suggesting your father *thinks* you

knit stockings. He is so busy trying to run his invest-
ments in town from a distance and will doubtless have
to travel back there frequently throughout the summer,
he will not check. As long as I tell him you are part of
the same ladies' circle as I, he will not bother to query
it and Clarissa is unlikely to want any part of it. She
hates volunteering for anything, so she will be none
the wiser. As long as you are careful, I see no reason
why you cannot continue your work and education in
the infirmary. The staff and Dr Warriner would have
to be sworn to secrecy, of course—but seeing as you
are so useful to them, I dare say they will.'

'You would lie to Papa for me?' Suddenly, the world
was not such a grim place.

'I've lied to your father about all manner of things
for years. Most wives do. As long as he hears what he
wants to hear, he will be perfectly content.' Her mother
wrapped her arms around her. 'Do you think you can
manage getting to the infirmary by yourself? Clarissa is
bound to get suspicious if you insist on bringing her as
before and your dear papa does like me to be at home.'

Bella would walk over hot coals if it came to it. 'I
will manage.' It was just a short walk across the square
and now she knew to keep a watchful eye out for roll-
ing vegetables. 'Thank you, Mama!'

Monday was running away from him. After a busy
morning surgery and two unexpected calls to opposite
ends of the village hastily tagged on to his long list of
scheduled visits, it was past three when Joe finally ar-
rived at the foundling home to check on Tom. He took
the stairs two at a time and dashed down the hallway to
the infirmary. If Tom was well enough to be sent back,

then at least he would have one less pressing matter to attend to for the rest of the week. A week which was rapidly filling up with more tasks. Joe really needed to employ an assistant, which meant he might have to start insisting on actual coin as payment. Either that or surgically split himself in two to be able to cope. He shouldn't have wasted an entire Sunday at leisure and he certainly shouldn't have bothered wasting his time calling on Lady Clarissa. Being told the family were not at home, when he could hear them plainly talking in the drawing room beyond, had been humiliating.

Inevitable, when he recalled how the Earl of Braxton had positively oozed hostility, and probably for the best. Joe had known his pathetic mooning was futile and he also knew better than to be goaded into doing something foolhardy by his irascible younger brother. It was a good thing Jake had no idea he had visited the house and then been denied entry, as Joe would never live it down. He doubted the charming Jake was ever turned away from a young lady's front door. Thinking about how he had felt on that doorstep, nervously twisting his hat in his hands in a desperate attempt not to be the placid Warriner his brother had playfully accused him of being, made him slightly queasy.

He could cope with being scholarly—but placid sounded so dull and insipid. Placid most definitely would not win him the hand of the fair maiden, not that he had ever seriously hoped to win it, and with hindsight he should have listened to himself and worshipped her from afar. Now he had to suffer the painful indignity of the two vexing Beaumonts knowing he had been sent away with his tail firmly between

his legs because he was nowhere near good enough to socialise with. Why the devil had he listened to Jake?

Joe skidded to an abrupt stop at the open doorway of the boys' ward and stared agog. Not only did Tom appear to be in fine fettle as he had expected, he was also cuddled in the arms of the younger Beaumont, who was laughing as she read to the boy from a large picture book.

Joe stepped quickly out of sight behind the door frame and simply watched the oddly arresting and surprising sight. She was so animated. Vivacious even. That laugh too loud and too boisterous to belong to a truly shy young woman. Little Tom was bestowed with the full, beaming glow of her stunning smile as he giggled on her lap, and even more shocking, the quiet, measured, scholarly Lady Isabella was acting out the story with different voices.

The noonday sun glinted off Captain Galahad's cutlass. 'Stand down, Brimstone! Unhand Miss Freckles!'

'Never!' the dragon roared as hot flames shot out of his nostrils, 'She is my prisoner and she will stay with me for ever!'

'Then you give me no choice...'

Her voice petered off as she sensed she was being watched, then her eyes warily locked with Joe's. The boy tugged at her dress impatiently. 'What happens next, Bella?'

Informal, too?

Interesting.

As soon as he thought the word, he remembered how Jake had teased him about preferring Bella and tried to conjure Clarissa in his mind just to prove to himself his brother was wrong about that at least. With

the bookish, dark-eyed, brunette Isabella there in front of him, his skin tingling and his mind instantly filling with erotic images of her lovely legs, that proved surprisingly difficult.

She'd also done something different with her hair. It was looser. Not as sensible. Thin plaits were woven around thicker coils of hair and arranged in a way that emphasised the almost feline slant of her eyes. Very pretty. Beautiful even. Disconcerting. More tingles.

'We will continue with the story later, Tom. Dr Warriner has come to check on you.' Hastily, she lifted the child back on to the mattress and made a great show of tucking him back into bed while he badgered her incessantly about the rest of the story. By the time she stood up she was all formal again, the lovely smile long gone. She was also, he noticed, edging slowly back towards the door almost as if she wanted to blend invisibly into the background or retreat from the advancing enemy unseen. He strolled into the room, grinning at the boy in an attempt to reassure her, too. 'How are you feeling, young Master Thomas?'

'I would feel a lot better if Bella finished the end of the story.'

'I am sure it will all end happily. The *Orange Blossom* stories usually do. Or the dragon will eat her. Either way, you shall have to wait.' He gently examined the outside of Tom's throat. Joe did not need to see the boy's tonsils to know he was fit and well. So fit and well he was practically bouncing on the mattress with unspent energy. 'Poke out your tongue, you rapscallion, and say *ah*.'

Tom managed this briefly between bounces. The tonsils which had been red-raw and blotchy only a few

days before were nearly back to normal. 'Does it still hurt to swallow?'

The boy shook his head. 'Not much now. The ice cream took the scratchiness away.'

'Ice cream?' Joe looked quizzically at the silent statue next to him and saw her blink guiltily.

'I thought the cooling properties would tame the swelling.'

'And where, pray tell, does one get ice cream in Retford?'

Tom answered for her. 'Bella's cook made it. She brought some this morning especially for me *and* she drizzled it with honey.'

'Did she? What a splendid treat. Is there any left?'

'No, sir. I ate it all after I took my medicine.'

'Well, clearly *Bella's* ice cream is exactly what was needed to aid your convalescence and I bow to her greatness.' Joe executed a mock formal bow from his seat on the mattress and watched her blink again, then stare at her hands. Was she embarrassed he had been turned away from her house? Joe certainly wasn't going to mention it. The humiliation was too fresh and he was still fuming about it, although as always he was bottling that anger up inside. Better to pretend nothing was amiss than give in to the temptation to hunt down her pompous father and give him a piece of his mind. Joe didn't allow himself to lose his temper often, but when he did it was something to see. 'When did he last have his medicine, *Bella*?' It was a tiny act of defiance and he liked the way her eyes widened slightly each time he said her name.

'He is due more now, Doctor.'

'I'm not taking it without ice cream! And make sure it's drizzled with honey.'

'Bella is not your slave, young man. Apologise immediately.'

She winced, making her perfectly straight nose wrinkle, and she still refused to meet his eyes. 'It's my fault. I used the ice cream as a bribe to get him to take it earlier because he had been very reluctant to have it otherwise. Just before you arrived, he promised to take his medicine...as long as I finished the story.'

'Master Tom, you should be ashamed of yourself! What a troublesome patient you are turning out to be. Poor Bella. If I was her, I would hold you down and pour it into your throat. And I would refuse to read you the rest of the story.'

The boy giggled. 'It wouldn't matter. She read it all the way through this morning.'

'All the more reason why you should be ashamed of your behaviour.' Joe casually picked up the prepared drink and began to spoon it into the bouncing boy's mouth. 'And did you find out if Captain Galahad rescued Miss Freckles from the dragon?'

'He did, sir. They had a magnificent battle with swords and fire. Captain Galahad was victorious.' The boy frowned. 'Then it got a bit soppy. The captain asked Miss Freckles to marry him, then they rode off into the sunset together.'

'I suspected as much. The *Orange Blossom* stories *always* have a happy ending.'

Joe shot Bella a grin as he tousled the child's hair and watched a pretty blush stain her cheeks. 'I think you are correct, Bella. Send this malingerer back to

the boys' dorm this very afternoon. He has become far too fond of ice cream and spoiled with fairy tales.'

'Woo-hoo!' The boy began to bounce again. 'I can finally take off this dreadful nightgown!' The offending garment was gone in a flash, much to his nurse-maid's consternation.

'Tom! At least wait until I have brought you your clothes!' But the boy was already off the bed and running around in excited circles, deftly evading her arms. He did not expect Joe to grab him and lift his wriggling body calmly from the floor. Joe held him securely tucked under one arm.

'Oh, to be six and unashamed to be naked.' Joe handed her the giggling nude bundle. 'Master Tom, there is a lady present. At least put your bottom away. A gentleman should never display bare cheeks to the world. It isn't proper.'

To prove his point, Bella was glowing like a tomato. With determined precision, Tom was swiftly encased in a pair of knee breeches and the loose, comfortable smock worn by all the younger boys at the home, then there was no stopping him. He dashed off to rejoin his friends the moment his little feet touched the floor, leaving them all alone.

'I am very sorry about that, Dr Warriner.'

The rosy blush and flustered state suited her as much as the plaits. 'A physician sees all manner of things as a matter of course and it is hardly your fault he decided to strip off. His exuberance is testament to his speedy recovery—a recovery which you had a significant hand in. Your liberal use of ice cream worked wonders, by the way, and is a remedy I will shamelessly steal in

the future. I am always on the lookout for a better way to do things.'

She gave him a brief smile and then turned and rapidly went about stripping the bed. 'I am also sorry about my father's behaviour yesterday...when you called upon us. I fear he has been listening to gossip.'

Chapter Seven

'Pay it no mind.' He smiled kindly at her. 'We Warriners are used to it. I blame my grandfather. He treated his tenants abominably and swindled all the local tradesmen. As did his father before him. And then, of course, my own dear papa was a famous drunkard who was too quick with his fists and racked up debts all the way from Lincoln to Nottingham. He also, if the gossips are to be believed, drove his wife to suicide— but then I am told my mother was selfish by nature and did enjoy a bit of drama. Which was probably why she married him in the first place. Whilst those scoundrels fester in the ground, this generation suffers for their sins. The gossip about the four of us is quite wonderful, too. I suppose you have heard the story about how my oldest brother, Jack, kidnapped an heiress and compromised her into marriage? Each time I hear it told I swear it has been further embellished. The one about my other brother James is equally scandalous. He seduced the vicar's daughter into sin and practically dragged her out of her father's house after beating the man senseless—or so I've heard tell. For the

record, neither account bears any resemblance to the actual truth, but who cares when the gossip is so delicious. I'm not surprised your father sent me away— I'm a danger to society. Frankly, I am surprised he has allowed you to continue here, what with me being the devil and all.'

He hid the note of bitterness well beneath a veneer of amusement, but his eyes gave him away. The gossip bothered him and rightly so. Bella now dreaded telling him the truth. 'Actually...' Shame made her dip her head and the silence hung for a heartbeat.

'Ah...I see. I take it he doesn't know you're here.'

'He thinks I am knitting stockings at the ladies' circle.'

He had turned his back to look out of the window, so Bella had no idea how he felt about her confession. 'And when he finds out the truth?'

'I shall cross that bridge when I come to it—*if* I come to it. My mother is fairly certain he will take her at her word without challenge.'

She watched his shoulders stiffen and a hand scrape across his jawbone, and she got the distinct impression he was angry, yet when he turned to face her again his expression was bland. 'With both his wife and his daughter lying to him, let us pray he remains blissfully in the dark.' His arms folded across his chest as he pierced her with his gaze. 'Tell me—*why* are you here, Lady Isabella? Is this some form of rebellion or a way of getting your own back on your father? An adventure, perhaps?'

The accusation stung. 'I am not that shallow, Dr Warriner, and I resent the implication.'

'Fair enough, I shall take you at your word, but there

has to be a reason why you are defying him and coming here, despite his express instructions to the contrary, and if I am expected to lie for you, which I presume I am, I should like to know I did so for a good purpose. After all, I dare say I will be the first person your father hunts down when your duplicity is uncovered and I doubt he will be inclined to be reasonable. Not with *my* reputation.'

She knew lies now would likely only serve to alienate him and Bella needed his compliance to stay. 'Since I was a little girl, I have had an interest in science and medicine in particular. Being here, helping these children, allows me to indulge that interest.'

His dark head tilted to one side as he searched her features for the truth. She tried and failed to hold his stare. 'What else?' For the first time he was not the affable and easy-going man she had always seen. This one had a stubborn set to his jaw, an edge of steel in his tone. He was offended and suspicious, the outer layer of calm belying his irritation, yet bizarrely the tight control he held over his emotions made her feel secure in his presence. Even angry, she knew he wouldn't hurt her and she knew it without having to think it like a mantra.

'There is nothing else.' Although her cheeks were already burning with shame at the flimsy explanation.

'You're lying.'

'It's not a lie!' At best it was a watered-down version of the truth. A watered-down version which skipped over a great many pertinent and humiliating details.

'You are prepared to risk your father's wrath because you have always had an interest in medicine and I am to risk bearing the brunt of it merely to *indulge*

you? I think it is best you go home, my lady. I have no desire to be blamed for luring you into disobeying your father and I do not have time to pander to your indulgence.'

He stalked to the door and was almost through it by the time the voice inside called out in panic, 'Please don't send me away. My work at this infirmary has been everything to me these past few weeks... I can't go backwards. Not now.' Bella wanted to cry and he heard it.

He halted and turned to face her slowly. 'Backwards?' His deep blue eyes were watching her intently, reminding her this man was more intelligent than any man she had encountered before, when Bella was used to being the most intelligent person in any room. 'Backwards from what?'

If she told him, would he think her mind addled like all the other doctors? The real her was tempted to trust him, because he was so different from the other physicians who had been thrust upon her, but it was too great a risk. A woman with an addled mind had no place tending to sick children, not when she could barely function as herself. More than one London doctor had told her family she had no place being in society any longer because the damage to her mind was too entrenched. A nice place in the countryside might be better, with people to attend to her every need. People who understood her particular kind of condition. Because the addled needed to be hidden from sight if they refused to be treated, in case they were contagious.

Bella tried to control her breathing and temper the panic in her voice. 'I have more than a passing interest in medicine... I have always studied it. But a career

in medicine is not an option for a woman. We are supposed to embroider or paint or press flowers, not read about stethoscopes or anatomy. Here I can pursue science in the only avenue available to me.' His face was now more curious than hostile. 'I have been learning so much—both from you and from the practical experience of nursing. If that is taken away from me...' Tears prickled at her eyes again. Endless days filled with anxiety stretched on the horizon. 'Please let me stay here. Just for a few weeks. I will be careful to make sure my father never knows.'

Jake's suggestion that gently bred young ladies enjoyed the thrill of dallying with a rogue had bothered Joe. Whilst he was almost certain he had no designs on Bella, the thought she might be using him to amuse herself or thwart her father with one of those shocking 'wild' Warriners hurt. He didn't want to be any society lady's entertainment again or bring any more unwelcome or unwarranted gossip to his family. Not when he was building up both his practice and his reputation against the odds stacked against him.

But his gut told him her distress might be sincere. Joe understood the burning desire to learn and to be thwarted. For years, he had been denied the opportunity of studying medicine properly because there had not been the money to send him to school. He'd never blamed his eldest brother, Jack, for the poverty. Jack had tried and tried to save enough to help him pursue his dream of obtaining a medical licence. Only after his eldest brother had married Letty did Joe finally fulfil his ambition and the sense of rightness had been all-encompassing. He finally became who he was destined

to be. Seeing Bella's distress, and realising despite her family's wealth she would be denied the opportunities he'd had based on her sex, brought him up short. That had been an obstacle he'd not had to contend with. Hell, if he was honest, it had never occurred to him before now. As a male, even a poor *Warriner* male, he had advantages over half of the population he had been blissfully ignorant of. The knowledge was humbling.

Bella was clearly a very intelligent young woman with a talent for healing. She had read extensively—good grief, she knew Laennec. That spoke volumes. Little Tom was walking proof of her knowledge and dedication. She had stayed all night to tend to his fever and been here every day since. Maybe she did have more than a passing interest? Enough of a need that unshed tears shimmered in her dark eyes at the thought of losing a fraction of what he took for granted every single day.

She was staring at him, waiting for him to pass judgement. One fat tear caught on her lower lashes and without thinking his palm cupped her cheek so his thumb could gently brush it away. The tingles shimmered from the pads of his fingers directly to his heart. In the same moment, her breath caught. He heard it because his caught a split second before. She blinked. The only movement as her body was frozen like a statue, but while her body was as rigid as marble her skin was as soft as velvet. Her widened eyes locked with his and Joe couldn't seem to tear them away. 'Don't cry. I'll keep your secret.'

'Thank you.' She swallowed nervously and he realised his palm still rested against her cheek. He dropped it, feeling self-conscious and oddly moved.

Suddenly, he had no idea what to do with his errant hands, and when no immediate solution presented itself he resorted to clamping them firmly behind his back while he stepped away and walked to stare out of the window again. Whatever had just passed between them was both unfamiliar and a little overwhelming. Definitely something which required further analysis. Lady Isabella had not flirted or batted her eyelashes once, nor used any of the man-traps her sister wielded with so much precision, yet he suddenly had the urge to kiss her. Where had that come from? He was supposed to be in love with her sister. How could he be hopelessly in love with Clarissa if he kept having these peculiar thoughts about Bella?

Behind him, he heard the rustle of her petticoats as she moved. It reminded him of her legs and the inexplicable urge to kiss her turned from something sweet and tender to something warm and physical.

Desire.

Joe knew the symptoms as well as any man and understood them more than most. A basic need of all living creatures, like the need for air or food, except this time it was led by his head, not his loins. Or perhaps he was merely having an odd male moment brought on by the sight of that single female tear. He turned to see if the urge waned or increased at the sight of her. She now had her back to him and was stripping the sheets from the bed, no doubt as a way of coping with the awkward atmosphere his wayward hand had caused by touching her.

He should probably apologise or, even better, brush it off with his customary professional detachment and pretend nothing at all was amiss, when his mind was

racing and his heart was hammering and for the life of him he couldn't recall what her sister looked like at all. For weeks he had been convinced he had been attracted to the ethereal, out-of-reach Clarissa, yet he had no memory now of her face or voice or scent. Three things which had resolutely occupied his brain had now disappeared like steam from a kettle after one brief touch of her shy and confusing sister. The conundrum.

Words failed him, so Joe simply stood and found himself gazing at her bottom as she moved. Like her legs, it was very nice indeed, rounded, womanly. Beautifully curved hips flared from a trim, small waist, yet he had not noticed those attributes before now. Raw, unadulterated lust burned hotter.

Unhelpful, unwelcome and totally unexpected.

A harried-looking Mrs Giles burst through the door and saved them both from having to talk about it. 'Oh, thank goodness! You are still here, Dr Warriner. One of the girls has had an accident!' One look at the older woman's face and he knew he couldn't dawdle. Joe chased the matron down the stairs and out into the garden.

When his sister-in-law Letty had first set up the foundling home, she had insisted the children have a proper area to play. A small crowd of concerned faces were gathered near one of the rope swings suspended from the sturdiest tree. As was so often the case, they parted the moment one of them spied him, allowing him to take in the scene and take charge.

His patient was one of the older girls of about twelve. He remembered her name was Molly because he had treated her for malnutrition when she had first arrived in the home almost two years ago. She was

lying flat on her back, her face scrunched up in agony, her right leg thrown out at a worryingly odd angle. Much as the situation concerned him, Joe was mindful never to let his patients witness his fears. He knelt beside the child and smiled.

'I might have known it was you, Molly. Were you swinging too fast again? When I was a boy, my brothers and I used to try to get our swing high enough to kick the clouds. It never happened, of course, but we persisted regardless.'

Joe kept up the inane chatter while he gently lifted the hem of Molly's skirt and assessed the damage. Her leg was unmistakably broken and it was a bad break. Blood was already caking around the woollen stocking on her calf and he could see a small part of the bone protruding from the wound. The poor thing must be in agony; moving her was not going to be pleasant.

'Can you boys get some clean sheets from the infirmary?' Bella's instruction came from behind him and he turned to see her smiling down at the girl before her eyes flicked to his. 'I thought we could carefully slide one under her and then use it as a makeshift stretcher—in the absence of a real stretcher, that is.'

It was a good idea. Seeing that she had already proved herself to be eminently capable, Joe did not hesitate to trust her. 'Carrying her upstairs might be problematic at this stage. Can you organise my things in the dining room? I will use one of the tables in there to examine her properly.'

Bella nodded briskly and hurried off, taking a few of the older children with her as helpers. Joe took off his cravat and carefully tied Molly's ankles together, hoping the good leg would provide some support for

the broken one when they came to lift her. The less the bone was disturbed between now and him resetting it, the better.

It was Bella who came back with the sheets and rather cleverly she had folded them into a concertinaed strip. With his help she was able to thread the fabric beneath the girl's waist, then they were able to slide the sheet open beneath her. Several burly market traders had been press-ganged into helping, so while Bella supervised and issued helpful instructions, Joe and the other men were able to lift the child without too much disturbance and carry her inside.

The dining room had quickly been turned into a physician's surgery. Most of the furniture had been cleared and fresh linens had been draped over the largest of the refectory tables. To one side she had also organised a smaller table for his equipment, which was all laid out in readiness, alongside bandages and a steaming bowl of water. He could smell the tell-tale aroma of gin and was impressed by her diligence. She had listened to him and learned, then put it into practice without hesitation. 'I have sent for ice and set the gardener to fashion some splints. I assume you are going to reset the bone.'

Tactfully, she had come up next to him and spoken in hushed tones so as not to distress Molly. 'The bone is protruding from her shin. This procedure will be very painful. I am hoping it is a clean break, but the fact it is now an open wound is a worry. Such fractures often turn gangrenous and end in amputation.' He kept his own voice quiet.

'Perhaps some laudanum might be in order before you begin? Enough to take the worst of the pain away.'

Joe agreed. Whilst it was common practice to keep a patient lucid during surgery, Molly was just a child and he did not want to cause her undue stress. They cleared the room of all but a few people. Two strong men to hold the girl in place if needed and, at Bella's insistence, Molly's closest friend. Bella gave the girl a few drops of laudanum, stroked her hair and soothed her. As Molly's eyelids began to droop, Bella stood and instructed the wide-eyed friend to continue in her stead. 'Avoid looking at what the physician is doing, Daisy. Your job is to chatter away to Molly to distract her. If she wakes, I want her to see a friendly face to ease her fears.'

Briskly, and without needing to be told, she handed him scissors. Joe cut away the bloodied woollen stocking and his worst fears were confirmed. A good two inches of bone stood proud from the wound, but on first inspection it did appear the bone had snapped rather than shattered. It was a small consolation. In the time it had taken to move the child to the house, the muscles in her leg had already contracted significantly, so those would need stretching back before the bone could be set in its proper place. Times like this always made him grateful for the years of having to labour on the family estate. Whilst poverty had been hard, it had given him a broad back and a strong pair of arms, two things essential when dealing with broken legs.

Once again, Bella anticipated what he needed without needing to be told. She brought the hot water and some gauze and helped him to clean the wound. It was a nasty one and certainly not for the faint-hearted, yet she never baulked once at the sight. The splints arrived. Two sturdy strips of wood secured at one end

with a smaller piece of wood joining them together, the width of a child's foot. How had she known to do that, when many doctors simply made do with a basic pair of splints? Then he remembered her reading had extended beyond the common medical books used in the home. The rigidity of these splints when bound would keep the bone straight and allow Molly to walk with it. She deftly weaved strips of bandage beneath the girl's leg, ready to tie them in place when the time came, then with the men, Bella held Molly immobile as Joe braced himself to set the leg.

'Once I align the bone, can you begin to strap it up?'

She nodded, clearly concentrating intently, and Joe got to work. Despite the laudanum, the girl cried out, yet Bella impressed him with her single-minded determination to ignore the cries and do what needed to be done. After what seemed like an eternity, the bone finally came together, but with Molly's muscles now quite contracted it took all of Joe's strength to keep it in place. Bella began quickly lashing the splint in place, her teeth clenched with the exertion of pulling the bandages taut across the wooden frame. By the time she had finished, Molly was thankfully unconscious, the leg was perfectly straight and it would take more than a simple pair of scissors to destroy their work.

'We should move her up to the infirmary now, before the laudanum wears off.' She issued orders sparsely, but effectively, he noted. Using the sheet on the table and simple, concise instructions meant the men could transfer the girl to a stretcher and carry her safely up the stairs without incident. Joe found himself with a bowl of hot water and soap to clean himself up, a cup of hot coffee put into his hand by Mrs Giles and

nothing whatsoever pressing to do. As Mrs Giles had never done either thing before without his asking, he knew he had Bella to thank.

'Does Lady Isabella drink tea or coffee?'

'Tea, Dr Warriner.'

'Then make her some, please, and I shall take it up to her.' They had both worked hard and needed refreshment. Especially as their work was far from done. 'And see if you can rustle up some biscuits. She is fond of those.' At the foundling home, at least, it appeared he now had an able assistant. Whatever else he was foolishly thinking about Bella was probably best ignored.

Chapter Eight

The last three weeks had been some of the best of Bella's life. She had managed to sneak away to the infirmary almost every day for a few hours without rousing her father's suspicions. If anything, he was buoyed at seeing her so purposeful and invigorated. Of course, he believed she was helping the needy through the ladies' circle, not nursing the sick at the Warriner foundling home, so she was careful never to so much as blink whenever any mention of the family was made.

But Dr Warriner had not only allowed her to continue, he had begun to teach her things and delegate certain treatments entirely to her. It was marvellous. Under his tutorage, she was learning how to discern the different sounds within the human body using her stethoscope, plan treatments and make her own diagnoses, and just yesterday—when she had claimed to be shopping for ribbons—he had allowed her to stitch a small wound closed using ligatures under his supervision. It had been daunting and thrilling in equal measure, yet the sense of accomplishment she had experienced afterwards had quite made her forget about

the incident or her close proximity to a man for the entire duration of the day.

The only day which had proved to be problematic was Sunday. Her father insisted they all go to church, then spend the day together as a family, which left Bella twiddling her thumbs and overthinking things. When she could, she sneaked back to her room and devoured one of the scientific journals Dr Warriner had lent her, but it was no substitute for practising medicine.

Or for seeing him.

Not that she saw him every day. Some days his heavy workload meant he did not make it to the infirmary before dusk, when Bella had left for the day. He usually left her notes telling her what he wanted her to do, detailed instructions written in his shocking spidery scrawl. The writing was often marred by ink spots and smudges where he had written the words with such haste he had forgotten to remove the drips from the nib. However, she couldn't help but admire his shoddy penmanship. It suggested he was far too busy and occupied with his work to have a care about such trivialities. Bella was coming to understand the scrawl regardless, and as she read each missive she could hear his deep, calm and patient voice almost as if he was stood beside her.

When he was stood beside her, usually either teaching her some new skill or discussing the children whilst they were both clutching steaming cups in the short, restorative breaks he allowed himself, Bella was constantly aware of him. Although bizarrely, not in the guarded way she usually had around men. Dr Warriner had become both a mentor and an almost-friend

since the odd moment they had shared a few weeks ago. Whilst she was convinced he had touched her and brushed away her tears out of doctorly kindness, the moment held more significance for her. It marked the first time a man had touched her in over a year when she had neither flinched, panicked nor wanted to bolt.

His palm had cupped her cheek, his intelligent eyes had locked with hers, then Bella's skin had heated beneath his fingers and her heart had skipped a beat beneath her ribs. There had been, she was certain, a moment of perfect clarity when she had known categorically he would never hurt her and that she trusted him. More than that, she realised with a jolt, she was physically attracted to him. His mind, those fathomless blue eyes, the broad shoulders, the large work-roughened hands and those spectacles. The real her inside did not need to tell her it was swooning, because she *was* the real her. Just for a few moments, she had crawled out of her hiding place within and stood facing him. Once or twice since, there had been similar moments, but no lingering, tender touches.

Just now, there had been another one. Her family had arrived at the church to attend the Sunday sermon and she had seen him stood outside in the churchyard with his family. As much as she hated doing it, they ignored each other as they queued to go inside, but as she passed him her gaze flicked briefly to his and he winked at her. It was so quick and so subtle nobody else noticed, but it reminded Bella there was something between them, although perhaps not entirely what the real her was coming to want.

The Warriner family pews were right at the front of the church as the Earl of Markham, despite the family's

ill-deserved reputation, was the highest-ranking noble in the district. In deference to his title, her father had been given a private row just over to the side. Those seats allowed her to watch Dr Joseph Warriner for most of the sermon whilst pretending to be focused on the malicious droning from Reverend Reeves.

It gave her a unique insight into the man when he was not being the capable physician. The devoted brother always ready to share a joke with a sibling or the doting uncle entertaining his five young and boisterous nieces and nephews. The two boys belonged to the Earl and Countess, the three gorgeous little girls to Captain James Warriner and his wife and the vicar's estranged daughter, Cassie. Like all the Warriner brothers, the children had thick ebony hair and striking bright blue eyes. Today Joe was sat next to his younger brother, Jacob, and, to the Reverend's complete consternation, the pair were openly playing cards.

Bella recognised it as an act of quiet rebellion and one that certainly appeared to entertain a great many of the congregation. The Reverend Reeves was maligning the family in his sermon and had alluded to them all being the spawn of Satan. Yet aside from the surly Captain who glared at his father-in-law menacingly, the rest of the family were unperturbed by the insults. The Earl—Jack—and his wife, Letty, sat arm in arm and smiling at each other as if the dreadful sermon was a big joke. The Captain's wife, Cassie, was rocking her youngest daughter to sleep in her lap, seemingly oblivious to the Reverend's fire and brimstone predications while lost in her own thoughts, and Joe and his brother were playing what Bella thought was speculation but couldn't be sure. She had witnessed similar versions

of this rebellion every Sunday since arriving in Retford and remembered how he had made a joke of their reputation. He participated in this ritual, but the accusations bothered him. She felt privileged to be one of the few people who realised that.

The youngest Warriner groaned and tossed down his cards and the handsome doctor grinned smugly. The grin earned him personal censure from the ranking priest.

"'You are of your father, the devil, and you want to do the desires of your father!'" The Reverend Reeves pointed at him with a quaking finger. 'John, Chapter Eight, Verse Forty-Four.'

Jacob Warriner patted his brother on the back as if he had just done something brilliant. Jack smiled at his wife as if it was still a big joke and the Captain glared. As if he could sense her watching him, Joe's blue eyes slowly moved to meet hers. Held. Then winked again. Bella felt that wink all the way down to her toes and back up again. Whatever nervous reaction he had triggered, it was warm and welcoming and oddly exciting. She suppressed the urge to smile shyly in response, resorting to chewing her bottom lip instead and staring at her hymn book for the rest of the interminable sermon.

Her father ushered the family out of the church swiftly at the end. Usually they would mingle with the parishioners, but this afternoon he was headed back to London on business. Even better, her sister, after days of pleading, was going with him. That meant Bella had at least a whole blissful fortnight ahead of her where she didn't have to lie, look over her shoulder or keep a

close eye on the time whilst at the infirmary. If she was lucky, much longer. She intended to celebrate by heading directly to the infirmary the moment the dust from their retreating carriage wheels settled on the drive.

'Did you see those boys playing cards?' Her father sounded incredulous. 'Have you ever seen the like?'

'The Reverend Reeves had maligned the poor family throughout the sermon, Papa.' This came from Clarissa. 'Under the circumstances, I was amused at the way they dealt with it. Very original.' There were moments when her sister forgot to be selfish, although the older she got, the fewer and further apart they became. The words warmed Bella.

'Outrageous, you mean.'

'Not at all. *Outrageous* was when he winked brazenly at Bella.' The fuzzy feeling of sisterhood evaporated.

'He did what!' Her father was instantly livid. 'I've a good mind to turn this carriage around and give the scoundrel a piece of my mind!'

'I saw him wink, too...' her mother appeared bored '...and fear you are quite mistaken, Clarissa. The wink was aimed at his brother after he had won.'

Her lie went some way to calming her husband. 'Well...even so, gambling in the house of God and grinning and winking like a rogue are not fitting behaviours for a man who calls himself a physician. The comparisons between that young man and Dr Bentley this morning in church were quite astounding. Now, there is a physician who knows how to comport himself at all times, especially in church. You don't see Dr Bentley grinning and winking.'

'That is because Dr Bentley is a crusty old fool who wouldn't know one end of a stethoscope from the

other.' One look at the stunned face of her father and Bella realised the real her inside had spoken the words aloud. She hadn't been so outspoken and opinionated towards her father since *the incident* and she found herself grinning at the achievement.

'Dr Bentley is a well-respected physician and member of this community, young lady, and one who has repeatedly offered you his help, only to have it turned down flatly!'

More words of rebellion tumbled blithely from her mouth. 'Dr Bentley is a money-grabbing fool and little better than a quack. Of course I have turned down his offers to treat me. Archaic and draconian remedies have no place in modern medicine. Do you know he refuses to treat a person, no matter how ill, unless they pay him up front?'

'The man is entitled to earn a living from his business.'

'Would you be saying that if he refused to treat you? Say you were a stranger wandering through here and had a carriage accident or were accosted by footpads who had relieved you of your purse. One would hope the local physician was a good Samaritan as well as a businessman. Dr Warriner now single-handedly treats all the poor people of this parish because Dr Bentley refuses to. His sister-in-law established and pays for the foundling home which rescues orphaned children from poverty. Those are hardly the behaviours of bad people. Yet *Dr Bentley* refused to help little Tom because he had the audacity to have been taken in by the generosity of the maligned Warriner family. Yet *he* has the cheek to sit piously in church as if he has the right to pass judgement over good

people more generous of spirit and deed than him. A church, I should point out, which is presided over by a man who has never acknowledged the existence of his three granddaughters when they are sat directly in front of him! Those are innocent children we are talking about.' Her papa's mouth moved as if to speak, but Bella could tell he was struggling to find strong enough counter-arguments. She was too riled with her old righteous indignation to wait for him to do so. 'You never used to be so pompous, Papa. Before I fell foul of that monster at Vauxhall, you used to pride yourself on judging all men on their mettle, not hear-say and gossip.'

Now the whole carriage was silent. Nobody ever referred to *the incident*, least of all Bella, yet she had just brought it up without feeling the crippling fear which usually accompanied the memory. She was as stunned as her family and searched her mind for signs of the usual fear. None were forthcoming.

Clarissa spoke first. 'I see Bella's acid tongue has returned with a vengeance. I, for one, have missed it. You have been very dull these last few months, sister dear.' The smile she shot Bella was genuine and the bonds of sisterly love returned unabashed. She might be self-centred and a tad vain at times, but her older sister had always enjoyed a sparring match with good humour and appreciated Bella's former spirit.

'I'm pleased to see it, too, my darling.' Her mother leaned across the carriage to pat her hand. 'You always did have fire in your belly and I am encouraged to see it burning again. Does Dr Bentley really turn the sick away when they cannot pay? That is truly awful and very unchristian of the man...' And just like that

they were back to being a harmonious family again, all talk of Dr Warriner and his tantalising wayward winking forgotten.

Two hours later and Bella was positively skipping up the steps to the infirmary secure in the knowledge her overprotective papa and meddling sister were well on their way on the road towards London. Buoyed by the sudden return of her pithy retorts and forthright opinions, she had almost managed to walk across the deserted market square without the customary trickle of unease, and when it came she simply took a deep breath and logically ploughed on. Satisfying progress and hugely reassuring.

After shedding her straw bonnet and shawl and hanging them on the hall hatstand, she headed directly towards the girls' ward to check on Molly. Thankfully, no doubt due to regular gin baths, the open wound on her leg had healed relatively quickly without any signs of infection, so poor Molly was bored senseless sat in splints away from her friends. 'I brought you some paints.' The expensive set of watercolours her father had bought her to take her mind off things were gathering dust in Bella's bedchamber. She had no patience for the finer arts and always preferred to read rather than be creative. 'I thought perhaps you could brighten up the place with some of your lovely artwork.'

Molly grabbed the package gratefully and tore open the oilcloth Bella had wrapped it in. Not only had she brought the paints, but brushes and paper, too. 'Can I paint something now?'

'I don't see why not. Why don't I set up a table by the window where the light is better?'

Bella dragged a small desk across the ward and was in the process of hauling a heavy but supportive chair when she sensed, rather than saw, Dr Warriner arrive. 'Let me do that.' He came alongside and lifted it with no effort at all. Once it was set in place, he turned and dazzled her with the full force of his smile. 'I wasn't expecting to see you again today.'

'I've had a reprieve. Papa has gone back to London on business. He's taken Clarissa with him.' She watched him carefully as she passed on this news, looking for signs he was bothered by her sister's absence, and she was pleased when she saw none.

'Then I suppose you will be getting under my feet a great deal more?'

'Indeed I shall.'

'And how are our patients today?'

'As you can see, Molly is in fine fettle. I've only just arrived, so have not yet been to see the boys.' An outbreak of chickenpox was spreading like wildfire in the younger boys' dormitory, which meant the boys' ward had seen a succession of little, itching cherubs come in and go out over the past week. Dr Warriner had spent a great deal of time examining the blisters on each child and was satisfied that as they were quite rounded, rather than depressed in the centre, then this was the harmless version of pox common in children. It was highly infectious and often accompanied with a slight temperature and general feeling of malaise, so Bella and Mrs Giles had spent the last week making soothing poultices out of oatmeal and smothering them on the children from head to toe.

'Then let us get Molly settled and visit the boys' ward together.' He helped the girl stand and passed her

the crutches he'd had made specifically to fit under her arms. Dr Warriner felt that it was essential she took some exercise despite the broken leg, believing the recovery would be much quicker once the splints were removed if her healthy muscles hadn't wasted as well. It made sense to Bella and gave Molly the freedom to take her meals with her friends and get some air every day in the garden, and it was yet another pearl of medical wisdom Bella had never read about in books.

There were just two boys left in the other ward and both were in the latter stages of chickenpox. After supervising Bella listening to their chests with her stethoscope, he pronounced them fit enough to leave the ward in the morning, which left precious little she could do with her time aside from sitting with Molly. He must have realised the lack of new cases left her twiddling her thumbs. 'In my experience, it is best to relish the quiet times as they rarely last long. The lulls give me the opportunity to read up on new things and restock my medicine cupboard. Which is exactly what I am off to do now. I'm running low on almost all my essentials and Sundays are the perfect day to brew potions. For some mysterious and thus far unfathomable reason, I am rarely called to an emergency on a Sunday in Retford. I like to think it is the Almighty's attempt to make up for the Reverend Reeves's damning sermons.'

'I could help you, if you wanted.' As soon as Bella said this she was torn. One half of her was terrified he would say yes and then she would be completely alone with him surrounded by unfamiliar walls, the other half desperately wanted to learn more. 'Seeing that things are quiet here and I am in no hurry to return home,' the real her said, 'it would give me the perfect opportunity

to learn some more.' Clearly the eager scholar half of her was winning despite her irrational fears.

'Even though my father is the devil himself?' Now he was smiling and that smile made her feel all fluttery and daft.

'That really was a disgraceful sermon.'

'Not one of his best. The better ones usually liken Markham Manor and the spawn thereof to Sodom and Gomorrah. Those can get quite exciting when the Reverend reaches his crescendo. He goes quite purple. Occasionally, he even foams at the mouth.'

'Do you think he might do one before the end of the summer? I should hate to miss it.'

'It's been a while. We must be due one soon.'

As they were both walking in the direction of the hatstand in the hallway, Bella assumed he was happy for her to accompany him. When he handed over her straw bonnet, she experienced a brief moment of panic and then decided she was being ridiculous. His housekeeper was bound to be there and they had spent hours alone together, save the patients, at the infirmary. Mixing medicines would give her another practical lesson which her books glossed over and the prospect of it was rather exciting.

Outside in the empty square, he offered her his arm and with trepidation she took it. He was merely being solicitous because that was what gentlemen did. Beneath the fabric of his coat his forearm was solid, as they walked her hip occasionally grazed his, but he didn't seem to notice or care. The distance between the foundling home and his surgery was short and in no time he was ushering her inside and helping her with her shawl before leading her past his consulting room

to another small room in the back. The house appeared very quiet and the stillness brought Bella up short.

'Where is Mrs Patterson?'

'I always give her Sunday afternoons off.' She swallowed and breathed deeply.

He has no intention of hurting you.

'Now that I think on it, it was remiss of me not to mention it sooner. I forget sometimes that you are a young lady and, as such, should be chaperoned. Should I take you back to the infirmary?'

Chapter Nine

'No. No, of course not.'

She didn't look particularly sure and Joe could have kicked himself at his thoughtlessness. The trouble was, the longer he spent with Bella, the more they discussed medicines and treatments and ailments, the more he thought of her as a fellow physician because she had such an astute scientific mind. Not completely, of course. He had lied when he'd said he forgot she was a young lady. As each day passed, he was becoming increasingly aware of the fact. Her scientific mind aside, he found himself watching her more. The way she moved, the way her long lashes framed her dark eyes, the tiny, iridescent flecks of copper in her irises, the way she pouted when deep in thought, the magnificent way she filled out her gowns. Just now, as they had strolled across the square, Joe had struggled to keep his voice from moaning every time her undulating hips had brushed against his thigh.

Inviting her here had been foolhardy and a trifle selfish, but he had been delighted by her offer to help him and perhaps even relished the opportunity to spend

more time with her. It seemed Jake might indeed be right and he did prefer Bella to her sister. He certainly hadn't given Clarissa a great deal of thought in over a fortnight. Today, when he had seen her in church, his eyes had resolutely sought out the bookish Beaumont. In fact, if he were honest, he hadn't really noticed Clarissa at all. Which seemed to rather prove Jake's point. The more Joe got to know Bella, the more she occupied his thoughts. The woman he had believed himself in love with now apparently no longer intrigued or interested him, when Bella did both and had, God help him, since the moment he had brushed that single tear from her cheek. The rapid about-face of his feelings was unsettling. Was this the woman his heart now desired? A real flesh-and-blood woman rather than an ethereal fantasy within his own head? Joe had never fallen for a real woman before. He'd done a great deal of thinking about the subject of late and was a little ashamed of himself, truth be told. But there was no arguing with facts. He was falling for the real Bella and in grave danger of falling hard.

'I am eager to learn, Dr Warriner.'

By saying that, Bella reminded him her interest in him was purely academic and once again he was barking up the wrong tree. She didn't want him any more than her sister did. She simply wanted to learn. Like a sponge, she was the most receptive and canny student he had ever met. Her mind was sharp and her memory sharper. Not once had he ever seen Bella write anything down, yet she never needed to be taught something twice. And he, for his sins, was now her sole tutor. Lucky him.

Self-conscious and suddenly awkward, Joe began

to reach for some ingredients from his shelves to make more tincture of laudanum. 'We should start with the basics. No medical kit is complete without a ready supply of laudanum. It is the most powerful painkiller yet discovered and can induce sleep in higher amounts. However, it should be used sparingly and withdrawn as a treatment as soon as the patient shows signs of recovery. The opium base makes it dangerously addictive and regular users become nonsensical.' Joe retrieved the brown leather journal he kept in a drawer and handed it to her. 'This is my medical bible. In here I have logged every single one of my recipes. This book is very poorly organised, I'm afraid. I keep meaning to start a new one...but, alas, I never seem to have the time. Over the years, with experimentation, I have tweaked quite a few. If you see one with a large cross drawn through it, then that means I have written a better version of the recipe later on. Towards the back is my current recipe for laudanum.'

She found it with little problem and began to read. 'There are two different recipes.'

'I make a different type for children. Less opium in view of their size and a great deal of sugar because it tastes foul and they take it better when it is sweet.'

'Yet you add no sugar for adults?'

'I want the taste to be unpleasant because...?'

'They are less likely to become dependent on it if it's awful on the palate.' She had a way of smiling and shaking her head when she worked out something. 'Which one shall I make?'

'A batch of both. Be careful not to put your fingers near your mouth after you handle the opium. It will make your head spin.'

Joe did not need to tell her to weigh and measure the ingredients meticulously. He already knew her well enough to know she would check each measurement at least twice. Bella didn't cut corners or approach tasks in a slap-dash manner. She did everything logically and in an impressively practical manner. He began to mix more of his honey salve while keeping a close eye on her. To his amusement she sniffed everything before adding it to her mixture, her small nose wrinkling in disgust at the over-perfumed smell of the opium resin. 'It is a mystery to me why some people take this stuff for pleasure.'

'Me, too, although I doubt it gives them much pleasure when they come to depend on it. Everything I have witnessed and read leads me to conclude the euphoria of opium is brief. In no time at all, it plunges the body into melancholy, often one so deep that it is difficult to claw out of without the complete cessation of the drug. Even then it takes the mind a time to heal.'

'Do you believe the mind can heal?' She stopped grinding the resin in the mortar to stare at him. 'If it is broken, I mean, rather than addled by laudanum. Lunatics, melancholiacs…hysterics?'

'An interesting question and one I do not completely know the answer to.'

'But if you had to speculate?' She had leaned closer as if his opinion was of great import and Joe found himself frowning in thought.

'I suppose it entirely depends on what is wrong with the mind and how advanced the illness is. I have seen some of the poor unfortunates in the asylums and confess I would not have the first clue as to how to help them. They seem to be locked inside their own heads

and oblivious to the world around them. Those suffering from diseases like syphilis are quite tragic and I fear there is no hope for them. Whatever the illness does, it appears to alter the human brain and send it on a slow and irreversible decline into madness.'

'Say, for instance, the illness is caused by trauma. Something dreadful which changes the person. I have read accounts of soldiers' minds damaged by the horrors of war. Can those minds be fixed or is the damage irreversible?'

Something Joe had a first-hand account of. His brother Jamie had come back from the Peninsula changed and prone to violent outbursts in the night. However, talking about his beloved elder brother's ordeal with anyone outside the family was disloyal, so he would have to choose his next words carefully. 'I believe the human brain is the most powerful organ in the body and, like any organ, can be damaged by trauma and sometimes heal itself afterwards. I believe the mind can construct horrible and entirely believable scenarios to trick its owner into believing them as reality. A person can build giant walls in their minds which can imprison them. The key to the cure in such cases depends on the patient and the particular demons which haunt them. They need to find a way to circumvent or demolish those walls to see clear sky rather than their fears.'

She was nodding in assent, almost as if relieved to know this. 'Hypothetically speaking then, say you encountered an individual who had suffered horrifically at the hands of another and had—how did you put it?—locked themselves inside their own heads and built enormous prison walls in their mind. What if

that person was irrationally terrified of everything and everyone? What treatments would you prescribe to help them demolish them?'

Jamie had needed time, patience and understanding. He had also, it turned out, needed the love of a good woman to begin to forgive himself for being broken. He had confided his deepest, darkest fears to Cassie and in doing so had faced his demons. Five years on and his brother no longer thought himself a danger to society and was happy. He still had the occasional nightmare and still had a gun hidden in his bedchamber, but now it was consigned to the highest shelf of a cupboard rather than under his pillow. 'I believe, in the first instance, I would encourage the patient to talk to somebody they trusted.'

'Talk?' This appeared to astound her.

'Why, yes. A problem shared is a problem halved. I believe talking through fears and anxieties allows the owner of those problems and anxieties to take them out and examine them for themselves. Perhaps a little more dispassionately. See them through somebody else's eyes. I think the first step has to be to face their fears in order to control them.'

'I see.' She picked up the pestle again and began to slowly grind the opium resin into a powder. 'What are your opinions on water treatments for the insane?' She certainly knew how to test his knowledge and was apparently in fine form today.

'Again, I suppose it depends on the water treatments. Taking the waters, sea bathing…anything which relaxes the body and mind are always beneficial. If the mind is stressed, it stands to reason relaxation must be a good thing.'

'In my readings, I have encountered physicians who advocate more severe kinds of water therapy for those suffering from ailments of the mind. Cold-water treatments, for example, are supposed to shock the patient out of their impaired mental state.'

'Good grief! Do physicians still do that? I don't have much cause to experiment with diseases of the mind here in my practice, but I should imagine restraining a poor soul and then subjecting them to—or submerging them in—freezing water is tantamount to torture. I see no benefit in traumatising a traumatised patient further.'

This answer appeared to please her and she smiled at him. Like all her smiles it transformed her pretty face into a thing of sheer beauty which made his breath catch and those damn tingles play havoc with his nerves. 'I'm glad you think so. I think they are barbaric also.' She looked away then to check his recipe and a companionable silence descended. For several minutes they worked side by side, content to say nothing at all.

When her laudanum tincture was steeping, she spoke again, perhaps a little tentatively. 'Do you believe female patients with addled minds might need different treatments to male patients?'

'Why would they?'

'It is a widely held belief, is it not, that because of their physiology women are prone to hysteria…a condition which impairs their mind and…and must be treated…accordingly?' He glanced at her, a little stunned that she would want to talk about such a delicate subject, and was not surprised when she refused to meet his eye. Her cheeks were already rosy and her embarrassed blush made her swanlike neck blotchy.

'I...um...I have read about it.' Good grief, were they really going to talk about this? He sincerely hoped not. Joe began to focus intently on mixing his honey salve into a smooth paste in case he also blushed. Men of science shouldn't blush over scientific topics.

'Have you ever had to treat a patient for...um... hysteria?'

'No.' Joe wanted to hide his face. Or leave. Quickly.

'Do you believe *treatment* for hysteria is necessary, Dr Warriner?'

The temptation to change the subject was overwhelming, because what she was asking involved discussing the parts of a lady which a gentleman shouldn't mention in the normal course of a conversation—but she was also a scientist. A woman, *undeniably*, yet a scientist first. Were she a male assistant asking the same question, Joe would happily engage in the debate. Share his knowledge of female anatomy—both as a physician and a man—and laugh at the absurdity of the proposition. The double standard bothered him. 'Ah...well...firstly, I think I would have to subscribe to the theory that hysteria—as a medical condition— actually exists.' And that the only way of curing a woman with the condition involved intimately massaging those parts he really did not want to mention. He'd heard ridiculous tales of London doctors earning a fortune out of the procedure.

'And you don't?'

Some things were less painful in the long run if you just did what was necessary quickly to get it over with. *Be brave, Joe. Answer the question like the cool, calm, collected academic you pride yourself on being.* 'Can I assume, Bella, you are familiar with the theory and

treatments of hysteria?' Because if she wasn't, Joe was certainly not going to apprise her of them. Another glance to the side confirmed she was now quite crimson everywhere, a hue he suspected he also shared. She nodded curtly and stared at the tabletop. The obvious hideous embarrassment did confirm she was fully aware of what they were about to talk about. The culmination of sexual gratification! *Le petit mort*—the little death. The ridiculous, yet common, idea that females became *hysterical* and went out of their wits because of the lack thereof. 'I am wholly convinced it is complete nonsense. I fail to understand why a woman would need the paid services of a physician to achieve what any decent lover would happily provide her for free.' Something he instantly regretted saying the moment the words escaped as Joe silently prayed she wouldn't ask him how. In case she did, he bumbled on. 'The idea that illness of the mind can be cured by treating the...um...nether regions with vigorous pelvic massage makes no scientific sense whatsoever.'

'I see.' She still refused to look at him. 'Good to know... Very good to know... I believe my laudanum is ready to be bottled, Doctor. Where do you keep the bottles?'

Two hours later and Dr Warriner's medicine shelves were pleasingly full. After the abrupt conclusion to the difficult conversation she had instigated, things had been awkward for a full five minutes before he had started to laugh, clearing the air. 'I cannot remember the last time I blushed like a beetroot, Bella. You certainly know how to confound a man.'

'I was merely curious.' For herself, although she

could hardly confess to that shame. 'I didn't mean to embarrass you.' He shrugged and continued to grin, which in turn made her smile, too. 'If it is any consolation, I also embarrassed myself in the process.'

'I saw the blush. It was very impressive.'

'I've always excelled at blushing. I wish I didn't.'

'It suits you. Makes you seem less formidable.' He nudged her playfully with his arm and his deep blue eyes twinkled behind the lenses of his spectacles. Bella wished he would take them off. The combination of easy genius and wickedly handsome man was unnerving and made it difficult to concentrate.

'I'm hardly formidable.'

'On the contrary, when I first met you I found you almost frightening. Very serious. Very studious. Very unapproachable. However, now I know you are really none of those things. Apart from studious—you are brilliantly studious.'

At the time, she had been flattered by the compliment, because to be thought brilliant by him was astounding, but had been unable to think up any response other than blushing again. Instead, she began a discussion about another medical topic until the blush faded. 'What made you become a doctor?'

'The need to fix things. My younger brother, Jake, despairs of my good nature, but I cannot seem to help myself. If somebody needs my help, I have to help them, even if they don't want or deserve it.'

Something Bella understood only too well and ultimately to her detriment. 'I suppose it would have been easier to set up a practice anywhere in the country, somewhere where the name Warriner doesn't mean anything.'

'Of course it would have. But I am also, apparently, a glutton for punishment and determined to always seek the good in people—or hope for some good in people.'

'Why do you think that is?' As they had been talking about the workings of the human mind, a topic she was now determined to understand, Bella wanted to know what had shaped his character. Because events did shape a person's character, whether they be in a negative or a positive way. Aside from how *the incident* had changed her, she had also seen how being declared an Incomparable had affected her sister. Clarissa now needed constant affirmation that she was still an Incomparable and could not see the label was ultimately nonsense.

Joe stopped what he was doing and gave the question some serious thought, as if he had never paused to consider it before. 'I suppose it stems from having such an awful father. I know he was a bad man with few redeeming qualities, but as a child I needed to make excuses for him, almost as if those excuses would explain why he was so wretched.'

'You wanted to fix him.'

'I did. I suppose I still do. Even now I try to convince myself he was a drunkard because he was heartbroken over my mother. It irritates all of my brothers, as they hate him unreservedly.'

'But you don't hate him?'

'I can't bring myself to. Don't get me wrong, I cannot love the man either. I just choose to believe he was human underneath it all. Lost, perhaps, but still there somewhere.'

Exactly how Bella saw herself. 'What about your mother?'

'She's an enigma. I don't really remember her at all.'

'How old were you when she died?'

He answered without hesitation. 'Twelve.' Then he promptly picked up a jar and began filling it with salve, the motion suggesting his mother was not a topic he felt particularly comfortable talking about. Odd when he was so open about his father.

'Twelve? Yet you don't remember her?' If he had said five, six or even seven, she would have accepted his explanation, but twelve—Bella had very clear memories of being twelve and younger. 'Do you remember nothing about her at all?'

'I remember she was very beautiful. She had lovely golden hair which was so different to the rest of my family. The four of us all take after our father in appearance. She was very graceful, very well spoken. Not really the usual sort of woman one would expect in deepest, darkest, dankest Nottinghamshire.' He sealed the final pot of honey salve decisively and pushed it to one side. 'Is your laudanum ready to be bottled yet?' Before she could answer, he was striding across the room to fetch the tiny bottles. 'We will need to measure out the dosage exactly. I make sure there is never enough in one bottle to kill a person.' The quick change of subject said a great deal. His mother had shaped his character far more than even he knew.

It was close to six before Bella reluctantly acknowledged she needed to go home. 'I should send for the carriage. My mother will send out a search party if I am not home for dinner.'

'No need. I could drive you home in my curricle.

It will be quicker than sending a message and waiting for the carriage to get back here.'

She dithered, suddenly nervous, and he laughed at her. A delicious warm sound she felt everywhere. 'Are you going to worry about propriety when we have been huddled up here alone all afternoon? Or are you terrified to be seen with me?'

Not exactly—but terrified still. He was watching her intently for her reaction. 'Let me put your mind at rest. The streets will be deserted at this time on a Sunday evening, and if I take the lane behind the square, I doubt we will encounter a soul. It will be lovely and quiet. Nobody will see you with a *vile* Warriner.'

Quiet *and* deserted. And he was a man. Three excellent reasons to say no. The last time she had been dragged to a quiet and deserted place by a man...

Bella took a deep breath and forced the memory out of her head. She had to face her fears, and would do so with logic. Refusing would seem churlish and unfriendly after he had been nothing but generous to her with his time and his knowledge. Part of her was coming to believe he was purposefully training her in the art of medicine and he had just called her brilliantly studious. He respected her brain. Nothing more.

He has no intention of hurting you.

His wise words also still resonated. She did need to face her fears and being alone in a quiet, tree-lined country lane with a man would certainly do that. What exactly was there to be afraid of? Logically, she understood if Dr Warriner harboured any intentions of attacking her, then he could have done so at any point over the course of the afternoon, secure in the knowledge nobody would come to her rescue because they

were safely ensconced in the back of his house. All alone. The addition of fresh air and a few bushes would hardly turn him into a monster. Besides, he was too kind and gentle to hurt a fly. She knew that inside. At least his driving her home would allow her to pick his magnificent brain further while taking another decisive leap forward on the road to recovery. 'If you don't mind, that would be lovely.'

'Of course, I don't mind. I always dine at Markham Manor on a Sunday evening, so I would need my curricle soon regardless. I'll go and fetch it and meet you out front in ten minutes.' With that, he was gone, leaving Bella all alone in his house hoping she would not come to regret her decision. She tidied away the last of the bottles and equipment and then located her discarded bonnet, deciding to wait for him at the front door. But on the short walk down the hallway, curiosity got the better of her and she found herself wandering into his private rooms instead.

The small sitting room was cosy and filled with evidence of his family. Children's drawings stood along the mantel: simple depictions of flowers or stick people. One had the uneven letters *Uncle Joe* scrawled across the top. On another wall she recognised the work of his brother. A painting of Dr Sensible, complete with spectacles and medical bag, dashing to yet another emergency. His medical degree was framed next to it. The Countess of Markham had mentioned he had graduated top of his class in just two years when Bella had first volunteered at the foundling home, a note of pride in her voice at such an epic achievement. The Warriners were a close family. A loving one.

Alongside a large, comfortable chair were medical

journals, many well thumbed. A few more bore evidence of his hurried spidery handwriting where he had written his own notes in the margins. She picked them up and leafed through them, and his scrawl on one made her smile. The physician's surname had been crossed out and next to it was the word *cretin*, while the title of the work had been similarly adjusted from *A Treatise on Leech Bleeding in Infants* to *A Treatise on How to Frighten Infants and Put Them off Physicians for Life.*

Dr Warriner's ideas on medicine were scandalously modern, but she liked them all the more for that. It suggested a man who weighed up all the evidence, tested the validity of results and refused to be cowed by the decrepit establishmentarians, like Dr Bentley, who rigorously adhered to the old methods because they were too lazy or too ignorant to learn the new. He was a man who might, if she could find the words to confide in him, help her fight to become normal again. Demolish the damaging walls in her head and finally see the sky. Did she trust enough? Riding in a carriage and confessing you were addled were two entirely different things and right now it would be more prudent to take things one small step at a time.

Chapter Ten

At the sound of the horses Bella felt simultaneously guilty for snooping and unnerved at what she was about to do. She understood it was a big step. A turning point. She was decisively facing her fears even if it was with a man her heart instinctively trusted. Before she allowed any of those fears or doubts to creep in, she hurried outside and found him stood next to the horses, aimlessly stroking the mane of one of them.

'This is Withering. He's a shameless flirt.'

'Withering? What an odd name for a horse.'

He smiled as her hand came up to stroke the animal. 'I named him after James Withering, the doctor who discovered the common foxglove could…?' He eyed her expectantly, testing her knowledge.

'Treat patients with heart problems. I've read his work. Can I assume the other horse is also named after one of your medical heroes? Laennec, perhaps?'

'No. I had not read any of Laennec's work when I purchased these two. This is Davy.'

'Of course, after Humphry. The chemist.'

'A great scientist. His work on phlogisticated nitrous

air intrigues me. The idea that physicians might use his gas during surgery to alleviate pain—just imagine the possibilities if such a thing were possible?'

His mind was fascinating. The way he looked when he was hypothesising was also fascinating. Boyish, brilliant, devilishly handsome. And he was not wearing his spectacles, she noted. Without them he appeared more rakish, a word Bella never would have thought to associate with him before, but one that suited him right this second. The bright blue-and-white racing curricle added to the dashing image and was again not something she would have attributed to him. 'This looks fast.'

'It is.' He grinned and it did odd things to her pulse. 'I purchased it specifically because it flies like the wind. In case of *medical* emergencies, you understand.' A blatant lie judging by his pleased expression. 'And so useful. I had the back modified to hold my medical supplies rather than a tiger. I have far more use for bandages than a footman.' There was a large matching blue-and-white box nestled between the back wheels, secured with a very sturdy padlock. 'This magnificent machine is practically a mobile hospital. You name it, it's in that box. A good physician should always be prepared for every eventuality.'

'Does the big box slow it down?'

'Not at all. It weighs less than the average tiger and these horses are lightning quick. If you are not of a nervous disposition, I shall treat you to full speed when we get to an open bit of road. It's the perfect day for it.'

'I'm not of a nervous disposition.' A blatant lie when this last year she'd had nothing but. However, the idea of racing down a country lane with him was thrilling

and certainly not at all the sort of pursuit two serious scholars ought to engage in. Which added to the excitement. Racing sounded naughty and frivolous. Freeing. Bella was almost giddy at the prospect. 'Would you let me drive it? Just for a bit?'

'I might be persuaded to hand over the ribbons. Come. Let me help you up.'

'Thank you, Doctor.' Gingerly, Bella stepped closer to the curricle, not quite believing that this was her, being so brave, so fearless, so like her old self, and his hands came to rest on her waist.

'Don't you think it's time we dispensed with the formalities? We are about to drive *scandalously* fast. Perhaps it's time you called me Joe?'

She nodded jerkily because he was touching her. He had such big hands. They almost spanned her waist and she could feel the heat of them all the way through her stays. It was, for want of a better word, rather nice. Her own hands automatically went to his shoulders as he lifted her effortlessly off the floor. They were very solid, the muscles bunching beneath her palms as he carefully deposited her in the seat. Like a little boy with a new toy, he bounded around the curricle and hoisted himself up beside her. His body took up a great deal of the small space, resulting in his broad shoulders lightly brushing her arm as he gathered the reins together. Then, before she had time to reconsider, they were off, trotting out of the deserted square and out on to the wide lane behind it.

For the first few minutes he allowed the horses to warm up before he beamed at her, his handsome blue eyes twinkling with mischief. 'Hold on to your bonnet, Bella. I'd hate for you to lose it.' She barely had the

time to comply. The horses kicked into a gallop and the nimble curricle bounced on its springs. A joyful giggle escaped her lips as they tore up the empty road, Withering and Davy going faster and faster, both enjoying the run as much as their passengers. 'There's a slight bend in the road coming up—you might want to grab on to something.' His laughing deep voice was louder to be heard over the rattling of the wheels. 'Because I'm not slowing down!'

Bella took one hand from her hat to hold on to the rail, then decided two hands were probably called for. The tiny carriage hugged the road tightly as they turned, the speed dislodging her bonnet to dangle loosely by the ribbons around her neck. She could feel the full force of gravity on her hairstyle, the wind and her smooth, slippery locks proving too challenging for the many hairpins her maid had secured it with this morning. She probably now looked a fright and couldn't muster the enthusiasm to care. This was thrilling and naughty and totally, wonderfully frivolous. When had she last truly had fun like this? Too long, she decided, and she wanted more. Fun made her fizz inside, tiny bubbles of joy which began in her tummy and popped out of her mouth in laughter. This was living and she had missed it.

When she suddenly felt the curricle slow, she ruthlessly suppressed the tiny shiver of panic, refusing to allow her vivid and toxic imagination to spoil the beauty of the moment.

'Would you like a turn?' Joe brought the horses to a stop and jiggled the ribbons in her direction, smiling from ear to ear.

'I would, but have to confess I have never driven a

curricle before.' Honesty was probably best, even if he withdrew the offer. His infectious smile never faltered.

'Ah. A novice. It's dead simple. Here, let me show you.' He passed her the reins and then began to explain how to control the horses, his hands directing hers lightly on the thin strips of soft leather as he did so. They hovered reassuringly close by as she set off at a pace reserved for octogenarians with rampant rheumatism. 'That's it. Loosen the ribbons slightly. The tighter you hold them, the slower the horses will go. Poor Withering and Davy will die of boredom from this sedentary speed and I assume you want to get home before the witching hour.'

Over the next mile her confidence grew. It really was easy. A bit like riding a horse, except from a small distance, and the scientifically named mounts were wonderfully responsive and obedient. Joe was now leaning one long arm along the top of the seat behind her shoulders in case she quickly needed his assistance, not touching but intimately close, offering pointers occasionally but perfectly at ease with leaving her in charge. She adored that he trusted her enough to delegate. Something he did all the time, whether it be mixing potions, treating tonsils or driving his precious curricle. With him, Bella rarely felt addled or irrational at all. His attitude was empowering, addictively so. When they approached the final hazard-free straight close to her house, Bella could resist the temptation no longer. He sensed she wanted to fly and adjusted his position accordingly, bracing his booted feet to hold his big body steady.

The trailing arm came around her waist, the other rested gently on her elbow. Very close. So close she

could feel his warm breath whisper across her cheek as he issued instructions. Bella felt herself stiffen for a second before the inconceivable happened. Instead of feeling frightened at being at the mercy of a man, she felt safe. Protected. Joe became a blanket of security which emboldened her to be daring because he believed in her. When the horses sprinted, her body was pushed back towards the seat and further into his strong arms, and the open fields and bushes sped past in a green haze.

The unexpected laughter was borne out of sheer euphoria. Bella felt completely free and unfettered for the first time in over a year. Empowered and invincible. Young and carefree. The horses' thundering hooves in tandem with the glorious beating of her own excited heart.

Joe helped her slow the horses as her house came into view, his chest and arms enveloping her back, and the feeling of safety disappeared. Suddenly, he was no longer her protector, yet nor was he a threat.

He was just a man.

A very handsome man who looked like sin and smelled better. Windswept and with his deep blue eyes shining, Joe was devastating and for the first time in her life Bella was not a scholar or a dutiful daughter or a less attractive sister. Neither was she a scared, wounded bird.

She was a woman.

A woman who was experiencing the very first stirrings of what she suspected was desire.

She had read about the symptoms. The erratic heartbeat, warm palms, fizzing nerve endings and overwhelming need to lick her own tingling lips surely could be nothing else. His eyes dropped to those lips

slowly and he blinked. His hands let go of the ribbons and he unwrapped himself from her body. The sudden exposure of her back to the soft summer breeze made goosebumps break out all over her skin. Or perhaps that had been caused by Joe? Bella didn't know, yet they added to the odd sense of anticipation and need.

Joe, on the other hand, had already jumped to the road. 'I assume you don't want to be dropped off any closer to home, what with your father and all.' He busied himself securing the reins before walking around to her side and offering up his arms to help her down.

Once again, those warm hands spanned her waist. Once again, she had to feel the strength in his impressive shoulders as he lifted her down, although it was more significant now that she was so aware of him and so aware of herself as well. When her feet touched the floor, she was scandalously close to him and she didn't care. Being close to Joe was good. Their bodies were inches apart. Her hands had slid down to his chest, marvelling at the feel of it beneath his thin waistcoat and shirt. His hands remained resolutely on her waist, seemingly content to linger there. Neither of them made any attempt to sever the contact and neither dared speak, in Bella's case because she didn't want to break the spell they were under. She had no idea why he was quiet. When those fathomless blue eyes dropped to her lips again, the air between them became charged. Her body warmed further and her breath became ragged. Although she had little experience of men, good men, she knew with certainty he was about to kiss her.

Bella felt herself begin to rise on tiptoes, felt his fingers flex on her waist, his heart hammer beneath

her fingertips, and then panicked. The real her inside was screaming at her to step forward and let it happen.

Revel in this marvellous, magical unexpected moment.

That Bella wanted his kiss. The other, frightened, broken Bella feared it.

In the end broken Bella won. Her hands flattened against his chest and decisively pushed him backwards until he released his hold. He looked befuddled. As if he were as confused by what had just happened as she was. His dark eyebrows drew together and he simply stared at her. A question in his eyes and one she didn't want to have to answer.

The awkward stiffness returned to her limbs, and without thinking her arms came up to hug her body as she began to back away like a frightened deer. 'I should go. My mother will be worried.'

'Yes. Of course.' He stared down at his feet, then back up. She could almost hear the brilliant cogs of his mind whirring, yet she had no earthly idea what he was thinking. Probably that she was odd. Which, of course, she was. He took a step forward and she winced. Something which halted him in his tracks. 'Is everything all right, Bella?'

'Yes. Yes, of course.' She wanted to run. To cry. Irrational fear began to claw at her gut. 'Thank you for bringing me home.' Bella didn't wait for a response. Waiting would mean explaining and she didn't have the words. She spun on her heel and began to march away. The march soon became a run and within seconds she was hurtling towards the gates of her father's rented house and didn't stop running until she was safely inside.

* * *

After a largely restless night in his old bedchamber at Markham Manor, Joe intended to complete his daily rounds quickly to get to the foundling home by late afternoon. In truth, there was nothing pressing requiring his attention there, apart from the dark-haired conundrum who was occupying an ever-increasing number of his thoughts. It had been Bella who was responsible for his lack of sleep and not all his nighttime pondering had involved her lovely legs and beautifully rounded bottom or her brilliant mind. A great deal of his night was spent remembering the terror in her eyes before she had run away. Why the hell had she run away? From him?

Yesterday, she had worked alongside him companionably for hours in his house, then dazzled him on the short drive back to hers. That infectious giggle at his irresponsible driving, the wonder in her eyes as they had flown down the road, the glorious sight of her hair tumbling over her shoulders like ebony silk— all of it made his heart stutter and his body yearn to know her better.

Then the dreadful reaction at the end of her driveway when he'd almost kissed her. The way her body had stiffened and her lovely dark eyes had become wary, darting between the road and him as if she couldn't wait to be rid of him; her small fists clenched, ready to pummel him if he dared come any nearer.

It was insulting.

Humiliating.

And, damn her, worrying.

Her rapid about-face from cheerful assistant to fearful woman bothered him much more than it angered

him, especially when moments before they had been getting along so well. The way she had sprinted down the driveway had made him feel like a Viking marauder again, yet for the life of him he had no idea quite what had happened to cause it. It was not as if he *had* kissed her. He'd almost kissed her. He'd desperately wanted to kiss her, but there had been several inches of fresh air between their lips at all times.

To the best of his knowledge he also hadn't flirted. He'd been tempted to. Driving her home, just the two of them, felt like something a courting couple would do and for some inexplicable reason that felt right with her. However, nerves and his conscience got the better of him and he decided against it. Joe might have resisted flirting, but he acknowledged he'd failed to resist the urge to touch her, so perhaps that had upset her. For half the journey his hands had enjoyed the warmth of her skin as he'd instructed her in the subtle art of curricle driving. Not such a subtle art in reality, but he had been a most attentive tutor, using any excuse to get closer to her until he had practically cuddled her in his lap.

That might have upset her—although at the time she had seemed perfectly comfortable with it. Then, of course, only a few weeks before, he had been fawning over her sister. Well, not quite fawning, he hoped, but he had tried to call on the family as a thinly veiled attempt to call on Clarissa. Something the intelligent, bookish Beaumont might have worked out when he had turned up on their doorstep uninvited. Joe supposed his sudden change of heart might appear disingenuous.

Maybe she had seen his attempt at dropping the correct formalities as an attempt at shamelessly wooing

her instead, mercenary and crassly contrived now that
his brief association with Clarissa had come to a crush-
ing end? Another clumsy attempt at courting an heiress
after failing with the first one. The world and his wife
were convinced money was all the Warriner family
wanted and there was no denying the Beaumonts came
with money. Such behaviour would naturally infuriate
a woman, so he supposed he could hardly blame her.

He was still furious at himself for allowing Jake to
rile him into calling on the family in the first place,
when he knew it was a mistake. But Joe had been angry
and wanted to prove Jake was wrong about his consis-
tently poor choice in women. He had also wanted to
reassure himself he did have real feelings for Clarissa
that were based on fact, rather than the construct he
had created of her in his mind. Yet Jake had had his
measure, it appeared, and that galled.

Joe had never lusted after Clarissa. Not once in his
wildest fantasies had he imagined her in the throes of
passion or rumpled in his bed. In his stupid head, she
was too perfect to dare to allow his thoughts to wander
in that direction. Not a real flesh-and-blood woman at
all. Therefore, the ethereal, mythical Clarissa had been
a construct. A shadow. A ghostly, untenable image of
perfection conjured out of nothing real. An enigma—a
boy's dream of perfection rather than the sort of woman
the man found attractive.

If he was being brutally honest with himself, had he
ever found the real Clarissa interesting? Conversations
about ribbons and parties were dull. Yet he enjoyed her
sister's questions and observations and had also en-
joyed more than one dream in which her shapely bare
legs were tangled in his rumpled sheets. Last night,

after seeing her dark eyes fired with excitement and her hair loose, his fevered dream about Bella had been outrageously vivid. All that glorious straight dark hair fanned over his pillows, mussed from where his fingers had tangled in it. Her pink lips plump and swollen from his kisses. Her lovely eyes darker still from passion rather than wary. His mind desperate to know exactly what was going on in hers. Burning lust and curiosity. Those intense feelings were uniquely about Bella, and the more he got to know her, the more she interested him and the greater he lusted.

Perhaps she had seen that yesterday and his blatant lust had got her dander up? It was possible. He had found his eyes wandering to her as she worked alongside him. He had sought excuses to touch her and hold her. It was feasible he had held her too close and for a moment too long. And he'd asked her to call him Joe—because he had wanted to be Joe for her. Joe the man rather than the more formal Dr Warriner. He had even intentionally removed his spectacles as he'd drawn the curricle outside his office, in a pathetic attempt to appear less scholarly and more...what? Handsome? Attractive? He might have come across a tad desperate. Perhaps, in his rampant enthusiasm, he had overstepped the mark, especially if she was not at all interested in him that way. Something as likely as it was humbling.

Should he apologise in case he had offended her or ogled or lingered? Should he set the record straight and tell Bella his infatuation with Clarissa had been a silly phase and one he had quickly grown out of? Which, of course, all his infatuations had been, so why should this one be any different? Dare he suggest he preferred

Bella now that he had got to know her? Only an idiot would admit that truth. Aside from the fact it made Joe sound fickle and indecisive, her father had forbidden both of his daughters from associating with the entire Warriner family, so this foolish attraction was also doomed from the outset, too, and he would do better to leave it well be. That would be the sensible course of action as he wasn't entirely sure what he was feeling any more or if his sudden attraction to Bella was as transient as it had been for her sister. All his previous infatuations had been short-lived, why on earth should this one be any different?

Although this did *feel* different.

Bella had flaws. She was hot and cold. Her erratic stand-offish behaviour, for example, was annoying when Joe had done nothing to deserve it. And she could be snippy and downright insulting when she had a mind to be. One minute they got on like a house on fire and the next she bolted as if she was scared of him. Scared of him! Joe. The most placid and soft-hearted Warriner. It didn't make sense. Yet he still liked her. Her other attributes more than made up for her unpredictable mood swings. She was clever, resourceful, kind and brave. She was actively disobeying her father to continue to work with him, which showed she had the courage of her convictions and cared deeply about their patients. Bella was dependable. Scholarly. Inquisitive. Practical. Had a beautiful smile. A gloriously naughty laugh, lovely eyes and those legs... All real attributes rather than imagined. His feelings more human than courtly.

And still ultimately pointless.

Regardless of what he was feeling, Bella had never

once given him the impression she reciprocated them
and he sincerely doubted she was similarly struggling
with a sorry case of inappropriate lust. After yester-
day's tense and uncomfortable end to their carriage
ride, he wasn't entirely certain what the blasted woman
was thinking. But he still wanted to kiss her. Good
lord, he wanted to kiss her so badly, the pain of want-
ing a bit like a toothache. Constant. All-consuming.

Yet he still did not know what to do about it!

He huffed out a sigh, earning him curious glances
from the two brothers sat with him at the breakfast
table, and pretended to be engrossed in his newspaper.
Joe turned the page and wished he hadn't.

Chapter Eleven

He stared at the headline with a sinking feeling. Smallpox was in Nottingham. Although that was nearly forty miles away, it was still far too close for comfort as far as he was concerned. The Great North Road joined the towns together, which meant the disease could easily travel in a carriage and wreak devastation. Definitely something serious enough to take his mind off the vexing Bella and his own maddening confusion.

'You look like the sky is about to fall down.' His eldest brother, Jack, dropped his own newspaper to stare at him. 'Why are you huffing and frowning? You've been doing it all morning.'

Joe turned his newspaper around so it could be read from across the table. 'Smallpox.'

'Ah. I see. Not good.' As always, his big brother tried to reassure him. 'But as you've insisted on us all suffering that vaccination stuff, we have nothing to fear. Do we?'

'No. Of course not. Everybody in this house is protected against the disease. But it's not this house I worry about. It's all the others. Don't you remember

the ruckus Dr Bentley created when I tried to offer it when I first set up my practice here? He put the fear of God in people.'

Quite literally as it turned out. As soon as the old fool got wind of Joe's plans to treat the whole of Retford with cowpox—a harmless disease which was proved to repel smallpox—Dr Bentley had declared it a scandalous travesty. Cowpox was a bovine disease infecting the skin and udders of farmyard creatures, after all, and therefore not human. To suggest wilfully infecting the entire parish with a bovine disease on the off chance it would keep them safe from the dreaded smallpox was outrageous, when everyone knew the best way to prevent it was to be inoculated by subjecting the people to a weakened version of smallpox itself. A human disease for human patients.

Joe had tried to be the voice of reason, explaining that the new cowpox vaccination held less of the risk of inoculation—which sometimes erupted into full-blown smallpox regardless—but he was a newly qualified physician, and a Warriner to boot, so his calls fell on dubious ears.

Then the consistently Warriner-hating Reverend Reeves had thrown his oar in and issued a blistering sermon from the pulpit quoting Corinthians. '"All flesh is not the same flesh, but there is one kind of flesh of men, another flesh of beasts."'

At the end, the parishioners were left in no doubt that mixing the flesh of a cow and a man in any way was the work of Satan and that Joe was one of Satan's own warriors.

Few took up Joe's kind offer of free vaccinations,

preferring to wait for Dr Bentley to call his trusted *inoculator,* a man who would treat you with the crusty old flesh of a diseased smallpox victim for a price. Something the Reverend condoned as it was human and thereby sanctified by God himself. In the end, the trusted inoculator had charged an arm and a leg for his cure, so only those with a fat enough purse were able to benefit. Huge swathes of Retford remained dangerously unprotected and vulnerable still.

'Perhaps now the threat is so close, I should try again. I have a better reputation now in some quarters. We all do. Maybe the people would listen this time.'

So far silent, Jake snorted across the breakfast table. 'You are a glutton for punishment. It'll serve the fools right if they catch it and then they'll wish they had listened to you in the first place.' A comment which earned him a stern look from the eldest Warriner.

'We rise above the nonsense, Jacob, and we do what is right. We are not our father.' Jack regarded Joe seriously. 'If you think the situation warrants it, then you should offer it again. As you say, we have come a long way in the eyes of the locals in the last few years. Your patients have enough faith in you to trust what you prescribe. You've helped enough of them to earn their respect and the rest of us will reiterate your message. Just as last time, Letty and I will cover the costs.'

'It'll be expensive.' The cowpox vaccination was made by one man, the brilliant Dr Edward Jenner, who had worked on his cure solidly for two decades. Joe had met him once and they corresponded occasionally. 'And I'll have to travel to Gloucestershire to get it. I'm not sure I can spare the time to ride a hundred miles

and back just yet.' The logistics of balancing such a journey with his myriad responsibilities would be difficult. He could trust Bella to do what was necessary at the foundling home, but his other patients were spread far and wide. Some needed regular monitoring. The long trip would eat up at least five days. Possibly more, when Joe could rarely spare five minutes.

'I would offer, but I don't want to leave Letty.' Jack's third child was not due for another two months, but he was constantly fussing over his wife, due largely to the fact she could not be trusted not to take too much on. With Jamie's wife, Cassie, also in an advanced state of pregnancy, he was also unlikely to want to be away for the better part of a week. Both Jack's and Joe's eyes fixed on the youngest Warriner expectantly.

'Oh, for goodness sake! I'll go.' Jake folded his arms sulkily. 'Heaven forbid I should enjoy my holiday at home uninterrupted.'

'Your whole life is a holiday, little brother.' Jake's life in London was a bit of a mystery and a great cause of concern to his brothers, who all believed he was worth more than the gallivanting he was widely reported to be doing. 'Maybe it's time to consider a profession like Joe rather than swanning about town in the pursuit of pleasure?'

'Whilst I'll admit to the swanning, it's certainly not *all* pleasure.' He grinned rakishly, looking decidedly pleased with himself. 'But it is significantly more pleasurable than your constant nagging, *your lordship.*' Jake stood, clearly unoffended, and as usual wouldn't be drawn on the subject further. 'I find I am suddenly looking forward to a jaunt to Gloucestershire. The sun is shining, the birds are singing and a few days entirely

free of criticism appeals. So much so, I shall leave this afternoon. How much of your dreaded pox do I need to procure?'

Bella's nerves had been on edge all day, meaning she jumped at the slightest sound in the sunny, near-empty infirmary. It wasn't fear or the usual anxiety which caused this state, it was embarrassment. After a pleasant and enlightening afternoon mixing medicines, a fabulous and daring ride in his curricle, she had succumbed to irrational panic because she had assumed he wanted to kiss her and she had wanted to kiss him right back. Then she'd run.

Run!

Exactly like the irrational and addled girl she did not want to be. With hindsight, she was mortified and totally ashamed of herself. Lord only knew what he thought when she now realised he probably had no intention of kissing her at all. She had seen with her own eyes the way he had gazed upon Clarissa. The Incomparable. The charming, beautiful Incomparable all men preferred. Thinking he would want to kiss her instead, the bookish and broken Beaumont, was laughable, except Bella couldn't find it funny. She had wanted to kiss him though, for a fleeting moment she almost had, then remembered she was terrified of the thought of kissing. With hindsight, she had no right to have panicked.

She knew he was a good man. A wonderful kind-hearted, clever and lovable man. He had done nothing to make her think otherwise, behaving like the perfect gentleman throughout all their encounters, and he deserved a grovelling apology for being treated like

a lecher after a perfectly lovely day in his company. The poor man must think her the rudest, most ungrateful and peculiar of women. Totally irrational and probably mad. There was no avoiding an explanation for her horrendous behaviour. For hours she had been mentally rehearsing an apology, trying to find exactly the right words to explain away her unwarranted reaction to a good deed after a perfectly pleasant, incident-free afternoon. Bella was dreading his arrival and yet wishing the whole thing already done. All in all, the waiting was excruciating.

'Good afternoon, Mrs Giles.'

At the sound of his voice on the landing she nearly leapt out of her skin. She slowly inhaled and exhaled in a failed attempt to calm her hammering heart and wished she knew what words would adequately convey her disgust at her own behaviour without enlightening him about the humiliating truth of her addled mind. Nothing she had rehearsed felt right. When he strode into the empty ward looking about as gorgeous and windswept as it was possible for a man to be, she also apparently lost the ability to talk in cohesive sentences.

'Dr... Joe... Good afternoon.' She would apologise in a bit, once the power of speech returned.

He paused midstep and regarded her warily. 'Good afternoon, Lady Isabella. How are our patients today?'

He was back to being formal—who could blame him after she had sprinted away from him as if her corset was on fire?—yet she hated the formality at the same time. 'As you can see, all is quiet.'

'Something we should make the most of. Have you seen this?' He unclasped his bag and pulled out a folded newspaper, which he handed to her on his way past.

Clearly he was not going to be the one to bring up what had happened. He was far too polite. Or annoyed. 'Smallpox is in Nottingham.' The matter-of-fact delivery suggested he preferred to keep things professional and detached. Both bothered her immensely. She didn't want to forget all of yesterday, just the tragic ending, yet he obviously did. She should apologise now and just get it over with.

'Surely Nottingham is far enough away that we do not need to worry?'

Coward! Coward! You make me sick.

The real her inside was jumping up and down with frustration, yet as much as Bella wanted to draw a veil over her atrocious reaction and end the brittle atmosphere, that would require admitting things. Embarrassing things. Grossly personal things. Her toes curled inside her slippers at the thought.

'On the contrary, epidemics of smallpox have been known to travel much greater distances in a very short period of time. I am worried. Very worried. I estimate at least half of the population hereabouts are unprotected against the disease. And it is summer. Something which all my reading suggests appears to have a bearing on the spread of such illnesses. With the virulent nature of smallpox, it would take only one or two cases to pass through here to potentially trigger an epidemic.'

She could tell by his expression he wasn't exaggerating and his obvious concern worried her. It also gave her a pathetic excuse to avoid apologising for a little bit longer. 'You think it that dangerous?'

'When I was studying in Edinburgh, I witnessed firsthand the devastation smallpox can cause, especially in the poorest areas of the city. No matter what we did, it

passed from house to house in a matter of days. It killed hundreds and we were powerless to stop it. I would avoid that tragedy here at all costs.'

'How do we do that?'

'With smallpox, prevention is better than cure. We need to offer widespread vaccination.'

'I've read about it.' Bella also knew it was controversial and vastly unpopular. 'You think this is the best method of prevention?'

'I do. I've already sent my brother on a quest to fetch enough of Dr Jenner's cowpox to protect the whole parish. When he returns, I intend to offer it to as many people as I can. We'll start here in the foundling home, as children are particularly susceptible to the disease. Some healthy adults can survive smallpox, but like many plagues, it devastates the very old and very young. Those that have been here a few years have already received the vaccination. I made sure of it. The old inoculation is too unpredictable, and whilst it works in a great majority of cases, there is less risk using cowpox to ward off the disease as it is harmless to humans. Most suffer no ill effects whatsoever. The old way of inoculating the patient with smallpox—no matter how weakened a strain it is—carries too much of a risk. Some patients develop the disease itself rather than build resistance against it, often with disastrous consequences. I do not want one case of smallpox. Not one. Therefore, the only sure way of protecting Retford is to use the new vaccination now.' He glanced at her and frowned, and Bella knew that frown was all about yesterday and not at all about the potential threat of an epidemic. His lips compressed into a flat line and he looked away, perhaps in disgust, and the

weight of her shame hung heavy. 'Mrs Giles should have a list.' He was already busying himself reading the day's notes, effectively dismissing her from his presence, but Bella was not ready to be dismissed. She still needed to apologise.

'Then I shall ensure I audit the list thoroughly and make a new list of all those in need of it. I presume you also would like me to make enquiries amongst the staff?'

Just say the words. Stop putting them off. Make this awful tension go away.

'Indeed.' He didn't look up. 'Stress that any person not protected endangers the lives of the children.' Bella could sense he did not really want to prolong the conversation. His tone was curt. Clipped. Who could blame him? He had probably expected an apology and when none was forthcoming felt justifiably aggrieved.

'I will need the vaccination.'

His head snapped up and he glared at her. 'You've not been inoculated?'

'None of my family have…Doctor.' Bella hated the formality. Hated the wall of tension between them. Enough was enough. 'I'm sorry about yesterday. Running away like that… I…'

Face your fears, Bella, and talk to him.

'I panicked… You see…' She was not ready to talk about what had happened in Vauxhall Gardens. That wall inside her mind was too big to tackle today. 'I'm not good with men.'

The lungful of air she had not realised she was holding came out in a whoosh. He merely blinked back at her, his clever eyes magnified by the lens of his spectacles. After a few seconds she realised he was wait-

ing for her to continue and explain why. Nerves made
her next words garbled. 'I panicked. Sorry... I thought
you were going to kiss me...' Oh, Lord, she shouldn't
have admitted to that! 'Which I know is preposterous...
because you much prefer Clarissa...and ours is an aca-
demic friendship. Professional...for the foundlings. As
I said, I'm sorry.'

He blinked again and screwed up his face. 'For
the foundlings. Yes. Of course.' The corners of his
mouth turned down and his eyes dropped to the notes
on the table. 'For the record, I don't prefer Clarissa.
I thought I did—not so long ago—but as usual I was
quite mistaken.'

'I see.' What did that mean? Did it mean he preferred
her or did he not think of either Beaumont that way?
Ask him. 'Probably for the best. Clarissa has her heart
set on a duke.' *That was just mean. Ask him.* 'How
long will it take your brother to return from Dr Jen-
ner's?' Bella found herself turning away and refolding
an already folded sheet rather than bolt for the door
as she wanted to, hoping he would pick up the mantle
and continue the awkward conversation and help her
make it all right.

He didn't.

'Hopefully by the end of the week. In the interim I
need to try to convince the people to agree to the vac-
cination.'

Ask him.

'Friday would be the perfect opportunity. It's mar-
ket day. Everyone comes into town on market day.'

'That's a good idea.' His eyes searched her face and
she couldn't tell what he was thinking. 'Not that I was
going to, of course, in view of our *academic friendship*,

but yesterday...I apologise if I gave the impression I was going to kiss you.'

'It was my mistake. Put it down to inexperience and the painful awkwardness of being Clarissa's bluestocking sister. As I said, I am not good with men.'

'I see.' He looked confused. For a moment it appeared he might say more, before he offered her a tight smile. 'I'm glad we cleared that up.'

'Good. Then no harm was done.' *Then why did she want to cry?* 'I shall go and check that list.'

Chapter Twelve

Bella avoided him for the rest of the week, or he avoided her. Either way, they were like ships passing in the night. A brief hello. The odd question. Nothing longer than a few seconds snatched between other tasks which they both found more pressing to do whenever they were close by. He went back to using her title and she stiffly replied with his. To compound the issue, aside from Molly and her rapidly healing broken leg, the infirmary was as silent as a grave. The outbreak of chickenpox had been minor and, with no new patients suffering that or any other ailment, there was precious little for Bella to do. Despite that, she still came to the foundling home religiously every day, admitting to herself the draw was more to do with the handsome and now decidedly aloof doctor than the desire either to improve her own mental state or to quench her thirst for knowledge. If nothing else, the fraught atmosphere had served to occupy her thoughts to such an extent, *the incident* rarely skittered across her mind. She was too busy chastising herself for being such an irrational and pathetic dolt.

Joe now seemed to occupy her mind as if he had moved in and had no intention of moving out again. During the day, Bella spent most of her time hoping to see him and wishing she knew how to undo the damage she had done to their relationship. At night, wholly different thoughts occupied her head, usually revolving around their almost-kiss and scandalously wondering what it would have felt like if he *had* kissed her.

As depressing as it was, she did take heart it was progress of sorts. A few short months ago the merest thought of a kiss would have been abhorrent, because it would require being in close contact with a man. However, now that Bella had been in close contact to Joe and had liked it, the prospect wasn't quite so daunting. No doubt it helped that her assailant had not tried to kiss her. He had been too busy clamping his filthy hand over her mouth in case she screamed, and too eager to violate her body, to try. It also helped that she had never been kissed before by any man, so, like driving a curricle or mixing medicines, it had begun to intrigue her. Although only with him.

Dr Joseph Warriner.

The man who had no desire to kiss her back and, thanks to her irrational, panicked behaviour, no longer showed any great desire to speak to her either.

Bella sighed and glanced at the mantel clock for the fourth time in as many minutes. It was nearly five minutes to ten o'clock. With any luck, there would be a decent enough crowd in the market square ready to hear Joe's speech about the threat of smallpox and the need for immediate vaccinations, a crowd large enough that he wouldn't notice her watching from afar.

Since Monday, notices had been posted around Ret-

ford and Joe and his family had been spreading the word to such an extent there had been an expectant buzz amongst the market traders when Bella had hurried across the square earlier. He had wisely decided not to disclose all the facts beforehand, as he wanted to cause neither unnecessary panic nor rampant, unhelpful gossip. Those important details would be shared this morning when he outlined both the problem and his intended solution. Bella intended to listen to it from the steps of the foundling home. Out of the way of both the crowds and the wary and bemused blue eyes of the handsome doctor whenever they came to rest upon her. She took a fortifying breath, steeled her shoulders and headed out of the ward.

Nobody in that huge crowd wants to hurt you.

And he doesn't want to see you.

Splendid.

There was indeed a crowd. A very large and noisy one. The entire population of Nottinghamshire appeared to be crammed in the tiny market square. At the far end, on the wooden platform which had been hastily erected, stood Joe flanked by his two elder brothers, the Earl of Markham and Captain Warriner. It was the Earl who brought the meeting to order on the dot of ten.

'Thank you all for coming here today.' The many conversations around the square began to peter out and he waited for complete silence before he spoke again. 'As some of you already know, there are grave reports of an epidemic of smallpox in Nottingham. So far there have been near a hundred deaths. As of this morning, we have heard news there are now cases in both Mansfield and Southwell.' He paused to allow the

gasps and exclamations to die down. Allowed the fear to settle in their minds. 'The disease is edging closer. In just a week it has travelled ten miles both east and west. In a few more weeks, perhaps less, it will have made its way here, too. Fortunately, my brother has a plan to stop it.'

Bella watched Joe step forward and saw his posture stiffen. Only those who knew him well would realise he was nervous. To everyone else here in the suddenly silent market square he would appear calm and in control. But Bella saw the way his hand clenched at his side, the way those magnificent broad shoulders rose and fell with his measured breathing as he tried to steady himself, and her heart went out to him. Part of her wished she were also stood on that platform beside him, offering her support and her strength. The old Bella would have been. She would have stood tall and proud, standing up for what she believed in and what was right. Except doing it now was inconceivable as it would mean being the centre of attention and exposed to danger rather than invisible and safe. It would also undoubtedly filter back to her father when he returned and alert him to her duplicity. Selfishly, it was much better if she kept her distance, although her cowardice under the dire circumstances didn't make her proud. Shame, she now realised, left a foul taste in the mouth.

'Ladies and gentlemen, shortly my brother Jacob will return from Gloucestershire, where he has been sent to procure enough of Dr Jenner's vaccination to protect the entire village. His vaccination is proved to render all those who have had it completely immune to smallpox within a few days, even if directly confronted with the disease. Because he sees it as necessary and

would not see any of you put at risk, my brother Jack has already paid for all of you to receive it. There will be no cost to yourselves.'

The poorest in the square were relieved, she could tell, and many were already nodding their assent. One man, Mellor, the respected local constable, spoke out. 'How do we get our hands on this vaccination?'

'As soon as it arrives, the doors of my surgery will be open and I would like to see every person and every child not yet inoculated against smallpox so that I can administer the treatment. If you have been previously inoculated, there is no need to worry. You are already protected and have no need of the vaccination. I should be able to administer the treatment swiftly to everyone as long as you all make yourselves available here as soon as you receive word. Dr Jenner's miraculous vaccination is quick, simple, relatively painless, and will render you safe from smallpox for ever.' The crowd all began to mutter at once, both in excitement and trepidation, forcing Joe to raise his voice. 'Time is of the essence. The swifter you are all vaccinated, the more effective the protection will be in the event of the deadly smallpox making its way here.'

'If it makes its way here!' Dr Bentley's voice boomed from the edge of the square. 'You are creating panic where none is needed. Retford has been free of the disease for twenty years and there is no reason to assume it will come here this time. We will build bonfires at the boundaries, as we've always done, and burn tar to purify the noxious air. Those precautions have always been good enough.'

'Bonfires will not stop smallpox. All the research lends itself to suggest bad air does not transmit the

disease. It passes through human contact. Retford is a market town and close to the Great North Road. We come into contact with strangers all of the time.'

'We haven't had an incident in twenty years...'

'This town has doubled in size in twenty years! We are no longer the quiet provincial village visited by the occasional travelling carriage. As many as fifty people stop here each week on their way to and from the new factories in the north.'

'I've been practising medicine since before you were born, *boy*. And I know these people better than you. I will not see them hoodwinked by a charlatan.' The throngs of people parted as the elderly physician made his way slowly towards the platform, scowling at the three Warriners before him as if they were a plague rather than single-handedly trying to prevent one. He stopped just shy of the platform and turned to face the crowd. 'I suppose once again the illustrious *Dr* Warriner is intent on experimenting with his *miraculous* stable muck. Am I right?' He turned his head slightly, his expression derisive. Whispers of the words *stable muck* were audible though the crowd, causing doubt in the people's minds. Dr Bentley was very pleased to see it. 'No doubt he has told you already he intends to use cowpox on you rather than the proved method of using smallpox itself. People weren't meant to be tainted with the blood of beasts. I prefer to fight fire with fire than experiment with people's lives.'

'There is no experiment.' Joe's tone was measured. Reasonable. 'Dr Jenner is a highly respected physician who was given substantial funds from the Royal College of Physicians to continue his work with his

vaccination. It is proved to repel smallpox in every instance…'

'But do you deny it is made from the infected pustules scraped from a cow's udders?' Dr Bentley was quaking with indignation. 'You would infect the blood of the good people of Retford with bovine blood. Cow's blood! You would hide the consequences of that action, too, no doubt! Did he tell you all what his vaccination entailed?' Heads began shaking with indignation. 'I thought as much. These Warriners are all the same!' More nods and some blatant hostility now came from parts of the crowd. 'Thank goodness I was here to educate them about your intentions and allow them the opportunity to make an informed choice before they succumb to your quackery, Warriner.'

'Is this true, Dr Warriner?' Mellor had pushed his way to the front, his beefy arms folded. The constable had a firm but fair reputation in Retford. He didn't suffer fools gladly—in fact, was known to deal with any shenanigans briskly and without much finesse—but if he agreed with you, then the people followed his lead.

With more patience than Bella would have shown, Joe attempted to explain. 'Cowpox is caught from cows, that is true, but it is a human disease, too. It has been around for centuries. It is a harmless disease in both man and beast, causing at most a mild malaise which quickly dissipates. It is also true that those who have had it are rendered immune from contracting smallpox. Those who work with cows have known such for decades. Dr Jenner merely found a way to pass that immunity on to the masses. He conducted a series of experiments many years ago and was able to categorically report the effectiveness and safety of

his vaccination. Thousands have received it with no ill health whatsoever.'

'Really?' Dr Bentley rudely turned his back to Joe and addressed the crowd instead. 'In the short-term, this *young man* is right. To an extent. But the *revered*, and now very *wealthy*, Dr Jenner is very close-mouthed about the lasting effects.'

'That is because there are none.'

'Of course!' Dr Bentley laughed cruelly. 'The horrific tales of the vaccinated sprouting horns which they have to file down and hide beneath their hats are exaggerated?'

As it was meant to, this comment caused a great deal of commotion from the gathered locals, the majority of whom were illiterate farm workers who were conditioned to take the word of their betters as gospel. In their minds, age went hand in hand with wisdom and they were easily swayed by Dr Bentley's lies. That doubt would be their undoing unless Joe could convince them otherwise.

'They are lies.' Joe shook his head in disbelief. 'Ridiculous stories put about by Jenner's critics to put people off his cure.'

'Then you admit this quack Jenner has many critics. Why, pray tell, is that?'

Bella closed her eyes and shook her head. Joe was playing into the old fool's hands by admitting Jenner's methods were controversial. He needed to stick to science. Reiterate the facts. The logic. Let them know, in no uncertain terms, what he was proposing was the truth and that Dr Bentley's accusations were ridiculous.

'People are resistant to new ideas...'

'Or perhaps they choose to ignore the man who was

awarded a medal from Napoleon?' The crowd gasped in unison. 'Why would Dr Jenner be honoured by Bonaparte—the sworn enemy of England and murderer of many of our brave English soldiers—unless he was in cahoots with the French?' Joe was denied the opportunity of continuing his answer to the preposterous accusation because the Reverend Reeves was now marching across the square holding up a Bible like an amulet and followed by a small battalion of parishioners carrying banners. For the benefit of those gathered who could not read the banners, they had been crudely illustrated with pictures of frightened people sporting horns. This caused a cacophony of noise from the onlookers, who were now quite distressed at the sight of both the church and the town's oldest physician protesting Joe's plan.

'"All flesh is not the same flesh, but there is one kind of flesh of men, another flesh of beasts."' The Reverend Reeves took his place next to Dr Bentley. 'Corinthians!'

A terrified hush settled as he glared at those amassed. One bony hand pointing to Joe and his brothers on the platform. 'The Warriners are the devil's own henchmen! They are abusing the tragic situation in Nottingham to do his bidding. Any who succumb and take this vaccination will be punished by the Lord!' He raised one quivering finger heavenward. 'Like the devil himself, you will be marked with horns and doomed to burn for all eternity in hell!'

What happened next could best be described as chaos. Joe, the constable and his brothers tried to calm the crowd but kept being thwarted by the joint interjections of the Reverend Reeves and Dr Bentley. For several minutes, all Bella could do was watch it all unfold,

feeling helpless and increasingly furious at the scene. Angry faces and angrier words were exchanged in the square. Captain Warriner jumped off the platform and stalked towards his father-in-law with murder in his eye, only to be restrained by the Earl of Markham. Joe stood impotently, trying to be heard over the ruckus while the people surged forward as one mass towards the platform like a swarm of wasps.

Out of the corner of her eye Bella spotted a familiar dark head arrive at the periphery of the square, sat on horseback and staring in shock at the nonsense unfolding. Before she could think better of it, Bella dashed down the steps of the foundling home and grabbed him by the leg. 'Jake! Follow me. I have an idea.'

Chapter Thirteen

Joe had no idea who threw the first punch, but the minor scuffle in the centre of the square was quickly turning into a full-blown fist fight involving close to ten people.

Jamie and a few of Joe's loyal patients were in the thick of it, although in Jamie's defence he had been walking away reluctantly moments before and had then been attacked by a screeching woman wielding a placard with Joe's face painted crudely on it accompanied by the words "'Evil men and impostors will proceed from bad to worse, deceiving and being deceived.'"

He knew the words well. They were one of the Reverend's favourite Bible quotes when denouncing the wicked Warriner family once a month from the pulpit. Although Joe had expected some hostility at his proposal, he certainly had not anticipated this debacle. His attempt at protecting the people of Retford was in danger of doing exactly the opposite. Unless the warring crowd could be brought to order, then he feared nobody would agree to the vaccination and an epidemic was imminent.

What a mess. One he could have and should have handled better. But how to make it right now, when fists were flying and his town meeting had descended into little better than a barroom brawl?

'Excuse me. Excuse me, please.' The proper and curt feminine voice was one he knew only too well. 'Excuse me!'

Bella squeezed out of the crowd in front of him, closely followed by a petrified-looking Mrs Patterson and his highly amused brother Jake, who must have just returned. Something about her haughty demeanour reminded those close by that she was a lady. The daughter of an earl. A few even removed their caps in deference to her rank and stood awkwardly as she regally climbed the three wooden crates which served as steps up to his platform, apparently oblivious to the small riot behind her.

He had no idea what she was up to, but he was grateful for it nevertheless, as the presence of Lady Isabella Beaumont—and she most definitely was *Lady* Isabella Beaumont this morning—seemed to have a calming effect on the crowd. Ingrained politeness caused many to be embarrassed by their behaviour in front of one of their betters, and a lady to boot, and one by one they stopped shouting under the weight of her imperious and outraged glare.

She turned towards the crowd and shouted, 'You should all be ashamed of yourselves!'

'Yes, you damned well should!' The constable's loud roar cut through the chaos. 'Next person who raises his fists will spend the next week in the gaol house.' Eyes dropped to boots at the admonishment.

'If you don't mind, Mr Mellor, I have something to say.'

'Listen to the lady!'

Bella smiled sweetly at the constable, then began to address the fractious crowd. 'There is a plague hurtling towards us and you think shouting and fighting like savages will help you?' Her tone, her manner, held their attention and the crowd began to still. Just ahead, Jack and Jamie finally managed to separate the last of the fighting men and stood forming a human barrier between the protesters and the rest of the people in case anyone dared to start it up again. Curiosity had got the better of the majority and they turned to stare at the small, yet formidable woman glaring down at them, her fists planted on her hips like a stern schoolmistress admonishing a naughty class. Even Reverend Reeves had ceased ranting about the devil to stop and watch her.

Bella turned to Joe with her head held high and her voice strong enough to carry across the crowd. 'I do not wish to die, Dr Warriner. I am *quite* decided on that. And none of this silly, unfounded scaremongering will deter me. I have read the facts and am satisfied in the validity of Dr Jenner's research. Therefore, I should like to be the first to take up your generous offer of a free vaccination against smallpox.' Joe blinked at her, a little astounded and unsure as to what to say or do next. Fortunately, the formidable Lady Isabella was in no doubt. She held out her hand and Mrs Patterson placed his vaccination pouch in it. Within was the small knife needed to make the tiny incision, a vial of gin to clean the skin to prevent the wound from becoming infected, metal tweezers and fresh bandages. '*Now.* If

you please. In *front* of all these people. Perhaps then they will see their fears about sprouting horns, cloven hooves and udders are ludicrous. Why, I shall even sit in the square for a fortnight afterwards to allow people to examine my scalp and check I am not filing them down or hiding any bovine adornments under my bonnet.'

As she was already rolling up the sleeve of her dress and at least a hundred pairs of eyes were watching them intently, he didn't dare disappoint. With slightly shaking fingers Joe took the package his brother was holding in his outstretched palm and began to prepare for the procedure. By the time he held out the blade he felt sick, until he glanced up at her solemn dark eyes and saw the trust in them. Bella believed in him and was prepared to incur the wrath of the entire town and her father to prove it. 'You might feel a tiny scratch.'

She nodded brusquely. 'Better that than smallpox.'

How right she was. Joe felt an eerie calm wash over him. Bella was trying to help him prove the vaccine was safe and every face in the square was watching them carefully. If ever there was a time to be a competent and confident physician it, was now. He tried to block out the audience and the protesters, as well as Bella, as he made the tiny scratch-like incision in her forearm. Right this minute, she was a patient and not the woman who had been keeping him awake at night for over a week. Then he carefully removed one of the threads from Jake's parcel, each covered in several dried droplets of Jenner's vaccine, and gently used tweezers to remove one. He took a calming breath, then inserted it into the wound.

All around them, people were craning their heads

to get a better view. Nobody spoke as Joe wrapped a small strip of linen bandage around her arm and tied it with a knot. 'It's done.'

'How do you feel, my lady?' Mellor asked in a voice loud enough to carry across the square and Joe realised the constable, at least, was on his side.

'Well, I don't feel like mooing.' Her fingers went to her head and probed. 'No sign of horns either. And frankly, I feel wonderful. I'm not going to die from smallpox and that is such a *relief.*' She beamed at him and then the crowd. 'I shall be in Dr Warriner's office for the rest of the day helping *him* to *help* all of you. I hope to see a great many of you there. Now if you will excuse us, Dr Warriner has urgent business to attend and I need to set up his surgery.' Like a queen, she dismissed the crowd and began to glide down the steps, leaving him with no words and no further need of any. She had sprinkled enough doubt on Dr Bentley's and the pious reverend's arguments to allow the people to mull it all over themselves.

Dutifully, many of those assembled began to turn away as there was an air the meeting was now concluded. Joe supposed it was. What else was there to say? The sea of people parted to allow her to walk through and he felt himself smiling. When she wanted to be, Bella was fearless and formidable, and right now that was exactly what everyone, including him, had needed. A dose of logical sanity in a sea of nonsense.

'Wait a minute!' Dr Bentley shouted to her retreating back. 'Stop right there, madam! Do not force me to tell them the truth about you.'

Her step faltered, but she kept walking.

'What truth?' someone shouted from the crowd. 'We deserve to know the whole truth!'

'Do not put your trust in Lady Isabella Beaumont. I'd sooner trust the word of a Warriner than her!'

She stopped abruptly and turned around. Where Joe expected to see outrage, the formidable Lady Isabella who had just silenced the masses, he saw a small, timid woman instead. One he barely recognised. Instead of fearless, he saw fear. Her face was suddenly pale, like a ghost, as her terrified eyes locked with the aged doctor's. The smile with which he answered her terror was pure evil. 'This girl is quite mad. Deluded. Her wits have gone. Isn't that right, Lady Isabella?'

She took a step backwards as if she had been slapped, but met the old fool's eyes bravely. 'I am not mad, Dr Bentley.'

'Then why are you here in Retford, pray tell? Your father rented that house in the hope a change of scenery would return you to yourself. He also engaged my services to try to cure your addled mind.' He turned to the gawping onlookers and shook his head sadly while Bella stood frozen. 'Services, I might add, she continues to refuse, so deep rooted is her hysteria. None of the doctors in London could cure her. For over a year now she has been insensible, the poor dear. Rendered quite irrational and frigid after being molested by a villain.'

'Stop.' Her voice was so small it tore at Joe's heartstrings and he knew, there and then, Dr Bentley had power over her. 'Please stop.'

'Stop what? Telling them the truth? Do you deny it, Lady Isabella? Do you deny the months you spent locked inside yourself? Your irrational fear of the outside world? Of all men save your father? Do you deny

the steady stream of London's finest head doctors despairing of you? The failed treatments?' He turned to the crowd again. 'She imagines things. Her mind plays tricks with her. Half the time she cannot discern fantasy from fact. She belongs in an asylum, not in your admiration. A creature to be pitied...'

The Reverend Reeves began to drone in his menacing monotone. 'The Lord will smite you with madness and with blindness and with bewilderment of heart...'

Joe knocked the Reverend to the floor. 'That's enough.' At some point during the cruel assassination of her character Joe must have leapt from his platform, because he found himself striding towards Bentley and grabbing him by his lapels. 'You will apologise to the lady now!'

'I will never apologise for telling the truth.'

'Yes. You. Will.' The older man's head snapped back as Joe lifted him briskly from the ground and shook him. 'If I have to beat the apology out of you, you will apologise!'

It was Jake who stopped him slamming his fist into the physician's face.

'We rise above the nonsense, Joe, remember. The people here need you. Bella needs you, too.' Through the red mist of anger he forced himself to listen. Knew the fury and his irrational need for violence would only serve to strengthen Bentley's words. The Warriners of old used their fists to get their point across. They were better than that. He was better than that. With a growl, he let go of the man's coat reluctantly and stepped back, his whole body trembling with the roiling need to tear the malicious old fool limb from limb.

'What sort of a physician are you?' Joe had never

been a violent person. He was the most placid Warriner and now he was proud of that. If being placid meant he did what was right, then so be it. However, he had never wanted to hurt another person as he did the man in front of him today. He had betrayed Bella. Humiliated her. He had to pay and soon he would. But that was not today when Joe was needed. Jake was right. She needed him more right this second. He allowed himself to loom over the frightened man and enjoyed the sight of him cowering. For once, diplomacy could go to hell.

'You disgust me, Bentley. Everything about you disgusts me, but I am thankful to you. Because of you I know exactly what sort of doctor I want to be and it's not you! I swore an oath to help people. To heal the sick to the best of my ability and to protect the dignity of all of those in my care.' He allowed one finger to prod the man's bony chest menacingly. '*You* do whatever it takes to feather your own nest. Whether that be to line your greedy pockets with coin or to ignore the poor because they cannot pay you or to shamelessly destroy the reputation of an innocent woman. A woman who cares more for this community than you ever have. Spread your malicious lies and disparagements about me. Do your worst. I don't care. My deeds will shout louder than your poisonous words—but if you ever utter another vile word about Lady Isabella, be warned. You will pay!'

Joe spun on his heel to go to Bella, only to see she was not there, and the fury burned afresh as he worried where she had run to. 'Go home! The lot of you! She was right. You should all be ashamed of yourselves! How dare you all stand there in silence while an innocent woman, a brave and selfless innocent woman, is

bullied by these malicious old fools who are supposed to help people!' He snatched a placard from one of the protesters and snapped it across his knee, then tossed it to the ground. It did nothing to calm his temper. 'Take this nonsense and turn it into kindling for bonfires, and pray for your souls, you are going to need both. Although mark my words, there are no fires hot enough or strong enough to stop this disease if it comes here, and if it does and you are not protected, then I sincerely hope God helps you. Because by then, he is the only one who will be able to!'

Bella had no memory of stumbling up the deserted lane towards her house. How could she when all she could think about was the dreadful public shaming Dr Bentley had subjected her to. For over a year, her family had done their best to shield her from gossip and censure while they had frantically tried every means to get her better, even moving away to the back of beyond to allow her to find herself again. Yet in the end it had all been for nought. Today all the people of Retford knew she had been violated and gone mad, by tomorrow that delicious piece of gossip would be dashing down the road to London, where it would bring shame to her father and render her permanently damaged in the eyes of society.

Eyes which would now look at her like a curious specimen under a magnifying glass. Her legs suddenly unsteady, she sank down on to the grass at the edge of the lane and buried her head in her hands. Everything was ruined. Even if, by some miracle, the scandalous truth failed to make it all the way down the Great North Road, they would have to leave Retford immediately.

Bella could hardly quietly convalesce in a town which now saw her as addled. The longer they dithered here, the worse the humiliation would be—however, that meant leaving the infirmary, too. Not that she thought for one second she would be allowed to stay. Irrational girls who could not discern fantasy from reality could not be trusted with the care of children or with dangerous medicines. These blissful weeks of learning and healing, both herself and those children she adored, had been cruelly ripped from her hands. The one thing she had found the strength to live again for, and in doing so had found the part of herself she had thought lost for ever, was gone. The pain of losing it almost impossible to bear.

With a sob, she remembered Joe's face as he had learned the awful truth. Saw the incredulity contort his face as his eyes had sought hers, Bella's inability to meet his gaze confirming his worst fears. Because he was decent, he had been angry on her behalf, but she had witnessed the way he had lurched backwards as if he had been struck by a blow when he'd heard the vile but truthful words spat at the crowd. Insensible, rendered irrational and frigid. Addled. Belongs in an asylum. In trying to help him she had inadvertently brought shame to Joe, too, but worse. Thanks to her, he would now command even less respect in front of the town. His plans to protect them from smallpox shredded to confetti alongside her own pathetic façade of a reputation.

How was she ever going to face the poor man again? Hopefully her mother would whisk her back to London in the carriage today and she wouldn't have to.

'Bella.'

So much for wishful thinking. He was here. She could see the dusty toes of his boots through the gaps in her fingers and her misery was complete. 'I'm s-s-so s-s-sorry.' Clearly it was not complete as she was now also snorting. Bella felt him lower himself to sit beside her on the verge and willed herself invisible, or dead. Perhaps dead would be better. At least then she wouldn't be hurting so very much.

'You have nothing to be sorry about.' And now he was being kind when he had every right to be angry. For once, she was not going to let him get away with it.

'Of c-course I do. I've ruined everything. I was t-t-trying to h-h-help and now I've made it...' *snort* '...w-worse.'

'There was already a serious bout of fisticuffs as well as a placard with my face on it complete with jaunty devil's horns. It was worse before you came along and bravely showed them they were being foolish.'

Bella didn't want nice. She wanted him to be furious. The niceness was pure torture and she wanted to smack him for it. Vent some of her own anger at the gross unfairness of life. 'Did you not hear what Dr Bentley said? It's all true, by the way. Every single bit of it. Since *the incident*, I'm not right in the head. I'm terrified all the time. I imagine danger lurking around every corner. I'm scared to go out. I'm scared of men. I'm scared of crowds and I'm scared of being on my own. I continually refuse medical treatments because they terrify me, too. It's been over a year and I'm still irrational. My head is filled with those brick walls. I'm not fit to be around decent people. Dr Bentley is one of a long line of physicians who has—'

'Dr Bentley is a fool.'

'Don't interrupt me!' Bella needed to be honest with him because at the very least Joe deserved that. She would tell him the truth about her condition because he had a right to know how his hard-earned good name came to be in tatters. Her selfish decision to try to fix her own addled mind with logic had now put an entire community at risk. What had she been thinking? 'Dr Bentley is one of a long line of physicians who has been engaged to help me find myself, yet I continually think I know better and...' His words seeped into her head and she risked lifting her covered face slightly so that she could see his expression. It was more remorseful than thunderous. 'What did you say?'

'I said he's an arse. He sabotaged today, Bella. Not you. And right now I'd like to do nothing better than pummel his smug, wrinkled face with my fists for spouting all that nonsense about cows and even more so for what he did to you.' He sighed and stared down at where his hands dangled loosely between his legs. His fists clenched, then unclenched. 'I almost did as well, so I'm not feeling particularly proud of myself. Doctors should heal injuries, not cause them. Except I can't help not feeling sorry for it and I still don't regret it.' He offered her the ghost of a smile along with a clean handkerchief. 'Which is a first for me. I'm not used to losing my temper, let alone allowing it the freedom to rampage. I pushed the Reverend to the ground. Then when my brother prevented me killing Dr Bentley, I smashed up a placard and gave them all a piece of my mind. Once I started hollering, I couldn't seem to stop. I told Bentley exactly what I thought of him, then went after that fool of a reverend again before turning on the crowd and spelling out in graphic language what the

disease would do to them if they failed to listen to reason. I might have even called the Reverend Reeves an unwitting accomplice to Satan. I'm not entirely sure. I was so enraged at the time I can't quite remember exactly what I said. I rarely lose my temper, perhaps once every decade, but when it goes it explodes. If I say so myself, I was quite terrifying. I left them all gaping in the square to come after you.'

'You didn't need to come after me. You have more important things to be doing than concerning yourself with...' The tips of his fingers lightly touched her lips to silence her.

'Right at this precise moment, there is nothing more important to me than you.'

Chapter Fourteen

Her heart gave a little skip in her chest and more tears fell unbidden from her eyes. Joe didn't try to stop them. Instead, he wrapped his arm around her shoulders and gathered her close. Bella instinctively burrowed against him before she considered panicking at the contact. Once she was there, her face nestled against his chest, cocooned in his embrace, she decided she couldn't be bothered to panic because being held by him felt too good and she needed his strength too much to relinquish it. She felt his lips brush against the top of her head and for a split second she was sorely tempted to tilt her face up towards them before she remembered she was terrified of male contact.

'I'm so sorry he maligned you so grievously. It's all my fault.' He was apologising to her?

'No, it isn't. You weren't to know the secrets I've been keeping.'

'They were *your* secrets, Bella. Dr Bentley had no right to break your trust. He's duty-bound to keep the secrets of those under his care. What he said and the manner in which he said it fills me with rage. I'm still

in two minds about hunting the charlatan down and spreading his nose over his face. One word from you and I will happily do so.'

What a lovely thing to say. 'Please don't. As much as I loathe Dr Bentley, I would hate to be the cause of you doing something so against your character. You are a brilliant doctor and, as you said, doctors heal injuries, they don't cause them.'

'That answer doesn't please me.' He sighed the words into her hair and she felt some of the tension leave his body.

'Dr Bentley needs his nose, Joe. Without it, what will he use to look down at us with? The wild Warriner and the witless woman.'

His arms tightened around her. 'You're not witless. Far from it, in fact. You are one of the most intelligent people I have ever met.'

'And you're not wild.'

'More's the pity. Today I would very much like to be. It would give me an excuse to go back after Bentley and then hunt down the scoundrel who hurt you.' He stilled and she could almost hear his clever brain whirring. 'You were…attacked, I assume?' A very tactful way of putting it. Instantly, Bella tensed as the constantly lingering memory pushed front and centre in her mind. 'Do you want to tell me about it?'

'It is as Dr Bentley said. I was molested by a scoundrel and it addled my mind.'

'I don't want to hear Dr Bentley's version of events. I want to hear yours. Unless you would rather not entrust me with it. I wouldn't blame you after how despicably your last physician just treated you.'

'I prefer to forget about it and pretend it never hap-

pened.' Not talking about it was safer. She never talked about it, although, in fairness, Joe was the first person who had asked. 'I keep hoping if I ignore it, it will go away.'

'But it hasn't?'

She shook her head against his chest and wanted to cry again. Sometimes the pain inside was intensely physical, forming a tight knot in her gut and making her throat constrict. He must have sensed her discomfort, because his next words were measured, almost as if they took a great deal out of him to say.

'When my brother Jamie came back from the war, he was broken inside... He'd been captured and tortured. It...it changed him. His behaviour for at least a year was irrational and it was dreadful to watch. He kept it all locked inside, you see, and instead of healing the pain he surrounded it in a barricade, where it festered and grew. Those walls in his mind got so tall they engulfed him. He withdrew from the world. From his family. For the longest time we despaired of...of ever seeing the real him again.'

Just as Bella despaired of ever seeing the real her again, too. She had seen Jamie Warriner with his wife and family. He didn't appear broken now. 'What changed things?'

'Time.' His hand came up to stroke the long tendril of hair which had fallen down her back during her frantic escape from the square. 'The patience of his family. The love of a good woman.' Her scalp began to tingle as he wound the stray strands idly around his finger. 'Finding the courage to talk about what happened... I think that was the real turning point. He confided in Cassie first and then that made it easier for him to

tell us. Once it was all out in the open, we could all understand what he was feeling and help in our own small ways. Brick by brick he demolished those walls.'

'My family and I have never discussed it. I wouldn't know where to start telling them now. Everything is so jumbled and confused in my mind.'

'Then unjumble it. Tell me what's going on in whatever order it comes out.'

He made it sound so simple, when it really was anything but. How did one explain the constant, unfathomable and inexplicable fear hovering on the outskirts of her thoughts? Or the random flashes of memory which rendered her frozen and panicked at the same time? 'I... That night... My mind...' She huffed out a sigh and gave up. 'I don't have the words.'

'Would it be easier if I asked you questions?'

Probably, although the mere thought of answering them, of churning up all that quagmire, made her stiffen and pull away. Bella shuffled across the grass to put some distance between them and hugged her knees. 'All right.'

'Where were you? When it happened?' His instincts told him to start with simple questions which required little explanation.

'Vauxhall Gardens. There were fireworks.'

'Were you on your own?'

'No. I was with my family. We were all stood together.' Her eyebrows drew together and she frowned at the memory, apparently angry with herself. 'I should have stayed with them.'

'But you didn't?'

'No. There was a man a little way away. He was dressed in rags. He was so thin...'

He watched her swallow and felt bad for making her relive the dreadful events, and as much as Joe didn't want to have to hear about them either, he knew from bitter experience such recollections were better out than inside. Inside they festered like a tumour. 'You felt sorry for him?'

Her eyes snapped to his and she nodded. Just once. 'I went to give him some coins. I have this pathetic need to help people. Or I did. Before.'

She still did. Her work at the infirmary, her selfless act in the square, volunteering herself to be vaccinated in public to allay the fears of the locals and help him. It broke his heart to see those generous and selfless gestures thrown back into her face. 'Then what happened?' He could feel his own muscles tense before he heard her answer and willed his professional veneer of calmness to remain in place. His legendary temper had no place here, even though it was bubbling dangerously close to the surface and desperate to break free.

'As I turned to walk away, his hand clamped around my mouth and he pressed a knife to my throat. He s-said...' Her body racked with an unconscious sob as she relived the moment and her arms tightened about her knees. 'He said, "Y-You're a generous sort, aren't you, lovely? I'm not done with you yet."'

Despite the warm July sun beating down on them, Bella shivered and closed her eyes to block out the images in her head. She lapsed into silence, her usually plump lips compressed into a thin line, and Joe desperately wanted to hold her. He resisted the urge to touch her because she clearly needed the distance, hugged into a tight ball and refusing to meet his eyes. 'Can you tell me what happened then?'

More silence and for the longest minute of his life Joe thought she would refuse. But then her words came, tumbling out of her mouth in a half-whispered rush. 'He dragged me through some bushes. It was pitch-black behind. I couldn't see anything. The odd flash from a firework. Nothing more. I could hear all the people on the other side. Laughing. Having fun. But I could smell him. I can still smell him. He was filthy. Rotten vegetables. Stale sweat. Breathing on my face. His dirty hand pressed hard on my mouth. He hooked his leg around mine and I fell backwards. He fell on top of me. It crushed my ribs, but I couldn't scream.'

Bella scrambled to her feet and turned to stare off into space. Her arms now wrapped around her body, comforting herself. Quietly, Joe also stood and followed her to the edge of the field beyond, where he came to stand beside her. He sensed she did not want to be touched, so he clamped his hands behind his back, lest he gave in to the urge to clench his fists and she saw them. He hoped his presence gave her some courage and promised himself he would commit murder if he ever met the faceless man who had violated her.

'His other hand was touching me everywhere. Grabbing and pawing at me.' One of her hands fluttered near her chest and her abdomen, mapping the assault back on to herself. 'He tugged up my skirts and he...he touched me there, too. I kicked and twisted, but he was stronger than me. I was pinned to the floor. Powerless. When he grabbed my thigh and pushed my legs apart, I felt...him pressed against me. He almost choked me as he undid his breeches. His hand rummaged between

us…he said he'd kill me if I kept fighting him and ruining his fun.'

Tears began to pour over her cheeks and her chest rose and fell in panic. It was an awful thing to see. It was a more awful thing to hear and for a second Joe didn't want to hear the rest, until he realised he was being selfish and her telling it to expunge it from her soul was nowhere near as horrific for him as the actual ordeal had been for her. 'He raped you.' To his own ears his voice was choked with a bundle of warring emotions. Pity. Anger. Raw, unabashed hatred. Horror. The visceral need to avenge her. Poor Bella. Her odd way around him now all made sense.

'No.'

The intense relief left him exhaling loudly. At least she had been spared that. 'He almost did. He tried to. I could hear my family calling for me beyond the bushes. A big firework went off above us and I saw the blade of his knife lying on the ground nearby. I grabbed it and stabbed it in his hand as hard as I could. He flinched. Let go of my mouth briefly. I screamed as loud as I could until he punched me in the face. I managed to bring my knee up and hurt him, then he punched me again. After that it's a bit of a blur. Someone must have heard, because people came through the bushes. He ran off. My parents… They took me home. They managed to get me away without causing a huge scene. They were able to hide what happened for the sake of my reputation.'

And then stupidly never spoke of it again, he'd wager, hoping they could blot it out of their minds and allow Bella to continue blithely on with her life. Joe felt a wave of fresh anger at the silly rules of society which

put a woman's reputation above what was morally right. He knew the answer before asking the next question. 'Was the scoundrel caught and brought to justice?'

'They felt there was no need to cause a scandal because nothing had happened. Not really. I was still… still…' she covered her face again, distraught yet clearly ashamed '…intact.'

Yet broken inside because everything had happened. In one fell swoop this gentle, caring young woman had been shown how disgusting life could be. Traumatised. Her trust in the world and all its male inhabitants shattered while the monster who broke her was still wandering free.

'To begin with, we all thought I was suffering from shock and the family physician assured us it was entirely natural and would pass, but as the weeks and months went by, my mental state got worse. I couldn't go out. Crowds bothered me. Noise bothered me. Not knowing what was around the corner or deserted spaces bothered me. Men terrified me. When I couldn't bear to sit in my own garden, my father became desperate and sought specialised help. At first I tried to accept the treatments, but being strapped down and almost drowned with cold water just made me more anxious. When the water treatments failed, they sent me to another doctor. Very well respected and expensive. He said I was suffering from hysteria and as soon as he explained how it had to be treated, that it would involve him touching me…intimately…I went quite mad and attacked him. That doctor washed his hands of me. So did the next. I begged my parents not to subject me to more doctors and convinced them I just needed to be away from London for a while. I

wanted to find myself again…my way. I've been trying to use logic to help me face my fears…and I was d-d-doing s-so well!'

Joe didn't bother fighting the urge to hold her this time, although deep down he suspected he needed the comfort more than she did. She stood trembling in his arms like a wounded bird, sobbing behind her hands, and for the first time since he met her she seemed delicate. Vulnerable and so very lost it tore him in two.

'You are doing well. I would never have known you had suffered all this. And you will continue to do well.'

'Not if I have to go back to town. This was my last chance, don't you see? If my way failed, then I promised my father I would listen to the physicians and accept the treatment they all threatened. It's been over a year since the incident. I should be over it by now. Everybody says so. My family fear the damage to my mind is permanent, and if I go back home, then I know it will be. London petrifies me.'

He found himself clinging on to her possessively. After everything she had suffered, subjecting her to the violations of the hysteria doctors was nothing but cruel. When her father returned from the city, he fully intended to tell him so, but for now all Joe could do was try to calm her down. 'You don't need to go back to town. There is no reason why you cannot continue to convalesce here.'

'The whole village knows of my shame. I cannot stay.'

'The whole village saw you bullied by a man who purports to be a healer. Whilst I can attest to the fact this town has a very long memory, I can also tell you

that there are a great many people who have the capacity for kindness as well. Those with half a brain will know what happened to you was not your fault.'

'You put a lot of faith in those people, yet didn't they just cause the small riot in the square? Those same people gossip and spread lies about your family. I'm not hopeful they will be quite as forgiving as you seem to think. I am a virtual stranger to them. Now, thanks to Dr Bentley, I am an addled stranger who has a tenuous grip on reality. Much as I would like to believe you, I am a realist. At best I will be the source of much gossip, at worst, shunned.'

'Those who know you—those who work alongside you in the infirmary, your patients—they will stick by you.'

She stepped back and stared at him as if he had gone mad. 'You cannot be suggesting I continue in the infirmary now that everyone knows I've not been right in the head?'

'I most certainly am suggesting that. You have been a godsend to both me and those children. I've come to rely on you.'

'But people will disapprove—'

Joe interrupted her by holding her at arm's length. 'Let them. The foundling home is owned and run by my family. I'm in charge of the infirmary. Not one of those children has a parent who loves them. They are all alone in the world, save us. Their care should be our main priority, not what a bunch of ignorant gossips think. The best place for you to recover from your ordeal, to find yourself again and to knock down those walls in your mind, is in the infirmary doing what you love. You are a talented healer, Bella. I also happen to

think you'd make a very talented doctor if the fools who run the universities would accept women. I'm happy to work alongside you and teach you all that I know.' He saw hope blossom in her dark eyes. Saw her waver. 'You told that crowd of doubters you would work alongside me and help vaccinate the people of Retford. I need your help, Bella, if I'm going to keep them safe. Don't let that idiot Bentley destroy everything you've achieved since you arrived here.'

'I'm not sure I'm brave enough to face them all again.'

'Yes, you are. Today you will go home and you will lick your wounds in private. Tomorrow I will meet your carriage in the square and escort you to my surgery. If anyone is brave enough to say anything about the state of your mind, then they will answer to me. However, I suspect you will earn their respect by returning. Dogged determination and the desire to do good, even when it is unpopular, are attributes to aspire to. Come.' Joe took her hand; it felt small yet so right in his. His palm heated at the contact, the warmth spreading up his arm and flooding his chest. 'Let me escort you home.'

Chapter Fifteen

Bella never expected to sleep. The horrible morning, the physical and mental toll her confession to Joe took, combined with the frank and tearful conversation she had with her mother straight afterwards, had left her nerves positively jangling. She felt like she had been kicked around like a football, battered and bruised yet oddly unbeaten. Unburdening herself to Joe had been cathartic. His reaction to her words had been wonderful. He had been both supportive and outraged on her behalf and adamant she was neither mad nor would remain lost. After her initial outpouring, it had emboldened her to confide in her mother as well.

Her mother, God bless her, had been relieved to finally hear exactly what had transpired that dreadful night and had wept with Bella in her arms afterwards, confessing that she had wanted to know everything from the outset but, with Bella's reluctance to talk and the passing of time, had not known how to initiate the conversation. When she'd heard the full details of Dr Bentley's treachery, her mother had been incandescent with rage and intent on tearing him off a strip on the

morrow. Whilst she wouldn't be talked out of the latter, she had promised not to write to her husband about all that had transpired and to wait and see what happened in the next few days before acting in haste and worrying him unduly. Like Joe, her mother's advice was to brazen it out and dare anyone to give credence to Dr Bentley's accusations.

'We are Beaumonts, Bella, and we shall behave as Beaumonts.'

Wrung out like a dish rag in a mangle, Bella had gone to lie down on her bed a little before six and had shocked herself by sleeping like the dead until her maid woke her the next morning.

Now she was dressed in one of her finest day dresses, at her mother's insistence, and turning the square in the carriage with her dear mama sat loyally by her side and looking every inch the formidable society Countess she was. Dr Bentley really had no idea what was about to hit him. Her mother at full tilt was something to behold.

The carriage slowed and Bella saw Joe standing waiting, just as he had said he would. Seeing him made her stronger and her silly heart began to beat faster at the splendid sight of him stood tall and proud. To look at him, no one would guess he had been accused of doing the devil's work the day before, or smashed up placards or manhandled Dr Bentley on her behalf or knocked the pious vicar on his backside. He was as calm as a millpond on a warm summer's day and as handsome as sin in his austere black coat and freshly polished spectacles, his intense blue eyes twinkling

with what looked like pride as he helped her out of the carriage.

'You came, then. I knew you would.' Acknowledging the silently staring people all around, all pretending to be busy but watching intently out of the corners of their eyes, he winked. 'Not much happens in Retford.' He then blinked in surprise at the sight of her mother as well, but he swiftly remembered his manners and politely inclined his head. 'Your ladyship. How lovely to see you again.'

'The pleasure is all mine, Dr Warriner, I can assure you.' Her mother grabbed him warmly with both hands and then kissed him on the cheek with what looked to Bella like genuine affection. 'The more I learn of you, the more you strike me as a wholly lovely young man and one I have decided I heartily approve of.'

A little startled, Joe slanted a questioning glance to Bella while her mother threaded her arm through his. 'I'm glad to hear it, my lady.' The poor man looked quite bewildered by the sudden change of heart. 'Will you still be joining me at my surgery, Lady Isabella?'

'Of course she will. I've insisted on encroaching as I am eager to receive a dose of your *miraculous cowpox*, Dr Warriner, before it's too late.' Her mother's voice was louder than was usual, no doubt to ensure those watching them with barely concealed interest in the market square as to her intentions. 'It's *very* popular in the capital, Dr Warriner. All the very *best* people are getting vaccinated. Who wouldn't? What a wonderful discovery it is, to be sure, and in this day and age, when towns are becoming even more crowded than they were before, we need it more than ever. Why, I read only recently about an epidemic of smallpox in

the East End of London only last year that killed thousands. *Thousands!* Can you imagine that?'

'Unfortunately, I can, my lady. Ignorance and the cost of prevention mean the majority leave it off until it's too late.' He offered his spare arm to Bella and she happily took it. Joe was comforting and solid, and today she needed both. 'I hope to avoid that here in Retford.' Wearing two Beaumonts as bookends, he walked them across the market square towards his office. As they walked past, many of the traders removed their caps and mumbled *my lady* as she sailed by, their expressions running the gamut between curious and embarrassed. Bella could not tell whether they were embarrassed by her addled condition or at the way she had been treated by Dr Bentley, but a few did look impressed that she had shown up, just as Joe had said they would.

They hadn't got halfway when the entire Warriner family appeared out of nowhere to join them. The Earl, Captain James Warriner and the youngest, Jake, took their places behind them, like a guard of honour. Letty and Cassie Warriner both commandeered Bella, grinning and chattering away as if yesterday the whole world had not found out she was addled and irrational. The solidarity and unquestioning show of support moved her and emotion tightened her throat. This was a public display of resilience in the face of adversity and one which said a great deal about the family. As it was meant to—it shamed the onlookers who had come to gawp and the square fell oddly quiet despite the number of people within.

Joe turned towards them as they reached the door. 'Ladies and gentleman, in a few minutes I will be open-

ing my doors and inviting all comers to be protected
from smallpox. I sincerely hope to see all of you. How-
ever, I also understand some of you may still have res-
ervations and some of you might be adamantly against
it. All I would ask is you respect the decisions and
wishes of all those who do wish to take up my offer.
The nonsense of yesterday should never have hap-
pened, you know that, and I am sure, like me, you are
disgusted by what transpired. It was not Retford's finest
hour.' Several people glanced down at their feet, others
nodded in agreement. Only a very few were affronted.
'Should any of you have any questions about the proce-
dure, then do come and see me this afternoon, where
I will happily speak to individuals and apprise you
of the facts. In the meantime, Lady Isabella has gra-
ciously offered to assist me in my endeavour, so if you
will excuse us, the doors will open promptly at eight.'

What happened next was organisation of a mili-
tary standard. It had apparently been decided that they
would behave as if they were expecting hundreds. Rope
lines were erected outside to ensure an orderly queue.
Inside, a series of tables draped in pristine white cloths
were already laden with bandages and bowls of Joe's
gin-laced water for washing. Jake and the Earl were to
man carts which would travel around the outskirts of
town and the rural farms beyond, bringing those un-
able to make the journey on foot directly to the square.
Letty and Cassie, with her mother in tow, went outside
to greet people and explain the procedure to them while
Jamie's role was to ensure there was, as he put it, no
funny business. He planted himself between the roped-
off lines at the surgery and the square and loomed men-
acingly. A few minutes later he was joined by Mellor.

The two men most likely to terrify the naysayers of Retford now reassuringly stood guard. Mrs Patterson was in charge of keeping an accurate record and, as promised, Bella was to be Joe's assistant, responsible for cleaning the area of the patient's arm prior to and then binding the tiny wound after the procedure.

A few minutes to eight, when it was just the two of them left all alone in his office, Bella succumbed to the urge to move the lace panel aside and look out of the window. She was pleasantly surprised. At least ten people were standing in line. Before he spoke, she felt Joe come to stand behind her. Even though there were several inches between their bodies, hers was very aware of his. Goosebumps bloomed down her back and on her neck, making her flesh prickle in the most disconcerting manner—yet it wasn't panic or fear which caused this reaction. It was simply him and the strange effect he had on her senses. Bella knew it was attraction. There could be no denying it. Somewhere in the last few weeks her mind had decided that Joe the man was neither her enemy nor a threat. He was kind, strong, loyal and...she couldn't put into words the rest because the feelings were so new and unfamiliar. Even before the incident Bella had never had such a reaction to a man. It was more than respect and admiration, went further than friendship, and, at times like now, it was accompanied by need. Temptation. A desire to knock down a wall.

'That's a decent start. People are a bit like sheep. Where one goes, the others soon follow.'

His warm breath caressed her neck, sending shivers down her spine and to other places which shocked

her. Was this desire now, too? 'And you are a brilliant physician who inspires trust. That helps.'

'You think I'm brilliant?'

'Yes.' Bella didn't dare turn around. Turning around meant gazing into those soulful eyes and, while her skin was so sensitive and her pulse was fluttering, she didn't trust herself to keep her reaction to him private.

'I think you're brilliant, too.' Her head began to turn at the compliment and she saw he was smiling. 'I'm so glad you're here.' His deep blue eyes locked with hers and Bella had to fight the instinct to run as the usual panic began to claw in her gut.

Not now! Don't spoil this lovely moment!

Before she could stop it, what she was suddenly thinking came out of her mouth.

'Do you think I will get better? My irrational fear of men, that is?' Because she wanted to. She wanted to feel brave enough to want a man's touch. His touch.

Joe's smile never faltered. 'You're not scared of me any more. In time, you will conquer all your fears.'

'Do you think I will conquer my fear of...of the physical side of things, too?'

The smile disappeared, replaced instead by a solemn expression she couldn't decipher. 'One day...you will find a man you trust, and when you do, that side of things will develop naturally.'

You trust him.

'You'll remember how nice a simple kiss can be.'

'No, I won't. To do that, one would need an example to recall.' Why was she telling him that? She could tell by his expression he was shocked by the admission, so she tried to be matter of fact. 'I worry that I've built it up so much in my mind that it's all so tainted

by the incident, that I will never be able to move on.' Bella closed her eyes, embarrassed by the admission and not wanting to see the pity in his face. 'I know I should face my fears.' Although kissing him might not be so bad, she realised. A huge part of her wanted to. Really wanted to.

'You should.'

She risked opening her eyes to see his so close and strangely darker than usual. He was still mere inches away, so close she could feel the warmth of his body. Her eyes dropped to his lips and she pulled them reluctantly back up. Her whole body felt odd. Heavy. Expectant. Her fingers itched to touch his face. Her lips felt swollen and hot. They wanted to be kissed even if her head wanted to run. 'In the interests of science, and to help me demolish one of the irrational walls in my mind, I don't suppose you would...' Oh, good lord, was she now begging him to kiss her? How sad and pathetic was that? She'd bet Clarissa had never had to resort to begging to get a man to kiss her or had ever felt terrified at the prospect of a kiss. Mortified, she turned away, only to feel his palm touch her cheek and slowly turn it back. His eyes dropped to her lips and lingered. Then he dipped his head and softly pressed his mouth to hers.

Having nothing to compare it to, Bella was unprepared for the intensity of the experience. It was like tasting something delicious for the first time or the rush of excitement she had felt racing down the lane in his curricle. Her eyes fluttered closed and she sighed against his mouth, duplicating the way his lips brushed gently against hers. Her hands came to rest on his chest and she could feel the rapid beats of his heart against

her fingers. Unconsciously she stepped closer and didn't flinch when his hands came to rest on her hips.

Her breasts felt peculiar and needed to be touched, so Bella allowed herself to rest them against the hard wall of his chest, something which made him sigh, too. By the time the tip of his tongue brushed the seam of her mouth, she was past caring about anything except the surprising new sensations within her body. She mirrored the movement and the kiss turned from tentative to passionate. Her fingers were in his hair, his smoothed up her ribcage and over her back.

'It's eight o'clock.' The opening door had them jumping apart and one look at Jake Warriner told her he knew exactly what they had just been doing, even though Joe was now several feet away and fiddling with the equipment on his table.

'Splendid. Splendid.' His eyes flicked to hers, he blinked and she wished she knew what he was thinking. 'I suppose we should get started, then.'

Of all the things he had planned for today, Joe hadn't been expecting that. To be honest, even if he had planned for it, he couldn't have anticipated the ferocity of his reaction. His poor, shocked body was positively throbbing with need and his wits were so scrambled he could barely talk straight.

What the hell had just happened?

One minute they were looking at the people out of the window, and the next, nothing had existed except her. A simple, chaste, scientific kiss should not have such an explosive reaction, yet it had. More confusing was the way the kiss had made him feel. Since he had seen her distraught and demoralised on the side of the

lane yesterday, Joe had been filled with the most possessive male urge to protect her. The healer in him had wanted to fix her and he had spent most of the night staring at the ceiling, his thoughts darting between worrying about her and ripping Bentley and that monster who had defiled her limb from limb for hurting her.

When she had stepped out of her carriage this morning, tentative and nervous, his desire to protect her had overruled all other thoughts in his head. His thoughts just now hadn't been the slightest bit protective; they had been purely carnal. If he was brutally honest with himself, they still were. She was busying herself preparing for the stream of patients they were about to receive and all he could concentrate on was that kiss. Those lovely soft moans of passion, the way her body moulded itself to his, the delicious taste of her mouth— he'd been on fire in seconds and he sincerely doubted the flames were likely to be extinguished any time soon. Not when her lips were still so red and swollen from his kisses, her sweet scent was filling the air and tormenting his senses, and her breasts were rising and falling in time with her rapid breathing. Evidence of her quick and gloriously passionate response. To him.

Her fledgling passion had awakened something primal within him, something which made him ache to possess her, as well as protect her and claim her as his. He was certain he had never experienced desire so all-consuming. If Jake hadn't interrupted them when he did, Joe's greedy hands would have been all over her, filling themselves with her womanly curves, and he'd have inevitably pulled her body flush against his painful arousal and would've probably scared the poor girl

to death in the process. Joe had never been so grateful and so furious at his younger brother in his entire life.

Or so baffled by what to do next.

Bella had asked him to kiss her—but in the interests of science, because she was distressed and wanted to get better. There was every chance it had been an experiment for her. Joe hadn't kissed her in the name of science. He had kissed her because she had looked so damn beautiful with the sunlight behind her. Because he could think of nothing else but tasting that lush mouth at that precise moment.

Had it been the moment? Had his reaction occurred in the intense heat of it? She walked to the door and greeted their first patient. Joe watched the way her body moved, the way her mouth curved up as she spoke, her quiet dignity, her bravery, her generous, kind nature, her clever brain, and he felt it all in his groin *and* his heart. Not the moment, then, but her. Something he would need to ponder seriously later, once today was done. For now, he had a job to do and only hoped his unexpected case of rampant lust and his suddenly heightened feelings would allow him to do it properly.

Chapter Sixteen

By late afternoon, the steady stream of visitors to the surgery turned into a deluge as word filtered around the town that a great majority of people were daring to go against the explicit advice of the local cleric and were availing themselves of the free vaccine. It helped that the midday post also brought news of yet another reported case of smallpox, this time in Carlton-on-Trent, closer still to Retford. It confirmed Joe's suspicion the disease would travel along the Great North Road. There had been a minor incident outside, when the Reverend Reeves had decided to issue a blistering sermon in the centre of the market square, but once the post arrived with the grave news and the constable had frogmarched the outraged vicar back to the rectory, more people were concerned about their lives than the prospect of growing a pair of cow's horns, and the vicar's prophecy of doom was largely ignored. Dr Bentley failed to materialise at all. Bella hoped that had something to do with her mother, who'd gone off to give him a piece of her mind before she went home, or better still because he was scared Joe might carry

out his threat to tear the fool apart. He deserved to know what fear felt like.

To their credit, nobody treated Bella any different to usual. She caught the odd sideways glance, one or two expressions of embarrassment, but not one person said anything untoward or refused to allow her to treat them. If anything, they were nothing but kind. At Cassie Warriner's insistence, they took a break for food and Joe decided they would be more effective if both of them administered the vaccine. He watched her closely with the first few patients, then in his typical delegating style left her to it.

She had no idea what he was thinking or even if he was thinking about the kiss they had shared. He never mentioned it once during the day. If anything, as far as Bella could tell, he was behaving as he always did, so perhaps she had imagined much of his reaction afterwards. Bella was hoping it had meant as much to him as it had to her, even though she had practically forced him into it in the name of science and pity. Regardless, it had meant something to her. It meant the whole world to her.

Not only did she now know she could endure a man's kiss—Joe's kiss—she could also enjoy it, if her body's splendid reaction was any gauge. It renewed her hope she might be able to be intimate with a man one day. As long as that man was Joe. He was a strange and intoxicating combination of safe and addictive at the same time. Bella had experienced the first stirrings of passion—she was sure of it. With passion, the natural next step was intimacy, although she hadn't really given much thought to either at the time. Her body's reaction had been leading her. Not her broken head, nor

her tender heart, but the gloriously physical response to a thoroughly wonderful kiss.

All day she had found herself stealing glances at him as he worked alongside her and wondering what would have happened had they not been interrupted. Would she have allowed his hands to roam freely across her body? Could she bear the feel of them on her skin? Her breasts? Just thinking about it made them feel heavy until her broken mind reminded her of the hands of that other man as it usually did and the irrational fear returned instantly. Her eyes flicked to Joe's hands. Big, capable and suddenly all she could think about was the perfect way they had felt against her face. It was all so confusing.

'That's the last one.' Mrs Patterson's voice made her jump as Bella bandaged the boy's arm she had just treated. 'It's past nine o'clock and you two need your rest. I've told the others to come back tomorrow.'

Beside her, Joe stretched and rotated his shoulders. 'I *am* dead on my feet, so I dare say that makes sense.'

'Shall I draw you a bath, Dr Warriner?'

His eyes flicked towards Bella nervously before he answered his housekeeper. 'Perhaps after I have taken Lady Isabella home, Mrs Patterson.'

Little balloons of excitement at the prospect bubbled in her tummy only to be burst by the servant. 'No need, Doctor. I took the liberty of summoning Lady Isabella's carriage an hour ago. It is sat outside waiting for her in the square.'

'Ah—good.' He didn't seem pleased. She knew him well enough now to know a false smile when she saw one, but she had no earthly idea if this was a positive or negative sign. Did he want to drive her home spe-

cifically? Had he things to say? 'Well, then, I suppose I should see you to your carriage, Bella.' As he didn't meet her eye as he said this, she took it as a bad sign. Whatever he might want to say was probably not what she wanted to hear. An apology, maybe, or worse a castigation for the way they got carried away or because she had put him on the spot with her unusual request and he had felt beholden. Perhaps he had noticed the longing glances she had been throwing him all day and wanted to remind her of the fact he had done as she'd asked only in the interests of science to help her face her fears. A kindly experiment. Physician to patient. Explanations too awful to have to hear.

'There is no need. I can manage well enough and Mrs Patterson is waiting to draw your bath.'

He frowned before nodding. 'If you're sure.' And then they both stood rather uncomfortably as clearly neither of them could think of anything appropriate to say and were both hideously aware of the needy way she had responded to his mouth. Bella broke the silence because she could stand it no longer.

'I'd best be off, then.' Without waiting for his response, she walked swiftly towards the hallway to fetch her bonnet and shawl. He followed, rather stiffly, and stood near the front door while she tied the ribbons hastily under her chin and bundled her shawl under her arm because it was far too warm to bother with, or perhaps that was because of the blush already blooming on her cheeks.

'Will you be back tomorrow?'

'Of course. If you need me.'

'Mrs Patterson turned people away this evening, so I dare say there will be a need tomorrow. We also

still have to vaccinate the children in the foundling home.' His posture was uncharacteristically formal and Bella recognised she was the cause of his discomfort. He could barely look at her for more than a second or two before staring down at his feet. His posture did not instil her with a great deal of confidence. Joe was obviously in the midst of a great deal of regret. Bella felt her toes curl inside her shoes and tried to appear nonchalant, something not easy when she could feel her face was as red as a beetroot.

'Why don't I do that?' Then she would be spared more of this peculiar new tension in his company as well as the inevitable polite words about the mistake which he had made this morning in agreeing to her odd request. The offer appeared to perplex him and he blinked at her through his spectacles. 'Unless you don't trust me to do it alone...'

'Of course I trust you—yes. Yes. You do the foundling home. I suppose that makes sense as we can cover more people that way. I shall have Mrs Patterson prepare everything you need and have it all delivered at the home before you arrive tomorrow.' A sure sign he had no desire to see her at all tomorrow now that an opportunity had presented itself.

'Right, then. I'd best be off,' she repeated herself. 'Goodnight.'

'Yes. Goodnight.'

Bella hadn't expected him to follow her to her carriage and jumped when she felt his hands on her elbow when she went to climb it. Sudden warmth spread up her arm at the brief touch. It sent her scrambling for the seat, then turning, far too primly, a tight smile pasted

on her face. His was equally as tight. 'Thank you for today. And yesterday. It means a lot.'

'You're very welcome.'

Joe began to close the door but stopped and opened it again. 'I'm very sorry about earlier. I can see you're upset. I never meant to upset you.'

And there was the answer she had been dreading. 'You haven't. It was a scientific experiment. A favour between friends. Nothing more.'

For a moment Bella swore she saw regret clouding his face, but it was so fleeting she couldn't be sure and then the door was closed and the carriage lurched away. Bella slumped in the corner and tried to ignore the tears swimming in her eyes.

Joe didn't see her at all the next day and only fleetingly in the days after. She had appropriated Jake and the pair of them went off in a cart to visit the outskirts of Retford, intent on vaccinating the wary in the comfort of their own homes. Whilst it made perfect sense to allow those intimidated by the fire-and-brimstone Reverend or the respected Dr Bentley to be treated away from the censure of prying eyes, now that almost a week had passed Joe couldn't help thinking she was avoiding him on purpose. All because of one kiss which had burned out of hand.

As he treated the ever-decreasing queue of people at his surgery, he couldn't help reliving what had happened and mulling over what it meant. Yes, he had kissed her passionately. He hadn't meant to. The last thing he ever wanted to do to a woman who was wary of men was scare her with the full force of his desire, yet despite his best intentions that initially chaste kiss

had soon turned into a full-blown outpouring of it. No longer just a meeting of lips, but a feast involving tongues and throaty moans. However, the more he thought about it, the more it occurred to him she had also taken part in it. Unabashedly. It hadn't been just his lips, his tongue, his throaty moans. His dreams these past seven nights had been haunted by her. Real, not imagined. Her hands *had* explored his chest and her fingers *had* mussed his hair. Things which made her reaction towards him at the end of the day baffling. She'd been aloof and embarrassed.

But then again, he realised, so had he. And he was the one with experience of passion and by her own admission that had been Bella's first kiss. She had granted him that honour and unmanned him with it at the same time. What had started tentatively had rapidly turned into the most significant kiss of his life. Nothing else had existed except her in that moment. Had Bella felt the same?

He should have asked her, he now realised. He should have told her what it meant to him. Joe should have been honest, when instead he'd been hesitant. Preferring to wait for her to make the next move. As if a woman who had been through what she had been through, who had never been kissed before and didn't know how to flirt or be coy, would be so bold as to suggest there be more.

Joe groaned at his own ineptitude and slapped his forehead with his palm. There was every possibility he had been the one to play the aftermath all wrong and her withdrawal and natural distress had been all his fault, too. Perhaps there was even the chance she was feeling as utterly wretched as he was, in which case,

only a fool would avoid her. Especially as his body hadn't stopped wanting her since that day. Hers had fitted so perfectly against his. If he closed his eyes, he could still feel the soft press of her breasts against his heart, the way her trim waist flared out to that delightful rounded peach of a bottom...

'You look utterly miserable, Dr Warriner.' His head snapped up at the sound of Lady Clarissa's sultry tone. She was stood in the doorway on the arm of her father. A man whose jaw was set rock hard and whose eyes were distinctly narrowed. Joe sincerely hoped the Earl of Braxton couldn't read his thoughts.

'Lady Clarissa.' Joe stood and bowed politely. 'Lord Braxton. You are back from town.' Talk about stating the obvious. 'To what do I owe the pleasure?' *Aside from the imminent pasting I am doubtless about to receive.*

'We have come to be vaccinated. Mama has insisted and, since Bella is who knows where with your handsome brother, Papa insisted we come here presently.'

'Then you'd best come in and sit down... Sir, if you would remove your coat.' Although surprised and unsettled to see them, Joe was grateful they had given him something to do and set about cleaning his hands and preparing his equipment, all the while conscious of the silent earl's piercing glare and his own guilty thoughts concerning the man's other daughter.

'The whole of Retford is abuzz with your performance last week,' Lady Clarissa purred. 'Apparently, you were quite masterful. And impressive. Mama is now quite taken with you, Doctor. She couldn't stop gushing about you from the moment we arrived home

a few hours ago till the moment we left to come here. As far as she is concerned, you are the saviour of the town.'

'Lady Braxton is being too kind. I am merely doing my job.' Joe decided to hide behind professional detachment while he learned the lay of the land. 'Who is first?'

At her father's curt nod, Lady Clarissa held out her arm and pouted. 'Will it hurt?'

'It's just a scratch. Nothing worse.' To prove it, Joe swiftly did what was necessary. Her skin was similar in texture and shade to her sister's, he thought dispassionately, yet devoid of the powerful *frisson* he always experienced when he touched Bella. Not a single tingle materialised. Her face, the one he had once thought the most beguiling in Christendom, bore similar features, but none was as lovely as Bella's. The bouncing blonde curls no longer held any allure, not now that he knew he preferred luscious ebony silk.

As a test he glanced briefly down at her mouth while he bandaged her arm and was unmoved. Not lips he had any desire to taste. Lady Clarissa was quite the wrong sister after all, which meant he had been a fool from the outset and Jake had known Joe's romantic mind better than he did.

Or had.

Joe had no doubt where his affection truly lay any more because his feelings for Bella were unlike any he had experienced in the past. Instead of dreaming about a hazy image of perfection stood high on a pedestal, he had fallen for a woman who deserved to be put on one, but he couldn't bring himself to do so. He didn't

want Bella out of reach and unobtainable. He wanted her feet firmly planted on the floor so he could dip his head and kiss her any time he saw fit. He didn't want perfect because he loved her imperfections.

Loved?

Good grief.

'All done.' His head spun as he cleaned his vaccination knife and hands. When had that happened? Joe turned, a little stunned, and his gaze locked with the steely eyes of Bella's father. 'Your turn, my lord.'

'Could you wait for me outside, Clarissa?' Ominous words, but hardly out of the blue. Lady Clarissa huffed as if it was a great inconvenience and glided out the door. Because he felt it was appropriate, Joe closed it and braced himself for the onslaught. The Earl eyed him coldly.

'Did you encourage my daughter to go behind my back and continue to work alongside you?'

'I did not.'

'Yet you did nothing to discourage her either?'

'No. Your daughter is a talented healer and wanted to learn. She insisted on staying and I agreed to teach her.'

'I see.' The Earl sat silently while Joe made the tiny incision in his arm, administered the minute jewel of vaccine and then wrapped the wound. When Joe stepped away and plunged his hands back into the water to clean them, the older man watched him. 'Was it your suggestion she should be vaccinated in public?'

'Of course it wasn't!' Joe couldn't disguise the flash of anger, knowing full well he never would have agreed to it if he'd known how Bella would be humiliated. 'Your daughter has a very determined mind of her own!'

'This I know.' The Earl sighed, defeated, and all at once no longer looked like a formidable peer of the realm, but an anxious and devoted father. 'I had thought that part of her lost for ever...after...' His voice trailed off and he stared mournfully at his hands. 'I know Bella chose to confide in you...and that she chose you...over her family makes me feel ashamed. I keep thinking I've let her down in some way when all I've been trying to do is protect her...from what happened.'

Or protect himself from the ugly reality of what his daughter had suffered. 'You cannot protect her from what happened. It happened. It was terrible and horrific, but to deny it happened doesn't change the fact it did. Bella needs to come to terms with it and to do that she needs to talk about it. Keeping powerful emotions bottled up inside is unhealthy. They fester.' In the Earl's shoes, how would Joe feel? Responsible. Guilty. Overprotective. All of those things and more. 'You responded in a way which is entirely natural for a father and I'm sure Bella was reluctant to discuss it at the time.' The man nodded.

'She was too distressed. For weeks all she did was cry and hide in her bedchamber. It was...heartbreaking.'

'It is difficult to bring up uncomfortable topics. As a society we never discuss emotions or feelings. We hide behind our English veneer of polite detachment and hope those things will go away.' This man didn't need more guilt heaped upon the tons of it already resting on his slumped shoulders. He was coming to terms with what happened as well and he hadn't forced Bella into all the invasive treatments she had been offered. He had given her a say in her own life. 'You did right

by her in bringing her here. The change of scenery, the infirmary, doing something she loves, all those things have brought about progress. Bella would be the first to say so.'

'You think I should have brought her here sooner?'

Joe shook his head. 'Not until she was ready and, from what I've heard, she was nowhere near ready to face her fears before now. Bringing her here sooner might have been a mistake. The brain is a powerful organ—yet it is still an organ. Like all organs when they are damaged, it takes time to recover. However, in my professional opinion I do feel Bella is well on the way to recovery. She has made great strides in the last few weeks. Almost a different person from the one I first met.' Although fundamentally the same underneath. Brave, clever and beautiful inside and out.

'Do you believe she will get better? Fully, I mean, and be like her old self?'

'I know it. What she suffered will always be there, but like the grief of losing a loved one or the pain of a broken heart, it will lessen with time.'

'All of the other physicians we have consulted were less optimistic. We tried some of the treatments, until she put her foot down and refused to continue.'

'Good for her. Bella is much stronger than she gives herself credit for and appears quite determined to face her fears head-on now. She has a great mind and can be formidable at times. The way she strode on to that platform and faced the crowd last week was...' The single, most selfless thing anyone had ever done for him. He smiled at the memory. 'Admirable. I'm only sorry she was then betrayed by Dr Bentley.'

'I called on him before I came here. Like a coward, he refused me an audience. But he *will* see me and he *will* answer for his actions.' The icy hatred lacing the Earl's voice told Joe he meant it. When he turned to face him, he could also see the remorse in the other man's eyes. 'I owe you an apology, Dr Warriner. Once upon a time I would never have listened to idle gossip. I would have judged the measure of a man by his actions and his manner. Since Bella was…attacked…' just saying it seemed to take a toll, but at least he was saying it '…I've seen every man as a potential threat to one of my daughters. Bella called me on it weeks ago, but I wouldn't listen. My wife, also a formidable woman when riled, has torn me off a strip twice for my idiocy. Once in a scathing letter summoning me home and then again, this morning, when I arrived. Quite rightly, I believe, and I am big enough to acknowledge when I am wrong. She has apprised me of how you leapt to Bella's defence in the square and how you helped her afterwards. That she was brave enough to face the world again cheers my heart and I have you to thank for that.'

'No thanks are necessary.'

'They are and I want you to know that if you did want to call on Clarissa again, I wouldn't offer any objection.'

Clarissa. Good gracious, this was going to be awkward. 'About that…'

I've blithely changed my mind and fancy your other daughter instead.

How exactly was Joe to explain his about-face without sounding fickle, insincere or shallow? 'The thing

is, while I admit I did originally call at your house to see Clarissa—'

'Papa!' The door slammed open and Bella was stood in the frame, looking wide-eyed and more than a little panicked. Her face was a tad flushed and she was breathing exactly like a woman who had been running. 'You're home!' Her dark eyes darted between Joe and her father, doubtless to gauge the mood. 'Are you...*well*?'

He embraced her and grinned. 'I am indeed well, Bella, and I am glad to see you are, too. Most well, in fact. Much more like your old *formidable* and delightful self. I was just saying as much to Dr Warriner, who I am extremely impressed with by the way. You were right about him. And I was wrong.' She appeared relieved and offered Joe a shy smile. The first smile she had bestowed on him since before they had kissed and it quite took his breath away. 'In fact, daughter, you will be pleased to learn I have relented and have granted him permission to call upon your sister whenever he sees fit.' Joe watched that sweet smile falter, disappear, only to be replaced by one of her pretend smiles which didn't touch her eyes.

'Well, that's splendid. I'm...glad.'

He wasn't. The temptation to stride over there and kiss her senseless and then apologise for being such a blind fool was overwhelming, but Joe couldn't bring himself to do it in front of her father. Not when he had no idea how to explain away his overriding stupidity adequately and had no clue as to whether she was truly glad or if by some miracle, like him, she was mortified by her father's offer.

'Are you finished for the day, Bella?' Her father

had taken her arm. 'I should love nothing more than to catch up on all of your news.'

'Yes, I am finished, Papa.' Her eyes flicked briefly Joe's way. 'Quite finished. Let's go home.'

Chapter Seventeen

Despite the impending threat of smallpox, the monthly assembly was its usual crush. On a positive note the crowds bothered her less. Unfortunately, they were the least of her problems. In the two days since her father had returned, Bella had remained staunchly at home, justifying her belligerent cowardice on three counts. Firstly, and most importantly, she'd had several long and painful conversations with her father which had been necessary and healing, but had left her emotionally drained and physically exhausted. Secondly, with Molly now back in the girls' dormitory and the infirmary completely empty for once, there genuinely had been no reason for her to go, and thirdly, and to Bella's complete shame and disgust, she couldn't bring herself to face Joe knowing she had kissed him, but he still preferred Clarissa.

He must have asked to court her for Papa to have granted his permission and that stung. If she was honest, a mere sting didn't come close in describing the dull, empty ache which had taken root in her chest and refused to budge no matter how many times she tried to reason with herself this was inevitable.

She had known he was besotted with her sister from the outset, despite his one claim to the contrary. Why on earth had she thought that might change? Bella was the bookish Beaumont. The decidedly less beautiful Beaumont and, who could forget, she was also the broken Beaumont as well. Getting better slowly, which was some consolation, but not worth the effort of wasting a healthy man's affections on. Not when he had been granted permission to call on the Incomparable with impunity.

Poor Joe was definitely barking up the wrong tree there. A few weeks in London had quite turned her elder sister's pretty head; the balls, the parties, the superior society and a brief dalliance with a handsome duke had made her less benevolent towards Retford and desperate to return. Something she had lamented constantly for two whole days and was currently still lamenting to her usual herd of admirers from their spot close to the refreshment table. A spot Bella was also stuck in because her sister's arm was presently threaded through hers, clamping her in place.

Now that the family had seen such huge strides of progress in Bella's mental state in such a relatively short period of time, they were all determined not to allow her to go backwards, which meant, in Clarissa's words, forcing herself to engage socially. Another way of saying, *it's time you started talking to men again.*

Bella was doing her best to look engaged, despite the fact she didn't give two figs about the *glorious* society of the capital or the opulence of the grand entertainments in comparison to this *minuscule* little affair. Clarissa's admirers hadn't noticed. Next to her sister Bella was largely invisible. Always had been, but now

that Joe preferred Clarissa, blending into the wallpaper had rather lost much of its appeal.

He had yet to make an appearance. The entire Warriner clan were in attendance, all bar the handsome doctor who had wormed his way into her heart and then stamped on it without realising, and in a show of public solidarity both her parents were laughing and joking amongst them. Jake had sought her out over an hour ago and gone to great pains to reassure her that Joe would arrive, just as soon as he had finished with a last-minute visit to a patient. Why he had chosen to single her out, rather than Clarissa, and quite what his reassuring undertone was meant to mean, she couldn't say. Unless Joe had set his brother straight about the kiss he had witnessed and now the youngest Warriner pitied her as well. Uncharitably, Bella hoped Joe had been called to a birth and that the babe would be reluctant to be born until the Beaumont carriage was whisking Bella and her decidedly more beautiful sister home.

'Stop gazing winsomely at the door,' her sister whispered from behind her fan. 'He'll arrive when he arrives and it will be good for him to see you chatting to other men.'

'I'm not sure what you mean.' Although her cheeks were probably already giving her away as Bella realised she *had* been staring winsomely at the door.

'Really? Then I suppose I've also imagined the sighing and the sulking? I must be mistaken. You are clearly not waiting for a certain dashing young physician to burst through those doors and sweep you off your feet.'

'I do not regard Dr Warriner in that way at all, Clarissa! Ours is a professional relationship based on our mutual interests in medical science...'

'Poppycock. You have always been a shocking liar, Bella, and a terrible actress.'

'I am not lying!' Bella turned her back to the dance floor to spare displaying her blotchy and glowing blush to all and sundry and tried to make her outraged hiss sound less hiss-like. 'I have no romantic designs on him or any other man. Just because I am finally returning to my old self doesn't mean I am ready for any of that nonsense, thank you very much. It will be years until I'm ready to consider a beau, if at all. In fact, I'm quite wedded to spinsterhood. A husband would only get in the way of my medical studies, and now that Papa has finally agreed I can dedicate time to science I am reluctant to consider anything else.' By the end of the monologue, Bella was reasonably proud of how convincing she had sounded. Clarissa simply regarded her blankly.

'I see.'

She plainly didn't. 'Dr Warriner is a friend. A colleague. That is the full extent of our relationship.'

'Then you won't care that he has just arrived and is currently striding in your direction.'

Pride made Bella stiffen her shoulders. If he was striding anywhere, then it was in the direction of her sister, the Beaumont whose face was not as red as a ripe summer strawberry. Perhaps she could scurry away in a manner convincing enough to make everyone think she urgently needed the retiring room? Because her silly body could sense him and was heating with awareness, while her stupid face decided to spontaneously combust, but escaping now was out of the question. Far too obvious. Far too much like defeat.

'Why, Dr Warriner! How lovely to see you again.' Clarissa slid her arm around Bella's in case she bolted

and pulled her close, forcing her to face him. 'We had quite despaired of you ever arriving. Didn't we, Bella?'

'Good evening, Dr Warriner.'

Floor, open and swallow me now.

'I trust you are well.'

'Yes. I am well.' His hair was mussed. No doubt as a result of driving his curricle too fast. 'Good evening, ladies.' His eyes locked with Bella's with such intensity, it made her more nervous. She couldn't tell what the odd look meant. The optimistic and deluded real her inside hoped it was something to do with the intense feelings he had miraculously developed for her since he had asked her father to court Clarissa. The pragmatic scholar realised it was probably doctorly concern for her unnaturally high colour tinged with pity for her poor addled mind. Because only the most pathetic of individuals would have to resort to begging for their first kiss in the interests of science.

'We are most well, although peeved that neither of us is dancing.' Clarissa's voice was filled with mischief. 'When I can clearly hear the first bars of the waltz.' Bella found herself shoved forward a few inches and was mortified.

His eyes darted from hers to her sister's, then slowly returned again. 'Lady Isabella—Bella—would you do me the honour of dancing with me?'

And now he was being polite and solicitous because Clarissa had forced his hand both saddened and enraged her in equal measure. Bella opened her mouth to curtly decline, only to find herself propelled further forward by her sister. 'She would love to.' Clarissa's voice was so loud people turned to stare, making refus-

ing impossible without causing a scene and, whatever she felt about Joe, she owed him too much to do that.

He sought her gloved hand from where she had instinctively buried it amongst the folds of her favourite silk gown, a gown she had stupidly worn for him and had regretted from the outset, knowing it was futile, and she felt his heat through the fabric where it seared her skin. Her jangling nerves were bouncing all over the place as he led her to the floor, not helped by the intense stares from both of her parents. This was the first dance since the incident. A major step in their eyes. It would have been a major step in hers, too, had she not been mortified to be so pitied by a man she adored and wishing she was dead. If she didn't die of embarrassment during the dance, Bella decided she was going to strangle her meddling sister as soon as she had her alone. Just because Clarissa now had her heart set on a duke didn't mean she could alter this kind physician's romantic feelings by foisting Bella upon him.

Joe was smiling when he turned her towards him, his big hand came to rest just above the small of her back and Bella fought not to remember the last time it had been there. When his lips had been touching hers.

Because she'd asked him.

'You really didn't need to ask me to dance out of politeness.' Her voice sounded snippy and sharp, and not at all the casual nonchalance she had been aiming for. 'I much prefer watching and Clarissa should not have forced me upon you.' Good lord, he was tall this close. Avoiding his eyes, she had chosen to stare dead ahead, which meant she was currently staring at his broad chest.

'I thought I asked.' He sounded amused. 'I distinctly

remember saying, *Bella—would you do me the honour of dancing with me?* Besides, I wanted to talk to you.'

'Is there a problem at the infirmary?' That explained things. 'I told Mrs Giles to send word immediately if something was wrong.'

'I didn't want to talk to you about the infirmary.' Now he sounded irritated. 'Or vaccinations or any other medicinal matters... I wanted to talk about what happened between us the other day...the kiss.'

Bella felt her abdominal muscles bunch as she cringed. 'I'd rather not talk about it, if it's all the same to you.'

Yes, you do. Face your fears and hear what he has to say!

'In fact, if you'll excuse me...'

She tried to break away, only to find her body firmly held by his hands in the position of the waltz—but closer. So close goosebumps covered her skin because his caressed her cheek.

'Not yet.' His fingers laced with hers. 'We need to talk, Bella. There are things I've come here to say. Things I should have said at the time, but...' His voice trailed off, but his gaze never faltered. Those brilliant blue eyes were troubled as they peered into her soul. He wouldn't need to look very far to see the truth. Bella *was* a terrible actress and her feelings about everything had been dangerously close to the surface since the day he had found her weeping by the roadside.

It was then she realised two things. She needed to hear him say the words, no matter how difficult that would be, and half of the eyes in the ballroom were currently watching the pair of them with interest. Un-wittingly, Bella was the centre of attention and she was

not brave enough to have her heart broken in front of half the town. 'Then say them in the alcove and be done with it. Don't make me a spectacle.'

Hardly words to warm his heart or give him much hope. Joe silently led her to the most secluded part of the assembly room, conscious of the ramrod and stiff way she held herself whilst purposefully ignoring his gaze, and gave some serious thought to not saying what he had come here to say, then realised he still had to say them. If there was even the slightest chance she might entertain him as a suitor, he was going to grab it with both hands.

There were still one or two people milling about within earshot and he didn't trust himself not to create a spectacle, so he gestured towards the back door left slightly ajar to allow the warm July air to circulate and trailed behind as she sailed through it.

Although almost ten o'clock, it wasn't yet fully dark, showing the empty lane behind the assembly room stretching out before them bathed in the last fading vestiges of the daylight. Bella walked a few feet ahead of him before turning and squaring her shoulders. 'What did you want to say?'

'I wanted to say…' How to put it all into words when his tongue wanted to wrap itself in knots under her regal stare. She was Lady Isabella again. The convenient suit of armour she strapped on whenever the occasion called for it. 'The thing is, I know you said the kiss was purely in the interests of science, but…'

She held up her hand like a shield and stopped him. 'It was only in the interests of science. To see if I could bear the touch of a man. I am grateful to you for your

indulgence and your participation because I was able to demolish another of those walls in my mind. I am also sorry if my reaction led you to believe it meant any more than that, but you have to understand I was greatly relieved to learn that I was not disgusted by the experience and…and…*and* that I remain hopeful that the damage to my mind is not going to be permanent and that one day I might be able to be i-intimate with the *right* man.'

Damning words indeed. A polite and categorical no, thank you, not in this lifetime, but there was something about the brief hesitation which gave him pause for thought. When her arms came up to hug herself unconsciously, just as she had in the lane that morning when he had found her distraught and she refused to meet his eye, he took a cautious step towards her.

What wasn't she saying? The Lady Isabella armour was hiding something and that something might well be important to them both. Dare he hope he was the right man? 'Bella, that kiss was not the sort of kiss which occurs simply as a result of an experiment. That kiss was much more than that…' Joe was less than two feet away when an expression of pure panic washed over her features.

'Stop. Please. I don't want to hear it. I thought I did, but I was wrong.' She turned her back to him, wrapped her arms tightly around her waist and walked stiffly towards the low stone wall which separated them from the lane. 'I know your affections lie with Clarissa. Have always lain with her. I've known that since I met you. For the sake of my pride, can we please just pretend that silly kiss never happened.'

Joe moved to stand directly behind her. 'Sorry. But I

can't do that. That silly kiss has been all I have thought about for a week.' He heard her sharp intake of breath and risked reaching out to smooth his palms down her arms. 'I bitterly regret the clumsy way I reacted after it, especially if I hurt you in the process, but if I'm honest, the kiss caught me off guard. *You* caught me off guard, Bella.'

Her hair smelled of crushed flower petals, the intricate plaited hairstyle left her neck exposed. His physician's eye could see the tiny but rapid pulse beating beneath her creamy skin—evidence of her nervousness, yet his reaction to the sight was distinctly male. He fought against the desire to press his mouth to where it fluttered and soothe it with his lips and tongue. 'And whilst I am being entirely honest, my feelings for Clarissa are—were—complicated, but not the slightest bit real. I have told you that before.'

She pulled away then, her head whipping around to finally face him. 'They are real enough to make you seek permission to call upon her again!'

'I didn't. I wouldn't. Not now.' His feet slowly edged towards her until they were toe to toe. His fingers found their way to her cheeks. 'I have no feelings for Clarissa. None. I'm sure she is a very lovely person—but the truth is she doesn't interest me. She and I have nothing in common, whereas we...' he gave in to the urge to tug a tendril of her hair out of its pin and wind his finger around it '...have a great deal in common.'

'That merely makes us friends.'

'No, it doesn't. Because I am fairly certain the other feelings I have are not the sort one has for a mere friend.' Her breath was coming in short gasps, but she didn't try to pull away.

'What sort of feelings?'

'The constant need to see you and talk to you.' Joe didn't want to frighten her, not when she had barely come to terms with her ordeal, yet didn't want to lie to her either. She needed to hear why his feelings for her were completely different to the ones he had had for her sister. 'I've missed you so much this last week. It's felt like an ache in my heart. I find myself thinking about you all the time, Bella. Day and night. I even dream about you.' Although he wouldn't share those with her just yet. 'If we are in the same room, my eyes are always drawn to you and always have been. Even when I stupidly thought your sister was the one I wanted.'

'So you just changed your mind? One minute, you wanted her and now you want me. A tad convenient, wouldn't you say, especially when every man wants Clarissa, but Clarissa wants a man with an impressive title and you don't have one!' She leant back a little, not completely pulling away but certainly creating some distance. Her eyes searching his for the truth.

'I never wanted Clarissa.'

'Yes, you did. You just said so…'

Joe placed his fingers softly over her lips. 'No. I didn't. My silly crush on Clarissa was as transient and flimsy as the early-morning mist. She was this vision of a perfect woman, someone to put on a pedestal and revere. There have been variations of the same throughout my life. A perfect woman who I worshipped from afar. Always out of my reach and I suppose purposely so. My head never really wanted to know them, because when I did I was always disappointed. Clarissa was another one of a long line of such women. A transient, ghostly shadow of a dream. Something to torture myself with.'

'Like your mother?'

Joe paused and considered it. The suggestion had merit. He knew enough about the workings of the human mind to know traumatic events could become warped and twisted in the aftermath. He supposed seeing his mother from a distance throwing herself into the swirling river and being powerless to do anything about it had left its mark. 'Exactly—although until you pointed it out I had never really considered the link. Deep down I know she was a selfish woman with no interest in any of her four sons. My other brothers say that all the time, but I have always preferred to think of her as a tragic, delicate soul. A stranger to me because she died when I was so young, when in fact the truth is she was a stranger to me because she chose to be.'

She smiled sympathetically. 'The fantasy is easier to live with.'

'And I have continued constructing the same sort of fantasies because I have always loved the idea of being in love with a perfect woman, yet never fully understanding the true meaning of what a perfect woman is. But she's you, Bella. You're perfect. You're perfect for me and I think I'm perfect for you. You're the one I want and I'm a fool for not seeing it straight away.'

'You think me perfect?' A smile played at the corners of her mouth and his heart soared. Her lovely face softened and her hand came up to rest upon his chest, then he watched the smile melt away and be replaced by doubt again. 'We both know I'm not perfect, Joe, not compared to Clarissa. I'm bookish and fade into the background. I'm…I'm not right up here any

more.' She touched her forehead and without thinking he kissed it.

'You're getting better every day.'

'But I am still a long way from healed. There is still too much irrational fear blocking the daylight. Clarissa is—' He silenced her with a kiss. It was brief and gentle, but it still set his blood boiling with need for the brilliant, beautiful and complicated woman in his arms.

'Will you forget Clarissa? Because I have. I forgot her a long time ago. In fact, if you want me to be brutally honest with you, now that I know what my heart wants I realise it never wanted her at all. Truth be told, I find her conversation dull.' He winced, hoping she wouldn't immediately leap to her sister's defence. 'She's vain. A bit spoiled. She surrounds herself with admirers for her own amusement and lacks the depth of character I love in you. And if you require further proof of how misguided I was, I honestly cannot recall a single time my thoughts towards your sister were anything other than...pure.' There really was no other way of saying it. 'I never wanted her—like a man *wants* a woman.' Her breath caught and she bit down on her bottom lip, and Joe hoped his admission didn't send her thoughts back to Vauxhall Gardens. Her wary eyes never left his, but again she didn't pull away.

'Are you saying you *want* me?'

He nodded. 'Body and soul. Every intelligent, formidable, beautiful inch of you.'

With a stunned gasp, she stepped back and he let her go, hoping that would reassure her she was perfectly safe with him, and tried not to feel hurt when she unconsciously wrapped her arms around her body

and looked worried. Because he recognised her need for space, Joe stalked towards the wall.

'I think I've wanted you from the outset. I found you maddening and fascinating then. As time has gone on and I've come to know the woman you truly are, I've come to care for you a great deal. The real you, Bella, not some fabrication of a woman I have created to keep my heart at arm's length where it cannot truly be hurt. What I feel for you is more than friendship and certainly more than a quickly forgotten and meaningless crush. I've never felt like this before. But this—us—it feels right. Ever since that kiss I can't stop wanting you. I came here tonight to tell you that. I thought it important you understand the full extent of my affections—I wanted you to know that what I feel for you is so very different to the nonsense I thought about Clarissa. I want you. All of you. Your clever mind. Your kind heart. You in my life and in my bed.'

Her eyes widened and he felt sick, both at the extent of his confession and at the strength of his desires. Even now, when she was frightened and vulnerable, he couldn't seem to stop wanting her. Perhaps he had said too much too soon? He should have waited. Slowly, over time, allowed her to see all the things which had just tumbled out of his mouth in a panic. The poor girl had borne the horrendous brunt of a brutal man's desires and only just been brave enough to talk about it. And he was suggesting—what? A romance between them, a future? Marriage and all that entailed, when the physician in him knew now was probably too soon. However, that was the problem. Around Bella the calm,

reasoned, pragmatic physician kept disappearing and leaving just Joe. The man.

But it was clearly the wrong time, if her horrified reaction was any indication. There was twenty feet of ground between them and she had instinctively taken herself back towards the door. Ready to run. The sight cut like a blade, so he turned, braced his palms against the wall and stared sightlessly out at the stars, wishing he could turn back time and not say all he had just said. 'I'm sorry. I should have keep my feelings to myself, but I wanted to be entirely honest with you. Be assured I would never act on my desires unless you wanted me to.'

He heard her feet crunch on the gravel before he felt her hand come to rest tentatively on his shoulder. 'I know that. I know you're not the sort of man to ever hurt a woman. You are good and kind. Patient. Gentle... I also know my feelings for you extend beyond friendship. I know that in my heart... My heart wants more.' Joe turned and smiled in relief until he saw her pained expression, then dreaded her next words.

'But?'

Her hand dropped away and her voice became small. 'But my head is...scared...of all the things which extend beyond friendship.'

'You don't need to be scared of me.' He reached out to touch her and she flinched, crushing him. She saw the hurt on his face and her expression became wretched.

'It's not you I'm scared of... It's what you want to do with me. The physical side of things. It's the biggest wall in my mind.'

'You didn't enjoy the kiss?' How could he have

missed that? He must have been so consumed with lust he had lost all reason.

Her hand came up to touch his face, her fingers brushed over his mouth while she stared mournfully into his eyes. 'I did. Very much. But he never kissed me, so my mind couldn't link it to him.'

That was something. Perhaps the rest would come in time. 'I'm in no hurry, Bella. Just as long as I know you have feelings for me, then I will wait for ever if that is what it takes.'

'For ever is a long time.'

'You're worth it.' As he said it, Joe realised she was. 'And I have faith in you. You're strong and brave, Bella. That brilliant mind of yours will work it out. We can knock that wall down together. Brick by brick.' The answer seemed to please her. Despite the tears swimming in her eyes, they no longer appeared despondent. She was tempted. Thank God. 'In the meantime, would you mind if I kissed you again?'

The tiny shake of her head was all the encouragement Joe needed. Resisting the need to drag her into his arms, Joe bent his head and joined his mouth to hers and felt her sigh against his lips as she relaxed against them. Only then did he allow one arm to slide around her waist. They would take this one step at a time. It didn't matter that she was nervous or scared of the physical; her heart wanted him. Right now, this was perfect. She was perfect. This kiss, this heartfelt, sensuous and magnificent simple kiss, was all he needed.

Behind them the door opened and Bella jumped away like a frightened deer. The sensuous spell they

were under ruthlessly broken. When Jake's dark head popped out, Joe's temper snapped.

'Go away!'

'I'm sorry, Joe, but you're needed. I think the worst has happened.'

Chapter Eighteen

Bella followed both brothers around the rear of the assembly hall and across the deserted market square to the inn. The other two Warriner men were waiting outside, both wearing grave expressions. Next to them, also stony-faced, was Mr Mellor the constable.

'The innkeeper came to find me.' Mellor got straight to the point. 'The guard on the evening post was unwell and the driver insisted he rest at the inn while the horses were changed. It was Nelly, the innkeeper's wife, who first noticed the rash on his neck. She sent for that fool Bentley, and when he refused to attend she sent her husband to find me. So far, the news is contained, but I doubt that will last long.'

'There's a chance it isn't smallpox. Chickenpox has also been doing the rounds and that can also make people, especially adults, feel very unwell.' The ever-optimistic Joe didn't look convinced. 'I'd best go and examine the poor fellow before we create a panic.'

Bella went to follow him inside and he shook his head. 'Stay here, Bella. I don't want to put you at risk.'

She listened for all of two minutes before she de-

cided to ignore him. If the man inside did have small-pox and he had come into contact with people at the inn or in the square, then they were not facing one case, but many, and Joe would need her help. Whether he wanted it or not, he was going to get it. Bella had read all of Dr Jenner's research in the last fortnight, research which suggested his vaccination was effective in days, so there was unlikely to be any risk to her at all. She pushed open the door of the inn and took in a sea of terrified faces inside, but no Joe. 'Where is Dr Warriner?'

'He's in the back room.' The innkeeper pointed. 'We thought it prudent to put the man in there, away from the rest of us.'

Bella recognised the innkeeper, his wife and son as people who had been vaccinated by Joe on the first day. They were safe. The barmaid and ostler she didn't know, but she hoped they had availed themselves of it while she had been out in the cart with Jake. The others were not from Retford and therefore probably at risk. 'Who here has been vaccinated or inoculated against smallpox?' All the locals raised their hands. As she'd feared, the strangers hadn't. One man appeared quite terrified. 'We were in the carriage. Does that mean we've got it?'

Probably.

'Not necessarily, but you will need to remain under observation for a few days in case the symptoms present themselves. Were you all in the carriage?' Four people nodded.

'I'm the driver, miss. I work with Charlie. He's been ill for days, but we both thought it was a bad chill. Up until today he was able to work.' He looked down at

his feet, ashamed. 'I'm sorry, miss, but we don't get paid, you see, unless we work. Charlie has a wife and a baby. He couldn't afford the time off, and as we only run from Lincoln to Doncaster every day, I could carry him and do his job, too. He'd do the same for me.'

Lincoln to Doncaster! Four hours at the most in a carriage. 'You do the same route every day?' Please say no.

'Yes, miss. Every day. We leave Lincoln every morning at seven and do the return run at two.'

'And do you always stop here in Retford to change the horses.'

The driver nodded and Bella's stomach sank to her toes. If the man had been ill for days and he had mingled with people here in the square and the inn on all those days, then there was a dangerously high chance a great many people had already come into contact with the disease. They were going to need premises big enough to house them whilst keeping them isolated from the rest of the community. If poor Charlie did have smallpox.

If.

Bella covered her concerns with a reassuring mask of calm. 'Nelly, why don't you move these people into the dining room and give them all some tea and food? I'm going to check on Dr Warriner.' She walked briskly into the room at the back, took in Joe's ashen face, the sick man sitting slumped in a chair, his face pale and waxy, his infected body shivering, and her worst fears were confirmed. 'You are in no doubt?'

She could tell Joe was considering ordering her out and pre-empted it. 'You vaccinated me yourself. You know the risk to me is tiny at best and most likely non-

existent, and I'm not moving.' His mouth settled into a stubborn line as he nodded. He wasn't happy about her decision but recognised it was hers to make.

'The spots are just beginning to show. His mouth is filled with them and many have started to burst. Those on his face and neck are dimpled, not rounded, which is unique to smallpox. He's also got dreadful back pain, a higher fever than one would not expect from a lesser disease, and you can see how he's clutching his stomach. Severe abdominal pain is also a sign. The cluster of symptoms leaves me in no doubt. The rash is usually the last thing to appear and by then, of course, it is too late.'

The patient seemed to be either sleeping or too ill to care what they were talking about, but even so Bella took Joe's hand and pulled him out of earshot. 'Will he survive?'

'Difficult to say. Some people do. They recover fully. More are doomed to suffer the terrible after-effects. Blindness. Lung problems. Gangrene. In many cases, smallpox is a killer. Children and the elderly are more vulnerable, but that is not to say a healthy adult is less vulnerable. There is no rhyme or reason to it. Thank God Nelly had the good sense to keep them all in here and that the inn was quiet because of the assembly.'

There was no way of softening the blow. 'Oh, Joe, if only that were so. Unfortunately, he has been through Retford twice a day for the last week and ill for at least two days, according to the driver. Aside from today's passengers waiting outside, and the many more who have had the misfortune to take that post carriage recently, he will have had contact with people here. Lots

Luckily, Nelly had heeded her advice and the tap-room was empty, giving Joe the opportunity to say what he needed to without causing the coach passengers undue alarm. He called to his brothers through the heavy oak door. 'I need you all to move back at least ten yards before I dare open this door.' He waited a few moments while they complied, then cracked it open enough that they could see him. 'It is smallpox, and whilst you are all quite safe from it, I have no idea if the disease can harm unborn children, so I daren't risk coming any closer to you. Anything which has been in contact with a victim—skin, clothing, objects—has the potential to spread it. From this point on, I must insist on strict quarantine.'

'How many people are affected?' asked the eldest, Jack.

'Difficult to say. There were four passengers in that carriage as well as the driver. However, we have a problem. A potentially dire complication. The victim has been travelling back and forth through Retford for days and they always stop at the inn. I have no idea how many locals they have come into contact with during that time, but as their carriage is always here around lunchtime, I suspect a great many.'

'Yesterday was market day.' This came from Jamie and the brothers shared an ominous look.

'Yes, it was, but as Bella has pointed out we have managed to protect at least four hundred with the cow-pox. Even those who have only received it in the last few days will have some protection against the disease, although they will need longer for it to be entirely effective. My biggest concern is for those who refused to be treated.'

'Surely we can do more than just stand around and wait for it to kill us?' Mr Mellor was all business. 'What can we do?'

'Bella thinks we should quarantine the town. Shut up shop and confine everyone to their homes.' He turned towards her and smiled, then reached for her hand. 'I think she's right.'

None of the other men argued or threw down objections or obstructions. Instead, they plotted and planned for the next twenty minutes to make it happen. The eldest was going to address the crowded assembly room with the constable, apprise them of the plan, ask for volunteers and then send everyone else home. Once that was done, all three of Joe's brothers were going to see to the evacuation of the foundling home, the only place big enough and equipped enough to be quickly commandeered as a hospital. The fifty children were going to be housed temporarily in Markham Manor, Jamie's house, and, at Bella's suggestion, with her parents. Mr Mellor was going to round up a team of men and barricade the roads. Nobody, he decreed, was visiting or leaving from tonight. Only then, and when the streets outside were deserted, did they dare move Charlie and the other passengers. Tomorrow, the Warriners would organise everything else so that Joe could do what he had been trained to do.

Together, Bella and Joe explained the situation to the unfortunate passengers and driver of the carriage. They were all understandably shocked and scared, yet because he had explained it so carefully and kindly, they were also all reassured that being in Joe's capable healing hands was the very best place for them to be.

* * *

It was almost dawn before Jake Warriner brought a cart to transfer Charlie to the foundling home. The rest were in good health and able to walk the short distance across the square.

'Once this is done, Jake will take you home, Bella. You need to bathe and have those clothes you are wearing burned before you can go to bed.'

'I'm too awake to consider sleeping. I will snatch some rest tomorrow after we have settled the patients in and—'

'No, Bella. You're going home and you are staying there for the duration.'

'I'm sorry?' She quashed the urge to be affronted in case she had misunderstood his words.

'This is too dangerous to risk exposing you to the disease. The fewer people who come into direct contact with smallpox, the better.'

Joe was protecting her, something which should have warmed her heart, but actually fired her temper instead. He needed her and, more importantly, those people needed her. 'There is no risk to me and you know it. I was the first person you vaccinated, so I'm coming with you!'

'You most certainly are not. I can manage well enough on my own. In fact—'

Bella didn't bother allowing him to finish whatever nonsense he was about to say. 'Really? Perhaps tonight you can manage, when only poor Charlie is ill, but what happens tomorrow if the rest of that carriage take a turn? Can you cope with six patients all alone? And what if the worst happens and in a few days you have a hundred patients? Will you single-handedly see

to all their physical needs, administer their medicines, mix all those medicines yourself, clean them, force them to drink? You're talking nonsense, Joe. You are going to need me.'

'Mrs Patterson can assist me and Mrs Giles.'

Bella folded her arms and set her chin. 'What a splendid idea. Whilst they are two lovely and dedicated women, they need constant instruction and do not have anywhere near my knowledge of medicine. You will ultimately run yourself ragged and then what?' Good gracious, she wanted to shake him by his broad, martyring shoulders. She settled for prodding him hard in the chest with her pointed finger instead. 'I'm coming with you.'

'I would rather not put you through the ordeal.'

'I've been through worse ordeals and lived to tell the tale.'

He opened his mouth to counter, then closed it and crossed his arms belligerently across his chest. 'I said no, Bella.'

'Stop being so selfish!'

'I'm being selfish?' His own temper was now hovering close to the surface, she could tell. It didn't scare or deter her.

'Yes. You are. It is very flattering that you are so concerned with my welfare, but this has nothing to do with me and everything to do with what is logical. The sick need you to be at your very best, Joe, if you are to save them. This town needs you to be at your very best as well. I will go home when this is over and not before. Until then, my place is in the infirmary. With you!'

Bella spun on her heel and marched to the cart. She

hauled herself in to sit next to Charlie's prone body and barked at the youngest Warriner, 'Drive!'

'Yes, my lady.' Jake tugged at his forelock and, with a shrug at his brother, did as she asked.

Chapter Nineteen

The first week flew past with Joe in a near-constant state of exhaustion. Charlie's condition deteriorated considerably within hours of settling him in the infirmary and the following morning the driver of the post coach also began to get ill, although less seriously. Whether or not his lesser presentation of smallpox symptoms had anything to do with the fact Joe had given him the cowpox vaccination upon admittance, as he had with the other four passengers, or whether that was merely coincidence, he had no idea. However, as only one of the carriage passengers had fallen ill since and had yet to deteriorate to any great extent, he was hopeful Dr Jenner's miracle was working its magic.

So far only three townspeople had been brought to the foundling home. All three were in the early stages of smallpox and, as regulars at the inn, must have collided with Charlie at some point. Thankfully, and Joe had everything crossed on that score, there had been no new cases in two days, which suggested they had isolated the cause. With the town voluntarily under strict quarantine and all roads into and out of Retford

closed, any further cases would be people who had already caught it rather than caused by fresh exposure to the disease. By his best guess, in ten days, all things remaining as they were, he would begin to relax and declare the crisis over. But until then, two days clear was promising.

Hence Joe was able to snatch a few hours to scrub himself in the bath, discard these clothes to be burned and grab some much-needed sleep. The last week had been intense, both physically and mentally draining. As the smallpox rash appeared, the sufferers were in intense pain and violently sick. For their sakes, he and Bella had distributed laudanum generously to allow them some relief while their bodies suffered the worst. Even drugged to oblivion, it was a dreadful thing to witness. Having seen it in all its terrible cruelty once before, Joe had wanted to spare Bella the heart-wrenching sight, but she dealt with it with the same calm sympathy she had displayed with Molly's broken leg, hiding the toll it must have taken on her sensibilities from everyone—including him.

Her brave stoicism humbled him and served as a reminder that this remarkable young woman was far stronger than most people he knew and definitely made of stronger stuff than she believed herself to be. In a strange sort of way, the Retford epidemic allowed her to shine and, although undoubtedly as tired as he was, he had seen her confidence grow as she faced all the adversity life could throw at them using her customary practical nature and calm logic. Bella would have made an excellent doctor. Her ability to separate her mind and emotions when the situation called for it,

and to seek solutions to problems rather than become bogged in the quagmire they presented, was a godsend.

Her suggestion to place the town in quarantine had saved a great many lives. On the odd occasion Joe had a moment to look out of the infirmary windows, the usually bustling market square beyond was eerily deserted and so silent it was unnerving. But it also gave him solace. Whilst those streets were empty, the people were safe. Bella was responsible for that. The whole town had come together to fight the deadly pestilence with their absence. A brave, select few fought it face-to-face.

Whilst Jake had offered his services with Joe at the infirmary, Jamie, Jack and Mellor were organising everything else outside its walls. Twice a day came the sounds of their small army of farmers, market traders and shopkeepers distributing bread, milk and other essential provisions to the locals. A constant supply of bed linens and fresh clothes arrived outside the foundling home, with hearty cooked food and a seemingly constant procession of cakes and pies baked by the women of the town. There seemed to be a tremendous amount of goodwill towards the family now that Joe's dire warning had come true and selfishly he hoped it would continue once the crisis was over. If ever the Warriners had proved their worth to Retford, it was now. This last week they had been its saviours. Certainly, the doors to the church had remained firmly locked and no offers of Christian charity had come from the Reverend Reeves. At least the Reverend had had the good grace to stay put. Dr Bentley had tried to flee the town on the first day of the quarantine and Jamie had chased after him on his fearsome black stal-

lion Satan, then with the help of the constable cheerfully confiscated the man's horses and his barouche box to help with the supply chain. Joe wished he had seen that, but, alas, his place was behind the thick stone walls of their makeshift hospital.

To keep his brothers' unborn children safe, Joe insisted they and their helpers were kept completely separate from the disease. If a person presented any of the symptoms, a message was left on their door and the two eldest Warriners passed the details on to Jake, who went to fetch them in the evenings in a separate cart and brought them to Joe. Since the night at the inn, their only conversations had been from a distance and that would remain the case until he declared the all-clear. Something he couldn't do until his patients began to shed the itching scabs which signalled the end of the illness. So far, only Charlie's spots had begun to burst, so there was still a long road ahead for them all. A long and arduous road to be sure, but Joe was hopeful the end was in sight. Tonight he needed to rest.

After lugging pot after pot of steaming hot water to the giant tub they all shared in the municipal kitchen of the foundling home, the prospect of soaking in it at the end of yet another eighteen-hour day was so appealing it felt almost decadent and made all the sweeter knowing that his was the last bath of the day, so he could lounge in it for as long as he liked without fear of interruption. Jake was on duty in the ward and would fetch him only in an emergency, while the rest of the skeleton staff of infirmary volunteers, Bella included, had been sent to bed two hours before. Like all the five volunteers here at the foundling home, she, too, had moved in to avoid inadvertently passing the disease

on to the outside. On that first night, with Joe, her father had tried to reason with her, but she wouldn't be budged. After declaring that she was a Beaumont and that Beaumonts did not surrender in a crisis, the Earl of Braxton relented and declared himself proud of her bravery. With hindsight, Joe would be for ever grateful she had ignored his pleas for her to stay away. She slept in the girls' dormitory, chaperoned by Mrs Giles and Mrs Patterson, and was temptingly out of reach.

It was disconcerting knowing she was sleeping somewhere close by. A week of working cheek by jowl with her, after they had both confessed to having feelings for each other, had been taxing. Not in a bad way, as Joe recognised she had been right about him needing her help. More than right. Without her he would have been lost. Buried alive under the huge weight now placed on his shoulders. A weight she carried with him. Bella had been an enormous asset to him since the outbreak started, sharing his workload, organising the small group of volunteers like Wellington at Waterloo and keeping the medicine chest stocked to the brim. Thanks to Bella, Joe could sleep. In theory, at least.

In practice, being so close to her and not being able to act on his feelings or explore hers was painful. It had absolutely nothing to do with lust, although that unpredictable emotion had surprised him once or twice, although usually when he was lying alone in his cot in the furthest end of the boys' dormitory. Usually, he was plagued with an overwhelming surge of tenderness for the resourceful and resilient woman he had given his whole heart to. On more than one occasion he had simply wanted to hold her, nothing more, yet couldn't

because they were never alone and a building full of
sick people hardly seemed the appropriate place to try.

Once this was over, he had some serious catching
up to do and fully intended to shower her in romance
and begin the process of chipping away at her fear of
the physical. Bit by bit, brick by brick, Joe was going
to woo her into the wonderful world of passion she
feared so much. Granted, it would undoubtedly take a
great deal of time and energy on his part, but that was
fine. Bella was worth waiting for, as long as the want-
ing didn't kill him in the process.

Joe tossed his towel over the back of the chair and
climbed into the bathtub, sighing loudly as he lowered
his aching bones into the hot water. He slipped forward,
dunking his head momentarily before attacking his
hair, limbs and upper body with the cake of soap, then
plunged himself back in again to rinse off the bubbles.
Only when he was satisfied he had washed off all traces
of his day did he arrange his long legs to dangle over
the end of the bathtub to enable him to rest his weary
head on the folded towel he placed beneath his neck.
Utter, utter bliss.

He awoke with a start when he heard the door open
in the passage beyond and realised his wonderfully
warm bath was now stone cold at almost the same mo-
ment he realised he was probably about to be caught sat
in it. To spare his blushes, and his unsuspecting visi-
tor's, Joe draped the damp towel he had been using as
a pillow over his privates as the footsteps turned the
corner and his visitor almost blinded him with a lamp.

'Excuse me!'

Bella hadn't been expecting to see the cause of her

insomnia when she'd come down to brew some tea. She certainly hadn't expected seeing him hair damp, blue eyes wide and naked from the waist up. He did look rather splendid if, indeed, a little startled. Those broad shoulders she had often admired looked much nicer uncovered, his skin appeared golden in the soft lamplight and the fine chest, more suited to a burly labourer than a doctor, had an intriguing dusting of dark hair which narrowed and disappeared under the water. Her eyes were positively drinking in the sight and were in no great hurry to stop.

'Hello, Bella. I didn't mean to frighten you.'

'What are you doing? It's well past midnight.' And he still looked tired. Something which had become an increasing cause for concern in the last few days. 'You promised me faithfully you would be in bed by ten.'

'I did, or I meant to be in it thereabouts, but I must have nodded off.'

He smiled weakly, making him look boyish and mischievous at the same time. Thank goodness he was not wearing his spectacles. A wet Joe was magnificent, making Bella quite dizzy and off-kilter. A wet Joe in his eyeglasses would be devastating. 'I don't suppose you could fetch me another towel, this one is no longer fit for purpose.' Her eyes followed his downwards to his lap. The linen towel across it clung translucent in places, further flustering her. He was naked from the waist down, too! Of course he was. He was in the bath.

'Yes. Certainly.' She almost tripped over her own feet as she scrabbled towards the cupboard. Grabbing a huge pile of towels, she scurried back and tried and then failed not to ogle him some more.

'What are you doing up?'

'I couldn't sleep. I came to make a cup of tea.'

'That sounds lovely. A nice cup of tea would warm me up. I'm freezing.' Words which made her notice the droplets of water on his erect nipples and the raised goosebumps on his beautifully sculpted arms. Goosebumps which made the fine dark hairs on his forearms stand up. All at once, she had the urge to run her hands all over them to see if he truly was as gloriously solid as she suspected.

'R-right. Tea for two.' Good gracious, Bella felt peculiar. All hot and jerky and scandalously grateful for the splendid sight of him sat in the altogether. 'Would you like something to eat as well? I think we have some fruitcake left. Would you like some fruitcake? Or I could make some toast. That might be better. The toast will warm you up.' Good lord! She was still staring at him and now he was grinning, as though he knew exactly what had sent her in a tizzy. 'I'll turn around!' Bella spun so fast she knocked her elbow hard on the table, howled in pain and then cringed as he laughed.

'I do like it when you blush.'

Blush seemed such an inadequate word for what had happened to her skin. It was burning so red, if she plunged it into the cold water in his bath, it would hiss and bubble like a kettle. 'You caught me unawares.'

'At least you are decent.' She heard the sucking sounds of the water as he stood up and tried not to imagine what a completely naked, wet Joe looked like. Thoroughly indecent, she hoped, and then shocked herself with the uncharacteristic carnality of her wayward thoughts. She heard him rub himself briskly with a towel and, after what seemed like an eternity, heard

the whisper of cloth being pulled over his skin. 'There. You're safe to turn around now.'

Relieved, Bella did and wished she hadn't. All he was wearing was a pair of soft breeches and a billowing shirt he hadn't bothered doing up. Where his skin was damp, it clung to the exact muscles she had wanted to touch moments before and the shadow of the dark hair on his chest and the tiny bit visible at his throat left her mouth dry and her tongue sluggish. 'Oil make… I mean, I'll make the tea them. I mean then— not them!' Not only was she talking nonsense, but her voice had gone high-pitched. Her face felt so hot she needn't bother with the toasting fork. If she held two slices of bread against her cheeks, they would be crisp and brown in seconds. If ever there was a time for a tactical retreat, now was probably it. 'Better still, I'll just go. I think I've made enough of a fool of myself for one night.'

'Sorry—but I can't let you do that.' She felt Joe's hand clasp hers and he gently tugged her to face him. 'Not when the sight of me in my birthday suit has… vexed you so.'

As there was no denying it, Bella covered her flaming face with her hands. 'I'm embarrassed.'

'I know.' She didn't need to see his expression to hear his amusement.

He knew she had ogled him. Of course he did. Not much got past the brilliant physician. 'I didn't mean to look.'

'And I didn't mind you looking.' The tone of his voice had dropped. Quieter. Deeper. Like melted butter. 'In fact, I am vastly relieved the sight of me didn't horrify you.'

How could it? The man was gorgeous. Six feet and more of golden muscle. Muscle arranged more perfectly than muscle had ever sat on a human skeleton. Not one of her anatomy books had prepared her for the sight.

'Would you be horrified if I kissed you?' Would she? Probably not. 'Only, it's been a week since the last time and you look so beautiful when you blush.' Bella felt his hands slide around her waist and felt no urge to pull away. She waited for him to make the next move, and when he didn't she risked peeking through her fingers, only to find him staring down at her affectionately. 'You have to be willing, Bella.' He caught her hands and placed them flat against his chest. 'You need to grant me permission to kiss you, else I won't.' That he was giving her control showed what a wonderful, intuitive man he was. Being out of control, powerless and at another's mercy still frightened her, even though she knew Joe and that monster were nothing alike.

'Yes.'

'Yes what?'

'Yes. You can kiss me.'

'Excellent news.'

He tugged her close and sealed his mouth over hers gently. Only when he sensed she was done with the soft, chaste kisses did he deepen the kiss, but when he did Bella forgot about her shameful staring and her ugly, scarlet blush and she certainly didn't allow any negative memories to cloud the moment. Joe's lips had a way of making her forget everything except him. At some point, he must have lifted her to sit on the kitchen table and her hands must have gone wandering of their own accord, because when he eventually lifted his head, her palms were burrowed under the

linen and pressed flush against his bare chest and his body was stood between her thighs. Not touching, but close enough she was aware of his desire.

Beneath her fingers his ribcage rose and fell in time with his laboured breathing. Those intense blue eyes swirled with longing. He wanted her. Like a man wants a woman, yet she instinctively knew he wouldn't take. Bella saw the truth of that, too, in his eyes. Instead, he placed a light kiss on her nose and then decisively stepped away. 'Time for that tea and toast, I think. I'll go cut some bread.'

Bella watched him go, a little incredulous at both what had just happened and at her earthy reaction to it.

Well, that was nothing like Vauxhall Gardens!

At the unwelcome memory, she wrapped her arms tightly about her middle and the magical euphoria Joe had created was gone.

Chapter Twenty

Charlie was crotchety. He wasn't delirious or in agony or so ill he couldn't talk, he was complaining about his itching spots, the uncomfortable cot and the beeswax ointment Bella was applying to help alleviate his discomfort. Her eyes locked with Joe's across the mattress and he smiled. He didn't need to tell her Charlie's foul mood was a good sign. The guard had been the first to succumb to the illness and had suffered the most. Blessedly, the rash had avoided his eyes, although Bella would have been hard-pressed to put a pin between the rest of the oozing spots. Spots which thankfully had now formed scabs. Charlie would be horribly scarred, but nothing more. His baby would grow up with a father. The rest of their small group of patients would also walk out of the infirmary alive. In a few more days they would no longer present a danger to society either. Both achievements made her proud.

'Be careful!' Charlie snatched his arm away and glared. 'I've had enough of your pawing.'

'Would you like something to help you sleep?'

He nodded belligerently and she smiled in sympathy.

She went to the table and poured him a cup of the warm sleeping draught she had prepared earlier and brought it back to him. 'Tomorrow I will draw you a special bath which should help to soothe your skin.' Joe's concoction of burdock root and other soothing herbs mixed with a generous dash of vinegar was proved to ease the dryness of some of the other patients' skin, but poor Charlie had had too many weeping sores to allow him it before.'

'When can I go home?'

Another good sign. 'If you continue to recover as well as you are now, you can go home on Friday.' They all could. Whilst Bella was looking forward to seeing her family again and sleeping in a comfortable bed, another part of her was sad to be leaving Joe. They had lived hand in glove for nearly three weeks now in the confined walls of the infirmary and, aside from the few hours she got to spend asleep in the girls' dormitory and the few minutes stolen here and there alone in the kitchen, they had not been apart.

The stolen minutes were the best part of her day. For over a week now they had taken to meeting late at night in the kitchen, where they chatted over tea and toast. More often than not, Joe turned the conversation towards the future, their future together, and Bella allowed herself to go along with the optimistic fantasy he painted. They were going to live happily ever after and work side by side in his surgery. Joe was going to train her to be a doctor in all but name, until the idiots in Parliament caught up and changed the law, allowing her to qualify properly. They were going to have an armful of children, boys and girls, all dark haired

obviously like their parents and all would be brilliant scholars.

They never spoke about how they would make those children and she was stupidly grateful he hadn't yet proposed. Whilst Joe appeared to be highly confident of her miraculous mental recovery, Bella didn't have the heart to tell him she didn't share his certainty and would adamantly not agree to any proposal while she remained broken. Because every night, after he had kissed her thoroughly and scandalously—a little more thoroughly and scandalously each night—the old memories would soon creep back to haunt her. Once they returned, banishing away all the warm feelings of desire he had skilfully created minutes before, they forced Bella to go to bed a little bit scared about their future after all. The wall in her head barricading her from physical intimacy was the tallest and strongest her mind had created, and while the others now lay in ruins, that last barricade blocked out all the daylight.

Behind her, Joe dimmed all the lamps in the ward. 'I'll go and put the kettle on.' Her pulse quickened at the promise of yet another thorough and scandalous kiss. 'Don't be long.'

'Can you bring me my tea before you two do whatever it is you do in the kitchen?' Jake was taking the watch tonight and was already lying awkwardly sprawled across two chairs he had pushed together to form his bed for the night. 'Last time it came tepid and I hate tepid tea.'

Bella instantly began blushing, but Joe brazened it out. 'Count yourself lucky you get any. You don't bring me tea when I'm on watch, tepid or otherwise.'

'That's because Bella brings it to you and the pair

of you cosy up like two lovebirds, staring at each other soppily over the rims of the cups.' He batted his eyelashes, clutched his heart and sighed loudly. 'It's nauseating.'

Joe shrugged, refusing to be baited, and disappeared out the door, leaving Bella with his brother while she finished up for the night. Jake was watching her thoughtfully as she made a great show of writing up Charlie's notes.

'I've never seen my brother so besotted. I think the pair of you make a fine couple. Both studious. Both selfless. Both cursed with enormous brains filled with knowledge which would make my eyes water. There'll be no banal chitchat about the weather at your breakfast table. It'll be all science and medicine. Remind me never to have breakfast with Dr and Mrs Dr Warriner.'

Bella didn't want to talk about the possibility of a breakfast table. 'If Charlie has a restless night, you can give him a few drops of laudanum at around three o'clock in the morning—but not before.'

'Will you be having a summer wedding, do you think?'

She shot him a warning look. 'We have not discussed weddings. It's far too soon to discuss weddings.'

'Is it? If history repeats itself, then I'm sure he'll march you up the aisle as soon as possible. Both Jack and Jamie met and married their wives in weeks and both by special licence. Which I suppose the pair of you will have to do, won't you? Seeing as there's not a cat's chance in hell the pious Reverend Reeves will allow one of the spawn of Satan to marry in his church. The Bishop of Nottingham married Jamie and Cassie...'

'Can we not talk about this, Jake?.' Talk of weddings

conjured up images of wedding nights and Bella could feel herself getting tense.

'But I'm going to need to have a rough idea of the date, seeing as I'll be the best man, and at some point I need to head back to London. If you want the banns read, I suppose you could always get married in Little Gringley—but then you'd be for ever having to tell people you got married in a quaint little place called *Gringley...*'

'You should head back to London, Jake. If there is going to be a wedding, it'll be months away. Maybe even a year.' Or two, or ten. 'We are not in any rush. Goodnight, Jake.'

Good lord, would Joe wait ten years? Was she being fair by allowing him to wax lyrical about their future together when Bella couldn't think beyond the here and now? Probably not. No matter how lovely it was to hear and no matter how much she wanted to believe him, she owed it to Joe to set his expectations. On Friday, when they left the otherworldly bubble of the infirmary, they would return to the real world and in the real world Bella was still—what? Broken? She didn't feel broken any longer. Most of the time she felt much like her old self. Driven. Inquisitive. Logical. Only when she thought about the physical did all logic evaporate as soon as it hit that enormous wall. The wall she couldn't seem to demolish even with kissing.

By the time Bella got to the kitchen, Joe had filled the kettle and set it to boiling. 'There you are.' He stepped towards her, his bright blue eyes filled with longing. His fingers found the waistband of her apron and he tugged her into his arms. 'I've been waiting all

day to kiss you.' His gaze dropped to her lips and his head bent.

'Wait.' Bella used both her hands against the hard wall of his chest and tipped her chin to look at him. 'We need to talk.'

'Let's talk after I've kissed you.'

'I'd rather talk now. I want to be fair.'

'Fair?' She had his attention, even though he was smiling at her choice of phrase. 'Fair about what?'

'Fair about what is realistic...in view of my mental situation.'

His hands left her hips and lightly locked behind her back, gently anchoring her in place. 'Go ahead.'

'I want you to stop talking about the future, Joe. I'm not ready to think about one yet...not when I can't bear the thought of the physical.'

His dark head tilted to one side as he considered her words. 'If you don't mind me contradicting you, all of this kissing and canoodling we have been doing is entirely physical. Things between us have got quite heated at times and at your instigation. You certainly don't kiss me like a woman who finds kissing me a great chore.'

'But that's just kissing. Kissing isn't intimacy.'

'On the contrary. Kissing is entirely intimate.'

Bella stepped out of his arms and put some distance between them. 'I simply think it's fair to tell you I might not be ready for more than kissing for years.'

'All right.'

His calm patience grated. 'No, it's not all right. We can't continue talking about children and growing old together, when the original purpose of marriage is...is...'

'Sex.'

'Yes. Sex. I can't face the idea of that yet.'

'I don't recall asking you to. Nor do I recall proposing. I know that part of things might take time and I respect that.'

Because she didn't know what to with her hands, Bella crossed her arms and stood stiffly. 'I feel like I am leading you on, when I still have this big wall in my head.'

'Hypothetically speaking, if we can demolish the wall, are you opposed to the idea of marrying me?'

'No, of course not, it's just...'

'Do you like it when I kiss you?'

'Well, of course I do, I wouldn't let you kiss me if I didn't enjoy it, but...'

'There is no but, Bella. Stop overthinking things and, in time, that wall will fall exactly like the others.' In three quick strides he closed the distance between them. 'In the meantime, let me kiss you. That's enough for me.'

An hour later, and her body still hummed from the kiss. The more he kissed her, the more intense her reaction to it, which she assumed was progress. The last one had been spectacular, so spectacular Bella had stumbled to bed on very unsteady legs, her body humming with needs she didn't fully understand and couldn't help fearing. One day, perhaps, she might even allow him greater liberties. Just as soon as she no longer kept thinking back to Vauxhall Gardens and that other man's vile touch, or the dreadful violations she had been powerless to stop him doing to her body. Instantly, Bella's flesh prickled and she found herself scowling in distaste. His hands had pawed at her breasts and

groped between her legs. His hands had been nothing like Joe's. Where Joe was gentle and appealing, that man had been rough and abhorrent. That man still made her body cringe. Joe made her body hum.

Joe made her body hum.

He also spoke a great deal of sense about facing her fears and rationalising the nonsense her mind kept conjuring. Each fear she had faced head-on, all bar one, had crumbled to dust in the last few weeks. A few seconds ago she had been daydreaming about a perfectly lovely kiss, her body had heated and hummed with need and then she had allowed her mind to wander. In fact, it suddenly occurred to her, she had practically dragged the memory of Vauxhall Gardens back to the forefront of her mind as a way to justify her own irrational fears.

Joe wasn't him.

She loved Joe. Trusted him implicitly. He put no pressure on her, nor forced her to do anything she didn't want to. Even when she was in the grip of irrationality he was always patient. He loved her and was prepared to wait.

Face your fears head-on.

Could she? If she stopped approaching her fear of physicality emotionally and faced the fear logically, then this final barrier would also dissolve and Bella would be free and normal again. There would be no more walls, just clear sky. Instead of regarding the sexual act through the eyes of a damaged girl, she should examine it entirely scientifically. Exactly like the kiss, or her fear of talking about it, or her discomfort amongst crowds. Her fear of all men. Exactly as Joe suggested.

There's a practical solution to this and you're tired of being broken.

* * *

'Joe! Wake up.'

He felt her hand nudging his shoulder and forced himself to stir. 'What's wrong?' His jaw hadn't woken and the words came out garbled. He opened one eye and instantly closed it as the brightness of the single candle was too offensive in the pitch-black darkness. Joe rubbed his eyes and shuffled to sit, wishing his sleep-scrambled brain would focus. He'd been in a deep sleep and being dragged from it was a shock to the system.

He cracked open his eyelids again and suffered the discomfort of adjusting to the light. 'What's happened?'

'Don't panic, this isn't an emergency.'

'Then why the blazes did you wake me?' The flash of temper was justified and he didn't care if he sounded sulky. 'There had better be a good reason.' She'd scared him half to death.

'Now that you've put it like that I feel bad. It can wait.' Her downcast face made Joe feel guilty. Bella wouldn't have woken him unless she thought it was important.

'No, it can't. I'm awake now. What's wrong?' He patted the edge of the mattress and she dutifully sat down.

'I've been thinking...'

'About?'

'Us, actually, and me in particular.' The way she was staring down at her lap made him uneasy. Earlier she'd been worrying about fairness and forcing him to wait and for a moment he had been convinced she might terminate their romantic relationship indefinitely. He'd distracted her then with a kiss which had left them both breathless. The temptation to do that again was

overwhelming, but impractical. If she had something burning to say, she had the right to say it.

'Go on.'

'Well, you know how I'm scared of…of…intimacy?' Unsure where this conversation was going, he simply nodded. 'Well, I've decided it's time to face my fears head-on and smash down another wall.'

Was she suggesting they be intimate? Now? His mouth went to speak, then he stopped himself when he assumed he had misunderstood and huffed, 'Go on.'

'The thing is, it has occurred to me that since I came to Retford I have overcome many of my issues, and in the main I have you to thank for that. You let me work here at the infirmary, where I felt safe and found the courage to be myself again for the first time in a year. Because of that I can walk across the square and talk to people normally and usually without panicking. I've spoken about what happened, confided in both you and my parents, and you were right. Talking helped and now the whole incident is out in the open and people have been so nice about it, it's given me the strength to move on. I was frightened of kissing. Partly because I had no experience of it… He'd never kissed me, so I forced myself to give it a go, in the name of science, and I think you'll agree, the kissing part of our relationship is very nice. I've even stopped being bothered when you hold me, because I rather like that, too. With you, I mean. I doubt I'd like it if any other man held me. The thought holds no appeal.'

'That's good…for the record, I would have a problem with another man kissing and holding you, so I am selfishly rather pleased it holds no appeal.'

Her eyes lifted from looking at her lap for a second

and she smiled shyly, then went back to staring at the riveting spot on her skirt. 'I didn't come here to talk to you about other men, Joe. The thing is...in view of the success of the other things...and because I would like to have that future with you...I think it best if I continue to approach my fears rationally, using logic rather than emotion... As this is the last wall left in my mind, I was wondering— I'm really not sure how to say this next bit...' She was blushing. Good lord, she was blushing and he was coming to suspect he hadn't misunderstood at all.

'Straight out is usually best.'

'Well, seeing that *he* never completed the act itself and my irrational emotions linked to the incident are clouding my judgement concerning the...um...sexual act itself, logic dictates *I* complete the act with you and, in doing so, banish him from the equation.'

There were no words. His brain had stopped working completely. Joe felt his jaw drop and he blinked. Repeatedly. She saw his reaction and her next words tumbled out in a rush.

'I know it's an odd request and it has come completely out of the blue, but I wondered if you would be intimate with me. Now, if at all possible.'

'I'm not sure it is possible. A man needs to be in the mood.' His head was spinning, although his groin felt odd. He was astounded to realise he was very much in the mood. 'Good grief...er... Bella, I don't quite know what to say.'

'You don't want to be intimate with me?'

'Of course I do, I just assumed it would occur naturally when the time was right.'

'The time is right for me.' Her eyes wandered to the

unmistakable bulge in the bedcovers. 'It also appears to be right for you. I have read extensively on the sub-ject, so know logically what to expect. My body was designed to accommodate yours, so I doubt it will be too awful, and there are accounts of some women quite enjoying it, which I find encouraging. And I am in the firm belief that once I have got it over with I will be...' Her slim shoulders slumped and she stared mournfully down at her hands, too ashamed to finish her sentence.

'This is hardly how I pictured it, Bella. I had planned to seduce you properly in a more romantic setting than here.' The place where the pair of them had spent most of their time together. Worked side by side. The place she had just said she felt safe enough to find the cour-age to be herself again.

Good grief.

Chapter Twenty-One

Realisation felt like a hammer to his head. Bella didn't want to be seduced. She needed to be in control, because control had been denied her in Vauxhall Gardens and in all the months since. Until she came here and learned to trust him. *Him.* And now she was being brave and strong again and wanted to face her final fear with him as well. Joe wouldn't let her down. His fingers found her hand and laced with hers. 'But I am happy for it to happen here and now, if that is what you truly want.'

She stared at their clasped hands for a moment before dropping them decisively. 'Yes. Thank you.' She couldn't look at him. 'I suppose we should get started, then.' She walked stiffly a few feet away and then she began to pull pins from her hair. 'Should I take all of my clothes off?'

'I can do that.' Aside from being something he had dreamt about constantly in the last few weeks, undressing her slowly would be less clinical in a situation which had suddenly become decidedly so. She dashed that hope with a frown.

'Probably best if I do it. It will be quicker and then you can get back to your rest without delay.'

Joe didn't argue. If she needed to be in control, he would concur now and save his energy for exceeding all of her painfully low expectations of what was to come. If the no-nonsense way she was dealing with those hairpins was any indication, Bella was of the belief the act itself would be equally as mechanical. Bizarrely, the sight tugged at his heart and tortured his loins in equal measure, because he knew he'd rather die a slow and painful death than do her that dis-service. Tonight Bella would be loved, whether she wanted to be or not. Already he knew she enjoyed being kissed. Thoroughly. A woman who responded with that much passion to a simple kiss had the ca-pacity to lose herself completely in bed. But there was no point trying to tell her that now. Not when she was being brave and scientific and needed to discover the truth for herself.

When her hair was loose, it fell in a straight, dark curtain to her waist, the single candle causing the ebony strands to shimmer as she moved. Just the sight of that had him breathing irregularly. Her hands went to the laces at the back of her dress and made short work of them, too, and in no time she was stood be-fore him in just her chemise, the prerequisite ten feet of floor standing between them. The temptation to jump out of bed and stride over there was overwhelming, but for her Joe remained rooted to the mattress. She had to come to him. This was her fear to face and it had to be her decision.

He wanted to smile when she inhaled and turned her back to him to slide the chemise from her shoul-ders. It slithered down her graceful back and caught on her hips. Her hands gripped the fabric in a matter-of-

fact brusque manner and pushed it over her delightful peach of a bottom until it pooled at her feet on the floor.

'I suppose you've seen a great many naked bodies, so I dare say mine is nothing new.' He could hear the nervous tremor in her voice before she steeled herself and turned briskly around to face him. She was wrong. The sight took his breath away.

Her pert breasts were capped with dark pink nipples which his mouth ached to taste, her waist was so small he'd bet his Warriner hands would easily span it, but the hips which flared below it were all woman. Sultry curves. Everything a hot-blooded man could want. An enticing, neat dark triangle of hair sat directly above the lovely pair of legs his body had first responded to. Tonight, he fully intended to worship every inch of them. And every beautiful, real and precious inch of her.

'Should I get into bed?'

He shuffled sideways in response and let his head fall back against the pillow to watch Bella slowly walk towards him and found his fingers gripping the sheets as if his life depended on it. His body was on fire, but Joe didn't want his rampant desire to scare her. Instead, he bit down on the inside of his mouth and tried to remember this was not about him. His feelings and needs were inconsequential because tonight had to be all about her. If he survived, he deserved to be a candidate for sainthood because the woman coming towards him was the single most beautiful thing he had ever seen.

She lifted the sheet and slipped in to lie beside him in the narrow cot. When he risked turning his head slightly to look at her, she was staring at the ceiling with the blankets pulled up to her chin.

'I'm ready.'

No, she wasn't. Bella was as far away from ready as it was physically possible to be. She was so tense he'd bet he could bounce coins off her tummy.

'What do we do first?'

She had to be in control. Both the physician and the man recognised that. 'We should start with kissing. Lots of kissing.' To stop himself from touching her, Joe tucked both his hands behind his head. '*You* should kiss *me.*'

He'd confused her, he could tell by the way he felt her leg muscles relax against his. 'Oh. Right.' The mattress moved as she turned on to her side and for the first time since she had roused him from his slumber her eyes truly met his. Despite the courageous determination shining in them, Joe could see the fear there, too. The trust. The trepidation. He smiled.

'You don't have to do this, I'm happy to wait.'

'No. I want to. My fear of intimacy is irrational, and unless I face it, it will continue to grow out of hand. This is necessary.'

'If you're sure.'

'I am. I want to marry you, Joe, and I don't want to have to make either of us wait.'

Before she gave in to the panic he saw in her eyes, she placed a soft kiss on his lips. Then another. Joe let her ease into the kiss before he kissed her back. When her breast brushed his upper arm and her hand came to rest over his heart, he couldn't stop the soft moan from escaping, but he kept his hands tightly locked beneath his head and let her be the one to dictate the pace. Because kissing was something she was used to, her body began to soften against his. Her eyes had

fluttered closed and her shy tongue was beginning to explore his mouth, just as it had only a few hours before. Only when she went to pull away did he allow one hand to lightly anchor her in place, letting her know that he was in no hurry to move on and that what they were doing was more than fine by him. 'Don't stop. I adore kissing you. Besides, we have all night.'

Bella sighed with relief and kissed him again. Her nipples were pebbled against his chest, a very good sign in his book, and her heart was hammering by the time they broke apart. Her upper body was sprawled across his, her creamy soft skin felt perfect against his darker, hair-roughed chest. All that delectable hair forming a silken curtain around them and separating them from the rest of the world. Their own private heaven. 'Now what happens?'

Satisfied she sounded as breathless as he felt, Joe grinned. 'Now we touch each other. This stage can take hours and hours. Because I am a gentleman, I shall let you go first.'

A delightful blush bloomed instantly, but she soldiered on, keen to eradicate her fears with her actions. 'Where do I touch you?'

'Wherever you want. There are no rules. Let your hands wander where they will. In the interests of science, of course.' She giggled at his wink and relaxed a little more. After a few seconds she smoothed the flat of her palm over his chest and up towards his shoulders, then lifted it away, self-conscious. He kissed her and gently pulled it back. 'Be fearless, Bella. A woman with such a keen interest in anatomy must be curious. How many naked men have you seen before? Without a wet towel covering their crown jewels?'

'None.' Her fingers were trailing down his abdomen. 'But I've seen pictures.'

'Were any of those scientific pencil drawings flesh and blood? Were they aroused like I am?'

'No.'

'Then I know you too well not to know you are burning with curiosity.' Her gaze drifted from his belly to where the blankets bunched about his hips. 'No need to worry. It doesn't bite.' Joe tried to sound teasing even though her delicate touch was driving him mad with lust. When she lifted the covers away and exposed his skin to the air, he had to grind his teeth to stop the guttural moan which threatened. Bella simply stared at him. At least half a minute ticked painfully by before she moved her eyes from his groin or spoke.

'It's much bigger than I expected.'

Joe couldn't help it. He laughed. 'An excellent response which flatters my fragile male ego greatly.'

'Does it hurt? When it's in that…state?'

'No. Yes. Difficult to explain really.' Good grief, the woman was going to kill him. She wanted to discuss the peculiarities of the male anatomy when his body was now completely disconnected from his scholarly brain. 'It wants. That is the best way of explaining it.' And to prove his point, his arousal was straining towards her hand. A hand which had drifted lower past his belly button and was still moving downwards at a virtual snail's pace. A hand he wanted to grab and wrap around himself and ease the clawing need. Joe closed his eyes tightly and prayed for strength, enduring the sweet pain of her touch by consoling himself he was doing what was right for her. He would take all night

if necessary, just as he had promised, unless he spontaneously combusted first.

When her finger briefly brushed over the tip, his hips lurched off the mattress and he grunted.

She pulled her hand away quickly. 'Sorry. Did I hurt you?'

'No, Bella. I want you to touch me. You have no idea how much I *want* you to touch me at this precise moment.'

'There?'

'Yes! There!' Joe sucked in some air and fought for restraint.

Tentatively, her hand reached down again and gently stroked him. 'Like this.'

'Yes.' His teeth were aching. 'Just like that.'

Her touch became bolder and firmer as the minutes ticked slowly by. And because watching her touch him, feeling those beautiful breasts occasionally graze his skin, was now causing him real physical pain, Joe kissed her instead until he could stand no more. With as much self-control as he could muster, Joe adjusted his position so that he could explore her luscious body, too, all the while conscious that he didn't want it to appear as if she had no choice in the matter. The monster who had attacked her had pinned her to the ground and roughly groped her. This experience had to be nothing like that. In fact, it was probably better if he didn't use his hands at all just yet. Keeping one hand loosely on her hip and the other propping up his head, Joe let his mouth adore her instead. It humbled him that she trusted him enough to allow him to kiss her without question.

He let his lips and teeth wander down her neck, nib-

bling his way to one breast. When his tongue found her nipple, her hand stilled and the surprised moan of pleasure which escaped her mouth sent him over the edge.

Bella had never really considered her breasts before. Up until Joe had started to kiss them she had assumed they were expressly for feeding children. Now she realised they were also the source of great pleasure and she sincerely hoped he was in no hurry to stop what he was currently doing. One of them was breathing heavily and, with a start, Bella realised it was her. Her hands had also found their way into his hair so she could hold his head in place while his tongue did wonderful things to her nipple and her body came alive.

When he stopped and released it, she almost complained, but then his clever lips found the other one and she shamelessly pushed that breast further into his mouth. By the time his hands replaced his mouth she didn't care. She welcomed them. Her skin was desperate for his touch, but while his palms were now filled with her breasts, his lips were elsewhere. Waking up other parts of her body to delicious pleasure, parts she had never known could be so sensitive. Her belly and ribs. Her navel. Wherever he kissed her suddenly became inflamed and needy as the nerve endings awoke to passion for the first time. His mouth found her hip and his tongue traced the curve of it. Each stroke causing her womb to contract.

Bella had come here tonight expecting a bit of an ordeal, one she was prepared to face and endure, but had hoped being Joe it would be nothing like it had been before. Nowhere near as awful. She had also expected it to be over quickly. Lord only knew how long they

had been here already—minutes? Hours? And they still hadn't done what she had come here to do, but right now, she was in no hurry to get this part over with. Not when the preamble was an education for her senses.

'Do you trust me?' His breath whispered over the triangle of hair at the apex of her thighs.

'Yes!' Was that her voice? Gravelly and desperate. Her hips instinctively straining towards his face. Joe must be about to do the deed. 'I trust you.'

He placed a kiss on the dark curls and lingered. She felt his hands on her thighs, felt him part her legs and tried not to panic.

This was Joe, not him.

This was a necessary part of human intimacy. She knew exactly what the act entailed. That big, hard, smooth part of him needed to fit inside the part of her buried below that she had never seen, but which he now could. All of her was now bared to his beautiful, kind blue eyes. Logically, she knew he would have to position himself so that his lower body would be flush with hers. He would push that part inside and then in a few minutes it would all be over.

Except he didn't move. Not his body at least. His mouth touched her again, lower this time, and his tongue found a part of her body Bella had not known existed before. A part which was apparently attached to every nerve in her body and one that rejoiced in his kiss. Her legs fell open at the same time she moaned, and when he kissed her again her heels dug into the mattress. 'What are you doing?'

'Kissing you. And you should probably know, Bella, I have no intention of stopping any time soon.'

'Oh… Oh!' His tongue was swirling around the

cluster of nerve endings he'd found and all rational thought evaporated. All that existed were wonderful new sensations which made all previous kisses pale into insignificance. Her hands clutched his hair and her body began to writhe against the sheets. It didn't matter that she was completely naked and totally exposed to his eyes, or that she was powerless to stop him doing what he was doing, because she had been pinned to the bed by her own wanton passion. Her breasts craved his touch, and when his hands remained on her hips, her own fingers shamelessly touched her aching nipples in his stead.

His fingers had moved to her core and, while his tongue continued to torture her, his healer's hands began to explore her wet heat. Her hips bucked as he slipped one finger inside her and began to stroke the inner walls of her body, too. She felt her insides clench erratically around it. Felt something build, then explode within her, then she was soaring amongst the stars which exploded to brilliant whiteness behind her eyes and crying out his name in exultation as she floated boneless back to earth.

By the time she came properly to, Joe was smiling down at her, his beautiful blue eyes just inches from hers. His body was covering her, in the way she had expected it to, yet it didn't feel daunting. She enjoyed the solid feel of his weight upon her. Their bodies were touching intimately. She could feel his maleness resting between her legs, next to the part of her body which still pulsed from his kisses.

'Do you trust me?'

'Yes.' Because she did. After what had just hap-

pened, being intimate with Joe was no longer as daunting. He would make it right. 'I love you.'

His expression became fierce, wonderfully so. 'I love you, too. But we don't have to do this now.'

'Yes, we do.' Bella kissed him, hoping the gesture would wipe away the concern in his eyes. 'I need to do this to move on with my life and I want to be with you, Joe, in every way. I'm done with being scared and feeling broken. This is the last wall I need to knock down. Help me to do that.'

'I can't promise this bit might not sting a little. But it will only be this one time. After that, I'll never hurt you again. I promise.'

He wouldn't hurt her.

He would heal her. 'Do it.'

'I want you to count to three, then take a deep breath.'

'One…two…' As she inhaled, his body slid smoothly into hers and he swallowed her tiny cry in a kiss. Bizarrely, it was more the surprise than hurt which had made her gasp. Joe had prepared her body for the intrusion and Bella had been so convinced it would be agony, the faint discomfort was nothing close to what her irrational mind had imagined.

'That's it, my love. There'll be no more pain.' He filled her completely. The alien sensation felt oddly right. Not unpleasant, nor pleasurable, but it had the potential to be. Already that hidden bud of nerves was tingling against him. She could feel the effort it took for him to hold himself completely still, his arms and body trembled. Bella wanted him to move. Her body craved it.

Brazenly, she trailed her hands down his back until

they rested against his buttocks. She pushed her hips towards his and watched his eyelids flutter closed. 'If you want me, take me, because I want you, Joe, and I want this.'

His gaze locked with hers as he began to move. Slowly at first, to allow her to become accustomed to his size and the intrusion, then deeper. Bella met every thrust, wantonly moaning as his hardness caressed the inner walls of her body, until she melted beneath him and became part of him. When she felt the delicious tension build within her again, she didn't try to fight it this time, preferring to revel in the moment. Revel in seeing Joe lose himself completely in her body and rejoiced as she stared into his soul, felt their hearts beat together, until they finally soared to those bright white stars together.

Chapter Twenty-Two

Joe saw his brothers properly for the first time on Thursday morning, after nearly three weeks apart. The four of them sat huddled in the big kitchen in the foundling home with Mellor the constable and Bella, of course, discussing bringing the quarantine to an end and counting their collective blessings that just seven people had suffered smallpox, only four of them from Retford. What could have been a horrendous and devastating epidemic had only claimed a single life.

He still couldn't believe the Reverend Reeves chose to die a painful, lonely death in the vicarage when help was just across the square. The volunteers had regularly knocked on his door and each time he had sent them away, muttering insults about the Warriners and their ungodly souls. When he stopped responding, they all assumed that he was ignoring them, but Jamie had become concerned as to why no candles were lit one night and he and Mellor had broken the door down. According to Jamie, he'd been dead for at least a day. They'd agreed to keep the tragedy from Joe because they knew he would blame himself for not being able

to prevent it. In many respects, they were right. Nobody deserved to die in agony—even a twisted and spiteful man like his sister-in-law's father.

Tomorrow, they agreed, the roads and the market would reopen and the hastily commandeered temporary hospital would shut its doors for good. The unfortunate six remaining victims would leave at dawn. All battered and weakened by the illness, all undoubtedly would take months to fully recover, but at least they could begin that long road in the comfort of their own homes, surrounded by the people they loved.

'I reckon this town owes you, Dr Warriner. It owes all of you and I sincerely hope they remember all you've done to help them.'

'Perhaps.' But one look at his brothers' faces confirmed his belief they all held out little hope. 'But old wounds run deep, Mr Mellor.'

'I'm hopeful this town might surprise you.'

Before Joe bade them farewell, they talked about how soon the foundlings could return to the building. 'Every piece of cloth, mattress and blanket will need to be stripped out and burned. Every wall, floor and stick of furniture will need to be scrubbed with lye soap.'

'And gin. We've completely run out.' Bella grinned at him. 'We're going to need plenty of gin to mix with the water.'

'Gin?' all three male visitors said in unison.

'Indeed. Joe is convinced the gin helps to ward off infection.'

The constable simply nodded. 'Well, Dr Warriner's newfangled theories had proved right before, who am I to question them? I'll send some men to Nottingham

today and make sure they fetch plenty back for the morning.'

'Even with it, the building will need airing for another week before we can consider bringing back the children.'

Once they had a plan, Joe and Bella headed back to the infirmary to make their own preparations. Mrs Patterson was sent home. Now the crisis was passed, the extra bodies weren't needed and selfishly Joe wanted Bella all to himself tonight. Technically Jake and Mrs Giles were meant to remain with them for the sake of propriety, but he had tactfully gone off to oversee the cleaning of the post carriage before its journey back to Nottingham in the morning, dragging Mrs Giles with him, and Jake had failed to materialise by the time they went to bed.

He did, however, wake them up in the morning. Together. Which made Bella blush to the tips of her toes, but didn't in any way faze his irascible brother.

Just after dawn, Jake loaded the three locals into a cart to take them home. A few minutes later, Jamie and Jack arrived. Jack was on his horse and Jamie sat in the driver's seat of the post, his black stallion Satan tied to the back, ready to carry him home once he had returned its weary passengers to whence they came. As Joe and Bella helped them aboard, Bella's family arrived.

Joe kept his distance while they hugged, busying himself with his patients, but when the big carriage finally rattled out of the market square, he wandered over towards them, feeling oddly nervous. It was not every day you had to stare into the eyes of a father whose daughter you had recently deflowered.

The Earl walked towards him with his hand outstretched, clasped Joe's and shook it heartily. 'Bella has been telling me about your endeavours, Dr Warriner. I am heartily impressed. Heartily impressed.'

Never comfortable with accepting compliments, Joe brushed it off. 'I was simply doing my job, your lordship. Your daughter deserves more of the credit. It was her idea to quarantine the town. Bella has been my rock these last weeks.' A rock he intended to anchor himself to for ever. 'I'd have been lost without her.'

'She seems...*well*.'

'She is well.' Those walls had been replaced with blue sky. A horizon they would head towards together.

'I need to thank you for that, too. You have been a good friend to her since we arrived here in Retford. Have dinner with us tonight. I know Bella would enjoy it and I'll wager you are eager to reacquaint yourself with Clarissa.' The older man winked and Joe winced.

'About that...'

'Dr Warriner!' Mr Mellor strode into the square with an angry-looking mob behind him. 'We want a word with you!'

Instinctively Joe's head whipped to his eldest brother. All the Warriners looked to Jack in times of trouble, but Jack appeared unperturbed. If anything, he seemed amused as the constable strode towards him. Bella, on the other hand, rushed to Joe's side and gripped his hand in support.

The constable stopped dead in front of him and pointed one beefy finger in Joe's face. 'Leave. Now.' Behind him the mob nodded in noisy agreement. They all wore angry expressions.

'I don't follow, Mr Mellor.'

The constable gestured behind him with a jab of his thumb. 'We want you gone, Warriner.'

None of this hostility made sense. Something must have happened. Joe moved Bella behind him and folded his arms across his chest, feeling his temper begin to boil. Yesterday, this man had claimed the town owed Joe a debt of gratitude and now he appeared to have brought most of them baying for his blood. After what had happened the last time Joe had addressed a crowd in the square, he was reluctant to be the cause of another riot—not with Bella so close by. Maybe diplomacy was the key while he assessed the lay of the suddenly shifted land?

'This building belongs to my family, so I'm not leaving.'

'Yes, you are. Your work here is done. Go home.' From behind his back the constable produced a bucket and grinned. That was apparently the signal the rest of the mob had been waiting for. Their angry expressions were replaced with smiles as close to a hundred people held up mops, brooms, buckets and bottles of gin. 'You and your fiancée have done enough and deserve a rest. We'll scrub the foundling home clean.'

Like a swarm of bees, a hundred feet clomped past him and streamed into the building behind. Many patted him on the back or paused to shake his hand as they went, leaving Joe more than a little stunned and completely overwhelmed by the time the unexpected welcoming parade had disappeared into the foundling home. Sensing it, Bella wrapped her arms around his waist and stood on tiptoe to kiss him. Like all their kisses, it got a little out of hand until they both realised they still had an audience.

'Fiancée?' The Earl of Braxton was gaping at them like a fish. 'But I thought you had set your cap at Clarissa.'

'I don't own a cap and my heart always wanted Bella.'

'It did?' Now it was the Earl's turn to be befuddled. 'Well, I suppose that's splendid, too... And this is what you want, daughter?'

'It is. I am resolved to be a doctor's wife.'

He loved the sound of the word *wife* when it came from her lips. Joe bent to kiss her again and pulled away with a groan when he heard Mrs Patterson's approaching voice calling him in a tone he recognised all too well. 'Dr Warriner! I'm so sorry to bother you, but Lady Fordyce has gone into labour and has called for you to attend her.'

'Lady Fordyce is Dr Bentley's patient.' She had far too much money to be one of Joe's. Joe's patients paid in hair combs or chickens, not shiny gold coins. Besides, he wanted to carry on kissing Bella.

'I did tell her husband that, Dr Warriner, but Lord Fordyce said, and I quote, he wanted a proper physician to attend his wife. One with modern ideas and upstanding morals. Should I tell him you are indisposed?'

For a second he selfishly wavered until the physician inside him sprang forth. Clearly he was for ever doomed to need to rescue people. 'No. I shall attend her.'

Joe glanced back to Bella apologetically. 'I'm afraid this is merely a taste of what it will mean to be a doctor's wife. I scarcely get five minutes to myself.' Perhaps he was the one being unfair? He could hardly dedicate all the time to being the husband Bella deserved when he knew deep down that this was who he was. 'My life is often frantic and—'

Bella silenced him with a kiss. 'I've never attended a birth.' She threaded her arm though his and beamed at his housekeeper. 'Mrs Patterson, can you have my fiancé's curricle brought around? And can you see that its medical chest is topped up?' Turning to her parents, she grinned. 'We might not be back for dinner. Births can be problematic, or so I have read, and babies do tend to come when they are ready.'

'Indeed they do.' Joe's hand came to rest possessively over hers as he led her across the square. Bella was exactly like him. His perfect match. Real, resourceful, a consummate rescuer and utterly brilliant. 'Breech births, for example, need to be dealt with swiftly else both the mother and the babe are in danger. Twins can be tricky, but most labours are straightforward. Once you've assisted me with a few of them, you'll soon pick it up.'

Joe stopped abruptly, a look of wonder on his face. 'You'll finally be able to hear the twin heartbeats I was telling you about. Where did you leave your stethoscope?'

Bella's fingers went to her pocket, where it always was. 'Right here. I would never leave home without my most important piece of medical equipment.'

His deep blue eyes swirled with amusement. 'That's my girl.' Which she was. And always would be. His. Heart and mind. Body and soul. 'Then you'd best follow me.'

'To the ends of the earth.' And into the brilliant, blue daylight stretched wide open in front of them. 'Can I drive?'

* * * * *

A WARRINER
TO SEDUCE HER

For Dave.
Welcome to our crazy family!

Prologue

Markham Manor—February 1803

'Why don't we go and walk in the orchard, Mama?' He tugged her hand, hoping she would cease staring at the river. While her distant mood and melancholy were nothing new, and nor was the route their daily walk had taken, the water was high and angry after the week of rain and the sight of it bothered him.

'When I was a young girl, Jake, we used to promenade along the River Thames at Putney. Sometimes my father would row us out onto the water, but more often than not we used to sit on the banks with a picnic. He used to love escaping the crowds of London and while away the hours on that pretty stretch of the river.' At least she was talking, albeit about the past again, which was a marked improvement on the painful silence he had endured for the last two hours.

But then it was always the same after his parents had been fighting, which they did with the same regularity as the sun rose in the mornings and set at night. His elder brothers Jack and Jamie always claimed it

was best to leave them both be afterwards, and although he knew they were probably right, Jake's bedchamber was next to his mother's and the familiar sounds of his parents' explosive, poisonous relationship taunted him and haunted him in equal measure. Her angry shouts and spiteful words, his father's drunken slurring, the short and terrifying bouts of violence which they both participated in and then the odd silence, broken only by whispers, intimate laughter and the inevitable rhythmic creaking of the bed frame. When his father left her soon after, as he always did to find more brandy or whisky or whatever cheap grog he had managed to procure instead, there would be more cruel words followed by his mother's noisy tears. It was so very hard to sleep with all that wailing going on and his poor childish heart wished he could make her happy, even though Jake knew that was impossible, too. His mother's happiness remained in the past, well before she had met his father and stupidly married him.

If he had been Joe, he could have read to her. Mama liked that—sometimes—but although only one year separated him from his closest sibling, Jake had struggled to learn his letters and his mother became impatient when he stumbled over the words. Jamie earned her smiles by painting her beautiful pictures, although he did that less and less because he said she was selfish and self-indulgent and he had no time for either. His eldest brother saved her from the worst of their father's daytime violence, by absorbing the blows in her stead, and took on the main brunt of the parenting because neither she nor his father could be bothered. The only thing Jake excelled at was making her

laugh or by being the ears which listened to her incessant ramblings about her old life, back when she had been happy and he could only do that by keeping her company.

'Tell me about London, Mama.'

As he'd hoped, the usually dead light flickered in her eyes. 'It's a grand place, Jake. So vibrant and exciting. Every night there is a different ball or party to attend and my dear papa made sure I had enough gowns for all of them. They were always in the first stare of fashion and the gossip columns frequently commented upon them. The dancing was my favourite. I was renowned for my grace as much as for my beauty...' She sighed and closed her eyes, picturing it all. 'It's the most wonderful feeling, Jake, swaying in time to the music and being adored by the lucky gentleman I had deigned to dance with...'

Jamie often said she was vain, too, preferring to spend hours having her hair dressed for dinner than spending any time with the sons she conveniently forgot existed. Jake secretly agreed, but felt guilty for agreeing, because she was always so sad he reasoned it had to be good that looking pretty pleased her.

'That's where I met your father. Without waiting for the proper introductions, he pencilled his name on my dance card. He was a wonderful dancer and so handsome.' Two of the few positive things anyone could say about him.

Her eyes fluttered open and she noticed Jake for the first time in an hour. Her hand came up and cupped his cheek. A rare and precious moment of parental affection in a home devoid of any. 'You're the most like him, you know. You have his smile and his way with

words.' As his father's words were always slurred or nonsensical from inebriation that comparison didn't particularly please him, but Jake didn't move or speak because at least she saw him. 'He was a charmer, too, just like you are... I dare say you'll grow up to be identical as well. His bad blood runs the strongest through you.' Her hand slipped back to her side and her expression soured. Because he reminded her so much of his father she looked away in disgust. That cold, dead stare out to nothingness reserved wholly for him for disappointing her so. How he hated that look.

'Go fetch him, Jake.'

'Not now Mama. It's still early.' Two in the afternoon was practically dawn by his father's standards. 'Let him sleep it off a bit longer. Tell me more about your picnics in Putney.'

'No, Jacob! Fetch him now.'

He never understood how it was possible for her to simultaneously loathe and love his horrid father at the same time. How could those opposing emotions exist together? He loved his brothers, sometimes they irritated him, but Jake never hated them. Joe reckoned this was because the love between men and women was entirely different from brotherly love. If that was true, then he wanted no part in that destructive other kind of love. Jake hated arguments. And bad moods. He preferred fun and laughter to tears and tantrums.

'Let's walk in the orchard instead.' Away from the dangerous, angry water which she seemed intent on staring at.

'I don't want to. I want my husband. Bring him to me! Tell him I will throw myself in the river if he doesn't come!'

And there it was, the usual threat. Mama was always threatening to end her life in whichever violent way was closest to hand to get her own way. Yesterday, she had threatened to stab her heart with her embroidery scissors, last week she was going to fling herself under a carriage. She never once tried, but his father still came running, after Jake had borne the brunt of his drunken temper at being awoken when his head still pounded. He would haul his dissolute carcass from his pit, dash to his woman and the pair of them would go at it again like vicious cats with their claws bared until they disappeared into her bedchamber.

With the threat of the customary angry punch from his hateful father and the petulant, dramatic whining he would hear from his mother if he refused, Jake nodded. Resisting was futile. This was the way of things. His parents hated each other and were addicted to each other at the same time. The emotions so powerful they blotted out and excluded everyone and everything from the personal hell they preferred to share together.

With heavy feet he trudged back towards the house and tried to fill his head with happy thoughts instead. Purposefully light and cheerful things which he would one day enjoy, but which did not exist in his miserable childhood. Parties, balls, dancing ladies in beautiful gowns, rowing boats and sunny picnics...

Instead of fetching his father he sat down to daydream, waiting long enough to ensure she believed his lie that dear Papa couldn't be woken. Another habit which earned him censure from both his parents. Sometimes that worked and she would march back to the house in a temper to give him what for. Other times, she scowled at Jake and called him useless like

his father, then ordered him straight back, but at least he had delayed the inevitable.

It was always inevitable.

With a sigh he stood and headed back to where he'd left her. As soon as he emerged from around the trees she turned and smiled, then promptly launched herself off the bank into the swirling water.

At first he stood frozen to the spot, but then realised the gravity of the situation. She had carried out her threat and he'd failed to fetch his father. His father might well be a roaring drunk, but he was a strong one and could save her. Now all she had was Jake, the smallest and most useless Warriner.

He sprinted towards the river bank calling to her, dropping to his belly at the edge and stretching out his arm. 'Mama! Grab my hand!' But she was too far away from his childish arms to reach, clinging to overhanging branches of the bare weeping willow as the river foamed and rolled around her, coughing violently as water splattered into her lungs.

He ran to the tree, screaming for help. 'Jack! Jamie! Come quick!'

His elder brothers were in the field somewhere, working because most of the labourers had left long ago. He had no idea where Joe was, but willed him here, too. Joe was cleverer than Jake and his quick brain would find the solution, although anyone else would be better than just him. In desperation, he clung to the sturdy trunk and leaned out as far as he dared, knowing that if he tumbled in then the raging river would take him and they would both be dead.

'You need to grab my hand, Mama!' Hot tears were streaming down his face. Tears of guilt and terror, of

shame at not being good enough and too selfish to sacrifice himself. 'Please!'

Her heavy winter coat and long skirts were weighing her down like an anchor. Jake could see that as well as he could see the fear in his mother's eyes just before her head plunged beneath the water. It bobbed up, but barely. Only her face was visible as she gulped for air, but her eyes locked with his and beneath her fear he saw the disappointment that he had failed her just as his father had so many times. In that moment, he realised she had never meant to die.

'Grab my hand...please!' Her chilled fingers were losing their grip on the slippery fronds, the fast current was greedily flowing around her, each new surge ebbing higher and higher as she struggled to stay afloat. Soon her fingers, then her face disappeared beneath the water and all Jake could see was the tangled whirl of her green skirts trailing like river weed among the branches of the willow.

He couldn't tear his gaze away from the dreadful sight, even for the thumping sound of racing feet behind him, watching powerless as his two eldest brothers selflessly risked their own lives to correct his mistake. Joe arrived soon after and was stood frozen behind, his face white and terrified. Like a statue, he was so still.

In his daze, the tragedy unfolded.

Jack, his eldest brother, waist deep in the water, holding Jamie's hand tightly on the bank as he tried to grasp her.

Jack carrying his mother's limp and bedraggled body towards the bank.

Jamie laying her out on the ground, pumping her

chest. The eerie gurgle of water trickling from her mouth with each push. Painful minutes ticking by before pressing his ear to her chest. Shaking his head.

Joe's pleading voice. 'We have to save her. There must be something we can do?'

His eldest brother's arms went around his shoulder. He didn't offer platitudes or false hope, simply his strength, and Jake leaned on him.

'This is all my fault.'

'No, it isn't. You did all you could.'

Which was never enough.

His mother's lifeless eyes as she gazed up from the mud. That final cold, dead stare out to nothingness. Disappointed for evermore.

Chapter One

Lord Fennimore's Mayfair study, on a very wet night in February 1820

Thanks to the splendid port, the cosy heat from the fire and a distinct lack of sleep the night before Jake would soon need a pair of matchsticks to prop open his eyes. Viscount Linford was droning on about the latest numbers of confiscated barrels of brandy in every coastal county the length and breadth of the entire British Isles, or at least he had been before Jake's mind had wandered off to greener pastures while listening to the man's soporific voice.

As always, the Viscount measured success in numbers, seemingly oblivious to the fact it made no difference how many cargoes the blockade men had seized this month compared to last. Those dull statistics were a drop in the ocean—albeit the English Channel—compared to the massive cargoes which slipped past them daily. For a small pile of coin, most people could be relied upon to be resourceful. But smugglers weren't most people, the piles they wanted

weren't small and their resources far outstripped those of the rag-tag disorganisation of the Board of Excise. Whoever the mysterious Boss was, his toxic network was proving near impossible to infiltrate. Crowbars wouldn't budge the terrified sealed lips of the few crews they had arrested and for every ship they seized another twenty sailed right past.

'All well and good, but can we trace any of those barrels back to Crispin Rowley?' Lord Fennimore's curt tone suggested he was as bored by the Viscount's bean-counting as Jake was.

'Not exactly.'

'Not exactly? What sort of an answer is that? Either we have a traceable link to the bounder or we don't.'

Viscount Linford began to blink at the challenge. 'We know that a substantial amount of those barrels were destined for the capital.'

'And?' Fennimore was losing patience. 'We are in the midst of the Season, when I dare say London consumes more than its fair share of brandy. Are Rowley or any of his associates transporting the goods further afield or selling the stuff in the capital?'

'Not that we can find. He's covered his tracks well. However, we all know he is the source.'

'Knowing it and proving it are two very different things. The Attorney General will sign no warrant for the man's arrest unless he has tangible evidence of Rowley's involvement.' Something they had failed to get in the six months since Crispin Rowley had come under the suspicion of the King's Elite, a small but highly skilled band of covert operatives created to infiltrate and take down the powerful, organised smuggling rings which threatened Britain's ailing economy.

Rowley was linked to a ring that they believed was funding the loyal last remnants of Napoleon's army, which was a great cause for concern. This group was intent on stealing the former French leader from his island prison and returning him to power, using funds raised from smuggled brandy on the shores of the very enemy that had brought him down, and at the helm was one man: the faceless, untraceable and powerful man known only as the Boss. As much as ten thousand gallons a month were finding their way into the public's glasses in the south-east, no duty paid and all profits heading directly back to the French rebels.

But this smuggling ring was not only supplying the capital. Every major city, the length and breadth of the British Isles, was benefitting from cheap spirits to such an extent the bottom had practically dropped out of the legitimate market. Most worrying was the persistent intelligence that hinted the group's tentacles were firmly embedded among the ranks of the British aristocracy. Men with the power, connections and means to distribute the goods widely. Lord Crispin Rowley was the first and only name from that dangerous list they had.

So far they only had the tenuous word of a French double agent, who up until recently had been completely loyal to Bonaparte. His sudden change of allegiance, combined with his hasty flight from France, did not instil a great deal of confidence in his intelligence. Not when the man had urgently needed asylum and was still too terrified to come out of the hiding place Lord Fennimore had provided him, lest his former comrades hunted him down and assassinated him as they had so many other informants.

As much as none of them trusted that man's word, there was a great deal about Lord Crispin Rowley which did not ring true and had set the intuitive Lord Fennimore's alarm bells ringing. Three years ago Rowley had been on the brink of bankruptcy. The government contracts he had enjoyed during the war years to supply grain to the British army were cancelled after Waterloo and with no market for his corn and prices plummeting, as with many of the landed aristocracy, Rowley had suffered gravely and become disillusioned with the crown, blaming his collapse entirely on the government's lack of perceived loyalty to those who had helped England win the war.

Crispin Rowley wasn't the only peer of the realm who had turned on the government. Others also felt betrayed and were vocal in their criticism. While Jake had some sympathy for the way those men had been treated, he was also a realist. The world was changing rapidly and to survive the aristocracy had to learn to adapt. Land alone would not sustain a fortune any longer. Not with the mills, mines and colonies proving to be more lucrative for canny investors with ready coin to spend and cheap foreign grain pouring into England's ports.

Rowley, like so many of his ilk, had appeared to be doomed. His fields remained fallow, his labourers laid off and his creditors lining up at his scuffed and peeling front door. Then, for no discernible reason as far as anyone could tell, his fortunes miraculously turned around eighteen months ago. The huge debts he had racked up had been paid off in impressive lump sums and the formerly penniless peer was now positively lording it up all over the capital.

And he suddenly kept some impressive company. Bankers, shipping magnates, dukes and foreign princes all now enjoyed Rowley's extensive hospitality and, if their intelligence was to be believed—and Jake had no reason to doubt it—there appeared to be no ulterior motive to the man's benevolence at all. He didn't own businesses outright, preferring to dabble in stocks and shares like much of the new money. He was, to all intents and purposes, merely an investor—yet the double agent was adamant Rowley's fortune was intrinsically linked to the free traders as their main distributor in the south-east of England.

'So we've hit another dead end!' His friend, and former Cambridge classmate, Seb Leatham slumped back in his chair like a petulant child and shook his head. 'We keep throwing mud at the man and nothing sticks. Nothing! Surely there must be a chink in the fellow's armour somewhere?' He and his men had been watching Rowley's every movement in the last few months and Seb's legendary patience was wearing thin.

'Not that I've found.' Lord Peter Flint sighed from his place across the table. Being the heir to a barony and an enormous fortune, Flint had managed to inveigle his way into Rowley's vast inner circle and had spent months socialising with him in the hope of being allowed into the inner sanctum. 'I'm starting to wonder if we're barking up the wrong tree and he is not the man we are looking for. I've plied his closest cronies with drink and asked them all manner of subtle probing questions and nobody knows anything other than the fact he likes to speculate.'

'He must have secret associates. We have to keep

digging. If we could get inside his house, watch the comings and goings, read his correspondence and private papers, we'll find something.'

Flint glared at his boss. 'I've searched his study. Repeatedly. There's nothing there.'

'Which is why we need ears inside that house. A slippery eel like Rowley is hardly going to leave damning evidence lying about in Mayfair when he's invited guests in. If we can bribe a servant or get someone on the inside during the day to snoop around, I'll wager that's when we'll find his weakness.'

'I've offered huge bribes to as many minor servants as we dare. All have been refused. The others are too close to Rowley for me to risk approaching them. They will only tip him off.' Seb Leatham always sounded angry even when he wasn't. Unlike the suave Flint he worked best in the shadows and had a knack for blending in with the lowest of the low. 'And we already know the place is guarded like a fortress. Right now, he's confident enough to make mistakes. We daren't risk shaking that confidence by breaking in.'

'Then we'll need to be invited, won't we?' Fennimore smiled enigmatically. A sure sign he had dredged up something thus far undiscovered. Whatever it was Jake didn't care. He'd spent the last eight months infiltrating a gun-smuggling consortium running out of the East End docks and, now that the lynchpins were all sat in damp cells in Newgate awaiting trial, blissfully unaware of how their empire had crumbled, Jake was due a significant stretch of leave. Hell, he'd earned it. It had been a dangerous assignment and one he'd barely survived without a bullet between the eyes.

Tomorrow, he would head north to Markham

Manor and see his brothers for the first time in almost a year. For some strange reason, he had a hankering for the north and for home in particular. Probably because he was tired. Leading a double life, a secret double life, was exhausting. In deepest, darkest, dankest Nottinghamshire he was just Jake. It would almost be as good to be that carefree young rapscallion again as it would to see his family. Three months of being himself, no hidden agendas, no danger, no responsibilities and no web of lies.

Except the one.

The rest of the Warriners had absolutely no idea the directionless rake of the family had worked for the British government since the day he left Cambridge, when Lord Fennimore had recognised he actually had some potential, albeit not potential which would ever serve a good purpose. Not strictly true. Jamie suspected. The questions he asked and the quiet assessing way he had about him suggested he was piecing together the hidden puzzle of Jake's life. Jamie hadn't vocalised his theory outright, because that was not his reticent elder brother's style, but he had abruptly stopped joining in with the litany of criticisms Jake had received about his lack of purpose on his last two visits home, which in turn had led to more guilt and made returning home harder. That and the desire to keep them all safe. His job was dangerous. The risk of inadvertently dragging some of that with him on a visit home kept him up at night, when he much preferred to sleep. And, of course, it meant he prolonged his absences further and made more excuses.

Five years of lying to the brothers he loved was driving a wedge between them because Jake was ac-

tively avoiding them. They knew him too well and saw too much. They had also all made great successes of their lives and despaired that he had not. He tried not to feel envious at it, knowing they deserved all the good things and more, but the sight of their lives blossoming was coming to make his own existence feel barren. Yet he missed them and every day he missed them more. At least now his last assignment was completed he could go home and relax, safe in the knowledge he was working on nothing else which might put them in danger, trip him up or force him to tell them another pack of lies which he doubted they truly believed.

He let his eyes wander around the stuffy study which served as the King's Elite secret headquarters until they fixed on the dancing flames in the fireplace and listened with less than half an ear.

Or at least he thought he did.

'Warriner!' His head snapped around to see Lord Fennimore's bushy grey eyebrows drawn together in a scowl. 'Have you listened to a damn word I just said?'

'Er...of course, sir...well, actually...no. Not really. My eyes glazed over somewhere between one thousand barrels in Sussex and Rowley's resistance to mud. Forgive me. I'm tired and as I'm about to go on leave I didn't think it mattered.'

'Your leave has been cancelled. I have a job for you.'

'But, sir...'

'No buts, Warriner. Only you can do this one. It's a seduction job, so right up your street.'

Leatham and Flint were grinning at him smugly, no doubt having sold his sorry carcass up the river to

avoid spending hours, weeks and months charming information out of yet another empty-headed smuggler's mistress. 'Now hold on a minute sir, I'm due leave. Urgently due leave. You patted me on the back only last week and said so yourself. I've made plans.'

'Plans change. You can have your leave as soon as you've exhausted this new lead.' There was no point arguing further. Fennimore never budged when his mind was made up. Never. 'Given the lady's age and experience, I dare say you'll have done the deed in less than a fortnight and you can head north to rusticate then.'

Two weeks wasn't so bad, even if it did mean letting his family down again. Something he had done all too often in the last few years, to such an extent he could already picture his eldest brother Jack's irritated shake of the head and hear, crystal-clear, the blistering lecture he would receive as a result.

When are you going to do something with your life? Being a rake is not a career.

Jake was so caught up in the imaginary conversation with his responsible elder sibling it took a few moments for his superior's words to sink in.

'What do you mean *age*?'

'You really weren't listening, were you?' Lord Fennimore huffed and began to snatch up his papers, signalling the meeting was over. 'Crispin Rowley has a niece. His deceased, much elder half-sister's child. The girl has been hidden away in a convent since she was orphaned, hence we haven't bothered with her before. However, her neglectful uncle has now decided he's going to give the chit a Season. My sources tell me he is doing so with the express intention of mar-

rying her off by the end of it and to someone of stature. She's recently moved into his house in Mayfair. Her name is Miss Blunt.'

'She's fresh from the schoolroom?'

'One assumes.'

'What does that make her? Seventeen? Eighteen?' Please God, not sixteen.

'I suppose.'

'You want me to seduce a child!'

'Eighteen is not a child and you only need to actually seduce her if other methods of persuasion prove fruitless.'

'Why can't Flint seduce her?'

'I need Flint to keep chipping away on the other side. He's making headway into the bounder's inner circle and all that would be put in jeopardy if Rowley disapproves of him courting his niece. Your reputation makes you the perfect choice. Besides, I can hardly send Leatham.' All eyes instinctively travelled to the jagged and impressive scar down Seb Leatham's right cheek. Even without the scar, his friend resembled a bare-knuckle fighter and was painfully monosyllabic around the opposite sex. Jake was nicely trapped and Lord Fennimore knew it.

'The girl has spent most of her life with nuns, Warriner, isolated from the manipulative machinations of the world. In the full glow of your legendary charm, she'll probably confide all her secrets with a few flowery words. A simple brush of the cheek will likely render her a melted puddle at your feet. It won't take long to pry a list of her uncle's associates from her or his day-to-day schedule. Perhaps you can even convince the chit to steal away a few stray letters and such for

a couple of hours so we can analyse them. I'm sure you'll work out how to get her to do your bidding without having to bed her. But if it comes to it, then I'll expect you to do your duty for King and country. You've never complained about that before.'

'That's because I've never been sent after a child before!'

'I dare say she's not a child. The young ladies mature so much faster than the young bucks and it's not unheard of for them to marry at seventeen or eighteen.'

'But you're not asking that I marry her, you're asking that I ruin her!'

'You're a resourceful fellow, I'm sure you can find a way to get what you need from Miss Blunt without having to lift her skirts. But the point is moot regardless. This is the first time we've had the chance of getting close to someone who lives *inside* Rowley's house. The fact she is also as green as grass and ripe for the picking makes it all the sweeter. It's a chance too good to miss.'

Incensed, Jake merely shook his head. 'And how, exactly, am I supposed to seduce this *child*? I hardly have the sort of reputation which allows me to frequent the type of sedate and proper soirées the fresh crop of debutantes do and, even if I do, the girl is bound to have a handler. A chaperon with a sharp eye for the wrong sort of suitor. Which I am. They won't let me within ten feet of her.'

Everyone including the bean-counter grinned, which didn't bode well. 'If you had been listening rather than wool-gathering, then you would know Lord Rowley has engaged the services of his great-aunts to act as chaperons.'

'The Sawyer sisters?' Two spinsters in their sixties, both highly connected but with a penchant for hard spirits and reputations as characters. Hardly the sort of women who would be up for the task. 'The *slurring* Sawyer sisters?'

'The very same.' Lord Fennimore looked rightly pleased with himself at Jake's obvious disbelief. 'I know. I can't quite believe our luck either, but with no wife or other suitable female relatives, Rowley could hardly use his mistresses to launch the girl and my sources tell me he is determined to have her married by spring. He's probably already got the groom in mind, hence the sudden haste to launch the girl. It makes a strange sort of sense to align the girl to the slurring sisters. Cressida and Daphne Sawyer are invited to everything.'

'Because they are guaranteed to make spectacles of themselves and the *ton* likes a laugh. I can't think of two worse chaperons for a girl as green as grass.'

Fennimore shrugged. 'Perhaps that's deliberate, too. If Rowley has set his sights on a particular future nephew-in-law, if all else fails his lackadaisical choice of chaperons might aid the process when the girl is inevitably compromised. I wouldn't put it past a slippery and conniving snake like Rowley to have factored that into his equations. Being with the Sawyers will certainly get the girl noticed and that's usually half the battle on the marriage mart. It also aids us. I doubt you'll find it overly difficult to make a move on the chit. Even more fortuitous, the timing is perfect. The chit is being presented tomorrow. At Almack's.'

'I'm banned from Almack's.' Something which had happened quite early in his career and of which Jake

was inordinately proud. Only the worst sort of scoundrel was denied admission to Almack's and the ban had done wonders for his bad reputation.

'Not any more, you're not. The patronesses have had a sudden change of heart. Here are your vouchers.' He slid them across the table. 'To be on the safe side I got you a month's worth.'

The sea of people at Almack's swirled by in a pastel haze, thanks to Uncle Crispin's ridiculous insistence she leave her spectacles in the carriage. The unfamiliar place, the surging crowds and her short-sightedness made every step precarious. Already she had tripped up the short step into the high-ceilinged ballroom and nearly flattened a footman in the process.

'Keep your head straight and *glide*, Felicity!' Great-Aunt Daphne advised in her usual theatrical tone. 'A lady should walk like a wispy cloud, floating across the sky.' Or at least Fliss assumed it was her usual tone seeing that she had only met her aged relatives five days ago and, in truth, they weren't technically any relation to her at all. But they were nice old dears who meant well, even if they were a trifle eccentric, and they had been very sweet while attempting to train her in the art of being a lady.

Not that Fliss had any desire to be a lady of the *ton*. She was perfectly content with the manners she had already. Perhaps she could be a bit abrupt and had an acid tongue when the situation called for it, but those minor faults were actually quite perfect in her role as the schoolmistress of Sister Ursuline's School for Wayward Girls. Some of those young ladies required a firm hand and many more needed her guidance

because they were prone to make poor choices—especially regarding men. Once this silly visit was over, those girls would need the Miss Blunt they relied upon. Not some *improved* version who was required to walk like a 'wispy cloud', whatever that meant.

Although why it was considered essential for a lady to walk as if she had a book balanced on her cranium was beyond her. For the better part of two days, Daphne and Cressida had made her walk backwards and forward in Uncle Crispin's ostentatious Egyptian-themed drawing room, with a Mrs Radcliffe novel perched precariously on her head, while they instructed her on the subtle nuances of etiquette she had never had use of before. Who knew that curtsies were graduated, for instance, saving only the deepest and most grovelling for dukes and the monarchy? There had not been much cause for curtsying in Cumbria, thank goodness. Nor for the baffling array of cutlery deemed necessary for every meal when a knife, fork and spoon had always served her perfectly well before, thank you very much. Before she had been a wispy cloud, of course.

'And smile!' Aunt Cressida nudged her with such force she lurched a little sideways. 'Think of yourself as a swan, my dear. Graceful. Elegant. *Effortless.*'

There was no point enquiring as to where the cloud had gone, because Aunt Daphne and Aunt Cressida rarely remembered what they had said five minutes before. However, she was sorely tempted to point out there was nothing effortless in gliding like a swan in a strange place *sans* spectacles, but Fliss smiled tightly and tried her best, holding her head so still it made her jaw ache. She was here for her mother. Uncle

Crispin had apparently made her a solemn promise upon her deathbed to give his half-sister's daughter a Season and, while she was fundamentally too old to be launched into society, the guilt had made her agree to the offer—the guilt, Sister Ursuline's insistence Fliss needed to go and have an adventure, and the desire to do something for the mother she struggled to remember fully yet had missed keenly throughout her life. For her tragic real mother, and her incorrigible surrogate mother, she would attempt to be a cloud or a swan or whatever other nonsense her new great-great-aunts came out with in the next few weeks and she would do it with all the enthusiasm she couldn't be bothered to feel.

The new corset she had been trussed up in like a ham about to be boiled didn't help. While it did serve to keep her from slouching, because bending at the waist was now quite impossible, it also constricted every organ from her lungs to her bladder. It had also pushed her bosoms up in a most inappropriate manner so they threatened to spill out of the neckline of her new, form-fitting white-silk gown. Of course, she had protested the unsuitable dress and the corset, but her aunts insisted such fashions were all ladies wore in the *ton* and *de rigueur* at Almack's. And from the amount of foggy cleavages she could just about see all around her, presented like soft loaves on a baker's tray, her new great-great-aunts appeared to be right. The knowledge did not make Fliss feel any better about exposing her own bakery goods to the eyes of the world.

And Fliss had definitely been thrust into the window of the bakery, despite repeatedly insisting to both the aged women and her stand-offish Uncle Crispin

that she had no desire to find a husband while in town. Never had and probably never would. After years of being on her own, and after watching her mother's disappointing marriage to her unreliable father, she could see no reason why she would want to relinquish her freedom to just anyone. If, by some miracle, she ever did find a man who wasn't controlling or unreliable, then perhaps she would reconsider. But if she did, it would be of her own choosing somewhere very far in the future. And finally, and this was completely unnegotiable, he had to absolutely adore her. She wouldn't settle for anything less. She had agreed to a Season, not to any matchmaking, therefore introducing her to all and sundry was pointless. Solid, dependable and trustworthy men would hardly waste their time in this crush. They would be far too sensible and nothing like the fops, dandies and pompous aristocratic versions here, so why her new aunts insisted on parading in a constant loop around the room was beyond her. Not only was she unlikely to remember the fifty different names of gentlemen thrown at her so far, without her spectacles, every one of the fifty faces resembled blurred pink blobs. Aside from the varying colours of hair or clothing, none of the many men she had met had any discerning features which she could recognise them by, should she need to.

Mind you, parading around the ballroom was better than standing near the refreshment table. Her aunts had a worrying penchant for the lemonade—which they mixed liberally with the brandy they hid in hip flasks in their reticules, while they regaled her with outrageous stories from their pasts—and had pressed so many glasses into Fliss's hand her head was begin-

ning to spin. Thanks to the rigid corset, that wasn't the only side-effect.

'I think I need to visit the retiring room.'

Both old ladies sighed. 'How very tiresome. Ever since the *great* ball at Osterley we have trained ourselves to take no notice of such things. Isn't that right, Sister?'

Cressida nodded sagely. 'Indeed. And a very prudent decision it has turned out to be.'

They often talked in riddles, too, sharing knowing looks and wicked grins about experiences from their pasts which they frequently assumed she knew about. 'That is all well and good, but the retiring room?'

Daphne flapped her hand to the left. 'It's over there.'

'Aren't you coming with me?' Because Fliss didn't trust herself to get there unattended. Not when she wasn't entirely certain where 'over there' was. *With* her glasses she had a poor sense of direction. Without them she would be hopeless. 'I'm afraid I might get lost.' An understatement. It was almost guaranteed.

'As long as you have a tongue in your head, Felicity, you will never be lost. Remember that, dear.' Daphne was also prone to issue random guiding words of wisdom at odd times. 'Head towards the alcove and you shall find it in the furthest corner.' The hand flapped ineffectually again. 'We shall wait for you by the refreshment table, won't we, Cressida?'

Of course they would. Because that was where the *lemonade* lived.

'Yes, indeed. Now that you mention it, I am a bit parched, Daphne.'

To Fliss's complete disgust, the older women imme-

diately left her on their quest for yet more refreshment. She stood impotently and watched their ridiculously tall and elaborate feathered headdresses disappear into the sea of people and allowed her irritation to bubble.

How perfectly splendid. She'd been abandoned by the only two people she knew in the room. Yet another thing to sour her already dour mood. She was stuck miles from home at a ball she didn't want to be at, wearing a dress she feared she was spilling out of, trussed in a corset she couldn't breathe in and, to make the occasion all the more perturbing, she couldn't see more than two feet past her nose. As soon as she got back to Uncle Crispin's soulless Mayfair house, she had every intention of penning a sternly worded letter to Sister Ursuline telling her the next time she had the urge to suggest Fliss have a *little adventure*, she could mind her own business.

Typically, within a few minutes of squeezing past the silk-clad throng she was hopelessly lost and it didn't feel polite to ask such personal directions of complete strangers. Aunt Daphne had said the ladies' retiring room was in a corner and Almack's was reassuringly rectangular. If she kept resolutely to the edge, she would doubtless find the dratted room eventually, even if that involved going around a few times. Retracing her steps to the refreshment table might be more problematic, but at least left to her own devices she was spared a few minutes of pointless parading, smiling and gliding like a wispy, blind swan. A slow smile bloomed on her face at the prospect. Suddenly, being lost held a great deal of appeal.

Chapter Two

In a secluded alcove in St James's

Jake was still sulking when he arrived at Almack's. Seducing an innocent, wide-eyed chit didn't sit right with him. And, if he was being entirely honest with himself, neither did flirting with one. While he was supremely confident in his ability to do both with exceptional finesse, he made it a point of principle never to dally with nice young ladies. Bawdy young ladies, experienced older ladies and anyone who ran the gamut between was fair game, but impressionable virgins had always been off limits.

For all the many notches on his bedpost, he had not been a single woman's first lover, nor had he ever wooed a woman who didn't know how the game of illicit courtship was played. He might well be a scandalous good-for-nothing scoundrel, but even scoundrels had standards. A line in the sand which they did not cross. Yet now he was being asked to cross it for King and country—another standard he held sacrosanct. Despite a whole day to ponder the moral dilemma he still wasn't entirely sure he was prepared to make an exception.

Lord Fennimore had no such reservations, but then Lord Fennimore was not the one who was going to be whispering sweet nothings into her inexperienced ear or trying to trick her tender heart into trusting a man who shouldn't be trusted. But if his gut instinct was correct, then her uncle deserved all that was coming to him. Aside from the French double agent, every single person who had brought them closer towards the dangerous smuggling ring had wound up dead. All in very believable circumstances, of course—a carriage accident, a nasty fall, drowning in the docks while roaring drunk—but all cases a little too convenient and too close to their investigation to be dismissed. It positively reeked of foul play and Rowley was at the heart of it. And they did have to stop him, the sooner the better, but Jake sincerely hoped not like this. The whole situation left a very bad taste in his mouth.

Careful to stay in the shadows in the alcove, he scanned the room for the latest crop of debutantes. Fortunately, they were easy to spot. They were all obscenely young, eager and clad in the palest silk gowns. They were also all wearing permanently awestruck expressions. With no clue as to what Miss Blunt looked like, he instead searched for the Sawyer sisters, a task which didn't take long. The two ladies were glued to the refreshment table, clearly enjoying their matching glasses of lemonade too much for the contents of their glasses to be purely lemon.

Lady Daphne was sporting what resembled a whole peacock's tail on her head, while Lady Cressida's coiffure sprouted ostrich plumes dyed pink to match her garish dress. The weight of both headdresses, and perhaps the hard spirits the two women had a legendary

fondness for, was making the feathers list. Or perhaps it was the ladies who listed. From this distance, Jake couldn't be sure. He watched them closely for a full ten minutes before he could say for certain they had already misplaced their charge. With nothing else to do, he propped himself against a pillar and settled in for a long wait. With any luck, the chit would have already been waylaid by a handsome fellow who'd have already swept her off her juvenile feet, thus providing Jake with a ready excuse to throw in Fennimore's face when Jake failed in his unsavoury mission. Surely they could get to Rowley another way? He could work his way through the man's changing parade of mistresses, seduce a willing and lusty maid—hell, if it came to it, Jake was even prepared to whisper sweet nothings into the ears of Rowley's housekeeper as long as the woman was not a complete hag. Anyone, in fact, but an innocent child.

It was the perfume which distracted him first. The heady scent reminded Jake of fat summer roses, fresh air and sunshine. Nothing like the stuffy smell of Almack's. His nostrils twitched as they sought the source until his eyes located her.

Now this was more the kind of woman *he* would choose to seduce. Too bad *she* was not his assignment. He'd even go as far as admitting the tantalising vision that had just turned the corner would be pure pleasure, for once, rather than business. Thick honey hair, sultry almond eyes and the lushest pair of lips he'd seen in a long time. And the sensuous way she moved drew his eyes and imprisoned them. Her own had a faraway look in them as she hugged the wall, trailing the tips of her gloved fingers along the plaster

as if she had all the time in the world and was in no hurry to go anywhere. He liked that about her.

Here in Almack's the ladies always had a higher purpose. To be seen. To be noticed. To make a good impression. To find a husband. This woman preferred the shadows and had no interest in the nonsense going on outside the alcove. Just like him.

She still hadn't noticed him, despite the fact he stood barely ten feet away, so Jake watched her gaze out towards the dancers and sigh. There was a distinctly dreamy look about her, as if she wished she was somewhere else, something he also empathised with. If he hadn't been working, he might have walked over and suggested they go elsewhere together. But alas, he was on a mission and needed to see it through as swiftly as possible no matter how distasteful he found it. Something which would not happen if he gave in to the overwhelming temptation to talk to her. Jake watched her scan the room again, this time with very narrowed eyes which made him wonder exactly what it was she suddenly disapproved of until she clearly saw something—or someone—she didn't want to. She darted behind a pillar and straight into a potted palm.

The clumsy manoeuvre made him laugh out loud. Her head whipped around in alarm at the sound.

'Don't worry. I shan't tell whoever it is that you are hiding from them.'

'I am not hiding.' But she didn't move from the safety of the pillar. 'Oh, all right, I am. Have they gone?'

Jake scanned the area and nodded. 'There's nobody here but you and me. If it's any consolation, I'm hid-

ing, too.' Hiding from the inevitable. 'What are you hiding from?'

'The gentlemen my chaperons appear intent on introducing me to. What are you hiding from?'

'Responsibility and duty.'

Those lush lips instantly turned up in a smile and she was prettier for it. 'You can't hide from those.'

'I can and I have for the better part of a decade. What's wrong with the men your chaperons are foisting upon you?'

'Nothing, I suppose, other than the fact they are being foisted upon me. I didn't come here to meet gentlemen.' That in itself set her apart from the sea of eager hopefuls in the ballroom.

'Then what did you come here for?'

She sighed and looked miserable. 'My mother. Apparently, it was her dearest wish that I visit Almack's— among other things. Although I fail to see the appeal of the place.'

'Such enthusiasm.'

'I have no enthusiasm.' The corners of those plump lips twitched again. There was the vaguest hint of the north in her accent, more northern than where he came from in Nottingham. Yorkshire, perhaps, or Lancashire? 'That is part of the problem. I got lost half an hour ago and I find myself surprisingly content with being lost and by default reluctant to be found again just yet.'

Intriguing. Much more intriguing than the onerous task he was meant to be doing. 'What is it about this quintessential society ritual which has forced you into hiding?'

Her nose wrinkled endearingly before she spoke. 'I

find the whole thing pointless and a little shallow, if I am honest.' Something he had a feeling she always was. A northern trait. Brutal honesty and the inability to suffer fools or foolishness gladly.

'I can see how the attraction soon wears thin. Especially as Almack's has so many tiresome rules one has to obey. How many visits to this stifling establishment did it take for you to become so jaded?'

'Oh, this is my first. I was presented to the patronesses an hour ago.' She smiled a little shyly, but leaned a little closer than was proper, treating him to more of her delicious perfume, more alluring now that it was closer to her skin. 'I am being *launched* into society tonight. Rather reluctantly as I am sure you can see.'

She looked nothing like the traditional debutante. For a start, she had at least five years on most of them and lacked the dewy-eyed innocence prevalent all around them which Jake found so distasteful. 'This is your *come-out*?' Laughter threatened at the preposterousness. She had to be well past the age of majority, but, age aside, she was too canny a woman. Too comfortable in her own skin and mind when all around her were awed and awkward girls.

'I can see, sir, that you are as staggered by it as I am and are racking your brains for a polite way to say I am a bit too old to be coming out. Which I patently am.'

There was no point in denying it. 'How come a matron of such *advanced* years is only just being launched into society?' As he had hoped, she smiled at the sarcasm. He had no time for people who didn't understand it. Irony and sarcasm were two of his very best friends.

'I confess, I honestly have no idea. One minute I

was happily enjoying my dotage in Keswick and then I was dragged here.'

Very north, then. The more she spoke the more he could hear it in the lilt of her voice. 'How awful for you. Were you dragged from the bosom of Cumbria against your will?'

'Not completely. When the invitation came, I'll admit to being intrigued. London is an adventure, I suppose, and I was due one. And I was curious about the city I was born in, but have no memory of. I wanted to visit some of the sights I've only read about. The Tower of London, the British Museum, St James's Palace...' She sighed dramatically to amuse him. 'But alas, my uncle expressly forbade any touring about until I was launched properly.'

Little flags raised in his mind. 'Your uncle?' Surely it was a coincidence?

'Yes. My mother's brother. I hardly know him really, but he wrote to me saying he had promised my mother he would give me a Season and, apparently, dear Uncle Crispin only remembered that solemn promise this year. Hence, I am undoubtedly the *oldest* debutante anyone has ever seen and feel much like an old trout, rather than a common or garden fish out of water.'

'Hardly old.' It was difficult to sound nonchalant when his mind was already reeling, both at his good luck at naturally meeting the woman he had been sent here to seduce and his relief at finding her a grown woman rather than a child. 'What are you...three and twenty?'

'Save your polite London charm, sir, it's wasted on me. I am five and twenty and look it. And happy

to be so. Although even when I was younger, I doubt I was ever quite as *young* as some of the girls I was presented with. They all seem so surprised and dazzled by everything. I've never met such a jittery crop of girls before in my life. Do they not let young ladies out here in the capital before they come out?'

There was an earthiness and healthy cynicism about her which felt familiar and made him oddly homesick. Jake had grown up around people who said what they thought without artifice. Here in London, the true meaning of a person's words was often buried under layers of the polite façade they presented to the world. 'Of course not. Gently bred young ladies are practically locked up and kept well out of polite society to avoid them being corrupted.'

'Yet overprotecting them makes them all the riper for corruption.' She frowned as she said this, and shook her head. 'No wonder those girls all appear overwhelmed. They have lived such sheltered lives and then they are brought here. A place where its sole purpose, as far as I can ascertain, is for unattached young ladies to be tirelessly paraded around like farm stock on auction day in the hope someone will notice them, then deign to marry them. And they are grateful to be put up for the gavel. Listen to them all twittering like excited sparrows at the prospect.'

'You sound as if you disapprove, Miss…?' There was the slim chance there was more than one Uncle Crispin in town.

'Blunt. Blunt by name and blunt by nature, I'm afraid.' Thanking all his lucky stars she was the right woman, Jake was suddenly ridiculously grateful he had had his leave postponed. Of all the women to,

quite literally, stumble into him he'd been blessed by Rowley's niece. Rowley's lovely, womanly and ripe-for-the-picking northern niece. Seducing this tart morsel wouldn't feel like work at all. This he would do for pure pleasure. 'I apologise if you find my frankness rude.'

'I am delighted to make your acquaintance, Miss Blunt.' He took her hand gently in his and kissed the back of it, confident she wouldn't care when he failed to let go. 'And I find your frankness refreshing. Like you I am from the north—deepest, darkest, dankest Nottinghamshire to be exact—my name is Jake Warriner and I loathe Almack's, too.'

She leaned closer again, her pretty face tilted to one side and her palm heating his through the thin fabric of her evening gloves. Awareness. Chemistry. Mutual attraction. Jake knew the signs too well to mistake them for anything else. He had the urge to kiss her. An urge which had nothing to do with Crispin Rowley and everything to do with his bewitching niece. 'Is it obvious I *loathe* it, Mr Warriner, only I have been trying exceedingly hard to appear as if I don't?'

'To me it is obvious, but then again, just like you I am loitering in the alcove and avoiding the sad crush. It hardly makes me a genius to have seen a kindred spirit.'

She gracefully disentangled his grip from hers. 'When you put it like that, I suppose it doesn't. Why do you loathe it?'

An easy question to answer with complete honesty for once. 'This place, the stifling, petty rules and the callous way an elite few decide who is worthy to be allowed in, grates on me. I hate the power those few

have over the others. If they take to you, you are guaranteed the best invitations of the Season. If they don't, well...' He left the implication to settle. 'It all strikes me as grossly unfair.'

'Those poor sparrows will be devastated by the cut. Some might never get over it.'

'But I get the feeling you won't be devastated?' Jake had a talent for reading people. Each tiny nuance and expression told more truth than lips usually did and Miss Blunt did not look impressed with being here.

She sighed and shrugged again, something she did a great deal and which made his eyes want to wander down to where her neckline met flesh. Soft, perfumed, pert, female flesh. Jake resisted—but only just. 'Is it terrible that I hope they thoroughly disapprove of me, then I will be spared the effort of coming here again? Or of receiving the best invitations of the Season. I fear my uncle has lined up a whole host of *entertainments* for me to attend, none of which I suspect I shall find entertaining in the slightest.'

'Not every soirée is as dull and constrained as Almack's.'

'Perhaps. But being paraded around town like meat on the butcher's board is not what I had in mind when I agreed to this visit.'

'It's just a visit, then?' Clearly Miss Blunt was not aware of the fact Uncle Crispin was intent on marrying her off.

'Yes. A month. Then I shall return to Cumbria where I belong. Perhaps two at the most, although after tonight I sincerely doubt I'll manage two. It has been less than a week and I already find London society suffocating. I find I am fiercely wedded to my

freedom, you see, while here it is stifled. At home, I can walk outdoors where and when I please, say what I think, do what I want.' Clearly Fennimore's intelligence was lacking, as Miss Blunt was even less of a convent miss than she was an eager debutante. 'Here I have chaperons and all these rules I have to adhere to.'

'Such as?'

'Where to start? How to dress, how to walk. The correct way to curtsy to a duchess, which is I now know quite different from the way one curtsies to a countess or a queen. Who I should speak to, who I shouldn't, how to behave when dancing.' Another put-upon sigh. 'I was promised I would have an adventure and so far it has been anything but. However, at least I was dragged here by my family and had no idea it would be this awful. What's your excuse? Seeing that you loathe the place.'

'I, too, was dragged here, in a manner of speaking.' To do his duty, a duty he was now very much looking forward to doing. He gave in to the urge to touch her again and scandalously allowed his thumb to caress the centre of her palm where it rested among the folds of her skirt. Her eyes dropped to the spot. Stared. When her lush lips parted slightly he raised her gloved hand almost to his lips. He gazed up at her with the hooded eyes women always found appealing, knowing the deep blue soulful depths were his best feature. 'Although now I am very pleased I was. Else I never would have met such a rare bird of paradise in this tiresome cage full of sparrows.'

If he said so himself, Jake was rather pleased with the symbolism even if the words themselves were a tad triter than he would have liked. But a seduction

was a seduction and there was no point in beating around the bush. The rakish smile he bestowed upon her was second nature. It suggested he had a poetic heart beneath the cynical irony she found so amusing. He had certainly amused her enough that she had happily confided in him. A total stranger. In his vast wealth of experience, the sensible ladies adored both a man who made them smile and one with romantic sensibilities who listened to them. A deadly combination which had served him well since the day he had turned sixteen. Being used to forthright and charmless northern men, she would doubtless find his easy, open manner disarming.

Her eyes locked with his.

Narrowed.

And before he could kiss her hand, she snatched it away.

'Are you flirting with me, Mr Warriner?'

'I would certainly like to, Miss Blunt.' His voice was low and silky, the practised tone in a timbre he knew to be his most seductive. 'Do you mind?'

'I most certainly do.' Both gloved hands came to rest imperiously on her hips, giving her more of the appearance of a schoolmistress than an intriguing temptress. 'I have remained lost these past thirty minutes to avoid such nonsense.'

'Ah—in the main here at Almack's it is reliably all nonsense, but that is because the gentlemen over at the auction block are all shamelessly on the market for a wife. It is contrived and insincere. Here in the alcove—like you—I was content to hide and had no plans to flirt with anyone until *fate* introduced us.' Had he not been here at Lord Fennimore's bequest

and had she not been Miss Blunt, the woman he had been sent here to seduce, he still would have wanted to flirt with her without the interference of fate. There was something about her which called to him. 'Do you believe in fate, Miss Blunt?'

'Good lord! Did you really just say that?' Her brows furrowed. 'Do I look as green as grass, Mr Warriner?' She was positively glaring down her nose at him in bemused outrage. And if he was not mistaken it was tinged with real outrage rather than the feigned outrage he usually encountered when he turned on the charm. Her green eyes hardened; her honey brow furrowed slightly. Tiny, physical nuances that could not be faked. There was no hint of interest on her face—only disbelief. Making him feel like a fool for flirting. That made him uncomfortable because it was so...so...unheard of. He always flirted as a matter of course and had never once felt foolish in doing so. But Miss Blunt-by-Name-and-Nature seemed to see right through him to the hard kernel of insincerity buried deep in his chest which he had never noticed before. Now that he had—well, frankly, he felt queasy. At a loss for charming words for once, Jake simply stared at her and she began to giggle at his shocked expression.

'Do such hackneyed and slapdash endearments garner you much success with the ladies, Mr Warriner?'

'While the prose might have been slapdash, the sentiment was not.' He could save this. He was a master in the art of seduction. A maestro. 'But usually I am not so overawed by the beauty of my companion that my tongue becomes twisted.' Once again the rote phrases sounded hollow and unoriginal, making Jake

want to wince at his own crassness. What the devil
was wrong with him? 'In the few short minutes I have
spent in your company, Miss Blunt, you have made a
great impression on me and—'

'Oh, goodness.' She snorted and covered the of-
fending sound with her hand. 'I must give you credit
for perseverance, but really...' She eyed him as if ex-
pecting him to finish her sentence. He schooled his
features into a look of the utmost sincerity although
his toes had begun to curl uncomfortably in his boots.

'I'm not sure I follow, Miss Blunt.'

'Oh, Mr Warriner! You are funny. Are London la-
dies so daft that they do not know a philanderer when
they see one? Why, I saw it the moment I first encoun-
tered you, you have the look of one. And the manner.'

'The manner?' Jake usually enjoyed the sparring.
It was part of the game and a part he loved. However,
sparring with the blunt Miss Blunt was making him
uncomfortable. Especially as she had his full measure
and he didn't particularly like the label of philanderer.
He was a rake. A proud one. Rakes were dashing and
roguish. Philanderer sounded sordid. Cynical. Oily.
Good grief! Was he oily? The urge to find a mirror
and check he had not turned into a simpering toad
made him self-conscious. 'And now I suppose you
are an expert on philanderers?' Why didn't he cor-
rect her and say rake?

'Indeed I am. So much so I could probably write a
book on the subject. The self-assurance and smug sat-
isfaction in your own allure was as plain as the nose
on my face—although while you *weren't* practising
your philandering on me I was prepared to overlook it.'

Blast—she *could* see right through him. He was

confident in his allure. So confident he had made a career out of it. Obviously he had become too complacent. A new and worrying development Jake was ill prepared for. He must have slipped up somewhere. He had probably bared his hand too soon to this canny northern lass because he was too used to the relative ease of the pampered society ladies. He was tired. Desperately needed leave—and, if he was honest, he had rushed things because he was attracted to her. Very attracted to her. 'Forgive me. In my haste, perhaps I have overstepped the bounds.'

'There is no perhaps about it.'

'As I said, forgive me. When I see something I want, I am inclined to listen to my heart rather than my head.' He knew instantly he had laid the charm on too thick again, he didn't need to witness her exasperated eye-roll or to hear her amused snort to confirm it. What on earth was the matter with him? Jake wasn't usually this ham-fisted. He couldn't remember the last time he had run roughshod over a seduction and she had called it correctly. Tonight he was no better than a hackneyed philanderer. Maybe there was still time to fix it? And maybe the damage was done and was probably irreparable. He stopped himself trotting out more banalities because of the inevitable humiliation which would follow. Rowley's gorgeous niece was not the normal run-of-the-mill society miss. Judging from her incredulous scowl, he was in for another skewering for the *heart and head* claptrap. Miss Blunt didn't disappoint. Those playful, inviting eyes froze again.

'You are in danger of ruining a perfectly pleasant conversation with your contrived, insincere—and

while I am being completely frank—tired, overt and practised attempts at seduction.'

That stung. Jake was the master of subtle. 'Hardly practised, Miss Blunt.'

'Oh, dear. I can see I have hurt your feelings and that was not my intention. I simply wanted you to be aware that I am more than accustomed with men of your ilk. You're not the first scoundrel to try your luck and I dare say you won't be the last. All the clues were there right from the outset. The oh-*so*-casual lingering hold of my hand. The heated look. The purposefully intimate and sultry whispering. And do not get me started on the crass and *unspontaneous* way in which you tossed my own words back at me to try to convince me of your sincerity. Kindred spirits and birds of paradise indeed. What rot. I'm sure a handsome man like yourself is used to gullible women falling for your lies, but...'

'I don't lie.' Although Jake was internally wincing at the falsehood. He lied so much nowadays he had to keep a notebook of what he said and to whom to avoid tripping up. He even lied to his own family and had done for years. Nobody had called him on it before, that was all. Because usually he was damn good at it. He forced himself to smile. Forced himself to appear amused. 'When you walked into that palm I was charmed. I'm still charmed, despite your inaccurate and mean assassination of my character. But I can see I have inadvertently insulted you with my honest enthusiasm, which I never meant to do because the truth is...' The gloved hand appeared palm up near his face and the lush lips were grinning behind it.

'Let me save you from further embarrassment, Mr

Warriner—I wasn't born yesterday. Save your insincere seductions for the silly girls in the ballroom. As undeniably attractive as you are, I have less interest in being seduced by a man of your ilk than I do for this cattle market. I am only sorry that all these young ladies are not as pragmatic about men as I am.' Her fingers went to the fan hanging from a ribbon on her wrist and for a moment Jake experienced the forlorn hope she might snap it open and use it to flirt over the top of in the customary manner he understood so well. However, she wielded it like a broadsword aimed directly at his ribcage.

'And for future reference should we collide again in the foreseeable future, if you are going to throw about bird analogies, I'm neither a feeble sparrow nor an exotic *bird of paradise*, Mr Warriner. If I am any bird, I am an owl. Wise. Older than the rest of these foolish girls and blessed with the ability to see danger coming from all angles. And you, sir, are a hawk, circling the sky for unsuspecting prey.' Her arms folded across her chest and the stance did wonders for her figure—just to taunt him further.

'You are a very charming hawk and I like you for it, but I am far too prudent to fall for your nonsense. Please, take my advice and heed it well. Never flirt with me again, Mr Warriner, else I will stop liking you and I would hate to do that. Now, if you will just point me in the direction of the refreshment table, I fear I have been lost long enough.'

Chapter Three

*In a soulless bedchamber at Uncle Crispin's
Mayfair town house*

Somewhere in the distance a clock chimed the hour,
reminding Fliss it was now three in the morning, but
she was still nowhere near ready to sleep. How could
she when her mind was still whirring with images of
the evening? The provincial plays she had seen paled
into insignificance when compared to the splendour of
the opera. Everything about it had been breathtaking,
from the sumptuous and vivid costumes to the aching
purity of the soprano's beautiful voice. And watching
the audience had been equally as thrilling. The Prime
Minister had been there and so had the famous Duke
of Wellington. Aunt Cressida had pointed out both
men in their private boxes just a few feet away from
Uncle Crispin's, although even if she hadn't, Fliss's
eyes would have soon been drawn to the spots where
everyone else was staring.

All around them had been a sea of people dressed
in their finery and, thanks to the opera glasses she

had been given upon entering the box, Fliss was able to see every tiny detail despite her lack of spectacles. Spectacles she had been politely banned from wearing in public by her stand-offish uncle and which her new maid, Kitty, had already *mislaid* twice the moment Fliss dared to put them down.

During the interval, she had drunk champagne for the first time. It had been brought to their box perfectly chilled and served in crystal glasses; the delicious bubbles tickled her nose and the alcohol went straight to her head, making everything sharper and brighter than before. She allowed herself a second glass. Her aunts smartly finished the second bottle while Uncle Crispin discussed business with an older gentleman who had joined them. The Earl of Redditch was a portly man who creaked when he moved, thanks to the corset he was squashed into beneath his evening coat. A coat which bore the stain of recently spilled food on one lapel. He had a profusion of wiry grey hair which grew at right angles out of his head and sprouted out of his ears. He also smelled a little musty and had a habit of spitting slighting each time he talked. Fliss was painfully aware of both things because he had been placed next to her during the first half, but as soon as the orchestra began to warm up, signalling the interval was over, she cleverly sandwiched herself between her aunts to watch the second act.

Just before the lights dimmed, she experienced the oddest sense someone was watching her and instinctively dropped her eyes to the stalls below where they locked with the intense blue gaze of Mr Jacob Warriner. There was a wry smile on his outrageously handsome face that did peculiar things to her insides. They

heated. As did her flesh, while her tummy fizzed with unwanted bubbles of excitement which were surprisingly reminiscent of those in the heady champagne. Then the lights had faded, casting him in silhouette, and the odd yet special moment was gone.

As much as she adored the second half of the opera, she was constantly aware of him. Every time she glanced down, he was gazing back at her in the darkness. Flirting with his eyes in a more tempting way than he had with his practised words two nights before. She made a half-hearted attempt at ignoring him when the performance ended, but that stare drew her like a moth to a flame. A secret smile played at the corners of his mouth when their gazes briefly met and, before she could turn away, he pressed a kiss on the tips of his fingers and then blew it towards her. Thank goodness nobody else appeared to witness it in the melee exiting the theatre, nor did anyone comment on the ferocious blush which decided to bloom on her cheeks in response to his scandalous lack of propriety in a crowded public place.

After that, and to her great chagrin, Fliss had practically floated home. The carriage ride had been silent. Her aunts were softly snoring from the after-effects of all the champagne they had consumed and Uncle Crispin made no effort at engaging her in conversation, so she had stared out of the window up at the stars, trying and failing not to notice that they twinkled like Jacob Warriner's eyes. Now she was lying on her bed, recalling every nuance of the evening, more awake than she had ever been in the small hours of the morning.

Yet thinking about him was not constructive. Twin-

kling eyes aside, he was a rake through and through and Fliss was too savvy to be seduced by a handsome rogue. At Sister Ursuline's, she had seen the consequences of seduction first-hand. Ruined reputations, scandal, broken hearts, divided families and, on more occasions than she cared to count, inconvenient pregnancies. A succession of wayward girls had spent their confinement hidden at the convent and then were forced to say heart-wrenching goodbyes to those innocent babes when the girls were dragged back into society by their parents. Sister Ursuline always found those cherubs good, loving homes, but Fliss still thought each incident a tragedy and one that could have been easily avoided if the young lady had the wherewithal to resist the scoundrel in the first place.

While she knew that not all men were so inclined, regrettably all the male role models in her life were also scoundrels. Her father had been one through and through. He might have done the decent thing and married her mother when he had got her into trouble, but from the moment he had placed that ring on her finger he had abdicated all responsibility. Like all the men Fliss had encountered since, he was inherently untrustworthy and proved time and again to be an unreliable husband and father.

Fliss had spent her formative years with her mother growing up in his crumbling house in the country, while he frittered away all the money in town. The only benefit to that situation was her mother was happy when there were a significant number of miles between her and her wastrel husband. Fliss rarely saw him and they conversed little when they did. Much like her fledgling relationship with Uncle Crispin.

Perhaps one of these days she would meet a man who didn't fit the mould? A selfless man whom she could truly depend upon in the same way she could always depend upon Sister Ursuline, and before that her mother. A man who would always be there for her. One who put his family above his own selfish needs. A man who absolutely adored her...

And perhaps one day humans would fly. Both eventualities were as unlikely as the other. While she liked some men for their wit or their intelligence, found some interesting and wise, nothing would ever tempt her to want one all of her very own unless he measured up to the same exacting high standards of dependency Fliss set for herself. In most cases, experience had taught her the best you could hope for with a man was that he entertained you and had a back strong enough to lift heavy things. You didn't need to marry them for either.

Her uncle wasn't proving her theory wrong. Already, after some serious thought, Fliss had come to the regrettable conclusion she didn't like him at all. The only thing she had been able to truly ascertain was that he was dependably domineering and emotionless. She supposed the signs had been there all along, because she hadn't heard hide nor hair of the man in years, but it still didn't sit right to completely dislike the only blood relative she had in the world. Or half-blood at least. She had hoped to see bits of her mother in him, when in fact he behaved more like her uninterested and feckless father.

After her mother had died, *dear* Papa had found having a grieving and ever-so-precocious ten-year-old daughter taxing, so had parcelled her off to Sis-

ter Ursuline's School for Wayward Girls without so much as a backwards glance. She had never seen the man again.

However, for years her childish heart had secretly hoped one day her uncle would come to rescue her and she had assumed for the longest time he was prevented from doing so because her father was still alive. Even after the demise of her sire, she continued to kindle the tiny flame of hope with regular missives to remind him she was still alive and still hoping. Still praying that he might miraculously become someone she could depend upon.

It was only after she turned twenty-one that she stopped sending him an annual letter at Christmas, by which time she had embarked on her new life as a schoolmistress at the same school she had called home from eleven, and couldn't muster the enthusiasm to feel anything other than mild disappointment any longer. Anything more for a virtual stranger was self-indulgent and Fliss much preferred to march onwards and upwards rather than wistfully glance behind.

When his only letter finally came out of the blue, she had been surprised and dismissive. Something about it did not ring true and as she was well past the age of majority she was under no obligation to acquiesce to the odd request. She had been on the cusp of writing him a brief thank-you, but no-thank-you note when Sister Ursuline had intervened.

A perpetual romantic soul at heart, Sister Ursuline was prone to see the good in all. Including feckless men—an odd trait for a woman who dealt with unwed and abandoned mothers, scandalously ruined young ladies and the most precocious and troublesome girls

society had to offer. What if her mother *had* tasked her uncle with giving her a Season? And what if the poor man had been so financially embarrassed he could not do so until now? She deserved some adventure and it was only right and proper she met her only kin. While a dose of healthy scepticism was necessary in a young woman, Fliss was in danger of being an outright cynic. What was the harm of spending one month with her relative to find out which of them was right?

It had only been a little over a week and she already had his measure. Uncle Crispin was detached, clearly didn't give two figs about his only niece and seemingly only cared about what others thought of him. His fancy and no doubt expensive box at the opera had been purchased only so that others could be impressed. He had less interest in the actual opera than he did in Fliss. A decidedly good thing, else he might have seen Jacob Warriner's scandalously blown kiss.

Oh, for goodness sake! Stop thinking about that man! Now there was an untrustworthy, undependable libertine if ever there was one. Eminently likeable, yet as dangerous to a young lady's virtue as it was possible to be. But it was too late. Her body was already misbehaving. The rapid heartbeat, the fluttering pulse, the overwhelming suffusion of heat…

Good lord, she was hot.

Fliss flung the covers off and threw out her arms and legs to cool them. After five minutes, during which time the unwelcome warmth did not subside, she flung her legs over the side of the mattress and padded over to her window. A bit of cold February air was exactly what she needed to banish all thoughts

of the dark-haired, blue-eyed rake who had lodged himself in her mind and stalwartly refused to leave.

She cracked open the window and stood directly in the draught. The icy breeze was delightful, as were the goosebumps which instantly prickled her limbs. Anything that brought down her erratic temperature had to be a good thing. The trouble with living in a convent was there was a distinct shortage of young men. Fliss collided with them infrequently—at the assemblies or parties Sister Ursuline insisted all the girls attended to help them cope better with social situations—but not on a day-to-day basis. Therefore, it was difficult to make oneself completely immune to their charms. Familiarity breeds contempt, yet the opposite sparks interest. Her traitorous body was interested in the dashing Mr Warriner. Too interested. And that simply wouldn't do.

Somewhere below, she heard a door creak open, closely followed by the sound of the gravel crunching as someone walked down the garden path. More curious than scared, because everything about her uncle's house was still strange, Fliss hid her nightgown-clad body behind the heavy curtain and peeked out through the glass. There was a man walking around the edge of the lawn. It was difficult to make out much in the pitch-black darkness without her spectacles, but from his silhouette he appeared to be wearing what looked like shabby workmen's clothes.

'Wait—we're not done.' Her uncle appeared, probably from the same door, although she couldn't be certain. From his tone, he seemed angry. 'Next week is not good enough!'

The shabby man stopped in his tracks and slowly

turned. Fliss squinted, but still could not discern his face. 'It's next week or not at all.' He had a London accent. A common one. His coarse diction matched his attire. 'I've other buyers, Rowley, and if you can't wait someone else will happily take your place.' He turned, but as Uncle Crispin came level with the Londoner, he grabbed the sleeve of his coat.

'Tell them I'll pay them double the usual. I need the goods now!'

'Double. Treble. Even if you quadruple it I doubt it'll make much difference. Dead men can't spend. And the boss won't like it if his cargo gets seized. He's lost enough already this month. There are many new eyes along the water. I told you, this is not the time for haste.'

'But you're in haste for my money! This costs me. It costs me dearly, damn it, every time a shipment is late.'

The man pulled his arm free with such force her uncle took several steps back, his posture wary. It made no difference, as the other man closed that distance quickly, grabbed his lapels and loomed over him menacingly.

'Don't get all brave on me, Rowley! If you don't like the boss's terms, then we've got plenty of others who'll happily step into your fancy shoes. If you're not *our* man...'

'I'm your man. You know I'm your man. I'm doing my best for you and the boss...just like you asked.' His voice came out a few octaves higher than usual and pathetically desperate. 'I didn't mean to complain... But I've made promises. People are relying on me. What am I supposed to do in the meantime?'

'You wait.' The Londoner slowly uncurled his fingers from her uncle's coat and made a great show of rearranging the lapels before he patted his head roughly. 'Like a good boy.' His gravelly voice sent involuntary chills though Fliss, her every instinct warning her he was a dangerous man. 'Be ready.' With that he left, disappearing into the shadows behind the shrubbery and into the night.

Her uncle watched him leave, the clenched fists at his side evidence his temper was barely controlled, then he stalked back towards the house and she heard the angry slam of the door in his wake.

It had been an odd exchange. She couldn't shake the feeling that it had been a bad one. Dangerous, even. If her relationship with her uncle had been better, she might have gone downstairs and asked what was happening, enquired if he was all right, but Fliss knew he wouldn't deign to confide in her. At best, he ignored her. If they spoke, he was curt and dismissive, or downright aloof. When she had first met him just a few short days ago, she had thought him a cold fish and he had done nothing in the time since to alter that opinion. If he was in trouble, then it was doubtless of his own making and therefore nothing to do with her. In a few weeks she'd be gone.

Besides, there was no point in allowing her vivid imagination to run away with itself. There was probably a perfectly reasonable explanation why Uncle Crispin had met with that man.

In secret.

In the dead of night.

Perhaps this was the way things were done in town? Having little experience of the world outside her

sleepy part of Cumbria, much of the ways of the capital baffled her. And she was tired. It had been a long day. Why, only five minutes ago her silly mind had been conjuring up images of kisses with an untrustworthy rake, so clearly she wasn't thinking entirely logically. Sleep would put a different perspective on things. A problem was always best considered when the mind was at its sharpest and had one of her charges at the convent confessed to Fliss the same emotion Fliss was currently feeling, with no other proof than the peculiar disquiet she was experiencing, she knew she would scoff and be dismissive of unsubstantiated flights of fancy conjured during the witching hour. She would send the girl to bed, which was exactly what she should do herself. With an uneasy feeling, she silently closed the window and crept back under the covers, certain sleep was considerably further away now than it had been a few minutes ago.

'Rowley has recently bought shares in another small shipping company. The Excise Men have boarded every one of their boats in the last three weeks the moment they have docked in British ports and performed thorough searches. There is no contraband. The cargoes are all legitimate and all the taxes are paid.' Flint was pacing back and forth as he spoke, his frustration evident in every step. 'That's three merchant fleets he's directly involved in, yet all apparently clean.'

'He's bringing the stuff in somehow. Perhaps those ships are decoys? Perhaps he deliberately bought those shares to take us off the scent?' Lord Fennimore's reasoned tone did little to calm Flint's tem-

per. 'There is a chance he is smuggling the goods in on other boats. The old way—in the dead of night and onto quiet beaches.'

That didn't make sense to Jake. This single band of smugglers had flooded the London market to such an extent they now dominated it. Both London and the entire south-east. 'The volumes of brandy alone make that impossible. Even if he were using rowing boats, transporting that many barrels of illegal French spirits across the country to the capital would be problematic. They would be seen. We've had men watching all the roads into the town for months. He's got to be bringing the stuff straight into London. By sea.'

'The Excise Men assure me they have searched every nook and cranny of every ship linked to Rowley. They've had the cargoes apart the moment they've off-loaded and found nought that hasn't been recorded on the ships' manifest. Those vessels are clean.'

'Too clean.' These were the first words Leatham had said in the hour they had been sat in Lord Fennimore's study. They all turned to look at him. He didn't say much, but what he did was always worth waiting for. 'In my experience, the best place to hide is in plain sight. I'll wager he's using those ships and bringing the goods right into London just as Jake said—right under the Excise Men's noses. They won't use the roads. Not when it makes sense to keep everything in the water. Quieter, darker and harder to stop.'

He had Lord Fennimore's attention. 'You think he's solely using the Thames?'

'I would.'

'The river police patrol those waters like hawks. He'd be taking a risk.'

Leatham shrugged. 'Maybe they offload the big ships well shy of London. Transfer the stuff onto local coasters or barges. There are thousands of smaller vessels which run those waters every day and never get challenged—just as generation after generation of Thames watermen have done in the past. If they can fool the Excise Men with legitimate loads like fish, bricks or hay, then I doubt a paltry few river police will worry them and that's assuming it stays on the Thames. There's also the Fleet, the Lee. Or the canals. There are hundreds of miles of canals, remember. There aren't enough river police to watch everywhere or to check every boat and everyone knows they focus on the big ships and the docks. The ones that cross the sea rather than the local waters.'

Lord Fennimore nodded thoughtfully. 'Smaller boats? There'd have to be a lot of them, a whole rotten network. Perfectly synchronised. But I suppose if they avoid the docks, once they are through the city they can move largely undetected and unchallenged throughout the country.' His bushy eyebrows drew together and he nodded decisively. 'Send some of your men to do some digging around the wharfs, Leatham, and see what you can find. Flint, see if Crispin Rowley, or any of his cronies, has any links in any canal companies or river hauliers. I'll arrange for the Excise Men to pay close attention to the Essex and Kent stretches of the Thames Estuary. Get them to covertly follow a few of the regular wherrymen. It can't hurt to explore the possibility further. Better safe than sorry, even if we are just shouting into the wind until we have credible intelligence on Rowley's *actual* business

dealings.' At that, Fennimore's head turned to Jake. 'How are things going with the niece?'

'We've met.' That awkward introduction still grated.

'Met? It's been a week. Have you lost your touch, Warriner?'

'Miss Blunt is not the sort of woman one rushes.' Because she saw right through flannel. 'I flirted with her tonight at the opera.' Well, he'd gazed longingly at her. 'And thanks to subtle enquiries—' which involved flirting outrageously with several well-connected society ladies '—I've managed to piece together most of her engagements for the next few weeks. She will be attending the Renshaws' Ball on Friday.' Where he fully intended to sweep the pithy Miss Blunt off her canny northern feet.

'Engage her in conversation about Rowley's business interests. See if she's heard any mention of canals over the dinner table.'

Jake rolled his eyes. 'Yes, that ought to do it. Nothing says seduction like talk of barges.' Although with hindsight, that might have been better than waffling on about birds of paradise. Anything would have been better than waffling on about those damn birds. 'Leave Miss Blunt to me. By the time I'm finished wooing her, she'll sing like a canary.' Another crass bird analogy! Good lord, he was doomed.

If only he'd been able to stop thinking about the delectable Miss Blunt, then Jake would be more on his game. But there was something about her which had got under his skin and, even when it shouldn't, his mind kept wandering back to her. It wasn't just her beauty which appealed, although there was no deny-

ing the physical attraction he felt. Tonight, he could barely take his eyes off her. From the moment she had appeared in Rowley's box, he had been transfixed.

She had looked stunning with all that honey-gold hair piled loosely on top of her clever head, outshining every other lady in the opera house. When the done thing was to appear bored, Miss Blunt had flown in the face of convention and been utterly charmed by the occasion. Openly smiling at the actors on the stage and swaying in time to the music. To do that when all around you were people behaving *properly* showed a tremendous amount of confidence. That confidence, that comfortable sense of self, made Miss Blunt very alluring indeed. The way she had closed her eyes in bliss at the taste of the champagne had done peculiar things to his nerve endings, creating all manner of un-welcome images of the vixen in the grip of pleasure. Images which resolutely refused to leave his mind now, when he was supposed to be concentrating.

Of course, it didn't help that the copper-silk gown had shown off her magnificent figure to perfection. Cut to sit off the shoulder, the acres of creamy peach skin had tormented him each time the lights went up and haunted him in the darkness. Skin he now knew blushed more beautifully than any skin had blushed before—and from something as simple as a cheeky blown kiss when nobody was looking. A kiss he had every intention of delivering properly, in person, at the first available opportunity. And not because he'd been told to.

Flint's fingers snapped in front of his face and Jake realised he'd missed an important part of the conver-sation. 'Sorry. I was...'

'Daydreaming about your conquest, if your expression was anything to go by.' Flint grinned. 'I *said* you might have some competition for Miss Blunt's affections, dear boy. The word among Rowley's crowd is he has her earmarked for Redditch.'

'The Earl of Redditch!' The very idea was disgusting. The man was in his sixties and smelled like feet. 'I sincerely doubt I'll have much competition from that quarter. Miss Blunt wouldn't entertain an obnoxious fellow like him.' Or at least he hoped she wouldn't. Not that imagining her in the throes of passion with the aged Earl was any more distasteful than imagining her in the throes of passion with any other man. The mere thought made him strangely jealous and, if he was entirely honest, a tad nauseous.

'Perhaps not—but her uncle is keen to make a match. I've heard he fetched her to town with the express intention of presenting her to the Earl. Redditch is recently out of mourning and has been quite vocal about his desire to marry again. His first marriage was barren, so it stands to reason he wants a wife young enough to give him heirs and he is as rich a Croesus. Despite his stinky disposition, he's still quite a catch and one Rowley seems intent on catching. Miss Blunt does make attractive bait.' Flint and Leatham shared a knowing, wholly masculine look which made Jake yearn to punch the pair of them for the heinous crime of having perceptive eyes.

'Miss Blunt is a woman with her own mind and well past the age of majority. I wish her uncle all the luck in the world trying to bring her around to his way of thinking.'

Lord Fennimore frowned. 'This is a dangerous and unforeseen complication.'

'Hardly.' Jake made a show of adjusting his cuffs. 'I'm easier on both the eyes and the nose, and much more appealing than the Earl of Redditch.'

'Not all women's heads can be turned by a handsome face, Warriner. In case it has escaped your notice, most of the *ton* marries for status and wealth. As an earl he has the status—and he certainly has the wealth. The girl has nothing aside from her beauty to recommend her and now that we know she has been on the shelf gathering dust you will need to act fast. An earl on the hook usurps a rake. Especially if Miss Blunt is as clever as you say.'

The words unsettled him far more than Jake was prepared to admit. 'She's too clever to settle for an old letch like Redditch.' Surely? Although she had told him she also had a pragmatic attitude towards men. A dyed-in-the-wool pragmatist might well see the benefits of marrying a rich old earl. She would outlive him, for a start, and enjoy the rest of her life as a very rich woman. Completely independent and free to do as she pleased. Maybe speed was of the essence after all.

Chapter Four

Bored, in Uncle Crispin's dining room before the Renshaw ball

This was the second night in a row that the Earl of Redditch had been invited to dine and the second Fliss had had the misfortune of being seated opposite him. Just as he had during yesterday's dinner, the Earl had slurped his soup, chewed with his mouth open and used his hand to cover said mouth only after one of his many belches had escaped. Meanwhile, her uncle fawned over the fellow as if he were visiting royalty, while Daphne and Cressida quaffed the wine like it was going out of fashion.

For the sake of family harmony and out of ingrained politeness, Fliss had put on a brave face and made a concerted effort to engage with the dull conversation about canals right up until her uncle had begun to extoll her virtues to the fusty old Earl in the same way one would list the attributes of a fine horse up for sale at Tattersall's. 'As you can see, my niece is a sensible girl. Well read and not prone to the silly be-

haviour many of the younger debutantes display. The extra few years of maturity set her apart from the rest.'

Why on earth was he giving her indirect compliments when he could barely tolerate to be in her presence most of the time? Unless he was attempting to project an aura of the doting uncle? Fliss pasted on a smile and tried to think of a suitable response. She was spared the effort by the Earl.

'I approve of sensible gals.' He said this with a spray of pastry crumbs from the apple tart he was in the process of demolishing. 'Can't be doing with chits who have no common sense.'

'Felicity has more common sense than most, my lord. She is also blessed with good health as well as a fine figure.'

Unless her ears deceived her, which she sincerely doubted as she had always enjoyed excellent hearing, she had a sneaking suspicion Uncle Crispin was doing a bit of matchmaking. Very unwelcome matchmaking. The Earl's eyes dropped to her bosom, another one of his odious habits which made her flesh crawl, and he leered.

'Yes, indeed. A very fine figure. So far, I find very little about Felicity which I do not approve of.'

'My name is *Miss Blunt* until I give you leave to call me otherwise, my lord, and while I appreciate your approval, it is wasted on me.'

'She's feisty too, Rowley.'

'Too feisty.' Her uncle shot her a warning look down the table.

'I like a feisty gal.' Now the old fool was positively ogling. To her horror his wrinkled face scrunched un-

attractively as he winked at her. This needed to be nipped in the bud.

'Sir, I sincerely hope you are not flirting with me. I take a very dim view of flirting at the best of times, but *you* are far too old to be engaging in such nonsense.'

'Remember your manners, Felicity.'

'My manners? Surely it is the height of bad manners to discuss a lady's figure at the table as if she were an item available to purchase from a shop?' She turned to the Earl and bestowed him with a sugary, insincere smile. 'Unfortunately, I am not for sale, my lord. Not now, not ever.'

'I like a woman with spirit.'

'And I prefer a man with all his own teeth.'

'Felicity...' her uncle practically growled as his cold, silver eyes bored into hers. 'Be *pleasant* to our guest.'

'A lady shouldn't drink spirits,' Aunt Daphne said, waving her wineglass in the air. 'They don't have the constitution for it. Could you pass that bottle of wine, please, Felicity?' Her aunt was blissfully ignorant of the tension between uncle and niece. 'I must say, Crispin, your staff are very lax at topping up the glasses. Guests shouldn't have to resort to serving themselves.'

'Nor should they be insulted by members of my family.' Uncle Crispin glared, then turned back to their guest. 'Perhaps now is the opportune moment for us to retire with our port and cigars. It will give my niece's hot temper a chance to cool down.'

Fliss grabbed hold of the bottle and considered smashing it over her uncle's head, before banging it

down on the table in front of Daphne and biting back the angry words on the tip of her tongue while both men stood. She waited until they had closed the door behind them before venting her anger out loud.

'How dare he try to broker a match between me and that awful man!'

Aunt Cressida turned and blinked at her tone. 'What awful man, dear?'

'Weren't you listening? Uncle Crispin has decided upon the Earl of Redditch as a potential suitor.'

'Surely not. The man is old enough to be your grandfather. I was of the belief you didn't want to hunt for a husband.' Cressida appeared dumb-founded. Or wine-addled. Either way she was clearly not complicit in the matchmaking.

'I didn't come here to hunt for a husband! I'm quite capable of selecting my own suitors should the sudden urge appear. Uncle Crispin barely knows me, so what makes him think he will know what will make me happy or lure me to give up my position at the convent? I've told him as much, too. It hasn't deterred him.'

'Men always think they know what's best for us, dear—' this came from Daphne '—yet they rarely do. Ignore it.'

'Difficult to do when it is happening right in front of me and Uncle Crispin appears determined to be persistent. He knows my feelings on the subject and understands I will be returning to Cumbria as soon as the Season is done. I'm not sure what he thinks he's playing at. It's as if he hasn't listened to a single word I've said.'

'That's where you're going wrong.' Daphne sloshed

more wine into her glass and over the tablecloth. 'You used words. Words are largely wasted on males and one should never try to reason with a stubborn man. They simply dig their heels in further. Men respond better to visual stimulus than anything audible. If he's selectively deaf, which Crispin most assuredly is, deliver the same message in other ways.'

'Are you suggesting I mime it, like charades?' Unfortunately, the only gestures she knew for *mind your own business* were those deemed too unsavoury for a gently bred lady to use, but she treated her incorrigible aunts to a few of them just the same.

Daphne cackled with delight. 'If only! You shall just have to be more devious in future. The key to manipulating the *simple* male mind is to appear to be compliant, but to behave in a manner quite the reverse. They soon get the message you are not to be trifled with. *Show* my supercilious nephew you cannot be swayed. Remember, Felicity, a lady's actions *always* speak louder than words.'

Surprisingly, it was a piece of advice sound enough to have come from the wise lips of Sister Ursuline and Fliss decided it did have some merit. So much so that when her uncle and the Earl returned she held her tongue in check and proudly *showed* her frosty indifference until she climbed in the carriage taking them to the ball.

Jake found himself a secluded nook in the alcove and watched the proceedings from a distance. The trouble with having to socialise while working meant you were denied the opportunity to arrive fashionably late in case something happened, which inevitably

left lots of time to twiddle the thumbs. He was hiding out of necessity. There were several eager young ladies and several more mature ladies who were always desirous of his company, yet he could hardly be seen flirting with one of them when he had to seduce Rowley's niece. From his first impressions, she wasn't the type of woman who would accept playing second fiddle and would regard evidence of his obvious philandering in a very dim light after calling him one.

Not that he was in the mood to philander. Since he had first seen her at Almack's, the indomitable Miss Blunt had rather taken over all his romantic thoughts and, until he had slaked the powerful desire he had for her, frankly no other woman would do. Normal rakish business would doubtless resume straight after. Jake's attention span for an affair was akin to a bumble bee's attraction to nectar. As a bee blithely buzzed from flower to flower, Jake hopped from bed to bed. He preferred things that way. No commitments, no expectations and definitely no complicated and messy feelings to contend with. Much calmer and less problematic all around.

While love had apparently worked out remarkably well for his three brothers, Jake knew in his heart it wasn't for him. The elder three Warriners deserved to find lasting happiness with the women of their dreams. They were good men. Worthy men. Men who had found the right path to travel and had marched down it with single-minded determination and all had reached the destination they had intended against all the odds. He admired them for that. Jake's path meandered, largely because he had no idea where he was going. Never had. Therefore, his dreams were filled

with transient lovers and as he was never quite good enough, and had been that way since birth, it was probably for the best.

He excelled at ultimately disappointing everyone he came into contact with as a matter of course—from his parents, to his brothers, to all the women he had charmed. He was the reliably unreliable Warriner, yet quite comfortable in that skin. On the exterior at least. Inside, he wasn't as blasé about it, but then he knew bits about himself which, with hindsight, he would have changed had the die not been cast a long time ago. Once a disappointment, always a disappointment and rightly so...

Good lord, he was getting maudlin. Another irritating side effect of twiddling one's thumbs was excessive time for introspection. Something he staunchly refused doing for exactly this reason. It served no purpose. The clock could not be turned back, but he could do everything in his power to avoid becoming his father, even though those character traits were as imbedded in his body as firmly as his identical bright blue eyes and jet-black hair. He used those characteristics to do good rather than wreak havoc, although lying to women and using his innate charm to seduce information out of them was perhaps not the dictionary definition of good. But he was working with the limited arsenal of attributes God had given him. Attributes which would rapidly deteriorate with age. A depressing thought indeed.

At this rate, he would sour his mood, which would seriously impair his ability to be charming and seductive, two things he did excel at and always had. Two things he now used for the good of King and country

to great effect. That thought cheered him slightly. Jake was about to risk a quick dash to the refreshment table, when the air in the ballroom shifted. That was the only way of explaining the peculiar sensation which directed him to turn to the staircase the very moment Miss Blunt sailed down it. And, by God, she looked stunning. So stunning he forgot to breathe until the air he had been holding in his lungs all came out at once.

Had that ever happened to him before?

Jake couldn't recall it if it had.

Miss Blunt was a vision in forest green. A dour choice for most women, but a statement on her. The plainness of the colour was lifted by the daringness of the cut. The bodice clung to her upper body and hung off her shoulders. One single, fat, jewelled pendant rested above the tantalising glimpse of cleavage on display. Once again, there was a faraway look in her eyes as she floated into the ballroom, almost as if she didn't care where she was or who was around her.

His throat clenched when he realised his wasn't the only head that had been turned. Every man she floated past gazed appreciatively at her, not that she appeared to notice, a few young bucks even going as far as nudging their companions and hungrily grinning at the sight. Jake wanted to throttle every one of them.

Her chaperons appeared at her elbow and then Crispin Rowley materialised and took up the rear as the party moved to a free spot in the furthest corner. Jake had to crane his head to keep watching, something a man trying to be inconspicuous shouldn't be seen doing, yet he did it anyway. He couldn't help himself. Jake could watch her all night and never get bored.

Rowley left to fetch the ladies' drinks. When he returned, he handed Miss Blunt a card along with her glass. Words were exchanged and her expression changed from faraway to annoyed. She went to say something to her uncle, but he marched away mid-sentence, leaving her glaring after him as he disappeared into the crowd. The Sawyer sisters appeared to sympathise. They patted her arm and tried to distract her, but for the next twenty minutes Jake was forced to suffer seeing her distressed when she should be smiling and he willed her to break free of her charges so he could seek her out and make it all better.

Being rebellious at heart, she eventually did slip away and backed herself into the opposite alcove and out of his eye line. Like a man possessed, his feet began to move instinctively and he found himself skirting the perimeter of the room to find her. She was hidden behind a pillar. Well hidden, yet his intuition pulled him to that exact spot without any trouble. Her back was turned away from him and she was staring intently at the card. His eyes devoured the expanse of golden skin on her back; the loose honeyed tendrils of hair which curled seductively at the nape of her neck. The rest of her glorious hair was casually piled on top of her head, giving him the distinct impression that the removal of one or two strategically placed pins would send it tumbling around her shoulders. Enjoying himself far too much to interrupt, Jake rested his own back against another pillar close by and savoured the beautiful sight.

She sensed him.

Turned around.

Then guiltily tore the spectacles from her face.

Spectacles!

He hadn't been expecting those. Spectacles which did peculiar things to his nether regions.

'No. Leave them on. I rather like them.'

Good lord—now his obligatory nightly fantasy involving this Cumbrian temptress would include those spectacles…and nothing else.

'Mr Warriner, we've spoken about the flirting.'

'We have indeed, Miss Blunt, but I am incorrigible.' The knowing grin he shot her was all male arrogance. 'Stifling my natural instinct to flirt with a beguiling woman would be as futile as suggesting I give up breathing. You are going to have to suffer it, I'm afraid. Especially as you *are* beguiling and have a fortuitous habit of lurking in the same alcoves as I do.'

She stiffened her perfect shoulders and sniffed. 'I am not lurking, Mr Warriner. I am pondering. *You* are lurking.'

'Sounds important. What are you pondering?' He pushed himself away from the pillar and sauntered towards her. 'And might I suggest you ponder in those spectacles. There is something about a beautiful woman in spectacles. It gives her an air of the superior…the stern schoolmistress…the prim and proper governess…' He flicked his wrist as if tossing the flirting aside. 'But I digress. You are hiding again and I am intrigued to know why. It's a fault of mine. I need to know everything about everyone.'

'I am avoiding the Earl of Redditch.'

'A very sensible thing to be doing, if you want my opinion. The man is a dreadful bore.'

'He also smells like feet.'

He laughed at that wonderfully blunt summary

which perfectly matched his own from just a few hours before, enjoying her brutal honesty and the half-smile she tried to cover. 'That he does. Has stinky Redditch taken a shine to you?'

She pulled a face of disgust and made a great show of shuddering. 'Unfortunately, yes. Even more unfortunate is my uncle's persistence in foisting the man upon me. He has even gone as far as pencilling the Earl's name on my dance card for the first waltz—' she waved it angrily in front of his face '—and I am currently in two minds about what to do about it.'

'And what are the two warring parts of your clever brain saying?'

'The cowardly half thinks I should remain hidden during that dance and then have it out with my uncle later. The rebellious half wants me to dance it out of spite—but with a partner of my own choosing—and then have it out with my uncle later.'

'My condolences to your uncle. Whichever you decide, he is in for it regardless.'

'Although I doubt he will listen. Uncle Crispin is stubbornly ignorant of my feelings. When I speak, I am convinced his ears fill with wool, because he always does what he thinks I want regardless of my repeated assertions to the contrary. Why do men do that, Mr Warriner?'

'I hope you are not tarring us all with the same brush, Miss Blunt? Some of us listen.'

'You certainly don't. I've asked you not to flirt and yet you still do it.'

'I'm not flirting now. I'm listening.' Although Jake wanted to flirt. Instead he lifted the dance card and leaned conspiratorially towards her. 'I wonder why

he wants you to dance with Redditch? The man is rich and titled, to be sure, but no more so than half the men in this ballroom. Did he give you any idea as to his motive?'

'Aside from telling me to be *pleasant* to the old fool I was not apprised of the purpose. My uncle is irritatingly sparse with his conversation.'

'Perhaps they are old friends?'

'I believe theirs is a business relationship. It is the main topic of conversation during the interminable dinners I have had to sit through.'

Jake's ears pricked up with interest. 'Who else was invited?'

'What difference does it make who else was there?'

Good lord, she was sharp and he was clumsy. 'It doesn't. As I just said, I'm simply a curious soul by nature. Was there any delicious gossip? I'll bet there was.'

She huffed and shook her head, the motion causing one stray gold ringlet to bounce enticingly by her cheek. 'If only... I'm afraid the conversation was as deadly dull as it always is. They talked of canals.'

Leatham had been right, then. 'Canals? Gracious, that does sound dull. Tell me, are you now an expert on the subject?'

'By default and quite unwillingly, yes—but I was brought up to believe it is the height of rudeness to snore at the dining table.'

'That it is.' He was on to something, but had to tread carefully. 'Although I doubt it is *dull* enough to help me.'

She folded her arms across her chest, something which did wonders for her figure. 'Help you?'

'Indeed. I've been suffering through a bout of insomnia, Miss Blunt.' Largely caused because of her. 'And am in dire need of some mind-numbingly boring things to think about in the wee hours to alleviate the problem. Indulge me with your dull expertise on canals. It might come in useful later tonight when I am tossing and turning and wistfully yearning for you. Only the dullest facts, if you please.' Jake assumed a stance of a man ready to learn and it earned him another smile.

'The Regent's Canal will be almost nine miles long on completion later this year.'

'A painfully short canal, then. Hardly worth all the bother of building it. Go on.'

'Although painfully short, it will link the Grand Junction Canal with the docks in the east of the city.' Docks which sat on the Thames and flowed conveniently out to sea. Smuggling boats could bring their contraband right into the city and then transfer it to barges to send it inland. Smaller boats wouldn't even need to unload. They could sail on unencumbered by the Excise Men.

'That is dull.' Jake pretended to yawn. 'Go on.'

'The canal will have three tunnels, the longest of which is at Islington, which is already built, and runs to nine hundred and sixty yards, which I think you will agree is a very long tunnel indeed Mr Warriner.'

A lovely, long, dark subterranean place to unload unseen. Not that Rowley would even need the tunnels. The fetid stench of most canals meant people tended to avoid them. 'Long and *deathly* dull, Miss Blunt. I already sense a good night's sleep coming on. I shall probably regret asking, but feel that I must—why on

earth are the pair of them discussing an unfinished, painfully short canal over their soup? Does one of them have shares in it?'

'I cannot tell you about *that*, Mr Warriner, as that is the most interesting part of the story and it might undo all of the good work we have done thus far to ease your sleeplessness.'

'Tell me anyway, because now you have me intrigued.'

'New investors had to be sought a few years ago when the promoter of the canal, a Mr Thomas Homer, embezzled all the funds. The Earl of Redditch snapped up a significant stake in the venture for a steal, or so he says, and is very smug about his brilliance for he has a *magnificent* fleet of barges which he intends to use on that same canal.'

Transferring goods to and from the docks would be a lucrative business indeed for any canny investor. 'And your uncle has plans to invest in this venture?'

'Apparently, one cannot have enough barges, Mr Warriner, or so the stinky Earl of Feet claims. Uncle Crispin is one of three investors bidding to extend the fleet. So until the deal is sealed, he is doing his upmost to fawn over the old fool and I am expected to be *pleasant* to him and endure my uncle's flagrant attempts at matchmaking.'

'Does your uncle invest in other canals that you know of?'

Chapter Five

In the Renshaws' stuffy ballroom

'Why do you care?' Because Fliss got the distinct impression he did for some strange reason. 'And what has this to do with either your insomnia or my uncle's matchmaking attempts?'

His expression changed. Briefly he appeared almost frustrated at her answer, harder, less flippant. Somehow more intelligent and, strangely, much more attractive. 'It's your fault. You promised me a dull story, then piqued my interest and now I want to know all the gory details. I'm fundamentally a nosy fellow, as you now know. All manner of things fascinate me.' He smiled again and the easy charm returned, making her wonder if she had imagined the glimpse at a very different man who lived within the same skin as the dashing rogue.

She probably had. And if she was brutally honest with herself, which of course she always was, she had likely done so because a tiny part of her wanted him to be more than a rogue. Aside from being the only person she'd had a decent conversation with since ar-

riving in London, the female part of her was physically attracted to him. But attraction was a dangerous emotion which couldn't be trusted alone. Sister Ursuline's was filled with silly girls who had succumbed to the lure of attraction and then paid the ultimate price when the gentlemen concerned turned out not to be gentlemen at all. After their last meeting, Fliss had made some enquiries about Mr Jacob Warriner and her aunts had confirmed her initial assessment of his character.

He was a rake.

Handsome, charming. Hedonistic. A man who pursued pleasure with the same fervour a great scholar sought knowledge. She failed to acknowledge that the two old dears didn't seem to disapprove of his rakishness at all. Quite the opposite, in fact. Cressida had sighed wistfully and declared that rakes made the very best lovers and then the pair of them had waxed lyrical about the startling array of scandalous gentleman they had enjoyed relations with. More shocking was their ability to compare notes on quite a few of them, which caused even more wistful sighing as they relayed all the gory and fascinating details. Details which conjured up images of sinful blue eyes which Fliss had not needed at all. Attributing deeper layers to such a man led to nothing but folly, especially when she knew better. The only thing such a man could be depended on to be was the sort no sensible woman could afford to be charmed by.

'Their conversation was exceedingly dull, Mr Warriner. Tediously so. I spent most of the meal completely excluded from it, counting the fleurs-de-lys on the wallpaper.' She had reached one hundred and sixty

before she had lost count as all the patterns began to merge into one. No mean feat when she had been callously separated from her spectacles again. Uncle Crispin took great issue with them and had briefly threatened to stamp on them if he saw them again on her face before smiling insincerely and reassuring her it was a joke. Regardless, she had taken to keeping them hidden, and always on her person, just in case he had instructed one of the servants to conveniently lose them.

'It was very rude of them to ignore you.'

'I thought so. I came to the conclusion my presence at the table was entirely decorative.' Fliss was stuffed into another new gown which was designed to show off her figure. While she much preferred the bold green silk from the insipid pastel frock she had been told to wear to Almack's, the neckline still displayed far more flesh than she was used to displaying. She had pulled it up as far as it would go the moment she had stepped into the alcove. The additional inch did nothing to cover her modesty. 'My uncle seems determined to find me a husband.'

'Which you are adamant you do not want. Why is that?' His dark head tilted to one side and for a moment Fliss found herself drowning in his deep blue assessing gaze before she remembered she was supposed to answer.

'I am used to living on my own and actually rather enjoy it. It is liberating to only have to depend on one's self, when others are nowhere near as reliable.'

'It sounds awfully lonely.'

'Not at all.' Although lately it had been. Most of her best friends had married and moved on. Now that

they had their own families to look after, friends, even the very dearest ones, tended to come second. Seeing them happy and content, embracing motherhood and all that came with it, did make a part of her yearn for the same. Not enough of a part to lower her high standards, of course, but enough to make her stop and think from time to time. 'My life is phenomenally busy.' Fliss got to look after other people's children— an ever-changing, moving stream of girls went in and out of the convent's doors.

'There is a chance he is not really matchmaking. Have you considered the prospect he is using you as a distraction to lure Stinky Redditch into choosing him as a business partner?'

'Of course I've considered it and I still resent it. I have no desire to be a distraction either, Mr Warriner.'

'But you are Miss Blunt. Very distracting.'

As he appeared on the cusp of laughing at his own words she couldn't help smiling back at him. 'If you were me, Mr Warriner, what would you do? Hide in the alcove or rebel?'

'Wherever possible, I would rebel, Miss Blunt, but then I am a rebel, too, by nature. I wouldn't dream of counselling you on the correct course of action and nor should you actively seek it from a man with my reputation. What does that intelligent, stubborn and vexing head of yours say?'

'I am erring on the side of rebellion.' Even after all these years, the precociousness still surfaced occasionally. 'It sends a warning shot over the bow to Uncle Crispin stating I am not to be trifled with.' Saying it out loud cemented her determination. Politeness had made her closed-mouthed about her clothes and

spectacles up to now, but her uncle kept taking liber-
ties. Now that she was secure in her growing dislike
for her overbearing, cold and calculated only relative,
there seemed little point in playing happy families
any longer. Actions spoke louder than words. 'I shall
dance the waltz—but not with the aged and fusty Earl
of Redditch.'

'That's the spirit.'

All Fliss needed was another man to waltz with. A
man who was the exact opposite to the one who had
been foisted on her. Someone young and handsome.
One whom her uncle would heartily disapprove of.
One she could nab quickly as, according to her dance
card, the dratted waltz was imminent. 'Mr Warriner,
I don't suppose you would dance with me?'

The sinful grin spread up his face slowly. 'I thought
you would never ask, Miss Blunt.' His eyes were twin-
kling with mischief. Outrageously blue eyes. Beautiful
even. No wonder the ladies fell for him in their droves.

'Don't get any funny ideas. It is just a dance.'

'It's not *just* a dance. It's the waltz, Miss Blunt. Re-
nowned as the dance of *love*.' He held out his arm and
she took it, unprepared for the way the simple gesture
would alter the dynamic between them. Jake was solid.
Much taller up close than she had realised. Although
patently not, against him she felt petite and because he
smelled as gorgeous as he looked, she had the urge to
lean closer and inhale him. Sensibly, she moved away
instead. Just a few inches, but he was having none of
it. He curled one warm hand over hers where it rested
in the crook of his elbow, anchoring her gently but ef-
fectively at his side. It was a solicitous, possessive mo-

tion other men had done many, many times before, yet none of those had felt quite as significant.

Fliss had never been so bothered by a man before. And she was bothered. Jacob Warriner was infinitely more dangerous to all her senses, if her rapid heart-beat was any indication. Even her tightly laced corset seemed suddenly tighter now that their hands touched. He dipped his head and whispered in her ear and her whole scalp tingled. Ripples of awareness shimmered down all her nerve endings the moment his hot breath caressed her cheek. 'You should probably be warned I am devilishly good at waltzing. Barricade your heart now, Miss Blunt, else you'll fall head over heels in love with me before we have twirled a complete circuit of the room.'

'Oh, I can assure you there is no danger of that happening. I would never be so foolish as to fall in love with a rake, no matter how dashing and charming he is reported to be. Dashing and charming are not dependable and I'll never fall head over heels for anything less.' She made the mistake of slanting a glance up and into his intoxicating eyes. They must have contained magnets or something, as once his eyes locked with hers, hers were powerless to look away.

'Never say never, Miss Blunt. Remember, even the mighty Achilles had a heel.'

Had Jake not been a little overawed by the intensity of the moment and his reaction to her, he would have patted himself on the back for the return of his smooth, subtle and effective charm. This time, it had been more successful, although he suspected there was a long way to go before he had the delightful

Miss Blunt eating out of his hand. Thanks to their enlightening conversation, he was also making headway on his mission. There was dirt to be uncovered on Rowley, mud that perhaps they might make stick this time if they could prove a direct link to him and the smuggling ring. Investment in a new canal was not evidence enough to secure an arrest warrant. The Attorney General would need more before he set the King's lawyers on a wealthy member of the aristocracy. So much more. A very good reason to keep his wits about him with Rowley's clever niece. Unfortunately, his wits were currently scrambled and had been since the first moment she had touched him.

Oddly nervous, he turned her towards him and slipped her hand in his, trying to ignore the excitement building within his body at the prospect of holding her close. Thinking calming thoughts weren't helping, so he tore his eyes away from hers and scanned the edges of the dance floor. There was no sign, as yet, of either the Earl of Redditch or Crispin Rowley, but Flint was there. A half-smile on his face and a quick wink towards Jake; a stark reminder that he had come here with a job to do. That focused him.

Sort of.

'Aside from your uncle, I know nothing about the rest of your family, Miss Blunt.'

'There is nothing else to know, Mr Warriner. For a long time there has been just me and my elusive uncle.'

'I take it you didn't see him often growing up.'

'See him?' She laughed. 'I believe that would have been far too much trouble for him. Until last week, I'd never so much as heard from him.'

Interesting—if sad—and he felt sorry for her. The

first notes from the orchestra filled the room as he slipped his hand around her waist and tried not to think about the lovely way it curved beneath his palm. 'Surely you corresponded?'

'I did. He didn't. But then I suppose he was busy as important men are prone to be.' Her tone told him she didn't particularly like Rowley, but was trying to be tactful with the truth.

'I doubt he was busy for the entire fifteen years you've lived in Cumbria.'

'How do you know I've been in Cumbria for exactly fifteen years?' Good heavens, she was sharp.

'You've caught me out. I have been asking about you.'

'I shan't ask why in case you use it as an excuse to flirt.' She stepped on his foot.

'Is that a warning?'

Her lovely green eyes lifted towards his and quickly dipped again as a rosy blush stained her cheeks. 'Actually…this is technically my first ever real waltz. I never learned it in Cumbria. Aunt Daphne has been teaching me, but as she is so often—' She clamped her mouth shut and those bewitching eyes widened slightly, and Jake just knew she was going to say the word *drunk,* but stopped herself.

'She is so often what, Miss Blunt?' The corners of his mouth were already twitching and as one they both glanced towards the refreshment table. True to form, both the slurring Sawyer sisters appeared to be already the worse for wear. Cressida's silk turban had fallen so far forward it almost covered her eyes and Daphne's whole body was definitely listing on the scuppers.

'Shall we change the subject?'

'Probably safest.' His thigh brushed hers and sent ripples of awareness directly to his groin. 'What would you like to talk about?'

'Why don't we talk about you, Mr Warriner?'

Did that mean she was interested in him? Jake certainly hoped so. 'What would you like to know?' She was staring at his face intently, a little too close than was proper. Now that he knew she needed spectacles to see, the close proximity made perfect sense, yet only a fool would fail to enjoy it. 'Did your obvious enquiries about me turn up anything intriguing?'

She didn't deny making them, which he also took as a good sign. 'I think I have the measure of the man you are now, Mr Warriner, but I am curious about how you came to be so. Tell me about your background— *before* you were a rake.'

'I have always been a rake.' She was an atrocious dancer. Delightfully atrocious to the extent Jake would have to take his handkerchief to his boots to remove all the dusty footprints she was leaving on them. She almost tripped over them again and he used it as an excuse to hold her closer. Relieved to be supported, she gripped his shoulder tighter and gazed up into his face with an expression of intense concentration.

'Nobody is born a rake, Mr Warriner. Rakes are made. We are all nurtured by circumstance. There is probably some pivotal moment in your past which shaped your future.'

There was, not that he'd ever tell her. 'Do you really think a person's character can be altered by circumstances?' He was trying to distract her from probing further, but typically she refused to be swayed.

'Of course. It has certainly shaped mine. I doubt

I'd be as stubborn and vexing if I hadn't spent fifteen years on my own. There has to be something in your past. A significant occurrence which set you on the wrong path. Why don't we start with your family?'

'Well, up until very recently they were a very bad lot, so perhaps we should blame them for the shocking way I turned out. At home in Nottinghamshire we are known as the Wild Warriners—a title which was earned thoroughly by every generation of my forebears going back to Tudor times. We are a rotten lot. Very bad blood.'

Rather than shocked, she seemed interested. 'How bad?'

'The worst. My father was a violent drunkard, my grandfather was little more than a trickster and my great-grandfather was exiled from the *ton* for all manner of nefarious shenanigans too awful to sully a young lady's ears with. The earlier ones were no better. I come from a long line of ne'er-do-wells and, if the family stories are true, a couple of out-and-out traitors. The family seat is built like a fortress. There is a twenty-foot wall surrounding the house, enormous impenetrable gates and even a priest hole, although I doubt it ever held any priests. Sir Hugo, a Warriner from way, way back, had it made to hide his own sorry carcass in when angry people came looking for him. That says it all. So you see, I was doomed to be a rotten egg long before I was hatched.' Jake spun her in a quick set of turns straight past her fuming uncle and the bristling Earl of Redditch, and she shot them both a defiant smile as they twirled away.

Slightly and attractively breathless, she then picked up the conversation exactly where they had left it. 'I

do not subscribe to the belief of bad blood. My own father was a wastrel, yet I have turned out all right. But then I had a good mother to see me through my formative years. Tell me about your mother.' Like a dog with a bone, she was determined to get to the root of his problem and she had inadvertently found his tangled roots straight away.

'I barely remember her.' A lie. 'She died when I was very young.' Because he hadn't fetched his father when she'd asked. 'My eldest brother Jack brought me up.'

'You smiled as you said his name. Are you close to your brother?'

'Brothers,' he corrected with a grin, 'There are four of us. I'm the baby of the family.' Fearing for his feet, Jake manoeuvred them back towards the alcove rather than back to her chaperons as was customary at the end of a dance. He both needed and wanted to talk to her more. She didn't seem to mind and allowed him to lead her to their secluded spot in the corner.

'Tell me about them.'

Thankfully, this was much safer ground so he happily complied by keeping things superficial. 'We are all the spitting image of our father, who despite being a scoundrel was devilishly handsome, but obviously, I am the most handsome Warriner by far.' She rolled her eyes, but was smiling and that smile warmed his heart. 'We also all have the same initials—J.L. Warriner— why I cannot say, but it makes receiving letters at home very confusing. I open my eldest brother's bills and he receives all the adoring love letters sent from all the women who desperately want to marry me. His name is Jack. He's the responsible Warriner. He

looks after everything and everyone. Did I mention he is an earl? We might be wild, but at least there is a title lurking in the background, although Jack doesn't like to use it. Too much bad history is associated with it and he's trying to rise above it. You would like him, he's very *dependable*.' She acknowledged this with a grin that made his chest swell to have caused it. 'Then there's Jamie. He's the brave Warriner. He enlisted in the army and fought against Napoleon, but now he's an artist who illustrates children's books for a living. And he's doing very well at it, too. The clever Warriner is Joe. He's a doctor. A very good doctor who recently got married to an equally scholarly woman. He and his bride are nauseatingly happy. All my brothers are nauseatingly happily married and settled. Jack has three sons and Jamie has four daughters and I dare say Joe will have a family soon enough. A new niece or nephew might be pending, but alas, I am a bit behind on the latest family news.' The numerous exchanged letters weren't the same.

'You miss them.'

'I do, but their life is in Nottinghamshire and mine is here.' Suddenly the pull of home was stronger than it had ever been. He missed his brothers and their noisy families, missed being part of that noise. More than anything he missed being him. Just Jake rather than the rake-cum-spy—or was it spy-cum-rake? He didn't know any more and he was suddenly tired of it. 'Would you like me to get you a drink?' Over which he would quiz her some more about her uncle's business interests to avoid getting maudlin and homesick.

'No. I'd best go back before Uncle Crispin or my aunts come and fetch me. I can't spend all night in

the company of a rake. No matter how diverting that company is, Mr Warriner.' She smiled somewhat reluctantly. 'Thank you for struggling through the waltz with me. I hope I didn't crush your toes with my clumsy big feet. No doubt I shall see you in another alcove in the very near future.'

Jake would have tried to convince her to stay a while, but he could already see a furious Rowley elbowing his way across the crowded dance floor to get to her. 'No doubt you will, Felicity, but alas, the cavalry is on its way to rescue you from my wicked charms.' He winked as he bent to kiss her gloved hand. 'By the way, most ladies call me Jake, because I am dashing. Like a pirate.'

She grinned and shook her head at his return to shameless flirting. 'Most enlightening, but I am not as susceptible to dashing pirates as most ladies. For the record, I prefer Fliss to Felicity, but you can continue to call me Miss Blunt as is proper. Especially when one is conversing with a pirate. Goodnight, *Mr* Warriner.' She slowly walked three steps away before turning back. 'Responsible...brave *and* clever?'

'I'm sorry?'

'An interesting choice of adjectives to use for your three brothers. Hardly *wild*-sounding Warriners at all. In turn you called them responsible, brave and clever. Admirable qualities. Noble. *Dependable*. Which beggars the question—if they are the responsible, brave and clever Warriners, what does that make you?'

For a moment, he wished he was more like his brothers and less like his father. Worthier. Admirable. But alas, fate had chosen this path for him and both King and country needed him to stay on it. He

covered the uneasy well of longing with his most rak-ish smile. 'Why, that's easy, *Fliss*.' The sound of her name was like heaven on his lips. 'I'm the *disappoint-ment*. Somebody has to look after the family legacy.'

Chapter Six

Seething in Uncle Crispin's phaeton

'If you don't mind, Felicity?'

Her uncle shot her his *get out of the carriage and give us some privacy* look. Fliss knew this because he had already left her twiddling her thumbs as she stood idly waiting for him to conclude his business three times already.

'Actually, I do mind. This is not at all how I thought I would be spending the day.' This morning she had awoken early because her uncle had promised she could finally visit the Menagerie at the Tower of London, a place she had been dying to see for as long as she could remember.

'I have a little bit of business to attend to, Felicity. We'll be on our way shortly and I promise my little surprise will be worth the delay. I am just waiting for one more thing and then I shall take you to Gunther's.' He said this as if she should be impressed.

'What is Gunther's?'

'The home of the finest ice cream in all of London.'

'You want to feed me ice in February?' Thanks to the sedate pace and lack of exercise, Fliss's fingers were already frozen inside her thick gloves.

'You might sound a little more grateful. Gunther's is *the* place to be seen.'

I don't want to be seen, I want to see the lions! Or the Elgin Marbles or the Changing of the Guard. In fact, almost anything which did not involve the rest of the fashionable residents of Mayfair.

Fliss bit back the angry retort because her uncle's business associate had pulled his curricle alongside and was doing his best to appear as if he couldn't hear their taut conversation. Uncle Crispin nodded to the man, then turned back to glare at her. 'Now if you will excuse us, Felicity, I shall be but a few minutes.'

For the fourth time she reluctantly lowered herself on to the path and took herself a few feet away. For good measure, she folded her arms and positively seethed at him, not that it had any effect.

Behind her she heard the snort of a swan and turned to watch it floating across the Serpentine, instead. For such beautiful birds, they had the ugliest sound. They didn't quack or tweet. The best way to describe the noise of a swan was a cross between a snort and an asthmatic cough. Nature's way of reminding the bird it wasn't perfect. Nothing ever was. Today was certainly turning out to be a thorough disappointment. Even though Fliss had awoken in a perfectly lovely mood, her uncle had spoiled it straight after breakfast and she was already regretting the compromise she had made in the spirit of family harmony.

Last night, after the Renshaws' ball, he had promised faithfully she could begin seeing the sights of

the capital, decreed that she could take the carriage and her great-great-aunts to visit the Tower with his blessing and Fliss had started the day believing him. With hindsight, she should have realised something was wrong when her maid had laid out a wholly inappropriate and showy outfit for her to wear. Kitty had been most insistent she wear it and Fliss had been equally as insistent that she didn't.

She'd rejected the thin silk ensemble specially designed for her by Madame Devy because clearly the modiste had never ventured outside in winter. To the maid's vocal consternation, Fliss had rifled through her own wardrobe for something more suited to a cold February morning of exploring. That flimsy pelisse and those thin-soled slippers would have left her hideously exposed to the elements and ruined her feet. Instead, Fliss had dug out the sensible navy-wool walking dress she had brought with her from Cumbria, complete with its matching thick coat, and paired it with her sturdy yet comfortably worn boots. Garments much better suited to traipsing around a damp castle and climbing up its ancient battlements. But when she reached the hallway to meet her aunts, she met her uncle instead.

'There has been a change of plan.' Her uncle was dressed in his expensive riding clothes and the smile which materialised on his face was not echoed in his cold, flat, grey stare. 'It occurred to me last night that we have not spent enough time together, Felicity. I wish to remedy that and I hope you will indulge me in my quest to get better acquainted with my only niece by asking you to accompany me this morning on a little adventure.'

She'd had an adventure planned, one which blessedly had not included him and the unnecessary restrictions he placed upon her. 'I don't ride and I want to see the lions.' The churlish response was the best Fliss could manage in the wake of the disappointment. Yet another day would pass and she would still be denied the opportunity of seeing the places she had specifically wanted to see.

'I have something more exciting planned and you do not need to ride. I shall drive my phaeton and take you to see a part of this fine city which is much more interesting than the Tower. You will be diverted. I promise.'

His jaw was tight and his gaze was frosty and Fliss was well and truly trapped. It would be unforgivably rude to turn down her host's invitation even though she sincerely doubted he really wanted them to become better acquainted. He was up to something. She knew that in her bones. 'If you insist, Uncle Crispin, then I shall postpone my excursion.'

'That outfit is a little plain for what I have planned.' His eyes rested on the spectacles sat on her nose and narrowed. 'I'm sure your maid can quickly find you more suitable attire.'

How splendid. Another battle of wills and directly after breakfast. The food had already begun to curdle in her stomach. 'Uncle, it is February and freezing outside. If I am going out in a phaeton, then I shall do so wearing wool or not at all.'

'Will you at least take off those ugly spectacles?'

'I thought you were taking me to *see* something special. If I take off my spectacles, then it's hardly worth going as I shan't see whatever it is you are so

eager for me to see at all.' As she had intended, he couldn't argue with sound logic and they walked to the phaeton in a silence so brittle, the merest puff of the cold February air would likely shatter it.

Since then, Fliss had been largely invisible to him. Uncle Crispin's apparent idea of a treat not to be missed was to join the fashionable crowd in parading up and down Rotten Row. A pointless exercise in her opinion if ever there was one. So far they had spent an hour either saying hello to people they had said goodbye to only a few hours before or, like now, he was discussing business and she was excluded. She had a good mind to take herself off to the Tower as a mark of protest, but with her atrocious sense of direction, going alone would doubtless end in disaster. There was no telling where she'd end up if she attempted the trip by herself on foot. Kent, probably. Or worse. It would be typical, for her useless nose would take her to one of the less salubrious parts of the capital where she'd end up accosted by footpads or garrotted in an alleyway.

Much as she loathed taking the coward's way out, a solitary expedition to the Tower of London was out of the question. With a sigh, she stared out over the lake and smiled at the sight of a solitary rowing boat drifting across the middle. Only here, in London, where people ate ice cream in February, would a person be daft enough to row across a freezing lake for pleasure. The gentleman in charge of the oars appeared to be flagging under the exertion, while the lady passenger was hunched inside her highly ineffectual but highly fashionable coat as if her life depended on it. It was a pretty coat, made in the exact shade of blue

as the eyes of a certain rake of Fliss's acquaintance. A rake she had dreamed about last night despite her better judgement and one she rather liked. For all his faults, Jake Warriner had rescued her at the ball and asked nothing in return.

And they had waltzed.

Even now her body warmed at the thought of it.

His arms been firmly wrapped around her body. They had needed to be to hold her up and to prevent her from seriously damaging his poor toes, yet he'd not mentioned her embarrassing clumsiness once, despite the fact she had stepped on his foot repeatedly. Although not all those footwork mistakes had been caused by her ineptitude with the waltz. At least two mishaps had occurred from being so close to him while staring into his beautiful bright blue eyes. Or perhaps it had been the solid feel of his shoulder under her palm which had made her pulse quicken and her feet fail? Thanks to Jake's raw masculinity Fliss had experienced a bit of a moment worryingly akin to swooning.

He smelled sinfully delicious, too, which was indeed a bonus when she considered what she could have been forced to sniff on that dance floor at that particular time. Whatever cologne he had applied before dressing must have contained some sort of magical ingredient, because it was more intoxicating the closer her nose got to it. At one point, during a dizzying set of fast spins, the urge to press her nostrils against his Adam's apple had been fairly difficult to ignore, but she'd struggled on. Valiantly. Making do with seductive wafts which emanated from his exceedingly fine person and chastising herself for being weak. Waltz-

ing with the rakish Mr Warriner had not been a chore at all. It had been, she was prepared to admit only to herself, the highlight of her week.

He'd hardly even flirted and yet still she had been charmed. Charmed and intrigued in equal measure because the more she got to know him, the more she began to suspect he wasn't quite as superficial as he seemed.

Jake did have a way of looking at a woman as if she was the *only* woman in the room, which had made her feel very special. She had also spied a few jealous glances from the other young ladies as he had twirled her around the floor; young ladies who would have given their eye teeth to have been in his strong and capable arms in her stead. Fliss was just vain enough to be flattered by this and rather liked being the frivolous centre of attention for once, rather than the responsible Miss Blunt who always set an example to her students. The former wayward girl made good. An inspiration to aspire to. Sometimes all that made her feel old and dull.

With Jake, for a few short minutes, she had been vivacious and gloriously young. That waltz had been an adventure in itself. Shameless flirting aside, he was also good company. Interesting.

Interested.

He listened to everything she said, whether it be her bemoaning of her uncle's persistent and irritating attempts at matchmaking or recounting boring details about canal tunnels. He had called himself a nosy fellow and that he was, but Jake also paid attention and knew how to make a lady feel special. And his name suited him. Piratical and dashing.

Of course, he was still a shocking rake and liking him didn't mean Fliss was less mindful of his wiles. One of the benefits of living among a succession of wayward girls was one became an expert on the sort of men who waylaid them. Fliss had trained herself to be adept at ignoring her body's natural reaction to men like him. She wasn't a man-hater after all. A great many males were exceedingly tolerable, Fliss just knew their limitations. Some men were dictatorial. Some men were unreliable. Most men, however, were fundamentally untrustworthy. It was embedded in their nature, like the female urge to mother, and they really couldn't help it. One could still thoroughly enjoy the company of a rake without succumbing to his charms. Like all successful rakes, Jake had all the attributes to make a female body yearn. Such things were down to biology, not logic, and she would never allow herself to be a slave to something as base and savage. Logic made him wholly unsuitable. Not that she was in the market for a man at the moment. If she were he would be the very last sort to settle down with. Still, she was grateful he had stepped up to help her in her moment of need. That had been noble of him. It was too bad he was untrustworthy, else she might have been tempted.

To keep her mind from being further seduced by his presence, Fliss had asked him questions about his past. Although his answers had been glib, she could tell they were purposefully so. Another benefit of living among wayward girls was one became an expert in the art of lying. Her students knew she was a master at uncovering deceptions. At Sister Ursuline's, her ability to spot a lie at ten yards was legendary, although

how she could spot one was a trick she kept entirely to herself in case the girls got wise to it and tried to camouflage the clues.

However, the simple truth was it wasn't really a trick, it was mere observation. There were little, almost minute physical tells which always gave the lies away. Each unique to the person, yet obvious to a master at reading them. To most people, Jake's casual and seemingly open answers would have sufficed, but Fliss wasn't most people and Jake's tell happened to be in those spectacular eyes which had a habit of taking her breath away. And by golly it was tiny. Had she not been staring wistfully up into them she would have missed it. But she had been, so she'd spotted it.

His pupils constricted.

In fact, they had constricted three times.

Once when he had blithely denounced his father as a violent drunk, suggesting he was making light of something which had not been in any way light at all. The second had been stronger, his black pupils constricting to a pinpoint for less than a second, and it had been in a throwaway sentence about his mother. The woman who had died when he was so young he *barely remembered her.* Fliss would wager all her savings on the fact he didn't *barely* remember her. That was a tactic to avoid talking about her and one Fliss sometimes used when new acquaintances inadvertently probed a sore spot. Like her, he remembered his mother keenly. Too keenly and it hurt.

So much so, she had taken pity on him and allowed him to direct the conversation to his brothers where he felt comfortable. Something she empathised with. Despite outwardly projecting otherwise, the rejection

of her father when she had needed him the most still cut deep if she allowed herself to dwell upon it. All those years of loneliness and of feeling abandoned. Rejected. Not quite good enough to warrant even the tiniest place in his life. That pivotal moment in her past had shaped her and left her wary of all men, just in case another broke her heart quite so thoroughly and this time the wound would never heal.

What Sister Ursuline called cynicism was the necessary fortress that protected that tender organ from further damage. It was easier to not challenge the comfort of her carefully constructed status quo than subject herself to the risk of further pain. Once upon a time it had been enough, the walls of the fortress impenetrable, yet as the years had marched on Fliss was honest enough with herself to acknowledge those same walls which protected her also imprisoned her as well. This unexpected trip away from the sanctuary of normality had weakened those defences. Heightened the disquiet which had taken root without her noticing and had made her increasingly dissatisfied with her life. Made her yearn to climb a ladder to peek over the battlements at the possibilities beyond. The possibilities Jake presented.

Of all the men to be attracted to, her foolish heart had selected a rake.

Perhaps Jake had constructed a new persona to protect him from history repeating itself, just as she had? And perhaps Fliss was frantically hoping that there were deeper layers to him simply as a means to justify her continued fascination with a man her instincts screamed was wholly unreliable.

Or was he? It was obvious he adored all three of

his brothers as his face lit with pride as he described them. Responsible, brave and clever. And then those brilliant, vibrant irises had constricted again when he had called himself the disappointment. In that instant she learned it was a label he wore openly, almost like a shield like her cynicism, but hated it nevertheless. It was on the tip of her tongue to question him about it, but her uncle had come and claimed her, and by the time they parted ways, the flirtatious look was back in his eyes and the peculiarly telling moment and the opportunity to explore it was gone.

Much as the foolhardy rower and his lady friend were now. Gone to freeze in another part of the Serpentine on their quest *to be seen*. With nothing better to do, Fliss went back to watching the swans and wishing she was somewhere, anywhere, else. Trying to ignore the image of twinkling blue eyes which constantly invaded her daydreams.

Chapter Seven

Laboriously plodding along Rotten Row

Jake had always enjoyed riding. Dashing across an open meadow, racing between steeples or simply meandering aimlessly along the open road at a leisurely trot never failed to lighten his mood. However, there was no joy to be had jostling his poor horse through the well-heeled crowds at Rotten Row at a speed little faster than the average arthritic octogenarian could achieve going uphill. He'd never understood the point of this aristocratic ritual, where the horses served as pedestals for the *ton* to display themselves. But Crispin Rowley was guaranteed to be here preening, because he always came here preening, which meant his fetching niece might be here, too. Or so he hoped.

He turned his horse towards where the congested gravel path arced around the Serpentine and plodded on, forcing himself to return the smiles of the many young ladies who made no secret of the fact they had their eye on him. However, for the first time in as long as he could remember, not one of them caught *his* eye.

That was odd.

Usually, at least one tempting damsel would lure him into furthering the acquaintance. The ladies loved a naughty boy, but while Jake had worked hard to become one of society's naughtiest boys for King and country, earning that reputation had hardly been a chore. He liked women. Really liked women, usually much preferring their company to men. Women, in all their shapes and sizes, intrigued him and distracted him in equal measure. The way they saw life quite differently from men, the calming influence they had, their resilience and intelligence, the way they smelled, moved, laughed. He was a healthy, virile, gloriously unattached man in the prime of his life. Why shouldn't he enjoy them if the opportunity presented itself?

Most knew he was not marriage material, accepted it and enjoyed him all the more as a result. The neglected wives, young widows and the occasional scandalous debutante who had been happily waylaid many times before he had arrived in their lives were immediately drawn to him for their fun and he was fine with that, too. Both parties got exactly what they wanted and had a great deal of fun in the getting. No matter whether he was bedding them for business or for pleasure, Jake treated all types of paramour the same and hopped cheerfully from one lover to the next like a bumble bee in a summer garden full of flowers.

At the first sniff of awkward feelings, Jake usually made his excuses and ran, because he was an honest rake beneath it all and didn't want anyone wasting their love on him when he wasn't prepared to take the risk of offering it in return. They might come to rely on him and nothing good could ever come of that,

although fortunately he was so successful at being a rake that few of his conquests were silly enough to truly try. They knew he was superficial and transient, which was half of the fun of the dalliance in the first place. For them he was forbidden fruit. For him, each new lover was a tempting diversion from the gnawing empty, growing void in his life and the guilt which quickly turned him maudlin if he allowed himself to remember the cause of it. Therefore, it stood to reason that as long as Jake kept lining up potential diversions, then everything in his disappointing garden was as rosy as it could possibly be and he could flit through life without accruing fresh guilt to add to his burden. Therefore, he always had his wandering eye open for the next welcome diversion and Rotten Row had always been a particularly fertile hunting ground.

Except there was only one diversion currently lined up in his sights right now. Fliss. The only woman he truly wanted to dally with was the one he had fortuitously been tasked with seducing. A unique situation he had not found himself in before.

That vexing woman was taking up too much space in his head and, if he wasn't careful, when this mission was completed he would have nobody ready to fill her clumsy dancing shoes and would be left all on his lonesome to contemplate his failings. Something which wouldn't do at all.

It was worrying, but clearly not enough for his fixated mind to wander from its chosen route. Since the opera, he had done nothing but think about her and her alone—or rather his overwhelming reaction to her. Not a single other lady had occupied his thoughts or tempted his body in all that time, something unheard

of and extremely unsettling. The damn woman had bewitched him almost as thoroughly as she appeared to see straight through him and he wasn't entirely comfortable with that either. Yes, she was still a diversion and, yes, he desperately wanted to seduce her, but there was an irritating and nagging part of him which wanted more from the canny Miss Blunt-by-Name-and-Nature than good sense dictated.

Bizarrely, for a man who purported not to care one jot what others thought of him, Jake wanted her respect as much as he wanted to make her smile. He wanted to kiss her senseless *and* talk to her for hours on end. He wanted to spend time with her. Lots of time. Considerably more than the few accumulated hours he usually allowed himself and to hell with messy, complicated feelings. Truth be told, he suspected he wanted her to have messy and complicated feelings for him. He wanted to matter to her as much as he now suddenly wanted to be a better man than the one he was whenever he was around her. A man with the admirable characteristics of his three brothers. The sort of dependable man she had set her heart on. More than anything, he wanted Fliss *not* to be a mission to be accomplished for King and country. A ridiculous notion he couldn't seem to dismiss. What was that all about?

There had been a moment before they had parted ways at the dance, when she had turned around and simply stared at him as if she was assessing him and all he had just said, and for the briefest moment Jake swore he saw her recognise the real him. The man riddled with guilt and plagued with self-doubt. As ludicrous as that terrifying thought was, he had struggled

to shake it off for the rest of the evening because he couldn't help wondering what she had made of the real him. He doubted there was a hope in hell she'd want to take a chance on the reliably unreliable Warriner any more than he wanted to risk opening himself up to the unpalatable complications which came with romantic love. Except for the first time, he was sorely tempted by those complications and that bothered him.

To add insult to injury, he had even dreamed about her again last night and what a dream it had been. Jake had awoken hot and hard and so blasted frustrated he'd washed in ice water straight from the pump just to cool his ardour. Ardour which flagrantly refused to be cooled and still plagued him now. Ardour which could have been readily spent elsewhere. Why was he torturing himself with abstinence when she was his mission and he'd never been loyal to a single woman— business or pleasure—in his entire life? Misplaced fidelity wasn't rakish behaviour.

But then, he was tired. That probably had something to do with his uncharacteristic confused state. And he was supposed to be enjoying his well-earned leave. Casanova himself must have been exhausted from time to time and thus less inclined to woo willy-nilly. The simple truth was Jake needed to be home. In Nottinghamshire, sleeping. Not here traipsing up and down Rotten Row, so it was hardly a surprise his libido had gone into hibernation or that every female face and form seemed to merge into one and none of them piqued his interest. It wasn't the vexing Miss Blunt who had rendered him ruined for all these other women. It was tiredness. Pure and simple.

Nothing to worry about.

'Why, *hello*, Mr Warriner.' The sultry redhead and he had been exchanging smouldering looks for months. 'Fancy bumping into you here?'

Come on, Jakey-boy. Make some effort. 'Why, *hello* to you, too.' He reached for her proffered gloved hand, easy to do when she had brought her pony directly level with his, and placed a lingering kiss on the back of it. A kiss that did nothing to fire the loins which had been ablaze a few scant days ago. 'How are you on this fine morning?'

'Very bored, Mr Warriner. I am in dire need of some *excitement*.' A blatant invitation to sin if ever he'd heard one, yet still nothing stirred in his breeches.

'I'm sorry to hear that. A beautiful young lady should never be bored.' The back of his neck prickled.

Awareness.

Jake turned his head slightly and saw her. Her dress was as plain as the grey February sky. Her hair was simply styled. Her bonnet austere by Rotten Row standards and she was wearing those spectacles which had haunted his dreams last night. Spectacles, which by rights should lessen her attractiveness—yet his gaze had never beheld anything so lovely and every drop of blood he possessed suddenly rushed to his groin, the overly friendly redhead already forgotten.

'What do you suggest I do, Mr Warriner?' Reluctantly he tore his gaze away from his canny northern lass and gazed back at the sultry vixen next to him. A woman who plainly wanted him naked and soon.

Nothing.

The fiery lust he had for Fliss fizzled out the instant he had turned back to look at the other woman. Clearly

Jake really was doomed. He could already feel the powerful pull of whatever it was only she possessed.

'I really couldn't say…if you will excuse me.' He tugged the reins and angled his horse to trail after Crispin Rowley's phaeton and the golden-haired passenger his heart was suddenly beating loudly for, keeping enough of a distance that he remained unnoticed in the crowds, but close enough that he could watch her.

She didn't appear to be very comfortable sat next to her uncle. There was a stiffness about her posture which suggested she wasn't very happy with him, her eyes and body angled away. When Rowley slowed the carriage to greet a group of people, Jake lingered behind a tree. Her eyes drifted away from the people her uncle was chatting to and towards the banks of the Serpentine. After another few minutes, those people drifted away and an unfamiliar man walked towards the carriage. Rowley and his perplexing niece exchanged what appeared to be terse words, then she climbed out of the carriage to stand with ill-disguised impatience on the path.

Jake knew he should be watching the men, but his eyes followed her as she began to walk towards the lake and his shady vantage point. Making a snap decision he hoped he would not regret, Jake decided to forget about Rowley and his acquaintance. He quickly dismounted, secured his horse to a branch, then sauntered towards her.

Fliss had her back to him as she watched some swans close to the edge of the water. Her neck curved gracefully, much like those of the swans. Something he would rather die than mention as it was yet another trite bird analogy, but he suddenly had the urge

to place a kiss on the exposed slash of skin between her bonnet and collar. He didn't, knowing full well it would probably be the last liberty she ever afforded him and because he was here on the King's shilling. Jake had a job to do and needed to stop being waylaid from the purpose of his quest by swanlike necks and spectacles and tiredness-induced yearnings.

Chapter Eight

On the chilly banks of the Serpentine

'Hiding again, Fliss? We must stop meeting like this.'

To her credit she didn't jump or startle, despite the fact he had crept up on her unawares, making him hope that she had experienced the same early awareness of him as he did her. Instead she slanted him a glance and gifted him with a smile which lifted the dullness of the day in much the same way a beautiful sunrise would. 'Good morning, *Mr* Warriner... Even though it is not morning by any sensible standards in the rest of England, but here in the capital it apparently still is.'

'I see you have escaped the clutches of your evil uncle.'

She frowned slightly, her perfect brows wrinkling for a split second before they smoothed and she appeared bored. 'Evil? Why did you choose that word?' The way she studied his face intently, waiting for his answer, gave him pause. Did she know or suspect something about Rowley's activities?

'Merely that he tried to force the Earl of Redditch on you at the ball. Why? Has he done more dastardly deeds I should be aware of?'

'I don't think so.' She stared back at the water, her expressive brows furrowed briefly again. Not a *no*, then. Interesting. 'But he has dragged me here, as far as I can ascertain, just to ignore me, although he claims we are going to get ice cream. In February.' Her eyebrows said all the things she stopped herself telling him. Now they were slightly raised. Not amused.

'People do odd things like that here in town. It takes a while to get used to their peculiar ways. Why are you stood here all alone?' They both gazed back at the intense conversation going on between Rowley and a man Jake was sure he recognised, but could not place.

'I have been dismissed while my uncle talks business. Again.'

'How rude of him.' Jake offered his arm. 'Would you care to take a little turn about the lake, Fliss? To help pass the time?'

She briefly flicked her gaze back to her uncle's phaeton, saw he was still engrossed in whatever social discourse he was embroiled in and nodded curtly. 'I do believe I would, Mr Warriner. Are you going to flirt?'

'Most assuredly.'

'How tiresome.' But she smiled as she took his arm and Jake purposely led her along the bank and away from both her uncle and prying eyes. He allowed the companionable silence to hang for a minute, quietly enjoying the way her undulating hips intermittently brushed against his as they walked.

'Forgive me if I am speaking out of turn, but I get

the distinct impression all is not right between you and your uncle this morning.'

'Is it that obvious?'

'To me it is. Every time I see you with him, your expression always tells me you want to be somewhere else.'

'I am trying to enjoy my visit here. It's just…' She sighed and shook her head. 'Why do I keep confiding in you, Mr Warriner?'

'Perhaps because I ask the right questions?'

'You do have a canny knack of hitting the nail on the head.'

'It's a northern trait. Like you, I say things as I see them and here that is a rare treat.'

She paused, then laughed. It was a throaty, earthy sound. Unpractised and without any artifice. Jake made the mistake of turning to look at her and when their eyes met he lost himself for a moment.

'It *is* a treat. I never thought I would miss northern honesty. It can be brutal at times. But I do. I miss saying what I think without first checking myself.'

'Then I am glad I came along to fill the void. Be brutally blunt, Miss Blunt. You know you want to. Unburden yourself by listing all the things you are not enjoying about your visit. Cry on my attractively broad shoulders.'

She stopped for a second, assessing him with amusement, before tugging gently on his arm to signal she was ready to walk again. 'I had hoped to see the sights today. The interesting sights like the lions at the Tower or museums and such, but instead I have been ambushed yet again by my uncle's personal agenda. Since I arrived, I have done everything he has wanted

and nothing of mine. I've been dragged to Almack's and *launched*. I've made a tiresome number of morning calls on strangers I do not know and have no desire to, eaten numerous dull dinners in the company of the awful Earl of Redditch, where I am forced to listen to dreary conversation about barges or have to suffer the old fool's unwelcome attentions. I'm coerced into coming here to Hyde Park rather than visiting the Menagerie as I had planned. Soon I shall be fed ice cream because Gunther's is apparently *the* place to be seen. But I don't want to be *seen*, Mr Warriner. I am desperate to *see* things before I run out of time and have to go home.'

His mission dictated he should press her about the dinner conversations, but her eyes were suddenly sad and he wanted to make her smile. 'No wonder you are at odds with your uncle.'

'I think I am doomed always to be at odds with my uncle. His matchmaking aside, we have nothing in common. All he cares about are appearances and business. Uncharitably, I am starting to believe the only reason he hauled me away from Cumbria was to give that stinky Earl someone to fawn over, for all my uncle cares about is how I look. Which is never quite good enough.'

'I can't think why. You look splendid.'

She shook her head at his rakish grin. It made a stray tendril of hair float in the faint breeze enticingly against the rim of her bonnet. If she had been any other woman he had been ordered to seduce, Jake would have given in to the urge to touch it and tuck it back where it belonged, knowing that brief intimacy would create a *frisson* between them. For some rea-

son, although desperate, too, he kept his itching fingers to himself.

'We have already had words about my dour appearance today. He thoroughly disapproves of my choice of outfit this morning. Who knew that warm wool was not suitable for a cold ride in Hyde Park? Clearly I am expected to freeze to death in one of the frivolous silk concoctions he has had made for me.'

Jake couldn't help sweeping his eyes down the length of her. The dress and her winter coat might well be sensible, but she filled them spectacularly. The way the wool clung to her pert bosom and trim waist made his mouth water. The dark navy was the perfect showcase for her golden hair and English rose complexion. She was beautiful, breathtakingly so. 'Your uncle clearly also needs spectacles if he thinks you look dour. That is a very lovely outfit despite being less draughty than silk.'

For some reason, she blushed slightly and her fingers went to her spectacles. Without looking at him she slipped them off and stared at them in her hands. 'He disapproves of these most of all. I know they are ugly, but I can't see further than my nose without them.'

They weren't ugly at all. They were achingly erotic. 'I like them. I've already told you I think they give you the air of a schoolmistress. All prim and proper and bossy.'

'I *am* a schoolmistress.'

'Are you really?' The profession suited her.

'Yes, I am. Back at Sister Ursuline's I teach literature and grammar to the girls, with a smattering of history.'

'And are you prim, proper and bossy?'

'When the occasion calls for it.'

Because they were now completely shaded by a patch of trees, Jake couldn't resist gently prising the spectacles out of her hand and placing them back on her face. Because he had to, he arranged that stray silken tendril to sit against the soft skin of her cheek. He wanted to kiss her. He wanted to haul her into his arms and kiss her till both felt their knees buckle— instead, he took a step back and pretended to admire his work. 'I'm intrigued. Professionally speaking, how would you deal with a naughty boy, Miss Blunt? A *very* naughty boy. Would you tell him off?'

'I suppose it depends on what he has done.' She shot him a saucy grin which heated his blood quicker than any kiss ever had. 'For a mild misdemeanour, a few terse words might suffice. For something outrageously bad, it would need to be more severe. Perhaps he would be sent to bed without supper and have all privileges withdrawn.'

'Would you spank him?'

She rolled her eyes, but played along. For all her northern bluntness, she had a mischievous sense of humour. She didn't take herself too seriously and enjoyed a laugh. He liked that about her. 'In my opinion, a good teacher should never have to resort to physical violence. The most effective weapon in my arsenal is my disapproval. A *really* disappointed expression works wonders.' She peered at him over the rims of her spectacles, those green eyes hardened like emeralds.

He shuddered for effect. 'That is a terrifyingly disappointed look. I'm positively quaking in my boots.'

'It's been known to bring even the most unrepen-

tant miscreants to tears. I can be fearsome when I put my mind to it.'

'Not to me. Now that I know I shan't be beaten if I'm naughty it's given me ideas to thoroughly earn your disapproval.' Rash and stupid ideas, which blessedly aligned with his mission. A mission he was coming to hate because he suddenly hated lying to her.

'Really?' She feigned boredom. 'I'm not in the mood for your infantile flirting, Mr Warriner. You'd do well to stop it now because my mood is quite foul and I can be very shrewish when annoyed, and despite the flirting, my anger is not directed at you, so it wouldn't be fair to let you take the brunt of it. Besides, I'm leaving it to ferment for the real culprit.' She stopped walking abruptly so that she could angle her head to look back at her uncle. Her eyes widened and those eyebrows Jake was becoming quite fluent in disappeared under her hair. 'Oh, for goodness sake!'

At her exasperated tone, Jake followed her stare and saw the Earl of Redditch hoisting himself into the small pillion seat on the back of Rowley's phaeton and making himself thoroughly comfortable.

'I should have known!' She groaned loudly and narrowed her eyes.

'Oh, dear. It does look as if you will be having a table for three at Gunther's.'

'He did it on purpose! The wretch prevented me from spending a perfectly pleasant day at my leisure so that he could foist Redditch on me again! He must have planned it last night at the ball. He wanted us to get *better acquainted* indeed. Every word that comes out of his mouth is a falsehood. I should have trusted my instincts and said no from the outset.' She was

ranting to herself now and pacing around in a small circle, her expressive gloved hand slashing the air like a rapier. 'When is my uncle going to get it into his thick head that I'm not interested in that awful man and resent the interference?'

Outraged she was magnificent. The emerald eyes were stormy behind the lenses of her spectacles, those lush pink lips were pouting and her generous bosom was heaving with each frustrated, angry breath. 'How dare he! He's gone too far this time. Too far…if he thinks he is going dictate to me where I go or to whom I speak, then he has another think coming… He promised me a surprise! I postponed my own plans at his insistence and this is how he repays me?'

Jake shrugged ineffectually because she made a damn good point. The way her uncle was behaving was outrageous and he felt for her. Nobody deserved to have an aged earl thrust upon them as a potential suitor, especially when she had repeatedly voiced her refusal, but some men thought it was acceptable to bully women. Jake's own father had been such a man and had made his mother's life a misery, so, his mission aside, he was predisposed to loathe Rowley.

However, as one of the King's Elite he also needed to closely watch the events play out as the scoundrel intended. The man's sudden interest in both his niece and one of the main investors in the new Regent's Canal was in no way coincidental. The best and most prudent course of action would be to stand back and allow events to naturally unfold. He would be her shoulder to cry on. A sympathetic ear. Whatever was afoot today, duty dictated he should encourage her to go back to her uncle's phaeton and suffer the un-

wanted attentions of a man nearly three times her age. At Gunther's, she might well hear information that unlocked the case.

'Is there something I can do to help, Fliss?' Not the words he meant to say.

She slowly angled her face to his and Jake could see the cogs whirring inside her clever mind. 'Perhaps…' She inhaled deeply, her eyes closing, and appeared to centre herself from somewhere deep within. When her eyes opened, he knew she had made some sort of decision about the best course of action, because they slowly turned towards him and a new resolute defiance was shining back out of them. 'What are your plans for the rest of the day, Mr Warriner?'

'I don't have any.'

'Would you like to see the lions with me?'

'I can think of nothing I would like more.' Jake's pulse quickened. They would be all alone. Together. For hours. Finally, he could properly seduce her just as he'd been tasked.

'Then do you think you can smuggle me out of here without my uncle seeing?'

'As a matter of fact, I do. I excel at skulduggery.' He held out his gloved hand and she took it, causing intense awareness to shimmer through his fingers despite the layers of leather between them. Business and pleasure. Too good an opportunity to waste on both counts. He'd deal with the uncomfortable guilt which had settled in his gut later. 'Follow me.'

Chapter Nine

Wandering towards Traitor's Gate at the Tower of London

Escaping proved to be scandalously thrilling. Inexcusably irresponsible and definitely childish, but more fun than Fliss had had in years. It had been a very long time since she had allowed the precocious and wayward part of her character to run free and to do so for an ill-advised and fleeting afternoon was exactly the right medicine to cure her irritation at her uncle's conniving.

After Jake had hidden her behind his horse, the pair of them had crept out of Hyde Park giggling like children. He'd found a ragged, dubious-looking fellow with an angry scar running down one side of his face and paid him a few coins to take his mount back to his bachelor lodgings, then flagged down a hackney to spirit them to the medieval castle.

The Tower had proved every bit as fascinating as Fliss had hoped and Jake was entertaining company. Together they marvelled at the four ragged lions as

they tore apart fresh meat, gawped at the elephant, stared at snakes, petted some monkeys and tried to invent stories as to why Old Martin, the curmudgeonly grizzly bear, was so bad tempered. Jake had then paid a Beefeater to show them the jewels and take them on a tour around the fortress. The fellow had been so knowledgeable that Fliss's feet were now aching and her head was swimming with interesting facts she was looking forward to sharing with her students. Finally they were left alone to wander freely and Jake was reading from the guide book he had purchased.

'It says here that Queen Elizabeth passed through Traitor's Gate after being accused of treason by her mad sister, Queen Mary. The poor girl was only twenty and must have been terrified. Especially after what happened to her mother.' The Beefeater's story had been particularly graphic as he had recounted the execution of Anne Boleyn on the green by the White Tower. 'I'm glad I wasn't born back then. History is so gruesome, don't you think?'

'The gruesomeness is what makes it so interesting. Poor Elizabeth. Was she a prisoner here for very long?'

Jake consulted the guide book again. 'Eight weeks apparently. Not sure I could stand being incarcerated here for eight hours. I can't imagine how she suffered. I bet your uncle and the Earl of Redditch would find the story riveting, though. Look, it says she was brought to the Tower on a barge.' He grinned. 'The pair of them do get excited about barges. I wonder why?'

His question reminded Fliss she would soon have to go back to her uncle's soulless house and answer for pathetically running away. 'I'd rather not talk about

my uncle just yet.' Although there was no getting away from it really. While she couldn't bring herself to care about Uncle Crispin's feelings, Daphne and Cressida didn't deserve to worry. She would need to apologise to them for causing them undue stress. 'I suppose I should head back. As furious as I am with him, my aunts will be anxious and it'll be dark soon.' February days were too short, she decided. Far too short. 'I still have no idea what I'm going to say to him about his duplicity. It's bound to be ugly.'

Jake picked up her hand and wound it around his arm. 'Hopefully, once his temper has cooled, he'll listen to your objections properly.' They began to stroll towards the gate they had entered a few hours before. 'Perhaps we can rehearse your argument in the carriage?'

'We could.' It couldn't hurt, although Fliss doubted Uncle Crispin would listen. 'Or perhaps I should simply tell him I think it is time for me to return home to Cumbria? I'm tired of his overbearing and dictatorial manner.'

His step slowed briefly and a part of her hoped he would ask her not to leave yet. The silly female part of her which was easily swayed by biology. The part that adored the fact he had singled her out for his attentions among all the other ladies this Season. That same part deflated with disappointment when he made no mention of her leaving. 'I can't even say he's doing it because he cares, Fliss. I suspect he is throwing you at Redditch for his own gain, yet for the life of me I cannot fathom why. There are plenty of wealthy and titled fish in the sea of Mayfair, most of whom don't smell like feet.'

'As you said, he is obsessed with barges, an area in which the Earl of Redditch is a very big fish. I believe I am merely the bait on the hook.' Something Fliss decided right then she needed to clarify with her uncle. Had he really dragged her all the way down the entire length of the country just to tempt a business associate? 'The man leers and ogles me shamelessly, something my uncle is happy to condone because he is so keen to supply those dull barges.'

'Your uncle is a wealthy man and must have many business interests. Maybe something else will suddenly occupy him and distract him from his current fixation with barges. What else does he invest in?'

A laughable question. 'How should I know? As Uncle Crispin barely speaks to me at the best of times, he's hardly going to wax lyrical about his stocks and shares over tea.'

'But you must have some idea? What business, for example, was he discussing in the park this morning? Who are his other business associates?'

'In case it escaped your notice, I was rudely expelled from the phaeton *because* he wanted to talk business. He didn't introduce me to any of the gentlemen he spoke to. Whatever it is he does, he does it very covertly.' Which was a worry.

They had reached the pavement where a line of hackneys waited to pick up the tourists. Jake took his time inspecting all the interiors until he found the cleanest and, to her body's consternation, lifted her into it. His big hands easily spanned her waist and the heat of them seared through the woollen coat and dress, through her stays and seemed to brand her bare skin beneath. It did odd things to her pulse. Be-

cause it took him a minute to apprise the driver of their destination and settle himself in the seat next to her, the rapid knocking of her heart lessened—right up until the moment she felt his hard thigh rest against her softer one. As he appeared unaffected by the contact, stretching out his long legs and crossing both his arms and his booted feet comfortably, Fliss let it pass. There was no point in lecturing him about propriety when this whole outing was vastly improper, yet he had been a perfect gentleman all afternoon. Why, he hadn't bothered flirting once. Something which she bizarrely found rather insulting all of a sudden.

The carriage lurched forward and they watched the Tower shrink through the window in comfortable silence before he turned to her, looking devilishly handsome and more than a little inquisitive. 'What makes you say his business is covert?'

'I don't know. Just a feeling.'

'Most feelings are based on a suspicion of some sort.'

'True.' She angled her body to be able to look at him fully. He was a man effortlessly at ease and the casual, informal way he was lounging suited him even if it did make her skin warm at the sight. 'This morning, for instance. He was being very secretive. And the men he discussed business with didn't seem to be very happy with what my uncle had to say to them.' A common occurrence, apparently. 'Perhaps that is why he chose to apprise them of it all in Hyde Park. Less chance of a scene with so many others looking on.' Another worry. It suggested a deviousness about her uncle which didn't sit right.

'Rotten Row is an odd place to meet to talk about

business, I'll grant you, not when most men tend to discuss it at either their club or in the privacy of their own study.'

'Uncle Crispin doesn't tend to work in his study. From what I can make out he prefers to work in his dressing room. At least that is where his secretary and solicitor tend to be directed when they come to call.' Another odd thing when her uncle had a perfectly good study crammed full of expensive objects to impress. Or were most of his business associates so unsavoury he didn't want them in the main part of house? The only one she had seen had sneaked out the back in the dead of night. 'Although he did meet one man in his study recently. I only know this because my bedchamber is directly situated above it and it's rare to hear anything coming from that quarter—but I was awake.' Thinking about Jake. Fliss made the mistake of glancing into his eyes and almost drowned in the fathomless depths, until the carriage bounced awkwardly, shaking her out of the spell and sending Jake sideways.

'I do believe I've found the worst-sprung hackney in all of London.' To prove his point they rattled over a series of cobbles with such intensity that Fliss had to set her jaw hard to stop her teeth from clattering together. They turned on to a blessedly smoother road and both simultaneous let go of the seat. 'Who was the man?'

'I don't know. A nasty sort.'

'Oh, dear. What about him made you think he was nasty?'

'His manner. He was very...' How best to explain the odd chill she had experienced when she had

watched the altercation in the garden? 'Threatening. The pair of them argued.'

'About?'

'Why does it matter?'

'I'm simply curious. I did warn you I was a nosy fellow.'

He said it with such nonchalance, but his pupils constricted. Fliss was sure of it. He was lying. It gave her pause. 'Why don't we change the subject? All this talk about my uncle is spoiling what has been a thoroughly lovely day.' If her instinct was correct, he would try to direct the conversation back to her uncle.

He'd pushed her too far too quickly. Her brows had set in a straight line like a barrier. Fliss was too smart to blindly impart personal family information without questioning why a virtual stranger would feel inclined to ask. He and Lord Fennimore would just have to make do with the interesting snippets she had let slip so far. And they were interesting. How had the mystery man got into Rowley's house late at night when Leatham had all entrances on close watch? At least they knew why Flint had never found anything in the study. They hit more painful cobbles which made him wince. 'Let's talk about *Sister* Ursuline's. That sounds scarily like a convent.'

Her golden brows twitched, a sign she suddenly doubted herself, but she was searching his face a little too intently for comfort. Thank goodness he'd had the wherewithal to stop probing when he had. 'It is a convent of sorts, although Sister Ursuline is the only nun in residence, but it's not attached to any church. It's a boarding school for wayward girls.'

'And how did you come to be a prim and proper schoolmistress in a school for wayward girls?'

'I grew up there.'

'You were a wayward girl?'

'I prefer precocious. I'll admit to being a precocious girl. After my mother died, that is, and I was all alone in the world. Sister Ursuline's is my home so it was a natural evolution to go from being a student to a teacher when I became old enough.'

That all sounded rather sad and lonely to Jake. While his own parents had had little involvement in his rearing, at least he'd always had the strong and loving bond of his three brothers growing up. 'I'm sorry. I didn't realise you were an orphan.' One Crispin Rowley had left all alone until it suited his plans to claim her as kin.

'I wasn't an orphan.' Her face changed. Acceptance. She wasn't bitter or angry, merely matter of fact, then a tiny nerve twitched in her brow line and Jake saw the matter-of-fact acceptance was an act. It bothered her. 'My father outlived my mother by another decade, but he was ill equipped to be a parent and, as I have just admitted, I was a tad precocious, so I was sent away. As it turned out, his decision was for the best as I doubt I'd have grown into the woman I am today without the guiding wisdom of Sister Ursuline. She has been both a mentor and a surrogate mother to me all these years.'

'Your father abandoned you!' The sudden surge of anger at yet another example of shocking fatherhood made his voice louder and more forceful than Jake would have liked—but it was an honest emotion and one she seemed to appreciate. She patted

his hand and smiled wistfully, trying to hide the pain in her eyes.

'He did—but practically upon birth. I rarely saw him growing up so his loss in my life was hardly a great deprivation. You should also probably know that I had a very happy life at Sister Ursuline's. I had friends and a nice place to live. She might be a nun, but she is not a conventional one.' The wistful expression changed to one of mischief as she grinned. 'She took Holy Orders at the age of forty-two and only after a scandalously successful career as a courtesan.'

'A courtesan?' Jake hadn't expected that and the bark of laughter surprised him.

'Yes, indeed. She was gently bred, but exceedingly wayward. So wayward her family despaired and eventually threw her out. But Sister Ursuline is indomitable and made the best of her situation. She was mistress to some very powerful men and accumulated a small fortune on the back of it. Money she used to build her school and help other spirited girls avoid making the same mistakes she did. Girls who would also have been abandoned if she hadn't have provided their families with a suitable institution to send them to, to help them curb their wayward ways.'

'While I respect your Sister Ursuline for taking on the burden, a part of me cannot help feeling angry that those families have abdicated their responsibility.' Like hers. And exactly like his parents, although they were at least there in body if not in spirit.

'I couldn't agree more, but that doesn't detract from the awful reality. Sister Ursuline's has provided the love and guidance missing in many a precocious girl's life. Mine included. I suppose I was a difficult girl,

but Sister Ursuline helped me to control my impulses without weakening my spirit. She taught me to be self-sufficient, resilient and resourceful. Three skills a woman alone in the world needs more than any others. It was an honour to be able to give something back and I enjoy being a teacher.' She shrugged and he realised she had been in the exact same boat as the girls she now taught. Her own kith and kin had offloaded her elsewhere and then had quickly forgotten about her. Both her father and her uncle had abandoned her. All his brothers despaired of Jake's rakish way of life, but they would never cast him out. He was loved. Always had been. He also had always had a proper home to anchor him, one that drew him more and more with each passing day away. What must it feel like to have no one? Was it any wonder Fliss was fiercely independent? She'd had to be. She'd made the best of the poor hand life had dealt her, just as he and all his brothers had, but she had done it all alone from the tender age of ten. The knowledge humbled him.

'Sister Ursuline sounds like a wonderful person.'

'She is. As you would expect for someone with such a colourful history, her stories are hugely entertaining, and because of her background her advice is relevant. She speaks from practical experience and is sympathetic to human weaknesses. Perhaps sometimes too sympathetic as she is prone to forgive most when they have not proved their worth. Of course, very few know about her past outside the walls of the school, so I would ask you to keep it a secret, but she was a wonderful person to grow up with. I admire her tenacity and her outlook on life. She has a great sense of fun and an annoying habit of seeing the good

in all people. I suppose that comes from the depth of her faith, which sadly I do not share. I am neither as trusting nor as forgiving.'

'Not a bad thing in this day and age.' Although a very bad thing for a rake like Jake. Seducing Fliss was proving to be a challenge because of exactly that. 'Beware those wolves in sheep's clothing.' Which was exactly what Jake was; an uncomfortable truth that was leaving an increasingly bad taste in the mouth.

She turned and stared at him. 'Thank you. Sister Ursuline says I am in danger of becoming a cynic, but I think caution is prudent when dealing with new people. I find few who live up to my high expectations.'

'Spoken like a true cynic with the highest of expectations.'

'Unlike Sister Ursuline, I have *realistic* expectations. Some people can't change, or won't, and it's better to accept that about them than hold out futile hope they will improve. If calling a spade a spade makes me a cynic, then I am one and gladly so. It is quite possible to still like a person and be mindful or wary of their character flaws. Let's take you, for example. I dare say a blossoming friendship between a scandalous rake and a schoolmistress from a convent is unconventional, but because I recognise and accept your flaws I can still thoroughly enjoy your company while remaining gloriously immune to your obvious charms.'

A comment which certainly put Jake in his place, although it was probably not meant to. She had called him a philanderer on their first meeting, a label which grated but was deserved. Something this canny, ill-treated northern lass was obviously very mindful of.

He should be grateful that she at least liked him despite that glaring character flaw—but he wasn't. 'My obvious charms will grow on you.' Or at least he hoped they would. Regardless of King and country, he still wanted to seduce her for himself. Fliss was becoming an itch which he couldn't scratch. 'I am famously irresistible to all women.'

Chapter Ten

Bouncing in a hackney through the city

'And yet here I am, resisting you.' One wheel hit a pothole and she groped for the strap to steady herself as it bounced out, forcing Jake to watch certain parts of her bounce as well. 'Gracious, this *is* a dreadful carriage!'

He grabbed his own strap as the tired, corroded springs did little to stop the shoddy road surface rattling his bones. 'You'd think in a city as rich as this one they could manage to make a decent road... Ah, look! We're passing St Paul's.' Jake put his hand up to point, then instantly used it to brace himself on the seat as they rumbled along possibly the worst stretch of road in the whole capital.

As she stared out at the massive cathedral in wonder, he took the opportunity to move closer, ostensibly to point things out, but more because the sight of one of England's greatest edifices reminded him that he was supposed to be seducing vital information out of her. 'Did you know it is the fourth St Paul's to sit

on the site? The first was built over a thousand years ago, some time after the Romans left.'

'Really?' Her head whipped around to grin at him, then quickly returned to the building. 'You truly are a font of knowledge on the history of London, Jake.' It was the first time she had used his name and he liked the sound of it on her lips.

'Everybody knows this building was designed by Wren, but few know he was still designing it even as it was being built. Especially the dome. He wanted to create the dome without any visible supports inside. You should see it. It's a shame we have run out of time today as I would love to show you around it. We could climb up to the top and whisper at each other across the gallery.'

'I'd love to.' She turned her head and he recognised the instant she became aware of his close proximity, because she unconsciously licked her lips and looked down at her hands. 'I'd have to bring Cressida and Daphne, of course. Today has been highly improper.'

If that was intended as his cue to move back to his side of the seat, Jake skilfully ignored it. 'Hardly improper. I've been a perfect gentleman. Why, I've barely even flirted.' But there were other ways to flirt which required no words and his eyes were currently gazing deeply into hers. 'But we have laughed a lot, haven't we?' Humour was another excellent way of cutting through a lady's defences. Jake had laughed a few into his bed in his time, too. A goodly few.

She smiled at him and began to relax in the seat. 'It has been a perfectly lovely after— *Ooh*!' The hackney lunged to the right and tilted, sending Fliss sliding across the bench towards him. Jake only just caught

her before they both slammed into the side, her forehead bashing against his chin and making him cry out.

'I'm so sorry!' As she looked up at him, her spectacles were dangling at an odd angle on her face. The engaging sight did a great deal to alleviate the brief, sharp pain of bone hitting bone. Because she wasn't looking through the lenses, she instinctively leaned nearer to see if he was hurt. 'Are you bleeding?'

'No. No, I'm fine.'

A lie. Being so close to her was playing havoc with his senses. That perfume—fat summer roses, fresh air and sunshine—so uniquely her and divine. Those stormy-green, short-sighted eyes. The honey-gold hair. Those damned erotic spectacles which haunted his dreams. Everything made his body yearn and his heart pump. Her fingers touched his lip. If ever fate had presented him with the perfect opportunity to kiss her, this was it. Yet he hesitated, feeling suddenly awkward.

'Are you sure? I gave you quite a clonk.' And now she was torturing him. The sensitive skin tingled beneath her gentle touch, her face inches from his as she studied his mouth.

'I have a very hard head.' Gentlemanly good manners dictated he didn't tell her which part of him was currently harder. Jake stifled the groan. His fingers went to the spectacles and righted them, then simply stared at her mouth.

Longingly.

He wanted to kiss her. Desperately wanted to kiss her. Slowly he moved his face closer, watched her lips part. Was she game?

Perhaps.

Her eyes drifted to his mouth again. She didn't move away.

Good grief, why was he lingering? His mission dictated he should jolly well get on with it... The bad taste and the uncharacteristic guilt churning in his gut made him sit back instead. She deserved better. Honesty at least. A sobering thought for a man who made a living from lying. 'I have a very stiff upper lip.' As well as a stiff bulge in his breeches. 'I'm sorry for my appalling choice of hackney...still at least it's an adventure. Of sorts.'

'It is that.' He watched her blink, her long lashes and fine eyes making his heart stutter. 'I hope we survive it. Being shaken to death in a hackney is not how I had planned on leaving this mortal coil.' She was so very beautiful he found himself looking away because he couldn't think of a single sensible thing to say which did not make him sound gauche. Not a single witticism sprung to mind. No flattering words. Nothing flirtatious. Just nothing. The memorised script of seduction had disappeared out of his mind, or been buried under a whole swathe of new thoughts. Questioning thoughts which had him second-guessing himself. Jake had never felt so strange in his own skin. It was as if it didn't fit. There were at least another twenty minutes till they arrived in Mayfair. Twenty painful, awkward minutes now that he had apparently lost his ability for seduction thanks to the distasteful flavour of his deception.

Perhaps if she hadn't told him about her lonely past and perhaps if he didn't genuinely yearn to have her for himself, Fliss would be just another mission for King and country. Somewhere along the way he had

developed both a conscience and she had thoroughly charmed him when he had failed so spectacularly in charming her. When had that happened?

Admitting momentary defeat, Jake shifted his bottom back to his side of the bench. 'Tell me about your work at the convent. What is your favourite subject to teach?'

It was easier to let her talk than to attempt to do what he had been sent to do. All the while she was talking about her love of books, Jake pondered his odd mood and his odder growing attachment to the bespectacled woman sat next to him. While she might not have any messy feelings for him, he had some for her. That was a revelation. Feelings that made his heart both ache as well as soar and which had sneaked up on him when he hadn't been looking. Warm and comforting feelings. A sense of rightness. Of wonder and excitement. Complicated feelings which were unlike anything he'd encountered and not entirely as abhorrent as he had always assumed such attachments would be. It was more than a desire to know her better or to lose himself in her body. Among those familiar feelings lurked others.

A need to protect. The last place Jake wanted to deliver her back to was Rowley's house in Mayfair—yet that was exactly where the British government needed her to be. There was also a worryingly possessive edge to it. He didn't want her being used by her uncle any more than he wanted her to spend her life hidden in a convent making the best of the hand that fate had dealt her. He wanted Fliss to have a wonderful life, filled with laughter and family and the sense of belonging she deserved to have. The woman needed a family of

her own. An adoring husband. A dependable, solid man of impeccable morals. Someone who recognised the precious jewel he had married and who spent the rest of his days living just to see her smile—except thinking about that faceless, lucky fellow filled his head with rage and irrational jealousy.

Now there was a thought. Possessiveness, the primal need to protect and irrational male jealousy were all emotions Jake had witnessed his brothers experience for the three women they had chosen to spend eternity with. Those and *romantic* love, of course. Jack, Jamie and Joe were all hopelessly in love with their women, too, the sort of love which transcended sibling love. All-consuming and passionate love, but in their case it had not turned malignant. Was it too risky to allow himself the same luxury? Probably. Because he knew there was a little too much of his father in him for comfort and he did have the reliable habit of disappointing people. Horrifically.

And now he could add maudlin to the awful yearning which had apparently numbed his powers of seduction.

Capital.

With Fliss, it seemed, he was doomed to fail on that score for ever.

If he could temper his odd feelings with the reassuring certainty that he was seducing Fliss with for ever on his mind, secure in the knowledge that he would never let her down with his own inherited selfishness, then he would seduce her now. Guilt free. And he'd put himself immediately out of his self-imposed misery. But Jake could never be guilt-free any more than he could fail to be a disappointment. Reliably unreliable

Warriners, of which he was merely one in a very long line, couldn't be trusted with the happiness of others. Especially when they were out to seduce them under false pretences in the first place.

'Oh, no!' They hit another unforgiving road of cobbles and Fliss giggled as she was thrown about the carriage. 'This driver should supply his passengers with anchors, or something.' Being lighter and shorter than him, the poor thing did seem to be bearing the brunt of his shocking choice of carriage.

'Here—let me help.' Jake wound his arm firmly about her shoulders and used some of his weight to hold her down, frantically trying to ignore how utterly wonderful she felt against him and how desperately he wanted to kiss her. 'When we visit St Paul's we'll take a smelly hackney and some nosegays.'

She giggled again. 'You do make me smile, Jake.' That smile rendered all the maudlin regrets temporarily forgotten and he chuckled alongside her. That smile, the warmth of her body next to him, the inexplicable lightness in his chest and the perfect feel of her beneath his arm proved to be his undoing. Lord, she was lovely. Just this innocent touch fired his body and soothed his aching heart. Made him temporarily forget all the reasons why he shouldn't be listening to his heart.

'Berkeley Square!' The driver's shout accompanied the sudden jolt as the carriage began to slow.

Reluctantly he let go of her, internally cursing the swiftness of the journey while simultaneously thankful he had resisted. Because if he hadn't then he knew that a mere kiss would be more than a mere kiss. It would be the start of something he didn't have the

strength to stop. A path he was too terrified to go down, yet so very tempted to that denying himself hurt. Deep in his chest. Dangerously in the vicinity of his black heart. Fliss reached for her small reticule and clutched it in both hands as she turned to him. Her smile this time was wistful.

'Thank you for today. For everything. Thank heavens you happened to be in Hyde Park this morning. You do have an uncanny knack of being in exactly the right place at exactly the right time. At times, you almost seem dependable.'

'Perhaps fate is trying to tell us something?' Something certainly seemed to want to tell him something. Jake was feeling decidedly off-kilter and didn't give a damn.

'I don't believe in fate. Coincidence, perhaps. But even so, today has been the best fun I have had since arriving in London.'

'It's been the most fun I've had in months. Years, probably.' As soon as he said them, he realised the words were true. Somewhere along the line he had become jaded and his profession as a seducer had become dull. Each seduction a memorised routine offering little challenge and culminating in less and less satisfaction. But then Jake usually only offered his body and kept his heart guarded. It had never beat with such purpose before, or stuttered in his chest because of a pair of wonky spectacles or a smile as bright and as therapeutic as warm summer sunshine. 'Don't go back to Cumbria yet.' An odd knot formed in his throat. Jake would be bereft if she left now. Perhaps even heartbroken.

Definitely heartbroken.

Her green eyes gazed deeply into his to see if the words were sincere and he saw the exact moment that she did. 'Oh, Jake…' Perhaps because it was now as necessary as breathing, his head dipped of its own accord this time. Jake had no control over it. He didn't recall a Lord Fennimore, or a Crispin Rowley or his well-used seducer's arsenal or his parents' toxic love. Instead, nature and the overwhelming rightness of Fliss guided his actions. His nose gently brushed hers. He nuzzled her cheek. Then he surrendered to the uncontrollable need to taste her.

By his usual standards it was a clumsy kiss. A little too eager. A little too fast and too loaded with meaning, but all the sweeter for it. The kiss was innocently soft, for both his own sanity and because he was too busy glorying in the perfection of the moment to push for more. Gentle and tender somehow seemed right as this was not a seduction, it was an exploration. An overture from his foolish, wary heart to hers. To see if it might miraculously want more, too, despite both their better judgements, but the moment her lips responded he was ablaze. The simple, chaste kiss became more significant than any other before. Obliterated all previous kisses and conquests completely from his memory until there were no other kisses. Had never been any other conquests. It wasn't the master seducer who was kissing Fliss. It was just Jake.

Heart and soul.

She tasted of ripe summer peaches, but was as intoxicating and as addictive as absinthe. Fliss melted against him, sighing into his mouth and splaying her hands on his chest to steady them as the dusty carriage shuddered to a stop. It shouldn't have been perfect,

but it was. It shouldn't have felt right, but it did. His aching heart swelled with the knowledge that this— right here and right now—was suddenly everything.

It took all his strength to pull away, but when he did, he was glad. Those lush, plump lips were parted. Her lovely eyes were wide and had darkened with desire. He knew women too well to confuse it with anything else. She wanted him and he wanted her. It was that simple and that wonderful. Whatever battle they had been waging was lost, yet Jake had no idea quite who the victor was. He traced the soft curve of her cheek with the pad of one finger, drinking in the wholly wonderful sight of her undone.

'That was a mistake.' Her voice was breathy, her chest rising and falling erratically. Those green eyes saying the exact opposite to her canny northern mouth.

'No, it wasn't.' He cupped her cheek with his palm and allowed himself to drown in her gorgeous eyes. 'It was inevitable. Fate.' As if drawn by some magical force they both inched together again. As their lips almost touched, Fliss broke the spell by scrambling across the seat.

'I should go. Aunt Daphne and Cressida will be worried.' Her clumsy fingers wrestled ineffectually with the latch.

'Let me help you.' He placed his hand possessively in the small of her back and she leapt away as if burned.

'No, thank you. I can manage.' The door swung open and she practically fell out on to the street, then tried, and failed, to compose herself. 'Thank you again for…saving me earlier. And for today…and…and… Goodbye, Mr Warriner.'

At the formal use of the word *mister* her eyes flicked to his lips again. He watched her swallow nervously, noting the becoming warm flush which heated her cheeks. She was flustered, but not angry. A little baffled, yet clearly stunned by her equally enthusiastic part in the proceedings. Her eyes finally sought out his in question and she stared for a few seconds incredulous, gloriously lost for words for once and that made him happy because he felt the same. A little baffled. A little giddy. Almost drunk with the power of it all. When her words came, they came in a squeak.

'You're incorrigible.'

'Yes, I am...but you like me anyway.' She didn't deny it. 'I've reserved an alcove at Almack's tomorrow. I shall see you there.' Nor did she answer. But she turned and scurried off, clumsily tripping over her own feet in her hurry to run away, emphasising how rattled she felt.

It mirrored Jake's own feelings. He was beyond rattled, yet strangely happily so and couldn't say why. He sat contentedly and watched her lovely bottom sway in time to her marching and allowed himself a satisfied smile. Fliss was neither prim nor proper, nor was she as immune to his charms as she repeatedly claimed and rather bizarrely, rattled or not, more than a little bit scared by it all, Jake was suddenly looking forward to Almack's for the first time in his life.

Chapter Eleven

Changing for another smelly dinner with the Earl

'Where is my blue gown?' Fliss didn't own many outfits, but the blue watered silk was her best dress and she wanted to wear her own clothes for tonight's ball, rather than any from the new wardrobe she had been gifted. Those bold clothes did not feel like hers. The day dresses were cut too close to hug her figure and the evening gowns, although stunning, were more daring than she felt comfortable with. Comfortable being the operative word, as she hadn't felt anything close in over twenty-four hours and was desperate to restore some equilibrium to her own off-kilter biology. Thanks to Jake, and a very foolhardy kiss, her natural, primal, carnal urges were creating chaos within her body.

Even the new shift she was stood in wasn't helping. The gossamer fabric was practically translucent and did little to cover her modesty, but as it was the only garment the young maid had brought to her after her bath, Fliss had had no choice other than to put it on

while her hair was dressed. It did serve to make her supremely conscious of her needy body though. Each time the wispy fabric whispered against the tips of her breasts, a fresh wave of desire coursed through her which inevitably led to her reliving that splendid kiss over and over again. In her own clothes, Fliss would feel more like herself, or at least she hoped she would, rather than this shamelessly wanton stranger who currently occupied her skin.

If only she wasn't so tempted. Sorely tempted. Not that she had any doubts about the unreliability of the man. Gracious, no. Fliss's feet were still firmly on the ground despite the lure of those twinkling stars in his eyes. Jake Warriner was a bad bet if ever there was one. However, she was not looking for for ever. Not in her wildest dreams would she contemplate such nonsense with a man like him but... Surely there was no harm in a mild flirtation? A tiny romantic adventure with a man who her instincts told her was noble and trustworthy despite his shocking reputation. A man who called himself a disappointment, but seemed angry to be one. A man who had the uncanny knack of being in just the right place at just the right time, saving her from her uncle's meddling or her own maudlin thoughts. That peculiar jolt of awareness she experienced whenever he was close by was as comforting as it was alarming. A man she was coming to suspect might be one she could truly depend on. All the time. Or at least her heart hoped he was. She was honest enough with herself to admit that. Perhaps it *was* fate that had decided Jake was destined to be Fliss's knight in shining armour? Her lips tingled in anticipation at the prospect.

Fate! Destiny! Knights! What in heaven's name was the matter with her to be so…so…ripe for the taking? She knew better than to kiss a rake. Or at least she had always believed she did. Until she had succumbed to one and now couldn't get the dratted kiss out of her mind. 'I need to wear my blue gown.' As both a reminder of who she truly was and as armour.

Her maid's eyes dropped guiltily to the floor. 'I believe it has been sent to be laundered, miss. I have taken the liberty of laying out a gown already for this evening.'

Fliss had just seen it and heartily disapproved. The emerald-green taffeta was scandalously low at the front and significantly lower in the back. She would feel practically naked from the waist up in that thing, especially if Jake Warriner saw her in it. Already that man had taken enough liberties with her person—or at least he had in her fevered dreams where she had happily let him because that one kiss had apparently set her fevered body into a carnal frenzy. 'If I remember correctly, Kitty, you said exactly the same thing the other night despite the fact it didn't need cleaning in the first place. I fail to believe that the laundry takes so long in a household of this size.'

Fliss couldn't leave a room without crashing into a giant footman. One in particular seemed to follow her everywhere. Uncle Crispin had more staff than one bachelor who usually lived alone could possibly need. He had ten maids that Fliss knew of and a veritable army of footmen and even with the addition of her aunts and herself as temporary guests, that was excessive. A cool draught made her newly wanton nipples harden further and she crossed her arms over them

in case the maid saw. 'Go and retrieve it, please.' The blue silk would cover up most of her suddenly heavy, over-sensitive bosom.

The maid hesitated and then shook her head. 'I'm sorry, miss, but his lordship has instructed that you must wear one of your new gowns tonight.'

'Has he now?' The very idea was preposterous after yesterday—unless her uncle desperately wanted a tongue lashing. He was certainly due one. 'I'm afraid his lordship has no say in my attire. In fact, now that I consider it, I think I would prefer to wear something warmer tonight.' Something that didn't make her feel bold and attractive and ripe. Something which might encourage her dashing rake to lose interest and the wanton peaks under the scandalous chemise to flatten.

Her dashing rake! Gracious. This was getting dangerously out of hand.

If her blue silk was missing, then Fliss would jolly well turn up for dinner and the subsequent ball in one of her plain day dresses. A very warm one over layer upon layer of sensible underthings. Actions *had* been speaking louder than words for days now, so much so she was beginning to enjoy watching her uncle's mouth set into a disapproving line.

It was the only communication they seemed to share which he listened to, but at least he noticed her, which had to account for something. Yesterday he had been furious when she had returned home, somewhat flushed thanks to her indiscretion, but still buoyed from her rebellion. They had exchanged words. His had been angry, hers had been matter of fact.

'I am my own mistress, Uncle Crispin, and I shall do as I please with or without your permission. If

that causes you a problem, I am happy to curtail my visit here.'

When he stormed off, Fliss knew she had won. She had refused to tell him where she had gone and who she had been with. She wouldn't make Jake take the blame when the decision to leave Rotten Row had been hers and hers alone. That, and a tiny part of her, a part wholly ruled by her reckless biology, didn't want to alert her uncle to any potential chance liaisons in deserted alcoves in the future. Or tonight as Jake had suggested...

And she was doing it again! Thinking of Jake when she was supposed to be cleansing him and her momentary lapse in judgement from her mind. It was just a kiss, for pity's sake, and certainly not her first. Hardly something to get so worked up about. She would brush it off just as she had his flirting. Just as she had brushed off countless similar overtures from gentlemen in the past. A meaningless kiss meant nothing, after all. Although if she was brutally honest with herself, which of course she always was, this one felt entirely different. Worryingly different. All-consuming and gloriously different. The exact opposite of meaningless.

Why was that?

'What about the pink gown, miss?' The flustered maid's face matched it in colour as she dragged another wholly inappropriate dress out of the wardrobe. 'I think Madame Devy has excelled herself with this one. I love the ruffles around the neckline.'

So did Fliss. 'If only the ruffles hid more from lecherous, old eyes, then perhaps I might consider it.' Appreciative, twinkling blue ones, for instance, she didn't

mind at all. Which was a great part of the problem. Being friends with Jake Warriner and being attracted to the scoundrel was a totally different, and entirely unsatisfactory, kettle of fish. Jake the Rake Warriner was too much like all the men who had waylaid all the wayward girls at the convent. The sort of man Sister Ursuline had been tempted by. The sort of man who had seduced her normally sensible mother and doomed her to a lifetime of marital disappointment. Jake was a charmer and a philanderer, entirely not the sort of man she would ever allow herself to become romantically involved with. She had more sense than all those wayward girls. More sense than her mother and certainly far more than Sister Ursuline had ever had in her youth. She would continue to learn by example, not from personal experience. She had to fight this unwelcome and visceral attraction for the sake of her own sanity, as falling for a rake, even a noble, and entertaining one, could never end well.

Fliss stalked over to the wardrobe and began to rifle through it for a suitable garment to inform Uncle Crispin he had no authority over her appearance any more than he could control her movements.

Not one of her dresses was there.

'Where are my clothes, Kitty? The ones I brought with me from Cumbria.'

'I can't say that I know, miss.' The young girl couldn't meet her eye, a sure sign she did know. 'Perhaps they are all being laundered?'

'My uncle has had them removed, hasn't he?' His petty revenge for her rebellion yesterday. Another way to assert his dominance over her when all else thus far had failed. How typical he would use the contents

of her wardrobe! His annoyance at the simple ensemble she had worn to Rotten Row had been evident in his expression from the outset and he had once again made a huge fuss about her insistence on wearing her spectacles. Spectacles she'd had the foresight to wear to read in the bath this evening, else they would probably have been sent to the *laundry* as well.

'I couldn't say, miss.'

The maid looked close to tears, but they both knew all her clothes had been in there this morning. Neatly organised according to the occasion. Gone were her favourite walking boots, the heavy wool pelisse she wore when climbing the Cumbrian hills, her favourite long-sleeved day dresses and sensible, soft slippers. The plain, navy outfit she had worn to Rotten Row and foolishly kissed Jake in. In their stead were an array of more new gowns stitched by the sought-after Madame Devy—because all the very best ladies in Mayfair wore Devy—but Fliss wouldn't any more on principle.

Uncle Crispin must have paid the modiste handsomely to have sewn an entire new wardrobe in less than ten days, but while the gowns were intended to turn heads Fliss had no desire to be the body stuffed inside them. Not when that body appeared to turn Jake's head as much as his turned hers. And certainly not when they made an old lecher like Redditch drool—her uncle's only reason for insisting she wear them in the first place!

As the anger bubbled, she rummaged beneath the rows of strange new shoes, heeled boots and the rainbow of satin slippers dyed to match the fashionable and revealing gowns and huffed out a sigh of relief

when she found the sturdy wooden box. At least that was still there.

Regardless, she still checked the precious contents inside. Her mother's few items of paste jewellery had been spared the cull, worthless to most but priceless to Fliss. As had her embroidered handkerchief, made by her mother's hand as a present for her only daughter in the final months of her life, and the small bundle of letters tied in a pink ribbon were exactly as she had left them. The last things Fliss owned which connected her to her past. But the purse containing her money was gone. It wasn't a great deal of money, enough to buy her passage back to Cumbria and to cover emergencies, but having none made her financially dependent on her uncle and conveniently trapped here until he deemed otherwise.

The rage was instantaneous. 'Did he steal my money as well, Kitty?'

'I don't know, miss.' The girl was already backing away towards the door, her eyes wide and guilty.

'Kitty!'

The maid bolted and Fliss went to go after her, but then remembered she was wearing nought but a see-through shift and there was bound to be a footman hovering close by. There was *always* a footman hovering close by. If her uncle seriously thought she would take this outrage lying down, he was vastly mistaken and his actions could go to hell. Tonight, they would be sharing more words. The final words ever to be uttered on the subject, or so help her God.

She snatched the green dress off the bed and hastily stepped into it. Like a woman possessed she wrestled with the difficult laces down the back and tugged

up the scandalous neckline as far as she could before stuffing her feet into the matching jewelled slippers, grabbing her spectacles in her clenched fist and stomping out of the room.

It made no difference that she had dispensed with the need to truss herself into a corset or that she had neglected to put on stockings. The clothes would not be on long enough to matter once she had put dear Uncle Crispin firmly in his place, then she would leave this godforsaken town, with its dictatorial relatives and tempting rascals, and never come back. She had tried to be part of the family. However, as far as her dear, matchmaking and aloof uncle was concerned, Fliss did all the trying. His sole mission was apparently to see her decorated like a mannequin for the lascivious entertainment of an old man.

'Where is he?'

The burly footman stood like a sentry in the hallway was startled by her venomous tone and nervously gestured towards the dining room. She slammed open the door without knocking. At least twenty faces stared back at her curiously. Patently there were more guests than merely Redditch tonight. Another unwelcome surprise in a day full of them.

'There you are, Felicity.' He smiled genially to the rest of the predominately male table. 'Didn't I tell you all that my niece was a beauty?'

At least six of the men ogled her shamelessly. One of them was the Earl of Redditch. 'She is a beauty, indeed. May I be the first to ask you for a dance at Almack's this evening, Miss Felicity?' His eyes dropped to her unrestrained bosom and feasted. She should have put on the corset. Her bare breasts felt exposed

under the thin material of the gown and above the low bodice. She clamped her arms over them and patently ignored the request.

'Might I have a word, Uncle?' Her tone was brittle, but her glare was granite. 'In private.'

'Not at the moment, Felicity. Dinner is about to be served and our guests have waited long enough for you to finish your *toilette*.' He turned to the handsome blond man at his right. A man she had seen a number of times in her uncle's circle, but whose name she hadn't bothered remembering. 'Young ladies and their vanity. Felicity always likes to look her best. A splendid attribute in a woman, I think you'll agree. Who doesn't enjoy a tempting morsel at dinner, Flint?' He winked and a couple of the men laughed.

'I'm afraid I must insist, Uncle.'

His eyes locked with hers with such cold intensity that for a moment she wavered. He suddenly scared her, but her pride wouldn't allow him to see it. He stood, tossed his napkin down and apologised to his guests. 'We shall only be a moment. In the meantime, enjoy the first course.' The well-trained servants snapped to attention, serving the soup as her uncle stalked past her with such speed he caused a small gust of wind as he headed towards his study.

Once Fliss was inside he closed the door. 'You have caused a scene.'

'You have stolen my clothes and my money.'

'I have bought you new clothes. More suitable ones. I will not have the *ton* gossiping about my niece's woeful attire. It reflects badly on me. Most young ladies would be grateful at the generosity.'

'I am grateful.' Hard to say with her teeth grinding.

'You have been *most* generous.' With his money, at least. 'However, that does not give you the right to take my things or dictate how I must dress, any more than it gives you the right to dictate my every movement. Your overbearingness is spoiling my visit. I should like the items back immediately.'

'Impossible, I'm afraid. When I saw the sorry state of those garments, I had them donated to the poor.'

How dare he! Her outrage returned and served to dim her new fearlessness. 'They were not yours to donate.'

He shrugged unapologetically. 'What is done cannot be undone. Thankfully you have an extensive collection of ridiculously expensive new gowns to make up for the loss, so I feel no guilt. The new clothes are yours to do what you want with. I shall not *dictate* which you wear as all of them are appropriate for a woman of your status.'

'Status! I have no care for status. Where is my money?'

'I know nothing about that.' He was lying. Nothing about his expression hinted at it, but Fliss felt it deep in her soul. Uncle Crispin was a man with a casual relationship with the truth. A consummate and compulsive liar. Another thing she had no evidence of, but felt inside.

'How convenient. You had my bedchamber stripped of every stitch of clothing and every shoe I own in petty revenge for yesterday, yet you have no knowledge of the coins hidden in the same wardrobe?'

His pale grey eyes pinned hers and Fliss wanted to shudder. Cruel. That was the first adjective which came to her and once that thought took root, she won-

dered why she had not seen it before. He was more than merely cold. Cruel, callous and calculated. If eyes were indeed the windows of the soul, then his soul was tainted. He was not a nice man and neither was he one to mess with. She knew that with the same certainty she now knew accepting his invitation to stay had been a big mistake.

'I have no need of a paltry few coins, Felicity, and I resent the implication. One of the servants must have taken them. Your maid, perhaps? I shall have her dismissed.'

'Kitty didn't take my money. You did. What I want to know is *why* you took it.'

He exhaled as if greatly put upon. 'Have I not provided for your every need, Felicity? Do you doubt that I will continue to indulge you? Tell me what you need and I shall buy it for you.'

'I do not want *your* money. I want *my* money. And as soon as I get it, I am going home.'

'A tad melodramatic for a petty theft, don't you think?'

'Not when the thief is family. I've put up with your dictatorial and stand-offish manner, put up with your flagrant attempts at matchmaking and the way you have used my good nature to dominate my time and force me to follow your agenda, but this time you have gone too far. You have no jurisdiction over me, Uncle Crispin. None. I am not beholden to you, or anyone, for anything. Yet here, I am bullied into dressing how you want, attending the entertainments you deem fitting and degraded again in front of your cronies.'

'Degraded? My, you have you mother's flair for the dramatic, Felicity.'

'Yes! Degraded. In front of Redditch, and those other men just now, you reduced me from person to a piece of...of...' Was meat too extreme? 'Visual entertainment.'

He didn't bother looking affronted, his features remaining impassive and cold. 'I am a man of business, Felicity. I do what is necessary to expand that business successfully. Hence I host dinners, flatter and fawn over my guests and, from time to time, I see no harm in providing them with—what did you call it? *Visual entertainment.* A pretty face, some mild flirting and the tantalising promise of more can help facilitate that. I fail to see why it offends you so.'

Where to start?

'For twenty-five years we have been estranged—and that is of your making, Uncle, not mine. I wrote to you for years and every letter went unanswered. What gives you the right to feel as if you can have any say in my life now?'

'I am trying to make amends, Felicity. The new clothes are surely evidence of my desire to atone for all the years I couldn't provide for you as I had promised your mother I would.'

Once again he was using her mother to justify his actions. 'I don't believe you. This house, all this opulence, these are things you have enjoyed for a goodly few years. Yet in all that time you failed to make any contact at all. Now, suddenly, we are family because it suits your ends and you use my mother's apparent words to bend me to your will. But you don't care about my mother's last wishes. Admit it, you dragged me here for Redditch, didn't you?' His flat stare confirmed she had hit the nail on the head. 'You did!

You brought me here to be paraded in front of that old lecher...'

'Is your tantrum done?' He made to walk away and she pulled on his arm.

'My *tantrum*? You are attempting to use me to further *your* business. I am your only niece, yet I am to be bartered for a few *barges*. Have you no heart? No shame? If my mother was alive...'

Uncle Crispin turned to her, his face an ugly mask of pure malice. 'Your mother was a fool. With her beauty, she could have had any man she chose. She could have married sensibly and hauled our family out of debt in the process. Instead she shamed herself with a penniless scoundrel and wasted her God-given gifts on a wastrel with no thought for me. I couldn't give a damn about what she might think of me now!' Hearing her beloved mother so shockingly maligned stunned Fliss into silence. While she had known the half-siblings were not close, she had never realised her mother's brother had resented her. Hated her even, if his hideous expression was to be believed. 'While I was delighted to learn you were the spitting image of your mother, I had hoped that you might have more sense than her. I had certainly hoped that your years in that convent would have made you less headstrong and difficult. Can you not see the Earl of Redditch is a very wealthy man? As his wife you could have all your heart desires.'

'You are mad if you believe I would ever agree to his proposal. I'm going back to Cumbria in the morning!'

His hands lunged out and he grabbed her firmly by her upper arms, his ghostly pale eyes narrowed. 'You

will not jeopardise my relationship with the Earl. Our business negotiations are at a critical stage.'

'They have nothing to do with me.'

'Yes, they have.' He shook her as she tried to free herself from his vice-like grip. 'I promised him a stunning virgin. A woman he could proudly parade around on his arm and salivate over in the bedroom. A malleable, pliable woman, not a rebellious shrew! He wants you, or at least the illusion of you that I have created, and you will stay here until our business is concluded and continue to drive the old fool mad with lust.'

Clearly he'd gone insane. Fliss finally managed to jerk herself free by planting her hands in the centre of his chest and pushing with all her might. 'Over my dead body!'

Her uncle stalked to the door and grasped the handle, but before he opened it he turned back. Those flat grey eyes hardened. 'If you want the money to buy your passage to freedom, then you will earn it by being pleasant to the Earl. The quicker you comply and reel the old fool in, the quicker you can head back to whence you came.' He neatened his coat and his expression became bland again, devoid of any discernible emotion. It was chilling to watch. 'You are excused dinner, but you *will* waltz with Redditch tonight. The carriage will leave at precisely nine o'clock.'

Her mouth fell open, but Fliss struggled for exactly the right words to convey her utter incredulity and disgust. Before the right words came, Uncle Crispin strode out the door and slammed it behind him.

Chapter Twelve

A cold corner of Hays Mews and Hill Street,
behind Berkeley Square

The moment Jake stepped into the dark lane Leatham
appeared out of the shadows. 'What brings you here?'

A certain honey-haired temptress and an over-
whelming desire to see her sooner. 'I had time to kill
before Almack's and thought it might be a good op-
portunity to catch up.' He eyed the line of waiting car-
riages. 'What's going on?'

'Rowley's hosting a dinner. There are around ten
other men including Redditch. Flint's there, so we'll
have to wait for the full list of names to investigate.'
The flash of jealousy at Flint spending time with her
around the dinner table while Jake loitered outside
yearning didn't help his mood and he grunted. 'How
was the Tower?' Leatham's bland expression belied
the wicked glimmer in his eyes. No doubt he, or one
of his Invisibles, had followed Jake's every move and
his monosyllabic friend knew exactly what had hap-
pened all too briefly in that hackney.

'I'm making progress.'

'Slow progress by your standards, Warriner. I'd have thought you'd have bedded the wench by now.'

Hearing her talked about like that made his blood boil, but Jake covered it with lazy charm. 'That's why I do the seducing and you get to lurk in the stables, my friend. You don't know the first thing about women. Fliss is not the sort of woman you rush.'

A knowing grin split the other man's face. 'Fliss, is it? Suits her. She's got to you, hasn't she?'

Yes.

'Of course not.'

'Then you won't mind that Fennimore's told Flint to try his hand with her, too. Belt and braces…'

'You know damn well two men trying to woo the same woman would muddy the water. What the hell is Fennimore playing at? Flint's got his mission and I've got mine!' And he'd happily flatten the charming Flint if he so much as laid one finger on her. At his furious glare, Seb threw his head back and laughed.

'It was a test, Warriner. One that you failed. Miserably. I saw the soppy grin on your face after you ravished her in that carriage. She's been wearing a matching one most of the day.'

She had? His silly heart soared.

'Have your fun elsewhere, Seb. I was *sent* to ravish the girl as you well know. So what if I enjoy my work? It's better than loitering in the gutters like you.' And Jake was digging himself a deeper hole by seeking to explain it so vigorously. 'Has Flint got into Rowley's dressing room yet?'

'It's his intention to try again tonight if he can distract the guards. There's tighter security inside that

house than outside. Rowley has a man on practically every door.' Which was why they were currently chatting at the end of the cluttered mews which served the whole of Berkeley Square and well away from Rowley's small fortress of a stables. 'He's going to try and hang back till after most of the guests and Rowley have left...unless he can inveigle his way into the family carriage.' His friend slanted him a mischievous glance, waiting to see if Jake would bite. When he didn't, he changed the subject. 'The River Police have doubled their patrols, not that it amounts to much. They're spread too thin and their resources are woefully inadequate to cope with an operation of this scale, but they are focusing on the smaller boats coming up from the estuary. There are currently three of Rowley's ships that have been moored at the docks for a week now and show no signs of either unloading or leaving. I've had men watching them and they say the crews seem to know they are being watched, which leads me to believe they want us to watch them. My nose tells me they're decoys or have already been unloaded, there to taunt us while the little *laden* boats sail on by.'

As Leatham's intuition was scarily accurate, Jake was not inclined to argue with his assessment. 'Which explains Rowley's sudden interest in the Regent's Canal. It'll open up a new route all the way up to the Midlands.'

'And why he's throwing his niece at the man.' Something Jake was becoming increasingly annoyed by. If it drove Fliss to return to Cumbria... The back of his neck prickled with awareness seconds before his friend frowned. 'Hold on...' He strained his head to

get a better look. 'Unless my eyes deceive me, that's her?' Seb pointed to the lone figure hurriedly crossing the next road along, her head darting left and right before she made a mad dash out of sight. 'What's she doing out all alone?'

Everything about the situation raised Jake's hackles, from the furtive nature of her movements to the fact she was out in the chilly February night without so much as a shawl to protect her from the elements. Jake immediately broke into a run, his long legs eating up the distance between them until he could see her properly in the darkness. Her skirts were gathered in her hands as she ran in what looked terrifyingly like panic.

'Fliss!'

She hesitated at the sound of her name, then sped up, blindly heading towards Park Lane, seeming oblivious to the dangers of the many carriages which were trundling along the thoroughfare. She wasn't wearing her spectacles, which meant she couldn't see properly. In the darkness, a horse might not see her until it was too late. It spurred Jake's legs to pump faster before he called out again.

'Fliss, it's me! Jake!'

She skidded to a halt as her head whipped around. Most of her hair was in disarray, but her eyes were as wide as dinner plates. 'Jake?' Her hands went to her mouth and, as he finally caught her and dragged her into his arms, she crumpled. 'Oh, Jake...'

Her skin was like ice. The delicate silk of her dress was already damp with the frigid evening mist. Jake shrugged out of his coat and wrapped it around her, then guided her towards an alleyway and out of sight. If

she was running, then there was probably a damn good reason why. Nothing fazed his canny northern lass normally, therefore he would err on the side of caution in case she was in some danger. 'What's happened?'

It took her a few moments to choke out any words. When they came, her voice was shaking. 'He stole my money…all of it.'

'Who?' Jake scanned the street for any signs of the villain. 'Where were you?'

'All my clothes are gone. My money. Everything is.' She clutched at his lapels and he saw the tears streaming down her cheeks. She swiped them away impatiently. 'The footmen are watching me.'

'Your uncle stole your money?' Or at least that was the gist he was getting from her breathless staccato phrases. She nodded.

'Petty revenge to get his own way. To keep me here. He wants me to be nice to Redditch.' She stared anxiously down the street she had just run down. 'I had to get away, Jake. He scares me… I c-c-can't go back there.'

'You don't have to go back there.' His mind was whirring as he enveloped her in his arms, the desire to take care of her warring with the urgent need to give Rowley a sound thrashing. 'I'll help you.'

She reached up to touch his face and he saw relief and total trust in her eyes. 'You always are in the right place, aren't you? I *can* trust you.'

Guilt strangled any answer because he couldn't bring himself to lie to her, so he hugged her fiercely instead. 'I have lodgings at the Albany, less than ten minutes from here. Why don't we get you out of the cold and then we can plan what to do next?'

'I know what to do next. I need to go back to Cumbria. Back to Sister Ursuline's where I belong. I'll walk there if I have to! All three hundred miles of it in these silly shoes!' The old Fliss was rapidly returning. The feisty, no-nonsense, indomitable Fliss. The one he knew he had to leave regardless of how much it hurt to watch her go. As long as she was away from Rowley, he could bear it.

'I'll take you back home. In a carriage. It'll save those silly shoes.' She offered him a tremulous smile, happily absorbing his strength and the heat of his body. When she rose on tiptoes and placed a grateful, soft kiss on his lips, a surge of wholly inappropriate lust hit him with such force Jake closed his eyes to guard against it. Beneath his hands he could feel the softness of her body under the damp silk—unfettered by stays—and knew that only that one layer of silk and one gauzy layer of linen from his shirt and the inconvenient buttons on his waistcoat separated their naked skin. Knowledge which he didn't need while he was trying to be selflessly noble. Her knight in shining armour. 'We'll leave tonight if you want to?'

'You'll take me all the way back to Cumbria?'

'Yes.' And then he would say goodbye. Why did that thought already make his heart ache?

'Not a good idea.' At the sound of Leatham's gravelly voice behind, Fliss stiffened, her fingers gripping Jake's back. 'We need to take her to Fennimore.'

'No. We *don't*.'

'*Yes*, we *do*, Jake.'

At the familiar use of his first name, Fliss's eyes swivelled from Seb's to his warily, that clever mind of hers already doubting him. 'Who is he? Jake?' Her

pretty eyes widened. 'I recognise him...the scar...this is the man who took your horse that morning. You *know* him?' She took a decisive step back, severing all physical contact between them, wrapping her own arms around her body protectively rather than stand any longer in his embrace. Her voice was all at once both mistrusting and brittle. 'What's going on?'

Jake felt sick to his stomach. Guilty, ashamed and furious simultaneously at both Seb, his own duplicity and this impossible dilemma he wished with all his heart he wasn't facing. 'This is my friend Seb Leatham. He is...' His voice trailed off. How to explain the truth without having her hate him?

'We work for his Majesty's government, Miss Blunt. You are quite safe with us, but I hope you understand we will need to question you before we arrange for your safe passage back to Cumbria.'

'Question me about what?'

'Your uncle. We have been investigating some of his business dealings.'

Jake couldn't meet her eyes. He didn't need to deny it because his body radiated guilt. His dark head was bent. Broad shoulders slumped. For a man always supremely confident in his own body, he suddenly didn't appear to know what to do with his hands. Shocked, Fliss complied and allowed the other man in ragged labourer's clothes to escort her down the back alleys of Mayfair as she tried to digest it all. She didn't recognise the mews they entered, or the stables they went through, but she recognised the bitter taste of betrayal and the heavy weight of humiliation as she accompanied the two men. Both strangers to her now.

Jake was blessedly silent and walked several paces behind. It was just as well. If he had offered her any empty platitudes, she would have happily slapped his duplicitous and handsome face raw for his part in this. They were investigating her uncle! It had all been a lie.

What a foolish, trusting dolt she had been. Jacob Warriner had a canny knack of being in the right place at exactly the right time because he was apparently paid by the King himself to be there. He wasn't dependable, he was doing his job. He had wormed his way into her affections only to extract information for the crown. Every charming word out of his tempting mouth was a lie. Every stupid thing she had imagined between them was a mirage, too. The odd sense of kinship. The mutual attraction. The seductive allure of temptation. The hope that his feelings for her were as deep as hers had become for him. The perfection of that kiss... Fate! It would be laughable if she didn't feel like crying.

His empty words would be galling if she wasn't bleeding inside. He'd played every trick in the successful rakes' book and she had fallen for them. Just as she supposed a great many other women had in the past.

And it hurt.

Fliss so wanted to turn around to look at him to see if he was hurting, too, as if the sight of his remorse would make her feel better about his treachery. Fortunately, her pride kept her eyes front and centre and her shoulders fortified with steel. As soon as they crossed the garden and entered the French doors of the smart Mayfair town house, she shrugged off Jake's offending coat, not wanting any part of him left touching her skin. She heard him bend to retrieve it, but refused

to look back as he did. Let him feel the frigid cold of her indifference. He was nought but an untrustworthy philanderer just as she had first thought. A consummate and cruel liar. A chameleon who adapted seamlessly according to his environment and the situation; a wastrel like her father and one who had misused her as grievously as her horrid uncle.

An older man with a serious face greeted her in what looked to be his study. 'Miss Blunt. I wish I could have made your acquaintance under better circumstances and I hope you will forgive us our cloak-and-dagger methods, but until very recently we had no idea that you weren't in any way involved in your uncle's skulduggery. I am Lord Fennimore and I head up an organisation called the King's Elite. Warriner and Leatham work for me. As does another operative embedded within your uncle's social circle. I assume you have met Lord Peter Flint?'

Now she knew who the handsome blond crony was. He had always smiled kindly at her, as if he felt a little bit sorry for her—now she knew why. He knew what Jake saw in her. Fliss nodded once, curtly, and sat primly in the chair Lord Fennimore placed in front of the fire. As she sipped the hot tea she had been given, she felt the soft wool of a blanket be placed about her shoulders and felt the painful tingle of awareness which told her which of the King's minions had put it there. She didn't bother thanking him for that single genuine kindness.

'I suppose you have a great many questions, Miss Blunt, and now that Warriner has assured me we can trust you, I shall do my best to answer them, but for now I shall cut to the heart of the matter...'

A cut to the heart. How apt. Hers felt shredded.

'The King's Elite is a secret branch of the Home Office. We are tasked with unmasking and bringing to justice all those who seek to undermine the British economy through large-scale smuggling. For two years, we have been desperately trying to bring down a very dangerous group who have flooded the market with brandy. While smuggled liquor is nothing new, what concerns us most about this particular bunch are their links to the loyal supporters of Napoleon. The same men who helped him escape from Elba are once again plotting to return him to power—only this time they are using British coin to purchase weapons and amass an army, coin raised from the thousands of gallons of French brandy smuggled onto our shores every single month. Brandy they provide. Until recently, we had no plausible leads to follow. You see, this gang are as brutal and secretive as they are powerful and every smuggled cargo we've seized has led us to yet another dead end. The smugglers either did not know who they worked for or were prepared to go to the gallows rather than betray their masters. However, six months ago, one of those smugglers gave us a name. The man who he claims is the sole distributor for the goods in London and the Home Counties. I'm sorry to tell you that name was Crispin Rowley.'

Jake's shabby accomplice lowered himself into the seat opposite her. 'We believe the brandy is coming through London via the Thames and suspect your uncle is responsible for finding buyers and distributing it from there. He is a significant link in a very long chain, but he covers his tracks well. All we can find are his legitimate business dealings, shares in mer-

chant ships, banks and the like. However, his choice of investments lends itself as the perfect cover for the real source of his impressive new fortune. We believe those same shipping companies are somehow bringing in the cargoes, but we do not know either where or how they are able to hide the contraband from the Excise Men. We are coming to believe he moves the goods entirely on the water and in very large amounts. Thanks to you we now know he is seeking to invest in the new Regent's Canal, which goes some way to confirming those suspicions.' Jake had charmed and prised that information out of her, claiming the dull conversation would cure his insomnia. One of his many lies. They tripped off his tongue with such ease, no wonder he was so good at his job. She could feel his eyes boring into her back, willing her to turn around, but his dishonesty sickened her far more than her disgust at her own stupidity did. If he had been a decent man to begin with, he would have told her the truth from the outset and she would have happily still told him everything. Honestly. Upfront. He wouldn't have needed to try to seduce it out of her!

But lies and deception were a rake's stock in trade and she had pathetically fallen for them as well as him, so instead Fliss clutched the blanket tighter, and ignored him, focusing back on his friend. All these years she had stalwartly guarded her heart, waiting for someone worthy, only to discover she had unwittingly given it to the unworthiest man possible. He wasn't simply a selfish hedonist taking his pleasure where he could. He was paid to seduce. Somehow that felt worse. Humiliating. Even more of a betrayal.

'So you see, any information you can add to what

we already know will be a godsend, Miss Blunt. Your testimony could help us infiltrate that gang, or it could help clear your uncle's name of any wrong-doing.' The scarred man hesitated, obviously con-scious of the fact that his every word condemned his friend further in her eyes. 'Jake said you overheard a meeting between your uncle and another man which bothered you.'

She shook her head and laughed bitterly. Had their every conversation been reported in great detail? Very probably. Snippets of the nocturnal argument she had overheard in the garden filtered back and suddenly made sense. 'Dead men can't spend.'

'I'm sorry?'

So was Fliss. 'I should have trusted my instincts.'

All of them.

Mr Leatham and Lord Fennimore sat forward in their seats with interest. 'Go on.'

'That's what the man said. Dead men can't spend. I did overhear a conversation between my uncle and another man in the garden a few nights ago. My bed-chamber is directly above his study and faces out on to the garden. It was past midnight and I couldn't sleep. I'd left my window ajar.' And now she hated Jake, too. It had been his fault she had been hot and restless, and all the while he had been tricking her into confiding in him. The Biblical snake in the Garden of Eden, lur-ing her to sin and damn near succeeding. 'My uncle was in a state. Desperate. He offered to pay double, then triple his usual for a shipment of some sort. The other man refused. Said it would make no difference because *dead men* couldn't spend. He said the boss wouldn't like it if his cargo got seized. That he'd lost

enough already this month because there were many new eyes along the water. Or words to that effect.'

'You're sure he used the words the Boss?'

'It is my judgement that has been impaired, Lord Fennimore, not my memory. Because the conversation was in the middle of night and out of the ordinary, it sticks in the mind.'

'What else did they say?'

'I got the distinct impression the other man was the one in charge of the situation. My uncle seemed scared of him. He was pleading with him, complaining he was out of pocket every time a shipment was late and saying that people were relying on him. Now that I come to think about it, yesterday morning in Hyde Park, my uncle discussed a great deal of business with some other gentlemen, none of whom looked particularly happy by what he had to say.'

'Their names are in the list I gave you,' Mr Leatham said matter of factly, letting Fliss know he had also been following her around the park, and probably to the Tower. All three men were probably well aware she had been silly enough to welcome Jake's kiss. Had lost herself temporarily in it.

'Were both of you tasked to watch me, Mr Leatham? Was one charming nursemaid not enough?'

He had the decency to appear embarrassed. 'My mission was to follow your uncle's movements, Miss Blunt, not you. Jake was assigned...' His voice trailed off as he looked at his boots.

'I am well aware Mr Warriner was tasked with seducing me, Mr Leatham. I am a fool, not an imbecile. I suppose that is the usual manner in which you operate?' Fliss forced a brightness in her voice she didn't

feel, because she refused to allow him to see how much he had hurt her. 'Assign a *dedicated* and highly *skilled* man to everyone. Already I have worked out that your particular skill, Mr Leatham, is to blend into the background—am I right?' The other man nodded. The tips of his ears blushed incongruously with the rest of his harsh exterior. 'Then it is hardly surprising that Mr Warriner would be assigned to question the ladies. How *clever* of the British government to utilise his talent for philandering so *thoroughly.*'

'The man your uncle met with—what can you tell us about him?' Lord Fennimore clicked his fingers and gestured towards his desk to hastily change the subject and save his man, and it was Jake who quickly fetched paper and a pen and pressed them into his hand. He took himself to stand behind the other two, directly in her eye line. She resolutely ignored him. 'We will need a thorough description, Miss Blunt. All you remember.'

'He wasn't a gentleman, my lord, by the accepted definition of the word *gentleman.*' Neither was Jake the Rake, henceforth to be known as Jake the Snake for ever. She shot a few daggers at him in case he was in any doubt she loathed him for his deceit but wasn't broken by it. She'd been let down before by men. Continually let down by them. Expected nothing less. 'He was a Londoner. His accent coarse like a working man's. His clothes were scruffy. He was big. He loomed over my uncle.'

'And his features?' Lord Fennimore looked up from his notes.

'It was dark and I wasn't wearing my spectacles. At best his face was a smudge.'

'Was he fair? Dark?'

'He was wearing a hat. I never saw. It was an odd and short exchange, my lord. Once it was over the man disappeared behind the shrubbery. I haven't seen him since.'

'What of your uncle's dealings with the Earl of Redditch? Is there a chance he is involved somehow?'

Fliss considered it, then dismissed it out of hand. 'If he was, then there would be no reason for my uncle to thrust me in front of the man's nose. Tonight he made it clear that his negotiations with the Earl are at a crucial stage and that he expects to use me as a bargaining chip. I am to be *nice* to the man, apparently. Allow myself to be fawned and drooled over while the negotiations are concluded. Drive him mad with lust to scramble his wits.' Just thinking about it made Fliss shudder and she unconsciously rubbed her arms where her uncle had gripped her. 'He intended to keep me a virtual prisoner until the contracts were signed.'

Chapter Thirteen

Suffering an Arctic chill in Lord Fennimore's study

Fliss rubbed her arms and the blanket fell. It was only then that Jake's eyes were drawn to the dark finger-shaped bruises marring her upper arms. The urge to kill Rowley was primal and visceral. 'He hurt you!'

Her eyes flicked to his, hardened, then turned back to Lord Fennimore. 'We argued after I discovered he had destroyed all the clothes I had brought with me from Cumbria and had taken the money I had intended to use to pay my passage back. Clearly he assumed that would make me more compliant, when instead it only spurred my desire to escape.'

'How did you get away? My men have the front and back entrances under strict surveillance.'

She eyed Seb with marginally less disgust than she had Jake. 'The whole house and all its occupants are under surveillance, Mr Leatham. My uncle's henchmen are disguised as footmen, I now realise. There is one posted on every door. They watched me like hawks, I believe I have been *assigned* one in particu-

lar who is irritatingly diligent, but like most men he underestimated the resourcefulness and tenacity of women. When I realised I was being watched, I pretended to be distraught and dashed up the stairs and slammed my bedchamber door. When he went to talk to the man guarding the front door, I crept back down and returned to my uncle's study because I knew it would be easier to hide in the darkness of the garden than it would be anywhere on Berkeley Square. I climbed out of the window and followed the route I saw the Londoner take as he left that night. Low and behold, behind the shrubbery is a convenient ladder which he must have used to scale the ten-foot wall between my uncle's house and the neighbour's. I went over it and followed the path alongside it and away from the house. At the back of that garden is another pathway—a servants' alleyway of some sort. It runs between the gardens of the houses on Berkeley Square and whatever street is behind. Eventually, I could hear the carriages rattling past, so knew that it must be one of the main roads rather than the mews, so I managed to scale the wall and jump to the pavement. Then I ran.' Her eyes turned to Jake again fleetingly. They were as hostile as it was humanly possible for a pair of eyes to be. No less than he deserved, he supposed, but they made him feel utterly wretched none the less.

To avoid her gaze and his own guilt, he turned towards his comrades, only to watch a telling look pass between Fennimore and Leatham. 'Does your uncle *know* that you have escaped, Miss Blunt?'

'As I was excused dinner to compose myself, maybe not yet, but I was told in no uncertain terms the car-

riage would be leaving at nine and he expected me to be on it, I'm assuming he's in for a bit of a surprise.'

'Then perhaps—'

'No!' Jake interrupted before Lord Fennimore could vocalise what he and Leatham were clearly thinking. 'She's not going back there!'

'We cannot let this opportunity pass.'

'I won't have her put in more danger.'

'It's not your decision to make Jake. It's hers.' Seb's tone was intended to calm him, instead it fired Jake's temper further.

'She's told you all she knows and we promised her safe passage back to Cumbria.'

'Think logically, man! Think about the bigger picture. She has unprecedented access.' Lord Fennimore reached forward and took her hands in his. 'I know this is a great deal to ask of you, Miss Blunt, but these are dire times and we desperately need your help. If your uncle assumes you will back down and comply to his edicts, I propose we allow him to think he has won…it is a matter of national security…'

King and country could go to hell. 'I said no, damn it! I won't let her go back to that man and see her forced to suffer more of his brutality.' Those bruises on her arms were injury enough and Rowley would pay for them. Jake turned to her then, purposefully ignoring the others. 'I'll take you back to Cumbria in the morning, Fliss. Just as I promised. You don't have to do this. I won't let you do this.'

Instead of appearing grateful, her face contorted in a sneer. 'I'd rather face a month enduring Redditch's drooling than spend another second in your lying company, thank you very much.' To spite him she turned

her head towards Lord Fennimore. 'What would you have me do? My uncle doesn't confide in me. To be frank, we barely converse at all. I'm not entirely sure how much use I could be.'

'You can be our eyes and ears inside the building. Monitor the comings and goings, memorise the names of your uncle's associates, pump the Earl of Redditch for more information about the potential partnership with your uncle. You said the man was taken with you.'

'He is. His eyes are on stalks whenever he's within ten feet of me.'

'Then let us use that to our advantage. Your uncle will be thrilled with your newly compliant attitude and the Earl will be beside himself to have such a lovely young woman hanging on his every word.'

Now things were getting out of hand. 'What you are suggesting is as deplorable as what Rowley was doing! I won't stand by while you put her in grave danger and at the mercy of an old lecher! She'll be all alone in there.'

Lord Fennimore appeared affronted at the suggestion. 'Hardly. Leatham will be a stone's throw away outside and Flint will be inside as much as he can be. The house and any movements within it are already under close watch. Miss Blunt will be under our full protection going forward. She'll be perfectly safe.'

'You cannot guarantee that. Nobody can. These smugglers are ruthless and she's a blasted schoolmistress, for pity's sake. She's hardly equipped with the skills necessary to spy on the lot of them. She'll slip up somewhere and then she will be entirely at their mercy.' Thinking of Fliss in peril, her life at risk, made

his insides clench painfully. He should never have listened to Seb. Never have brought her to Lord Fennimore's house. Jake had put her in this danger when he should have listened to his heart and helped her to escape. 'She's better off back home where she belongs.' As far away from her cruel uncle and his bloodthirsty associates as it was possible to be. 'We'll find another way to infiltrate Rowley's web.'

'Not like this we won't.' Seb placed a reassuring hand on Jake's shoulder and then sighed when he furiously jerked away. 'Think about it, Jake. We've been trying for months to get on the inside. Flint is occasionally there, but the best we've really managed is to cling on the periphery. We've learnt more about his business dealings through Miss Blunt in one week than we have by throwing all our resources at it for six months. Even if she just sits by her bedchamber window night after night we'll find out more about this Londoner. He has to be the link between Rowley and the Boss. He will lead us to where they hide the cargos and eventually to the mastermind himself. Within weeks we could have all the keys to unlocking this case and bring the empire to its knees.'

'She's spent her entire life sheltered in a damned convent, Seb! She's not up to this!'

'She had the wherewithal to escape unseen from Rowley's fortress.'

Fennimore nodded. 'She is also incredibly intelligent and astute.'

'She's not doing it!'

'*She* has a mind of her own and the ability to use it!' Fliss sprang to her feet, her hands clenched into tight

fists she looked intent to use at any moment. 'Stop talking about me as if I am not here!'

Seb and Fennimore instantly apologised, but Jake was too furious and too concerned to back down. 'She's not cut out for any of this and I strongly recommend we put her on the first available coach north.'

Later, Jake would recall that those words lit the fuse which caused the full force of her temper to explode directly in his face. 'I *strongly recommend* you take your *strong* recommendations and place them elsewhere.' Her finger jabbed him hard in the chest. 'How dare you speak for me! If there are any decisions to be made and any risk to be taken, then they are mine to own and mine to take, *Mr* Warriner! How dare you say I'm not up to the task! If *you* can be a spy, then I doubt it is that hard to do. What are the main attributes of one? To lie? To sneak around? To flirt? To say one thing when I mean another? To shamelessly use my attractiveness to the opposite sex to seduce information out of them? Hardly skills which require a great deal of intelligence and, if your example is anything to go by, one doesn't need to have a great deal of finesse either!'

She was hurting. He'd hurt her and in doing so had mortally wounded himself in the bargain. 'Fliss, I'm—'

She didn't give him a chance to say sorry. 'I'll do as you ask, Lord Fennimore.'

After that the decision was taken firmly out of Jake's hands. While he silently seethed and flailed himself for his incompetence at handling the situation, Leatham and Fennimore briefed her on everything they suspected, what to listen out for and how mes-

sages could be quickly and covertly passed between them. As the chiming clock signalled their brief time was nearly up, it was agreed that Seb would escort her back to the street they had found her on. If the coast was clear, she would re-enter the garden in the same way she'd left it. They had a story all worked out so she could explain her appearance and where she had been should they have missed her. All Jake could do was stand by and impotently watch it all unfold.

'Godspeed, Miss Blunt.' Lord Fennimore walked her back to the stables and personally helped her into the shabby carriage they kept for such occasions. 'We are in your debt.'

As Leatham was already in the driver's seat, Jake went to climb in beside her, only to find his arm stayed by his superior. 'Best to leave this to the pair of them, Warriner. Too many bodies will only serve to arouse suspicion if you're seen.'

'I won't be seen.' Before he could put his boot back on the step, the irritated, stubborn minx in the carriage slammed the door closed. She did it with such force even Lord Fennimore was taken aback.

'Come on, man. Leave the girl be. While your concern does you credit, the bad feeling between you is not good for this mission. Leatham and Flint will look after her now. She's in good hands.'

They weren't Jake's hands. 'I'll work with Leatham and the Invisibles.'

'Do you think that is wise? She could do with some distance to get her head around things and focus on what she needs to. I suspect the last thing she'll want to see is you for at least the next few days and we all need her to be calm and rational. Her safety depends

upon it.' More words Jake didn't want to hear. 'For now, your part in this is over. I know you feel bad about the way things have turned out, but the mission has to come first. You know that. Take that well-earned leave I cancelled. Have a rest. In no time at all she'll be out of there. You can explain it all then. Rationally. When you are both calm and the danger is past.'

'If you don't mind, sir, I'd like to explain a few things now.' And Jake would do his level best to talk her out of this madness before it was too late. 'You owe me that.'

His superior consulted his pocket watch, then rolled his eyes. 'Two minutes, Warriner. But it is a mistake.'

Jake swiftly opened the door and quickly inserted himself into the small carriage in case she had a mind to stop him, then promptly closed it behind him. Fliss was still incandescent with rage, although it was quietly white hot now rather than raging red, and regarded him from the opposite seat with cold contempt. He steeled himself for the onslaught and prepared to do some serious grovelling. 'I wanted to apologise for lying to you.'

Silence.

'And I wanted to explain that...' What? Not everything had been a lie when the foundations were rotten? The friendship had been real, even if it had been contrived. So had the kiss. Very real. Although he had been tasked to kiss her and had been frantically planning exactly how to go about it just a few minutes before. If only they had met under different circumstances. 'I know this looks bad, Fliss, and I know you probably hate me right now, but...' As he struggled to find the right words to fully convey his own disgust

at using her while assuring her he had some seriously complicated feelings he didn't fully understand himself, she slowly turned her head away to look out of the other window. That cold, dead stare out to nothingness his mother had always done so well. The utter disgust at who he really was. His stomach lurched at the comparison.

'I understand. It was your job.'

'Yes, but not entirely… The thing is…' She turned back to look at him, or rather look through him, and her expression cut him to the quick. It wasn't hurt. It wasn't angry. It was resigned. As if she had been expecting to be grievously let down all along and had fully expected nothing less. The trust was dead. Its corpse a foul stench that hung between them in the air. 'It wasn't all a lie, Fliss. I promise you.'

'I know that.' His silly heart soared. 'Among all those lies, all those convenient chance meetings and all hose tempting glances and poisonous kisses, there was one irrefutable grain of truth which I should have listened to. You *are* a disappointment, Jake. Perhaps the biggest I have ever met.'

Well, that was a well-aimed dart and one he couldn't argue with. 'You don't have to do this, Fliss. There is still time to back out. Go home to Cumbria. Be safe. This is not your fight, it's ours.'

She sighed, her face for once inscrutable, then reached over his lap to open the door. This time she didn't fumble clumsily. The lock gave quickly. 'Your part in this is done. As are we. Take your leave, Jake. I dare say you've earned it.'

Chapter Fourteen

Somewhere in Piccadilly, one week later

Fliss forced herself to smile at the Earl of Redditch, even though the smell of the man in the confined space of her uncle's carriage threatened to make her retch. Her uncle still persisted in playing silly games, as if his decision to secretly swap carriages with the Earl so he could go home early had really been sudden. It had all the subtlety and finesse of a blacksmith's hammer, but for King and country she would make the best of it. 'That is fascinating, my lord. One hundred tons of cargo in one year alone! No wonder you need to increase your fleet of barges.'

The silly old fool preened at the compliment.

'Indeed, Felicity, and I expect my *own* fortune to be doubled as a result.' Since she had resigned herself to her uncle's threat, Redditch kept dropping in little hints about his wealth in the hope it would make him more appealing. It didn't—Fliss had maintained a healthy disinterest. She doubted her scheming uncle would be convinced by an abrupt about-turn and de-

cided a mildly belligerent stance would ultimately be more convincing. At best, she tolerated Redditch and reluctantly allowed him one dance, although much to her uncle's chagrin it was never the waltz, and her tongue still dripped the same acid, but with a sugary smile on her face.

While her behaviour added a layer of authenticity to the proceedings, the charitable part of her also wanted the Earl to get exactly the same message. She couldn't bring herself to give the poor man too much false hope, yet he still persisted in trying to impress her with his money, which served to do two things. Firstly, it made her pity the Earl. To feel that one's worth was inextricably linked to money was a very sad state of affairs, and, despite the fact Redditch was still an ogling, repulsive and shallow man with little respect for her beyond the sight of her now shamelessly displayed bosoms, Fliss couldn't help feeling sorry for him. He was also a sad, ageing, childless man who was clearly happy to settle for a woman who *only* wanted him for his money. That smacked of desperation and the more she was forced to get to know him, the more she wanted to take him to one side and tell him he was going about finding a wife all wrong. *Bathe more often, lift your greedy eyes and look at the woman in the face for once rather than the chest, listen to her rather than constantly bragging and then perhaps you will find the personal happiness you seem to crave.*

The urge to be honest with him for his own good was a double-edged sword, because the other thing it made Fliss ponder was how truly miserable Jake's deception had made her. She doubted his shocking

lies had left him feeling a quarter as guilty and dishonest as hers now did; rakes who did their raking for King and country had to have hard hearts and no conscience. After a week of attempting to find evidence of her uncle's criminality, Fliss now appreciated how dangerous and precarious such work could be. Half the time she was on tenterhooks, the other half simply terrified and both states were exhausting. She had never been so conscious of every word she said, every nuance, every movement and, aside from now knowing the ins and outs of the river-haulage business, she had gleaned precious little for all her hard work. Spies clearly needed vast wells of patience as well as nerves of steel.

However, knowing she had been nought but a job to be done, when she was still grieving the loss of *him*, made her feel ridiculously foolish, naïve and—if she was being entirely honest—more than a little bit heartbroken. While he had been busy working, Fliss had been nurturing a friendship which had quickly spiralled out of her control. Somewhere during their brief but eventful liaison her guarded heart had let its guard down, then had usurped her sensible, pragmatic head. Jake the Snake had become so much more than a friend. He'd been her Knight in Shining Armour. A man she had confided in and allowed to kiss her. That kiss had changed everything. In that one heady and unexpected moment she had begun to hope he was more. A few hours later, those dreams had been crushed just as brutally as all her childish dreams had before.

One day, she would be able to look back on the whole sorry affair and sagely warn her students of

the sort of techniques the most dangerous and predatory philanderers used to woo the unsuspecting. Or at least Fliss hoped she would get to that point, because right now, she sincerely doubted she could even confide her misery to Sister Ursuline without weeping like a pathetic victim and flagellating herself for her own stupidity.

'My future wife will enjoy all of life's comforts.' The Earl had smiled and settled himself back against the seat and his eyes drifted back below her chin again. Fliss ignored the compulsion to drag her thin evening shawl around her. Like the calculating Jake, she now also had a job to do and one which was easier if her lecherous companion was occupied. His tongue was looser when it was hungrily hanging out of his mouth. Something which did nothing to make her feel any better.

'Tell me, my lord, while I appreciate business is business and that you make coin by hauling the cargos of others, do you have some mechanism to rigorously vet what is carried.'

'Why would I do that?'

'I have heard stories about smuggling. Apparently, it is still as rife as it ever was, yet more secretive. What if the smugglers were using your boats to transport their goods? Are you not concerned for the consequences?'

His eyes flicked back to her face for a second before he shrugged and returned to staring at her décolleté as it gently moved with the motion of Uncle Crispin's well-sprung carriage.

'Why should I be? As a gentleman, I do not concern myself with the day-to-day machinations of *business*.'

He pulled a face as if such a thing was below him. 'I merely provide the capital. The barges are leased by the wherrymen who benefit from the numerous opportunities my good name provides them. I offer hold space for hire. The price is fixed according to the distance regardless of the contents carried. I get half of that fee and the wherrymen get the other. If anything, being able to categorically state I had no clue as to what is being transported means the Excise Men cannot blame me, any more than they can attribute blame to any of the other gentlemen of business who invest in the same trade.'

'But these are illicit, ill-gotten gains, my lord. Aren't you worried it will end badly for you if the Excise Men board one of them and seize the cargo?'

'If the crews are silly enough to take the risk of transporting something illegal, then that is down to them as they will ultimately pay the price. New crews are ten a penny. Especially when a business is as lucrative as mine.'

Fliss began to feel less sympathy for the man. 'Surely you wouldn't want boats sailing under your name to carry illegal cargo and rob the crown of its rightful taxes?'

'Better the coin falls into my purse than the Treasury's. They get more than enough from me as it is, so I shall not complain if I inadvertently get a little something back?'

'Even if it brings down the British economy?'

He laughed, flinging himself back into the seat in a musty waft and smiling at her in that patronising way sanctimonious men did when they thought they knew better. 'Oh, bless your good heart, Felicity! Your

strong morals are one of the many things I adore about you, but you have a scant understanding of the workings of the British economy. Smuggling is inherently part of it. The free traders have operated within it for centuries and will continue to operate for centuries more.' He pointed to the intricately patterned lace laid over the burgundy silk of her tight-fitting bodice. 'Where do you think that exquisite trim came from? Chantilly lace is a small fortune and few pay the extortionate prices from the merchants who are silly enough to pay the duties. And after the wars, we prefer not to *openly* trade with the enemy. While the *ton* loves its fripperies, smuggling will continue to flourish. Everyone knows the best lace comes from France.'

'So does the best soap.' Next to him, Aunt Daphne was blatantly wielding a perfumed vinaigrette in front of her nostrils and wearing an expression of complete distaste. 'You might consider using some!'

The Earl laughed, assuming Daphne's words were a joke just as the carriage slowed as it turned into the narrow lane which housed the mews servicing Berkeley Square, and like a fool Fliss allowed her gaze to drift out of the window. Although she had promised herself faithfully she would *not* look again tonight, her silly eyes had a mind of their own and of course they briefly locked with *his* before she resolutely turned away, heartily disgusted with her wayward urges.

In scruffy workmen's clothes, Jacob Warriner was no less attractive than he was in his evening finery and her silly heart gave a little sigh before she hardened it against him. Those beautiful blue eyes were liar's eyes and she would not be relieved or reassured by the sight of him. Not when she had Mr Leatham

and Mr Flint close by to help her should she need it. Jake the Snake was the last person Fliss wanted standing guard. Or within one hundred miles of her for that matter. He was history. The past. Done and dusted. Why couldn't the man have taken the leave he'd been offered? Why did she have to see his dratted face day after day, night after night, popping up wherever she went. Watching.

Why, she had already had to suffer the knowledge he had been in the alcove of the very ballroom she had just left! Did the man race his horse across Mayfair night after night and change his clothes en route? The very last image she wanted in her confused and exhausted mind was the thought of him shrugging out of his splendid evening clothes in some darkened alleyway and then pulling on the roughened ensemble he wore to blend into the mews, only the moonlight illuminating his broad shoulders and the muscles on his strong arms. Coarse clothes which should not make him appealing, but which suited him just as well. Oh, how she loathed him for his magnetic attractiveness and diligent persistence to see the job finished!

Nor did she want to think he was there because he cared. About her rather than his mission. Except his heated and poignant looks led her to believe he might, which made her waver in her resolve to loathe him for all eternity, constantly flitting between disappointment and raw hatred and a disturbing and foolish desire to put herself in his big, fibbing and fetching boots, hoping to find a way to forgive him for the unforgivable. He would be so much easier to despise if she wasn't confronted with those troubled eyes every single day.

Watching.

Protecting.

While she doubted he cared about her in quite the same way as she had been coming to care about him, Fliss was prepared to concede he did seem to have a genuine interest in her safety, else why would he be everywhere when he could be at home.

Instead, he had become her shadow and whenever she was out she could feel the intense weight of his stare as he followed her every movement. At balls, he seemed to become particularly stern whenever Fliss danced with another man, something she had taken to doing a great deal now that hiding in alcoves was out of the question. She justified her sudden transformation from reluctant debutante to eager social butterfly by telling herself that it reassured Uncle Crispin that she was partially abiding by his rules in her own rebellious way and in so doing was attempting to drive the Earl of Redditch mad with lust. However, it didn't hurt that the sight of her laughing and flirting with a succession of handsome new gentlemen made Jake's sapphire eyes harden and narrow while he watched her like the hawk she had once accused him of being.

Fliss had spent the entire interval of the opera yesterday giggling with Lord Peter Flint and had barely cast the traitorous Mr Warriner a glance. As the lights had dimmed for the second act and she had pulled her opera glasses up to cover her face, she'd needed to bite very hard on the inside of her cheek to avoid smiling at the splendid vision of Jake's hands clenched into tight fists on his lap. The wayward part of her hoped he was burning with jealousy. The sensible part wished she didn't care either way.

Lord Flint, of course, had some pity for his friend and used every opportunity to quietly reassure her that Jake was worried about her and that he was sorry for having to keep his true identity at secret. Neither comment made Fliss more inclined to feel any leniency towards him because he hadn't apologised for not telling her the truth sooner. A true friend would have.

It wasn't all a lie, Fliss. I promise you…

Ha! Roughly translated, that meant a great deal of the silky poison which oozed out of his mouth to loosen hers had been and she would not be the sort of dolt who sought clarification. It made no difference to her which bits had been true.

It didn't!

It wouldn't.

The tiny hairs on the back of her neck prickled, alerting her to the fact that the dratted man was still staring at her and willing her to glance back. 'Oh, for goodness sake! Why have we stopped?' The driver had brought them around the back because the lines of carriages going into the square had been horrendous. 'This was supposed to be the quicker route home!'

The Earl of Redditch reached over and patted her knee. 'The whole of Berkeley Square are doubtless all coming home at the same time. We are in the thick of the Season and Saturdays are always the busiest nights. I suspect there is quite the queue. On the bright side, we get to converse a little longer…'

Fliss offered him a tight smile and then glared at the offending palm which was still resting possessively on her leg. Fortunately, Aunt Cressida had spotted it, too, and thwacked him smartly over the knuckles with her folded ivory fan. He retracted the offending appendage

immediately only to face the outraged wrath of Aunt Daphne as well. 'Keep all of your digits to yourself in future, my lord, else I'll have you banned from my niece's company!' While they all knew Uncle Crispin would do no such thing, the Earl certainly didn't and the threat was enough to make him apologise.

'Dearest Felicity, I meant no offence. The close confines of this carriage make it very difficult to move without encroaching on another's person.'

Daphne pinned him with a withering look. 'Idle hands are the devil's workshop, my lord, and yours seem quite possessed. I suggest you sit on them in case they are tempted to wander again. Do you remember Nuneaton, Sister?'

Cressida glared imperiously. 'Indeed *I do* and we'll have *none* of that here today, my lord.'

Fliss gave both old ladies a thankful, enigmatic smile even though she didn't have the first clue what they were talking about as was so often the case. They had become the two guards she found she was grateful to have. In the week since the awful night when she had discovered the true hideous measure of both her only living relative and the only friend she had made in London, Fliss had come to rely on the comforting presence of these two eccentric, formerly scandalous and often useless chaperons. They meant well, seemed to have the same low regard for Uncle Crispin as she did and had appeared to understand her predicament—or at least some of it—without her having to tell them any of it. They assumed she had been bullied by their nephew into suffering the Earl while he concluded his business and Fliss didn't have the heart to apprise them of the terrifying reality. Her

uncle dallied with murderers, stole from the crown and was not averse to practically imprisoning and blackmailing his only niece for his own profit. It was bad enough that Fliss knew some of the tangled web of danger they were all in—alerting them to the real truth was asking for trouble.

The Earl of Redditch wore a sad puppy-dog expression which she assumed he thought was charming and guaranteed to earn him her forgiveness, so purposefully looked away so that the obnoxious fellow knew he had overstepped the mark on this short carriage ride he shouldn't have been on. When she found her eyes drifting back towards the handsome scoundrel still stood on the corner of Hays Mews, the one who had very definitely overstepped the mark during *their* carriage ride with her blessing, she stubbornly pulled them back. For five long minutes she sat but a stone's throw away and ignored him. Fliss didn't realise how much of her strength that took until the carriage eventually edged forward and she finally allowed her tense muscles to relax.

In the seclusion of the Rowley stables, Fliss made sure she clambered out of the carriage before the creaking Earl, thwarting any attempt at his lifting her down, and stood to the side waiting as her aunts alighted, too. They were soon met by the butler, a man who rarely ventured out of the house, who bowed politely to the Earl. 'My lord, his lordship sends his deepest apologies, but begs you understand he cannot continue to entertain you this evening. He has been afflicted with a sudden chill and has gone to bed. Your own equipage has been readied to take you home immediately.'

The temporary relief at being spared more time in the Earl's company was overshadowed by her unease. Her uncle never went to bed until the small hours and in the few weeks Fliss had been a guest in his house, she had never known him to pass up on an opportunity to impress the man he desperately wanted to do business with. As her uncle had also been as fit as a fiddle less than an hour ago, she smelled something rotten and, for once, it wasn't Redditch.

With her mind racing, she suffered through the polite goodbyes and made her own excuses to head to bed. A crack of light bled out from under her uncle's rarely used study door, but with several footmen guarding the hallway and his door, she dared not attempt to get any closer and rouse their suspicions. In her bedchamber, her maid insisted on helping her into her nightgown and plaiting her hair, and Fliss made a great show of going to bed. Twenty painful minutes ticked by before she heard her bedchamber door quietly open. Only when Kitty heard the slow, deep breathing of a woman lost in slumber did she leave. Fliss heard her mumble something to the footman on the landing and a few minutes later she heard his heavy tread move away from her door. Now that she knew the ritual of her gaolers, she knew he would take himself to the strategically placed chair at the end of the hallway and, if he was satisfied his charge was sleeping, he might nod off.

On silent feet, Fliss went to the window, slid her hand behind the heavy curtain and released the window latch. She never dared open it more than half an inch in case it could be seen below, then she threw water on the fire burning in the grate and snuffed

out the single candle Kitty always left burning in the corner. Only when her bedchamber was shrouded in blackness did she risk cracking open the curtains and peering out into the garden.

It was empty, but the soft lighting in her uncle's study illuminated the ground directly below, suggesting that he still had a guest. Fliss fetched the glass from her nightstand and stealthily rolled up a corner of the Persian rug covering the wooden floor. On her hands and knees, she pressed her ear to the glass and struggle to listen.

The sounds were too faint and muffled to discern more than male voices speaking. After five minutes of straining, Fliss gave up and sat back on her heels. She had to get closer somehow. Even if her bodyguard was asleep, taking the main staircase was pointless. Not only was his chair directly next to them, there were more footmen posted downstairs, none of whom could risk the luxury of a sneaky forty winks. She supposed she could pretend to go fetch a book or a drink, but then one of them would undoubtedly assist her and then escort her back. However, the kitchen did lead out to the garden.

Deciding to take a chance, Fliss carefully opened her door. The burly footman's head was leaning heavily against the wall, his eyes closed. In the last week, because she had been compliant, she had lulled him into a false sense of security and she thanked her lucky stars she'd had the wherewithal to do that one small thing. Keeping to the wall, she edged out of the room, mindful of gently closing the door behind her. Instead of heading towards the main staircase, she crept in the opposite direction, hoping the servants' staircase might lead her where she needed to be.

The narrow stairs were as black as pitch on the upper floors, so she used cautious feet and hands to feel her way down them. At the bottom was a dingy corridor with doors leading out to different parts of the house. Her appalling sense of direction made her dither. If she went out of the wrong door, then the game would be up. In desperation, she closed her eyes and tried to picture the house in relation to the route she had just taken. If the servants' stairs were behind her, then the garden had to be to the left. The kitchen had to be nearby.

Fliss stopped at the second door to the end and put her ear against it. Only when she was certain there was no sound coming from behind did she dare open it. The room beyond was blessedly empty, but well shy of the kitchens. The silhouette of the enormous gilt harp and the expensive Italian pianoforte told her that she had stupidly managed to get herself to the room furthest from the kitchen. The Music Room was the least used and most ostentatious of Uncle Crispin's showy entertainment spaces. The only other door led directly out towards the main staircase and the biggest concentration of guards. She was about to retrace her steps when the moonlight disappeared behind a cloud, plunging her into complete darkness again. Her eyes drifted to the windows. At least they overlooked the garden, although wholly in the wrong place... This new knowledge made her dizzy as Fliss heard her own heartbeat bang loudly in her head. Before she could talk herself out of it, she had pushed open the sash, hoisted up her billowing and flimsy nightgown, then clumsily lowered her body out.

The February cold made her skin prickle with

goosebumps, although the rush of excitement and the forbidden made her hot all over. Taking a convoluted route behind the screen of shrubbery and flowerbeds, it took a few minutes to get to the wall directly outside her uncle's study and she pressed her back against the icy brickwork, willing herself to look like a brick in a feeble attempt to blend in.

Barely breathing, Fliss shuffled a little closer to the window, then closer again until the back of her head came level with the frame. With her heart in her mouth, her pulse drowning out all other sounds, she had to give herself a stern talking to. Several deep cleansing breaths later, she was finally able to hear something. A London accent. Broad and flat. Common. More menacing now that she knew who he worked for. She concentrated hard on the sounds, trying to discern the non-existent consonants from the vowels. Eventually Fliss was able pick out one or two words, hearing them clearer because they kept being repeated.

Tomorrow and *fobbing*—whatever that meant?

The scrape of a chair and the sounds of movement had her leaping away, hugging the wall until she risked darting behind the skeleton of a rosebush and crouching low in the prickly branches to avoid the pristine white linen of her nightgown being discovered by the transient moon. As an afterthought, Fliss dragged off her spectacles, too, in case their lenses reflected the light, and squinted as the door to the garden opened and the Londoner appeared out of it.

Thanks to her poor vision and the hat pulled low, casting shadows over his face, she still could not make out his features and within seconds he had disappeared

into the trees. She considered following him and decided against it. Just this had been terrifying enough and she was in no hurry to die. She had two words more now than she had had before and the King and Lord Fennimore would have to make do with that for now. In the meantime, she had to get back into the house unseen and then count the hours until she could surreptitiously pass the information to someone from the King's Elite on her morning walk.

Chapter Fifteen

Hidden in the mist on Fobbing Marshes

Jake methodically tried to close all the gaps in his greatcoat for the hundredth time, then pulled his thick woollen scarf up to the rims of his eyeballs. After close to six hours exposed, he was prepared to do anything which might make his frozen body less cold. Beside him, Seb seemed cheerfully unaffected by the temperature and his legendary patience was driving Jake insane. 'What time is it?'

'Probably ten minutes on from when I last checked.'

'Can you look at your damned pocket watch?'

'I find time moves much more slowly when you watch it tick past.'

'It'll be light soon.' Which meant that Jake would have wasted an entire night for nothing, worrying about Fliss the whole time and wishing he was there in Berkeley Square, in case she needed him, rather than here hoping to end her torment once and for all.

Seb rolled his eyes, then promptly closed one to stare through his telescope. 'We've got at least another

two hours before the dawn breaks. A lot can happen in two hours.'

'Because so much has happened in six! And what have you got to be so blasted cheerful about? There must be something wrong with you that you are incapable of feeling the cold.'

'I feel it, but like the time I choose to ignore it. What can I say? Some of us are cut out for field work and some of us aren't.'

'I've spent years working in the field.'

'Yes—but your fields have feather eiderdowns and perfumed sheets.'

Jake didn't want to be reminded about those again, not after Fliss had made him more ashamed of what he did than anyone ever had before. His friend must have seen the flash of pain cross his face and assumed it was because of their situation. 'You did insist on coming here tonight, so you only have yourself to blame for your current predicament. You could be tucked up in a nice warm bed somewhere and have left this to the Excise Men.'

'Just as you could have. But like me you knew they're likely to make a ham-fisted hash of it.' The eager bunch who had been assigned to chase Fliss's sketchy intelligence were currently dotted around the marshes, hiding just as Jake and Seb were, waiting for their signal to move a muscle. 'We need the blighters alive, not peppered with musket balls.' So that Jake could shake the truth out of them and then snatch Fliss out of that monster's house.

If only they had more to go on. While Fobbing was a small village sat conveniently on one of the many marshy tributaries of the Thames, it was large

enough to mean they could be in entirely the wrong place to see the smugglers if they turned up. Just because the Norman-built tall tower of St Michael's Church behind them had once been a beacon guiding the boats into these treacherous waters didn't mean it still did. The Excise Men firmly believed they had eradicated free trading from this stretch of Essex nearly twenty years before. The increasing sea defences built since had blocked off many of the small inlets which the boats used and much of the marshland had been drained to make way for grazing land. But they were currently camped near a shallow creek, one of the few barely navigable ones left. One which had been getting progressively deeper over the last couple of hours as the tide came in and tides only came from the sea.

'Tell me what if feels like to be you right now? I mean, it must be quite alien for you to desperately want the love of a woman and to be confronted with the cold shoulder of abject disappointment and total disgust.'

It wasn't. Something which caused his chest to constrict painfully every time Fliss looked through him. The disappointment in her eyes eerily mirrored that of his mother's, except this time it wasn't caused because he merely happened to look like someone. Fliss's disappointment was real and well —earned. With hindsight, Jake wished he had broken ranks and told her the whole truth early on. The deception now created a chasm between them which he didn't know how to breach because she wasn't the usual sort of woman he dealt with. She was frustratingly resistant to his charms. She saw right through it and Jake only had

the truth left in his arsenal. Truth which she had no interest in hearing because she had already worked out most of it for herself.

'I want her forgiveness, not her love, Seb.' Although the latter should frighten him, his heart craved it none the less.

His friend grinned, clearly enjoying his misery. 'I doubt she'll ever forgive you for pretending to want her and then pursuing her relentlessly till you wore her down. I'm no expert on women, but I should imagine a woman like her, one who prides herself in her own common sense around men, would be furious at falling for a man who was only kissing her because he had been told to do so.'

'That wasn't...' He clamped his mouth shut, but it was too late. Seb was staring at him incredulous.

'Good grief... I never thought I'd see the day... You have *genuine* feelings for the girl. Proper romantic ones. You *do* want her to love you back!' He chuckled softly and shook his head. 'Now your belligerent mood makes perfect sense. Jacob Warriner is in love! And with a woman who now loathes him! Oh, how the mighty have fallen.'

'I haven't fallen.' Although he was beginning to suspect he had. This last week had been pure torture. Jake had followed her everywhere, hoping he would see a chink in her frosty, indifferent armour and when he hadn't it had hurt. Real pain. A constant knot in his chest. A head which ached because of his constantly furrowed brow. A tightness in his throat. Hell, last night when she had glared at him as if he were as abhorrent as something foul she had stepped in, he had experienced the overwhelming urge to hide himself in

some dark corner and weep. He was even displaying all the irrational behaviours he had watched his normally sensible brothers go through when their hearts had been lost to the women who were now their wives. Jake couldn't sleep, eat or think straight because the only thing on his mind was her.

Her. Her. *Her.*

Blunt by Name and Nature.

The woman he very probably loved.

Good grief, he was doomed.

The knowledge came with a wave of nausea so acute that for a moment Jake thought he was about to lose his long-ago consumed dinner. How had he let that happen? And, more importantly, what was he going to do about it? She hated him. Rightly so. He'd lied to her from the outset. It didn't matter that he had always lied to women, justifiably for the good of the nation, but Fliss wasn't most women. The second bout of nausea was accompanied by the depressing knowledge she would likely never forgive him for using her. Like every man she had knowledge of he had been wholly undependable in the end. The knot in his chest throbbed painfully and the urge to weep into his frozen hands sprung afresh. He'd made a hamfisted hash of things...

The pathetic sound of one of the Excise Men attempting to mimic a herring gull, the call they had insisted would not arouse suspicion, made a welcome diversion from his maudlin introspection. Someone must have seen something. Seb scanned the waterway with his telescope until it fixed on one spot. 'There,' he whispered, pointing. 'I see a lantern.'

Jake soon saw it for himself, although barely.

Smugglers were very good at blacking out all but the essential light and this one was no bigger than a shilling, flickering as it passed through the long marsh reeds. It made slow progress as it navigated the shallow creek, the long flat-bottomed hull of the barge sitting low in the shallow water. After an interminable age it finally moored at the bottom of the very hill the church stood on.

In the gloomy silence, one man jumped off the boat and raised the miserly lantern in the air. Only when he was satisfied they were all alone did he signal his mate. For the next ten minutes Jake watched the two men offload barrel after barrel from the vessel. When Seb nudged him, Jake readied his pistols and nodded, focusing on the scene in front while his friend moved towards them under the cover of the grass. It was quite a haul, but as yet nobody else had arrived to collect it. They couldn't make a move until they did.

'Put your hands in the air! In the name of his Majesty!' At the shout behind him, Jake wanted to scream in frustration. The Excise Men had jumped the gun and jeopardised the whole mission. The smuggler stood on the deck of the barge immediately dived over the side into the water and disappeared out of sight. The man on the shore partially raised his hands, but appeared ready to bolt at any moment.

'Hold your fire!' Jake stood up and raised one fist in the air to stay the idiots behind, pointing one of his own pistols directly at the smuggler's head. 'Stand still or I will kill you!'

The man paused, his gaze furtively darting from left to right as the Excise Men lit all their own lanterns and exposed him to their eyes. He took a step

backwards towards the water's edge, then yelped as Jake's warning shot sent the turf next to his feet spraying in the air.

'I said stand still! Don't do anything silly...'

In his peripheral vision he saw Seb less than twenty feet away from the man, ready to strike, and calmly raised the second pistol in the air, making sure the smuggler saw the slow cock of the hammer and the deadly aim of the barrel. They couldn't afford to lose this man, too, now their only link to Rowley and the Londoner, and by default Fliss's safety.

Seb inched closer, his head finally emerging from the reeds. A genuine herring gull call spooked the smuggler and he took another clumsy step back, his hands groping at his belt. Jake heard the blast of a shot behind a split second before it exploded in the smuggler's chest, flinging him back into the water. He held his breath while Seb plunged in to retrieve the body and felt the boiling fury course through his veins when his friend shook his head. Their only link was now dead.

'Which one of you fools fired?' Jake grabbed the closest Excise Man by the lapels and shook him. 'We needed him alive, damn it!' This was about more than a few paltry barrels of brandy. The woman he was head over heels in love with was in danger! Grave danger and this was Jake's one chance to get her out swiftly.

Their captain stepped forward, unrepentant. 'He was reaching for his weapon. My man did the right thing. At least the cargo has been seized.' He gave a signal to his men and they all came towards the now-crewless barge, only to be stayed by Leatham.

'You can board it once we've looked it over and not before.'

* * *

For the next half an hour the pair of them searched in vain for clues before reluctantly handing the vessel over to the others. All they could find were tankers filled with brandy. As the dawn began to break they made their way wearily back to the horses they had left almost half a mile away, exhaustion, the cold and Jake's ridiculously heavy heart making each step an effort. He'd failed her again. Now he would need some divine intervention if he was to—

Jake paused and pulled Seb's coat. 'Why were they here? Specifically here?' He stopped and turned full circle and took in the desolate marshland. There was the odd cottage, but the only building of any significance was the church. 'One of us would have seen something if a welcoming party had arrived.'

'Not if they'd heard the gunfire beforehand. Those idiots probably scared them off.'

'But what if there wasn't a welcoming party?' An idea was germinating in Jake's mind. 'We're assuming they came here because the creek runs off the Thames—but what if they came here because that church also used to hide contraband in its cellars?'

As one, they started up the hill. The heavy oak-arched doors were open, as church doors were often prone to be offering sanctuary to all comers, but at this early hour the church was deserted. They wandered past the silent pews to the vestry, locating the entrance to the cellar under a large, threadbare rug.

Jake squeezed his body into the small opening first and allowed his eyes to adjust to the pale lamplight as his friend followed. Ahead a long, narrow tunnel disappeared into the darkness. Together they moved

along it, crouched at first as it twisted and turned, but then it evened out and widened. Eventually they came to a crossroads of sorts as the tunnel veered both left and right. Knowing they'd have to follow both, they turned left and followed it to the end. The wooden door in the ceiling came out on the edge of desolate marsh land. Not a sign of human habitation marred the landscape. There was water, though. Plenty of it and a solitary wooden quay built of strong new timber. In the distance, Jake could make out the sails of the ships traversing the busy Thames beyond and the miniature signs of civilisation that dotted the banks as the river wended its way directly into London.

The second tunnel took them to another cellar, although thanks to a heavy barrel placed over the trap door, they couldn't see more than a small glimpse of the room beyond without dislodging the barrel and potentially alerting its owners to their presence. It was obviously a storeroom. A smuggler's storeroom. Barrels and boxes were piled several deep along the edges. Above that were the sounds of people. Lots of people. Metal plates and mugs clattered as they were plonked down on tables, the smell of ale and beer hung heavy in the air. All they needed to do now was work out the name of the inn.

It was a little past ten when all hell broke loose at Uncle Crispin's. One minute Fliss had been quietly reading in the drawing room, waiting for her aunts to surface, and the next the silence was filled with the angry growl of her uncle's shouting and what sounded like furniture being thrown. She immediately went to investigate and was held at bay outside his bedcham-

ber door by a shocked footman who politely suggested she make herself scarce until he had calmed down.

The cacophony persisted for almost ten minutes and was so loud it succeeded in rousing both Cressida and Daphne from their sherry-induced deep slumber. After that, while the ladies quietly discussed the possible cause of his fury, Uncle Crispin locked himself away for the rest of the day upstairs and Fliss watched a succession of harried-looking footmen disappear in and out of the house ferrying messages.

Close to seven, and in the middle of dressing, Fliss was informed that they would no longer be expecting guests for dinner and that neither would they be attending Almack's as had been intended. With no way of colliding with either Mr Flint or dropping a paper message for Mr Leatham to find, Fliss could do little other than worry and speculate, convinced that, somehow, she must have been the cause.

Her uncle didn't appear at the quiet, tense dinner table or in the hours after, and by the time Fliss pleaded a sudden headache and excused herself for bed in order to stress about it all alone, he was firmly ensconced in his study. The place he only holed up in when he was expecting his menacing nocturnal visitor.

Kitty, much like the rest of the staff, was nervously preoccupied. A full hour after putting her charge to bed, she had still not materialised to check Fliss was asleep and Fliss couldn't stand to waste one more minute. Something was up and as each hour ticked by, it seemed less and less likely she had come under any suspicion. If anything, it was the staff who were

marched into his office, if the steady stream of them leaving with pale, drawn faces at the end of the inquisition was anything to go by. When she could stand the waiting no more she raided her wardrobe and, using another nightgown, pillows and a filigree shawl which she hoped might pass for hair in the darkness, made a body-shaped lump in the bed. After extinguishing both the fire and the candle, she cracked open her bed-chamber door and, seeing the coast was miraculously clear for once, crept out.

The rain fell in a miserable, erratic drizzle which quickly seeped through her shawl and thin nightgown. Fliss ignored it while she found a place behind some bushes to watch her uncle's study. He was alone. Pacing furiously and wringing his hands. Far from being angry, he looked scared, his angular features pinched with worry. Several times he stopped and went to the window, his pale eyes nervously searching the garden.

His nervousness increased her own, heightening all her senses. She felt the air change before she heard the ominous sounds of boots crunching on the gravel in the distance and pushed her body further into the bush instinctively as she heard him scale the wall and drop with a thud as he landed on the ground.

He strode less than three feet in front of her, his big body vibrating with anger, and for the first time Fliss saw his features in profile. Dark hair, fuzzy whiskers covering both his cheeks and curling into a thick moustache under his nose. That nose was bent as if it had once been very badly broken, the large nostrils flared as his breath came in heavy bursts, but it was his hooded eyes which petrified her. They positively burned with hate.

Her uncle recoiled as the Londoner ripped open the French door and stalked inside; it slammed behind him with such force the pane quivered. Fliss watched, horrified, as her uncle was grabbed around the throat and smashed against the wall. The Londoner spat something in Uncle Crispin's choking face, then let him go. Both men began to speak in a rapid tattoo which she could neither hear nor follow from her spot a few yards away. The Londoner did lots of finger pointing, her uncle mostly cowered, and everything about the exchange smacked of something very important. Something urgent.

With her heart in her throat Fliss darted towards the wall and, exactly as she had two nights previously, she edged her body closer and closer until she could hear what was being said. Thankfully this time, because of their respective anger, neither was whispering.

'A month's hard work is gone because of your incompetence!'

'I've told you—I never told a soul outside of the usual few where the boat was headed!'

'You have a leak, Rowley! A big one! Someone tipped off the Excise Men and it sure as hell wasn't me or any of my men! The place is crawling with them now. The tunnels, the inn! We've lost everything. All the stock, our supply route…and all because someone in this house couldn't keep their trap shut!'

'My staff wouldn't dare talk. They know better. I pay them to know better…'

'What about Redditch eh? You've been cosying up to him a lot of late! Maybe you let something slip?'

'I promise you I didn't. I wouldn't. You know full well why I tolerate the old fool. It was you who put me

on to him in the first place! Why would I jeopardise all the effort I've put into wooing the man? The leak has to have come from somewhere else.'

'Mayhap you've employed someone else. Fresh eyes who see too much?'

'There's nobody new. I run a tight ship. Everyone in this house is exactly the same as they were last month, and the month before and the year before that...*unless*...' Fliss covered her mouth in case the cry escaped. Her uncle was no fool.

'Unless what?'

'Forget it. I was going to say my niece might have said something, but I have her under close watch. She doesn't go anywhere or speak to anyone now without me knowing about it.'

'*Now?* What the hell does that mean?'

Fliss felt tears sting her eyes as her uncle regaled him with how she had escaped, how she had rebelliously refused to comply with his demands. It didn't take long for the finger of suspicion to point firmly in her direction. 'I'll expect you to deal with it, Rowley.'

'You can't be suggesting...?'

'I am. You knew what you'd signed up for. You take the Boss's shilling. You carry out his justice. Plug the leak. I want her silenced for good. And tie up the loose ends. All of them. The two old ladies, too, in case she's talked to them as well as the authorities!'

'I can't kill family! What if we're wrong? What if—?'

'We can't risk what if! Put the three of them in a carriage tomorrow. I'll deal with the rest.'

'But...'

The sound of a body hitting the wall again and her

uncle's involuntary squeal suggested the Londoner had resorted to violence again. 'No buts. No excuses. No loose ends! Or do you want me to tell the Boss you are prepared to put his entire operation at risk for the sake of a bunch of women we both know you couldn't care less about…?'

Fliss didn't bother waiting to hear the rest of the conversation. She ran as fast as her legs would take her back to the window of the Music Room, all the time praying she could find a way to save Daphne, Cressida and herself before it was too late.

Chapter Sixteen

Aunt Daphne's bedchamber

Soaked to the skin, terrified and with her words tumbling over each other, Fliss managed to explain the whole story to her aunts in less than five minutes. Their initial disbelief was soon replaced by the same urgent fear which pushed her on. 'We have to escape! Now! Tonight!'

'But all my clothes are in my bedchamber.' Cressida gestured to her nightgown and her hair wrapped tightly in rags. 'I can't leave the house like this!'

'We don't have time to change! It was hard enough sneaking back into the house and rousing you both without the servants seeing, we daren't risk letting them see us prepare for an excursion!' Although the house had been ominously quiet as most of the footmen were now gathered in her uncle's study. They had one opportunity to escape. It was now.

'To be honest, if the servants see us in our nightclothes, we can pretend to be in need of a night-time beverage.' At least Daphne saw sense. 'How do you propose we leave, Felicity?'

'Through the gardens. We have to climb over the wall into the neighbours, then there is an alleyway and...'

Daphne held up her hand and shook her head. 'Out of the question. It is one thing for a lady to be outside in her nightrail, we've all *done that* a time or two, but quite another to be scaling walls. We shall leave by the front door as is proper.'

Cressida nodded enthusiastically. 'Yes, indeed. With my rheumatism I can't be climbing walls.' Before Fliss could argue, Daphne held up her bony hand again.

'Think, Felicity. The front door leads us on to Berkeley Square. My nephew can hardly murder the three of us in full view of the *ton*.' A valid point. 'And if your Mr Leatham has men watching the front then there will be someone around to save us.'

'But how do you suppose we get past the footmen?'

Daphne grinned. 'Do you remember Lord Wivenhoe's house party, Sister?'

A mischievous smile appeared on Cressida's face. 'I do believe I do, Daphne.'

And so it came to pass that Fliss found herself blindly following the lead of two incorrigible old ladies in their hasty bid for freedom. Daphne collected an array of assorted items from around her bedchamber, including a tiny lady's pistol, and concealed them about her person. Fliss was stripped of her soggy nightgown and swathed in the one her scandalous aunt claimed she kept for special occasions. If Fliss had thought her new underthings daring, this billowing, sheer confection made her reconsider. Without the matching silk peignoir, it left little to the imagination,

but it was nightwear and therefore apparently essential to the old ladies' plan so she didn't argue. If it came to it, she would run out of this house stark naked.

Daphne handed the poker to her. 'Hide it in the folds, dear, and do not use it until I give you the signal.' She executed an exaggerated wink, the agreed signal for mayhem to be unleashed.

Cressida retrieved a bottle of rum from her sister's trunk, popped the cork and took a healthy swig. 'I'm ready.'

With more calm than Fliss could muster she sauntered to the door and began to sing loudly as she swayed into the hallway waving the bottle.

'*The Dey of Algiers, when afraid of his ears, A messenger sent to the Court, sir. As he knew in our state the women had weight, He chose one well-hung for the sport, sir.*'

She giggled as Fliss and Daphne chased after her.

'Aunt Cressida. You are ill. Let us put you back to bed.'

'Sister, dear, come. Sleep it off.'

As they had hoped the noise drew the attention of the footmen on duty in the hall below and they rushed towards the staircase to help.

Cressida pointed at one and wiggled her finger at him suggestively. '*He searched the divan till he found out a man—* Whoops!' She tripped for effect at the bottom step and drunkenly pushed the footman towards the front door. '*And he lately came o'er from the Barbary shore, as the great Plen... As the great Plen...* Oh, dear I always get stuck on that last word.'

She leaned heavily on the footman and grinned up at him while the second footman supported her elbow,

and Daphne and Fliss gathered around to help. They were less than six feet from the door.

Daphne winked and Cressida threw out her arms, smacking the footman in the face with her bottle as she sang at the top of her lungs, '*As the great Pleni- potentiary*!'

Fliss cracked the second footmen over the head with her poker as Daphne whacked the first smartly with a full bottle of rum that hadn't been opened. Both men staggered woozily from the blows, leaving the three of them free to make a dash for the door.

They had the late hour and the element of surprise on their side, but not for long. There were so many bolts to slide, that it took all three of them to get the thing open before they tumbled out into Berkeley Square.

'Help! Help!'

Fliss scanned the darkness for the watchmen Lord Fennimore had promised her, all the while dragging her aunts with her into the night. When nobody appeared, they ran to the corner where a solitary hackney stood waiting, while back at the house there was already the sound of panicked shouts calling for help. Fliss managed to stuff both old ladies in as one of the footmen ran haphazardly from her uncle's house. His forehead was bleeding and he clutched at his head. Behind him, three more men hurried out and sprinted towards them, far too close for comfort. From the shadows, some shabby men appeared, but no Mr Leatham. They dashed towards her uncle's men, grabbing them and slowing their pursuit and giving Fliss just enough time to throw herself into the hackney. She screamed at the coachman, 'Just drive!'

Panicked, he cracked his whip repeatedly and the coach lurched forward the moment her feet left the pavement and thankfully didn't stop as one of the footmen came perilously close to grabbing the door handle. The horses picked up speed and the carriage clattered out of the square. Blessedly they were soon flying along the deserted streets away from the danger. Thanks to Mr Leatham's men, nobody appeared to have followed them. Eventually, when they were a significant distance away, he slowed enough to ask directions and Fliss barked the address of the only place she could think of. The only place her heart wanted to be.

'The Albany! Take us to the Albany!'

The city was wide awake as Jake finally wove his way to St James's practically dead on his feet, the sun valiantly poking its head through the miserable blanket of clouds for the first time in weeks. Typically, the fine weather decided to appear now, rather than overnight or the whole day before when he might have benefitted from it. After the discovery of the underground tunnel system, they had sent to London for Lord Fennimore and reinforcements, believing the smuggling gang might be spooked by the loss of their cargo and suspecting they would move swiftly to relocate their reserves. That suspicion had proved correct. The moment the darkness fell, the innkeeper and his staff set to work shifting the barrels towards the deserted quay he and Seb had found in the marshes, clearly waiting for some boats to come and retrieve it all. Jake and Seb spent another freezing, wet, sleepless night watching and waiting in the reeds with Lord Fenni-

more. At dawn, like the jumpy innkeeper, they realised those boats were never going to come. The Boss would rather relinquish that supply chain and those profits rather than jeopardise his entire operation.

They'd rounded up the terrified publican and his accomplices for questioning, seized everything in the cellar and left the Excise Men crawling through the tunnel like a colony of ants. While it wasn't the satisfying conclusion they had hoped for, Jake was philosophical. At least they had enough circumstantial evidence to arrest Rowley on suspicion of aiding and abetting free traders and, despite Jake's soggy clothes, aching body and heavy heart filled with worry, Lord Fennimore now finally agreed Fliss's work was done. As soon as Jake was washed, shaved and presentable, he fully intended to head to Berkeley Square and find some way to get her out of there.

When the doorman told him he had visitors, his first instinct was to pat the pistol on his belt as his hackles rose. Upon learning those visitors were female, three of them and all in nightgowns, he practically sprinted up the stairs in a blind panic. Something must have happened in his absence and he prayed it wasn't bad. But if three of them were there...

He burst through the door to see his valet pouring brandy into two outstretched teacups.

'Don't be stingy, there's a good fellow. We *have* been through an ordeal.' Daphne Sawyer's head turned and she smiled at the sight of Jake, her grey hair still wound in curling rags. 'Ah, finally! We've been waiting for you for hours, young man. Hours and hours. I suppose you've been out gallivanting.' The smile quickly turned into a frosty frown of disapproval. 'You

could have timed your urges better. We were almost murdered in our beds and would have been had Felicity not had the wherewithal to get us out! My nephew has gone quite mad, hasn't he, Sister?'

'Yes, indeed. We had to overpower the footmen and flee in a hackney.' Cressida swigged the entire potent contents of her cup and held it out for more. 'My nerves are shot to pieces.'

'Where's Fliss?' Because her absence in his tiny bachelor parlour petrified him. 'Has she been harmed?' If she had, someone was going to die.

'She is as well as can be expected under the circumstances and quite determined to go home today.'

'She is unharmed?' Jake barked out the question.

Watching his worried face, the old lady smiled. 'You *do* care! That *is* encouraging.' Both ladies shared a knowing smile. 'Since we arrived here, she's been in a foul mood and was getting more agitated by the minute. I thought she was going to wear a groove in the floor with her pacing.'

'But where is she now?' Their amusement irritated him.

'Gone to find some suitable travelling clothes in your bedchamber, sir.' His valet gestured backwards with an incline of his head. 'I've already sent a message to Lord Fennimore appraising him of her whereabouts.'

He didn't wait to ask more questions. The only thing he cared about was seeing her. Jake crashed through the door and stopped dead in his tracks as the sight of one very feminine, very bare back caught him completely by surprise. Fliss squealed and clutched the front of the nightgown quickly to her chin before she

turned around, oblivious to the fact the weak February sun streaming through the window made the gossamer nightgown translucent. Every mouth-watering curve was shown in stark silhouette and the dusty peaks of her breasts were easy to find.

'Don't you believe in knocking!'

'I was worried about you.'

'Oh, please! I doubt you've given me a single thought in the hours you've been out philandering!' The snippy, jealous tone buoyed him. 'Why—your shirt is undone and you're not even wearing a cravat. It's obvious you have just fallen out of some hussy's bed!'

'I haven't been out philandering and I haven't been in anything resembling a bed in days.' He quietly closed the door behind him and leaned against it, enjoying the way the daylight picked out the rich caramel tones in her hair as it tumbled over her naked shoulders. 'There have also been no hussies. Nor have there been since the night I met you at Almack's.' After his epiphany on the marshes, he had promised himself he would tell her nothing but the whole truth going forward—if he was ever given the chance to. Now that she was here, there was no time like the present. 'I fear you have ruined me for all other women, Fliss. I've missed you.' At her disbelieving eye roll he smiled. 'If you must know, I've been in Fobbing.'

'Fobbing is a place?'

'A very cold and damp place. Filled with smuggled brandy ferried down the Thames on barges.' As he spoke she wiggled her arms back into the nightgown and tightly tied the ribbons at her neck. Jake decided not to tell her it made precious little difference.

Thanks to the blessed return of the sun his view was still spectacular and the wiggling, combined with her presence, was doing wonders in taking his mind off his exhaustion. As were the erotic spectacles she had primly placed back on her delectable nose. 'Thanks to you we intercepted a fresh delivery and then discovered where the rest of the contraband was hidden.'

'Ah... My useless information proved not to be useless at all, then. I did wonder if I was responsible for my uncle's irrational behaviour yesterday.' She sank down to sit on the bed. His bed. The home of those fevered dreams and yearning. The irony was not lost on him. 'Hardly a surprise, then, that suspicion fell on me.'

Jake should have anticipated that and the guilt was instant. 'I put you in danger and then wasn't there for you.' Instead, he had insisted on accompanying Leatham when he should have remained watching over her.

For the first time since she had discovered his mission, Fliss smiled kindly. 'I seem to recall I put myself in danger. You were dead set against it. Mind you, I might not have been so gracious had I known my uncle and his associates would happily kill me and those two dear old ladies out there to save his own sorry hide. Still, we escaped. I didn't know where else to go.'

'I'm glad you came to me. Fliss, I know now is not a good time, but I need to explain.' Her eyes lifted to his—they were so troubled and sad he had to go to her, but as he sat down on the mattress beside her, wrapping one arm around her shoulders to draw her into his embrace, she folded her arms across her chest and angled her body ever so slightly away from his. The

message was clear. She didn't want his comfort. Coming here had been a last resort. The knowledge cut like a knife into his poor, confused and ill-prepared heart.

'There is nothing to explain.' She stood and, still hugging her body, calmly put several feet between them. 'They are dangerous men and the world will be a better place with them off the streets. You did what you had to do. What you are trained to do. We don't need to discuss it.'

'But, Fliss...'

'Please, Jake, don't.' Her golden eyebrows pleaded with him to stop and her eyes glistened with pain, then both faded only to be replaced with that flat, emotionless stare which destroyed him.

'We do.' He rose and edged towards her, his palms flat, imploring. He owed her the truth. What she did with it was up to her, but if there was any hope for them it had to start with honesty. 'To begin with, my pursuit of you was a mission, but from the outset I struggled with it. Before I knew who you were I was drawn to you, and then...' He sighed, not quite knowing how to put it all into words. The feelings he had for Fliss were so new and so different from any he had wrestled with before. They had broadsided him. 'I wish I'd been honest with you sooner.' Although would he have been? Knowing there were messy and complicated feelings involved, he knew himself too well to believe he'd have done anything differently if he'd have had any whiff of what was happening to his heart. If anything, Jake would have panicked and doubled his efforts to seduce her quickly so that he could get away. He'd spent a lifetime avoiding the painful emotion which came when a man and a woman

became too attached. 'And I wish I had been able to tell you the truth myself. The way you found out... the timing...well, it was not as I would have wanted.'

'If wishes were horses, beggars would ride. I wish I had never wandered into that alcove in Almack's.'

'You don't mean that.'

She shrugged and walked to the window, denying him the chance to watch her face to know for sure. 'I saw him. The Londoner, I mean. He was dark. Swarthy. His hair was black, I think, and he had bushy whiskers and a moustache. His nose was quite Roman. If I were to hazard a guess I would say it had been badly broken many times. He wasn't as tall as you, maybe an inch or so off six feet, but much stockier. Very big hands. Very frightening.'

Slowly, Jake had come to stand behind her. He resisted the urge to touch her, sensing it wouldn't be welcome. 'Information you can tell Lord Fennimore when he arrives. I want to talk about us.'

'There is no us, Jake.'

'I want there to be.' When she didn't respond, he risked putting one hand on her hip before allowing it to coil possessively around her waist. 'I know I am the very last sort of man you want. I have a past. One I'm not particularly proud of now. But the truth is, my heart...' His throat choked with emotion. Every messy and complicated feeling was suddenly clawing its way up his neck and demanding to be let out. It was both terrifying and humbling, but at least it was honest. She shifted round and was staring into his eyes so intently he felt vulnerable and exposed, and he couldn't bear to see her expression in case she rejected him. Instead he closed his eyes. 'The truth is

my heart is yours now. I… I love you, Fliss.' He exhaled, then instantly sucked in a breath to hold as he waited for her response.

She turned away and her head fell back to rest on his shoulder while her eyes stared out of the window. For several long moments, they simply stood there. Jake waiting. Fliss thinking. When she stiffened he knew he'd lost.

'I don't trust you, Jake.'

She gently prised his arm away and turned to face him again. He could see the doubt warring with some other powerful emotion. He hoped it was affection or temptation for him. Her lovely face was etched with pain. Seeing his wise northern owl with a broken wing of his making was eating him from the inside like a cancer. 'Do you think you might be able to? One day?' Again, she didn't respond straight away which gave him some hope. The tiny flame warmed his battered heart. A decisive flat no would have taken no thought.

'I don't know, Jake.'

That had to be enough until he worked out a solution and there and then he decided he *had* to find a solution. He had to find a way to make the badness good. A way to earn her forgiveness and her trust again. Even if it took him a lifetime.

A lifetime!

Good grief, he was doomed. Or blessed. Or just plain mad to be contemplating for ever with any woman, let alone the one who saw straight through him. Yet in her time of need, she had come to him first. That had to count for something.

'I'll make this right, Fliss. I swear it.'

Her lovely eyes searched his for the truth and he

held her stare this time, willing her to see it. Jake wanted to hold her and reassure her it would be all right. He took a step forward to do exactly that, but the soft knock on the door was followed by his valet's voice.

'Lord Fennimore is here and so are the others. There has been a complication, sir.'

Chapter Seventeen

*On the Great North Road, bound for
Nottinghamshire*

Fliss stretched out her aching neck and opened the carriage curtains. The sharp shard of sunlight made her wince and drop it back in place. This was the second sunrise she had witnessed in this carriage and the second night she had attempted to snatch a few hours of sleep on the uncomfortable bench as it sped north, barely stopping long enough to change the horses and fill their bellies with food.

As uncomfortable as the three ladies were, every mile away from London couldn't come soon enough. The more miles the better. Each one helped to relieve the enormous knot of fear which had formed in her chest when she had first learned she was a loose end to be tied and had doubled when she had learned that the Londoner had murdered her uncle for the very same reason and probably within hours of Fliss's epic escape.

Since then, the whole world had been turned up-

side down. At least that's what it felt like. She was no longer a naïve schoolmistress from Cumbria or an unlikely spy for his Majesty's government. Now she was a target. The only person still alive who could identify her uncle's murderer and his links to the dangerous underworld he had become involved in.

When the astounding news came that Uncle Crispin had been found hanging in his study within hours of her watching him, nobody believed it was suicide. Not when there were meaty hand-shaped bruises apparent beneath the silken bell-pull wrapped around his neck. Uncharitably Fliss knew he would have happily seen Daphne, Cressida and herself garrotted by convenient footpads to save his own skin. When push came to shove, he might have even done the deed himself, he was that cold and self-serving. So she couldn't find it in her heart to grieve for him and fully blamed him for the danger she now found herself in. There was no room in her mind for grief; having a price on one's head was petrifying.

Thank the Lord she had escaped and fled to Jake's, because he had been reassuringly adamant about her continued safety since Lord Fennimore, Mr Leatham and Lord Flint had arrived that morning at the Albany. At his insistence, they had left the capital that morning. The carriage they were travelling in bore the colours of the Post, so the sight of it speeding up the Great North Road would not arouse suspicion. Knowing he and Mr Leatham were driving it, that they were both heavily armed and that a huge escort travelled both ahead and behind them also made her feel better, although only marginally. Until she was safely locked within the fortress he had assured her he had grown

up in, and many, many weeks had passed, she doubted the crippling and all-consuming fear would begin to subside. Lord Fennimore was hopeful Fliss's final destination was obscure enough to be safe but, with what was highly likely to be an enormous bounty for her whereabouts, there was still the chance somebody might tell them she had gone first to the Albany and then from there perhaps they would link her to Jake.

Another group was being led by Flint and headed further north to Sister Ursuline's, to evacuate the school and lay in wait should the Londoner attempt to search for her there. Local battalions of Excise Men were also being drafted in to stand guard in Cumbria. Both Jake and Mr Leatham were of the belief the shadowy criminal behind it all, the elusive Boss, had men or informants from within their ranks and so involving the Excise Men while neglecting to apprise them of her true location would lure the men to the convent and ultimately to their arrest.

As the carriage began to slow, Cressida stirred beside her and gazed bleary-eyed around the dim carriage. 'Where are we?'

'I have no idea, but it's morning.' Fliss lifted the curtain again and forced her tired eyes to adjust to the brightness. They were no longer on a main road. The narrow lane was flanked on either side by dense trees. Eventually, a twenty-foot wall loomed in the distance. When they passed through it there was an orchard, orderly lines of trees echoing with the sounds of children's laughter. The carriage came to a halt and Jake jumped down. For the first time since they had begun this arduous journey, neither he nor Mr Leatham had

warned them to keep the curtains closed as they had at the busy inns they had stopped at.

Fliss took the opportunity to lower the window and poke her head out. Their scruffy-looking entourage rattled past the giant, sturdy gates which stood wide open. As the last cart of Mr Leatham's Invisibles trundled through, Jake, Leatham and several men began to close them. It reassuringly took a great deal of strength.

'I think you might be lost...this is private land.' A man the spitting image of Jake, only slightly older, limping and draped with little dark-haired girls, approached the carriage. His deep blue eyes flicked to hers first, then towards the gate. 'Jake? Is that you?' The sight of his brother sporting several days' worth of beard and dressed in the red uniform of the Post men clearly amused him. 'Our big brother will be pleased that you've finally got yourself a job.' His face fell when he saw the gates shut and he instantly wrapped his arms around his daughters. 'What's wrong?'

Jake strode towards his brother and hugged him. 'Too complicated to explain here. Where are Jack and Joe?'

'Both at home as far as I know as it's early, but you know Joe.'

'Round them up, Jamie. I'll see them inside.' With that he climbed back in the driver's seat and the carriage lurched forward again.

Within minutes they had reached an impressive Tudor manor house and were met by servants at the door. Another dark haired and blue-eyed man came to greet Jake with a beautiful woman still in her dressing gown. A riot of blonde corkscrew curls hung loose

over her shoulders. As the men talked she came towards them smiling. 'I'm Letty Warriner—Jake's sister-in-law. I can see you are exhausted. Come. Let us get you inside. Chivers, our butler, will fetch tea.'

After that, Fliss and the Sawyer sisters were made a huge fuss of. Hot tea and breakfast came in quick succession, which Fliss fell upon gratefully, and then sighed with relief when she was shown into a beautiful bedchamber. A steaming bath had been drawn and wafted a deliciously floral scent about the room. A selection of clean clothes and a beautiful embroidered nightrail had also been laid out.

'Jake said you haven't slept properly for days, so if you want to sleep then please go ahead and do so. We are very informal here.' Letty laid a soft hand on her shoulder and it appeared to have the power to trigger the waterworks. Tears streamed down Fliss's cheeks and, to her acute embarrassment, she couldn't appear to stop them.

'I'm so sorry.'

'Oh, don't be. You've been through an ordeal. I was kidnapped once, so I completely sympathise. I've often thought female tears are more a release of pent-up anger and frustration rather than a sign of weakness and from what I can gather you have been quite brave enough so far.'

Another woman burst through the door at that exact moment, copper hair tied back in a single ribbon and her freckled face smiling. 'Apparently we are in the midst of a crisis, or so my curmudgeonly husband tells me, so I brought cake. I know it's early but everything is better with cake, don't you think? I'm Cassie Warriner and I made this myself.' The sight of the charm-

ingly wonky concoction only made Fliss's tears worse and she began to hiccup and snort as she wept into the pretty handkerchief her hostess had just pressed into her hand. 'Clearly I've arrived just in time. I've sent Chivers for more tea. You can't have cake without tea.' Unfazed by her overtly emotional state, Cassie wrapped an arm about her shoulders and squeezed. 'Get it all out. Bottling stuff up inside is never good. Bella will be here soon. She's finding mornings a bit trying at the moment.'

The butler scratched at the door and didn't blink an eyelid at Fliss's grizzling as he deposited the second tea tray on the bedside table. He was closely followed by a dark-haired woman who looked worryingly green around the gills. 'Sorry I'm late to the party. I am counting the days till this morning sickness fades. Joe is adamant that it's not unusual for it to continue past three months and it's at least four months now and the slightest thing sets me off. Is that cake?' She eyed it suspiciously. 'Move it out of the way, Cassie, or I will disgrace myself in front of our guest.' A guest who would welcome some company in the disgracing. 'My goodness, you look pale…'

A large black medical bag appeared out of nowhere and the third Warriner wife rifled in it. She produced three bottles. The first two she measured out on a teaspoon and dropped in Fliss's tea. 'A few drops of these should help with your mood. Gorse relieves despair and willow apparently eases the tendency towards self-pity. I mixed them with plenty of sugar so even if their therapeutic abilities are dubious they will make your tea taste nice. But this…' Bella grinned and wiggled the third bottle '…is heaven in the bath.' She pulled

out the cork and, after depositing the whole bottle into the steaming tub, the scent of lavender tickled Fliss's nostrils. 'A nice cup of tea in the bath is just what you need.'

'I happen to think my cake in the bath will be more beneficial than your grass in her tea, Bella.' Cassie Warriner was already sawing off a slice which she placed on the side table she had dragged next to the bathtub, next to Fliss's tea. 'And then when you are fully refreshed we shall all gather again and get to know each other.'

'Yes,' said Letty as the three walked towards the door. 'We are all intrigued to learn about your dealings with our dear brother Jake. None of us has ever seen him quite so...ferocious before.'

Joe was the last to arrive and took his place at the scarred kitchen table where they had always held important discussions. In the hours since Jake had come home, they hadn't pressed him for information, merely aided him in making the grounds secure without questioning why. That solid, loyal reinforcement was exactly the reason he had brought Fliss here. When you messed with one Warriner, you messed with them all and together they had always been a force to be reckoned with, although he was dreading telling them all he'd been lying about for five long years.

Jack's quirked eyebrow signalled they had waited long enough. 'Why have we battened down the hatches and why is there a small army encamped on my lawn?'

'I've not been being entirely honest with you all.'

'You don't say?' His elder brother folded his arms across his chest, a sure sign his patience was wear-

ing thin. 'There are a lot of guns out there for a mail coach. What the hell are you involved in?'

There was no easy way of saying. 'I suppose the best way of explaining it is to tell you that I've been working for the government. I have been since Cambridge. I belong to a secret branch called the King's Elite. We work with the Home Office, the Foreign Office and alongside the Excise Men tracking large-scale smuggling operations.'

Two pairs of blue eyes stared back at him agog. Only Jamie didn't appear the least bit surprised. But then only Jamie had alluded to knowing the truth before.

'And you've done this for five years?'

'Yes, Jack. I was recruited almost as soon as I left university.'

'Why?'

Now came the part he was dreading. 'They recognised that some of my skills might be useful in procuring difficult information.' A painfully convoluted and shoddy description which he hoped might be enough. Typically, Jamie understood straight away because he'd done similar in the Peninsula, although he had nobly kept his clothes on.

'So you are a spy?'

'You're a spy!' Joe was flabbergasted.

'That's the long and short of it, yes.'

There was a painful beat of silence while they all digested this, and then, of course, came the narrowed eyes. 'What skills?' Because Jack knew he possessed few and frequently lamented his lack of attempting to acquire more.

'My way with the…ah…ladies.' Saying it out loud

made him feel like a doxy for hire, only it was the crown, not a client, who left the money on his nightstand.

'You lucky devil!' Joe threw his head back and laughed. 'Only you would land a job which allowed you to be horizontal most of the time.' He slapped him on the back jovially. 'All these years we've nagged you about being a rake isn't a career and all the while it was! That's priceless. You've always had the luck of the devil.'

'I wouldn't call myself lucky. I hardly had a choice as to whom I...' Oh, good grief, this was painful. For years he had told himself he was pleased with being a rake. He got to enjoy women without any of the messy complications, but now he felt sordid—a shameful philanderer, just as Fliss had first said.

'The young lady upstairs, I take it she is one of your *assigned* conquests?' Jack didn't appear the slightest bit amused at his confession.

'Yes. No!' Jake ran an angry hand through his hair. 'It's complicated. I *was* sent to seduce her. Her uncle was involved in a major smuggling ring which we believe is funding Napoleon's supporters. We had been trying for months to get deep into his inner circle and I was drafted in when they dragged Fliss into the mess.'

'Fliss?' Another cocked eyebrow. 'How very cosy. Does she know you bedded her on the King's shilling or are we expected to help you perpetuate the charade?' As the devoted father of four girls, Jamie's stormy expression conveyed his outrage at such a situation perfectly.

'I haven't bedded her and, if you must know, at this point in the proceedings I am highly unlikely to.' Get-

ting her to actually talk to him would be something. He and Fliss hadn't exchanged anything other than essential words in days. It was as if she had erected an invisible yet impenetrable wall around herself, one which let most people in except Jake. This morning she had barely looked at him and the widening chasm between them was killing him. 'She currently loathes me because she learned about the King's blasted shilling. I wish I knew what to do to fix that!' Three pairs of dark eyebrows rose at his frustrated tone and Jake wished he couldn't speak fluent eyebrow, or that the world would suddenly be completely eyebrow free and thus spare him from reading the meaning of one ever again. Embarrassed, he went on the defensive. 'Anyway, whether or not I bedded her is by the by. She's in danger. Grave danger and it's all my fault!'

They listened intently as he told them all about Rowley, the murderous Londoner and the mysterious and ever-elusive Boss. Jake left nothing out of the whole sordid story, knowing that each of them deserved to know the full truth because he was bringing that danger to their door. Their families. His family. To their credit, none of his brothers passed comment when he told them how he had sought Fliss out, how he had teased information out of her or how he had allowed her to walk alone into the lion's den after he had promised her he would help her. Three awful truths where he wished with all his heart he had behaved more honourably—as the three of them would have undoubtedly done in his shoes. By the end of the tale, he hoped he had adequately and dispassionately conveyed the seriousness of the situation. 'If you want me to move her, I completely understand. Just let us rest

here for a few hours because I am dead on my feet and I can't protect her properly if I am not on my game.'

Everyone looked to Jack to make the decision, just as they had always looked to Jack their whole lives, and he made them wait while he considered all the ramifications. 'This affects you all. Jamie's and Joe's houses lie within the walls of Markham Manor.' Both men nodded slowly. '*If* we do this—and it's a *big* if at this stage—then I think it's safest you all move back into the main house until the danger is past. It might also be prudent to attempt to convince the ladies to move away temporarily. For their safety.' The second nod was less decisive as all three knew there was little chance of dislodging their devoted and determined spouses. Especially if they banded together, as they were prone to do, and dug their heels in. More silent seconds ticked by until his eldest brother pinned Jake with his stare. 'Give me one good reason why we should invite trouble to our door for a stranger.'

'Fliss is...she is...' Emotion clogged Jake's throat.

'You love her.' It was a statement, not a question.

'With all my heart.'

All three sighed in that matter-of-fact way he also loved about them and regarded him with pity. Joe and Jamie simultaneously wrapped strong arms about his shoulders while Jack huffed out a deep breath. 'Then I suppose we need to start the preparations for a potential siege. Jamie, dust off your arsenal, I fear we might need it, and then we'll tackle the ladies. I suspect your smugglers might be easier to defeat.'

Chapter Eighteen

Around the dinner table at Markham Manor, eating Letty's traditional Foul à la Braise

'Could you pass the salt?' Too late Fliss realised it sat next to his hand. Jake smiled and passed it to her, but in her clumsy hurry to grab it as quickly as possible, their fingers brushed and she ended up yanking it away as if she'd been burned. Which she had. The instant warmth zinged up her fingers and bounced around all her nerve endings before blooming into an embarrassing blush on her cheeks. A blush she willed away by concentrating hard on sprinkling a few grains of the dratted salt over her potatoes. Good gracious, she had never felt so awkward, but then again she had never before sat down to a dinner with three strange women who had recently seen her blubbing like a baby and a scoundrel who had kissed her and made her fingers zing without trying and his entire family. It was beyond unnerving, yet apparently only to her. Nobody else appeared particularly fazed.

According to her generous hostess, whenever there

was a significant occasion, good or bad, the Warriners gathered together and ate chicken. It was a tradition and one which gave them strength, apparently, so Fliss found herself very much the centre of attention around their giant dining table. All the adults, aside from her vexing rescuer, were unsubtly watching the peculiar atmosphere between her and Jake.

She had done her best to reassure the ladies after her bath that she and Jake were merely acquainted through circumstances and that she was nothing more than a mission to him. She was grateful for his rescuing her, of course she was, but that was the full extent of their brief and odd relationship. But then, when she had related everything which had happened to her in the last few weeks, her uncle's treachery and the threat to her life by the Londoner, Fliss had conveniently left out how she had welcomed, then come to depend on, Jake's friendship. In her story, they happened to collide. They never danced, or ran away and spent the day laughing at the Tower, and they certainly never shared an earth-shattering and inappropriate kiss in a hackney.

In glossing over the truth she had hoped to maintain her dignity—the last thing she wanted was them knowing that most of those noisy tears had been shed because she was heartbroken. The constant knot in her chest she had carried since she had discovered he had been lying could be nothing else. And if she was brutally honest with herself, which of course she always was, she couldn't be heartbroken unless she had given her heart in the first place and somewhere in a ballroom, or in Hyde Park or in the worst hackney in the world, Fliss had given Jake hers and he had stepped

on it repeatedly—just as she had his feet during their one and only waltz. If only he wasn't a professional liar and if only she had not been stupid enough to ask for salt! Her silly cheeks were still glowing crimson.

Joe, the nearest brother in age to Jake, seemed to find the spectacle highly amusing and was making no attempt to disguise the fact he was studying their behaviour, much like an ornithologist would scrutinise rare nesting birds in the wild. Jack and Jamie were making a better show of uninterest, but even they had smiled at the salt incident. The wives put on a good show, but then they'd had a hand in placing her purposefully just opposite their untrustworthy brother-in-law and then distributed themselves specifically to get the best view, so that hardly counted. They all had their suspicions and she sincerely hoped Jake the Snake had been discreet in his own explanations. Surely he owed her that much?

The other end of the table was worse, so Fliss tried her best to avoid glancing left. Daphne and Cressida, already pickled in several glasses of wine, were openly grinning at her gauche and guilty reactions and Jake's feeble attempts to appear normal as he picked at his food. Periodically, though, his eyes would lock with hers and all manner of inappropriate emotions were visible in those intense swirling-blue depths. Each one of them doing strange things to her heart, which she was determined to harden against him and was failing to do with alarming frequency. Past him, several sets of identical bright-blue eyes were openly staring at her. All of them under the age of seven.

It didn't help that the nieces and nephews had insisted on sitting close to Jake, because he was a charm-

ingly doting uncle with a wonderfully patient way with children. The sight of him so obviously affectionate and paternal was making her womb ache and her mind wonder. Damn him for being a natural father! Jake didn't need any more points in his favour. That one was now noted alongside fiercely protective, quick witted, intuitive, devilishly handsome, always there when she needed him and a splendid kisser. Her heart wanted to add beautifully contrite and tortured in his remorse, but if she relented and added those then she would have to allow her sensible head to believe his sweet and heartfelt declaration of love was real when he had resolutely refused to meet her eyes when he said it, which meant she was doomed to surrender and he would have won. Although doomed didn't seem half as bad now as it had a few days ago and a growing part of her was coming to hope he might give up his womanising ways if the right woman came along. Was she the right woman?

Clearly, Fliss was now suffering from the blind naivety that had afflicted many of the wayward girls, Sister Ursuline and her own beloved mother, if she believed that nonsense, and she knew full well how all those liaisons had turned out.

Badly.

She had to be strong. Rise above her biological urges and uncharacteristic romantic tendencies. Ignore the persistent knot in her chest and the urgent call of her womb. Call of her womb! Biology was quickly becoming her least favourite science. He had not looked her in the eye and, deep down, she knew that meant he was probably lying. 'How long do you think it will be before I can return home to Cumbria?'

Jake's head snapped up because they were the first words she had directed towards him since they had sat down half an hour ago. 'I suppose that depends on how swiftly the Londoner decides to tie up the last remaining loose end.' And there it was again, that fierce, protective gleam in his eyes. 'When he is standing on the scaffold—unless he meets his maker before.'

'What happens if you can't find him?'

'We'll find him.' Certainty. Roiling hatred on her behalf. 'Until then, you are safe here. You don't have to live in fear, Fliss.'

'Can I call you Auntie Fliss?' The eldest son of Letty and Jack asked this with the innocent face of an angel.

'You may call me Fliss, as that is my name and we are friends now.'

'But when you marry Uncle Jake you will be my aunt, won't you?' There was an audible hiss as the entire table collectively breathed in.

Fliss didn't dare look up. 'I'm not marrying your uncle, poppet.'

'Mama says you will. If Uncle Jake apologises properly.'

Her eyes flicked to Letty, who had the good grace to look sheepish at the end of the table before she glowered at her son. 'I *did not* say that, Jonathan!'

'Well, if you didn't Papa certainly did. I heard him discussing it with Uncle Jamie. He said it was about time the notches on his bedpost had finally caught up with him.'

The eldest two Warriners' eyes widened as they struggled to find the words to apologise. However,

young Jonathan was far from finished turning the screw.

He tugged on the now-furious Jake's sleeve. 'Why do you have notches on your bedpost, Uncle Jake?'

Letty shot to her feet. 'Right, I think it's past your bedtimes, children. Come along!' She sent a mortified glance at Fliss while everyone else stared at their plates, except for Joe, who watched Cressida frantically chase a lone pea around her plate with her fork.

Fliss did the same, but found tears prickling her eyes. Tears she would never allow him to see. 'I think I shall retire, too. It's been a trying couple of days... Goodnight, everyone.'

She scraped her chair back too loudly and the sound reverberated around the dreadful silence like a hammer on an anvil at the crack of dawn. In her hurry, her skirts got tangled and she almost stumbled as she tried, and failed, to glide like a swan out of the room with the last vestiges of her dignity holding her ramrod straight. So straight she feared her shoulder blades might snap.

They all knew what had happened.

With her innate skills at reading people, she could see it written plainly on every face. The straightened brows, the chewed bottom lips, the downcast eyes, their irises brim full of pity. Because they knew. He'd told them. How she'd almost become another one of those silly notches. Every hideously shameful detail had been shared with his family, because he was lucky enough to have the luxury of one.

Suddenly all those intuitive and identical Warriner eyes bored into her soul and stripped it bare and she had to get away. She didn't look at any of them as she

swept out of the dining room. Alone, Fliss could curl up into a ball and cry. She heard more wood grinding against floor and purposeful footsteps behind her, and picked up her pace as she reached the staircase. The dratted tears fell regardless, silently and miserably, spurring her onwards.

'Fliss, wait!'

'Leave me alone, Jake.' At the top of the stairs she forgot about pride or propriety and simply ran towards her bedchamber. With his longer legs he was right behind her as she reached the door.

'We need to talk. Please.'

'You told them, didn't you? I'm so humiliated! Do they all know you were paid to kiss me?'

'Fliss—it wasn't like that—'

She cut him off by slamming the door in his face and resting her back heavily against it.

'Don't make me talk to the door.'

'Go away. I honestly have nothing to say to you. Just g-go away.' Fliss hated that her voice cracked. 'I wish I'd never met you, Jake Warriner! I hate you!'

That comment was met with silence, but when she craned her ears she could still hear his soft breathing outside. To her horror more tears fell, when she had never been one for crying. Silent, devastated tears of self-pity. For everything. Her situation, the danger, Jake's lies and the humiliation of knowing the last vestiges of her dignity now lay in tattered and public ruins at her feet.

'If it's any consolation, I hate myself, too.' His voice was a muffled whisper, as if his face was also laid against the door. 'I can't eat. I can't sleep. My mind keeps rolling, searching over everything and suggest-

ing a hundred different ways I could have done this or that. I loathe myself for hurting you and for lying and for letting you go back to your uncle. I wasn't there when you had to escape and I hate myself because you had to deal with that all alone. The danger you are in now is gnawing at me, too. I keep running through every scenario and imagining you hurt, and I blame myself for that, too. If you hadn't escaped, you would have been murdered that night just like your uncle. I can't get that image out of my mind. If I'd said no to Leatham and taken you straight back to Cumbria like I promised then you'd still be safe and none of this would have happened.' His voice sounded choked and her heart went out to him.

'That is my uncle's fault, Jake, not yours.'

'I could have stopped it.'

'Could you?' Without thinking, she traced her fingers over the wood his voice hid behind. 'Who's to say my uncle wouldn't have tripped up somewhere and those men still would have headed north to tie up loose ends? I would have been all alone, unsuspecting and unguarded. Maybe fate intended this to happen all along.'

'You don't believe in fate.'

'But you do.' Or at least he had claimed to when he had been tasked with seducing her. Her hand dropped back to her side and she felt betrayed all over again. 'When it suits you. It's impossible to separate the pretty lies from the facts.'

She heard him exhale slowly. 'You seem to always have my measure, Fliss, and that terrifies me because I'm stripped bare before you. You've always seen through the charm and the bravado, but actually

I do believe in fate. That is a fact. I believe that sometimes we have no control over things even when we try with all our might to direct them. The honest truth is I'm painfully aware of my own failings. I always have been. My brothers are right. I've spent my entire life avoiding emotional entanglements and responsibility.

'Growing up, I watched it destroy my parents. They both loathed and loved each other to the exclusion of all else. My father couldn't handle responsibility either and sought his solace at the bottom of a bottle for all the mistakes he made. My mother lived in the past and resented the life he had dragged her into. They were always arguing, often violently, and that constant battleground slowly killed both of them.

'My mother committed suicide. Or at least that's what the world believes. In reality, she was always threatening to harm herself in order to get my father's attention and it always worked. She would cry and he'd come running, then the pair of them would fight and then lose themselves in passion, then the toxic vicious circle would begin all over again.

'As a child I found it exhausting and terrifying, and I have no doubt those early impressions have stuck with me as I've grown. On that day, as she had on so many others before, my mother told me she was going to throw herself in the river and sent me to fetch him, but because I wasn't keen on facing my father's wrath I dawdled, and because of that she died.

'I'm not asking for your pity. I know I don't deserve it. My brothers tell me it was her choice to do what she did. That she was a selfish woman who never cared for any of us, me least of all because I was so much like my father. Another pretty liar with little else of

substance behind him. But even so, that event has left deep scars. That dreadful day, their relationship, it left its mark on me and shaped the man I became.

'I never wanted to live with all that angst and drama ever again. It's too painful. Too destructive. I like life to be simple and uncomplicated. I'm not good with guilt or anger or introspection and I certainly never wanted to become my father, although I also know, deep down, that I do not possess any of his worst traits. I would never be intentionally cruel and I'm not violent or unable to discern right from wrong. But I am selfish. I've selfishly protected my heart. I've lived my life ensuring that none of that messy emotional nonsense ever touched me. Aside from my brothers, I've kept everyone else at arm's length. Purposefully so. But then I met you and all those necessary defences dissolved and that terrifies me.

'I didn't want to get involved, yet I did regardless. I didn't want to show you my true colours, but you saw them anyway and the very last thing I ever wanted to do was fall in love, because I knew I couldn't bear the heartbreak if it went wrong and I was right. I'm dying inside, Fliss, because I love you so much and you quite rightly hate me. But know that, despite you loathing me, I will fight till my dying breath to keep you safe. If you cannot bring yourself to trust me with anything else, please trust me to do that, Fliss. I can't face living in a world that you are not in.'

Fliss wanted to believe him. Desperately. But with a solid oak door between them she couldn't see if he was telling the truth. She pulled open the door and sought his eyes. They were blue. So blue they were almost black. His tell-tale pupils were large and awash with

tears as she stared into them. One solitary drop fell off his lashes and slowly ran down his cheek. She saw his pain because it mirrored hers exactly. His misery was real and visceral. But alongside that raw, undisguised emotion swirling in his irises Fliss also saw something else. Something as irrefutable as it was unexpected. Something her heart yearned for and which her sensible head couldn't overrule. Something she'd wanted all her life. Waited for. Would never settle for anything less than. This man—this loyal, incorrigible, flawed man—absolutely adored her. Those beautiful blue eyes of his couldn't lie to her.

It was her feet that closed the short distance between them. Her hands that reached out to cup his face. Her lips which brushed his first. But it was both of them who lost themselves in the honest beauty of the moment before burning, biological need took over.

The second her mouth had touched his, Jake was on fire. His wary heart was bursting with joy that she wanted him and might well have forgiven him; his battered body yearned to join with her. That first kiss had ignited it all—love, desire, longing—and that first kiss was yet to end. What had started gently had simmered as they didn't break apart. Together they had stumbled back into her bedchamber, failing to pause when Jake had kicked the door closed, and tumbled breathless on to the bed. He had shrugged out of his jacket, then set about pulling all the pins from her hair while she clumsily undid the buttons on his waistcoat, before tugging the tail of his shirt roughly from his breeches.

Now, with all her hair gloriously loose he rolled her on top of him so he could fumble with the laces

at the back of her dress. As the fabric loosened he smoothed it off her shoulders with his palms, revelling in the warm, silky texture of the skin of her bare arms. He wanted to look at what he was touching, but that meant prising his hungry lips from hers and like a starving man at a banquet he couldn't. So he let his hands see instead, running them greedily down her ribcage, then back up again to cup her breasts while Fliss reached behind and attempted to undo the ribbons of her corset.

She giggled into his mouth and collapsed against him, her breasts squashed wonderfully in his hands. 'It's knotted. Take it off.' An invitation he didn't need to hear twice.

Jake shuffled into a sitting position and tackled the mess, but she was right, the ribbons were hopelessly tangled and his hands lacked the finesse or the patience to solve the puzzle. In desperation he groped for the knife in his boot and in one swift motion sliced through the ribbons to the delight of them both and tossed the offending garment to the floor.

Knelt on the bed in just her chemise, golden hair tousled and smiling, she was a picture. Her gaze never left his fingers as he reached out one hand and slowly tugged the bow on the low bodice. He teased them both by gently tugging the fabric lower, enjoying the way it resisted and strained across her nipples. He let his thumb slip beneath the lace to graze one and had the satisfaction of hearing her sigh at the brief touch. Another tug and the flimsy fabric pooled at her waist and he drank in the sight of her bared before him. Every inch of her was perfect, as he had known she would be. Flawless peachy skin, saucily

jutting breasts tipped with dusky pink tips, undulating curves which nipped in at the waist and flared out at the hips. All better than his wildest imaginings or his fevered dreams.

Reverently he bent his head to kiss her again, gentler this time because she deserved better than the rushed and hasty loving he had so far subjected her to. He trailed soft kisses down her throat and over the swells of her breasts, pausing long enough to worship each nipple. The throaty, staccato moans told him she thoroughly enjoyed that, so he lingered longer until those lovely breasts were rising and falling rapidly in time to her erratic breathing. As he nibbled the underside of one he let his fingers wander lower until they rested in the golden curls at the apex of her thighs. She stilled as they wandered lower, but she allowed him to nudge her legs open and gave a lovely whimper of pleasure as he caressed her, but when Jake sat back to look she clamped them shut again and hastily covered them with her chemise. 'What are you doing?'

The prim, missish reaction amused him after her obvious enjoyment thus far. 'I'm fundamentally a nosy fellow, as you know, and I need to see you, Fliss. All of you.'

'Why do you get to see all of me before I get to see all of you?'

'Because you are so beautiful I fear I won't be able to control myself if we are both naked just yet and I want to see to your pleasure first. Try to trust me, my love. It'll be worth it. I promise.'

He sensed her trepidation as she forced herself to relax, a rosy blush of embarrassment pinkening her cheeks and her neck as she allowed him to slide away

the last bit of clothing, but the trust in her eyes humbled him and exulted him at the same time. This time when he caressed her, she was tense, but he soon eased that away and she let her legs fall wantonly open as her breathing became more laboured and her hands gripped the sheet beneath her.

Jake knew exactly how to ease her frustration. He also knew enough about the female body to know that the more he built the anticipation, the sweeter her release would be. When he sensed she was close, he lazily smoothed his hand back up her body and went right back to kissing her. As he'd hoped, it was not enough. Her hips bucked and she arched beneath him, but he wouldn't be swayed. His talented mouth and hands remained resolutely above her waist until she was writhing beneath him.

It was Fliss who lost patience first, shamelessly sliding her hands under his shirt and raking her nails over his chest and back, making earthy noises which almost sent him over the edge. 'I want you naked, Jake.' Her green eyes were stormy with desire and her mouth was swollen from his kisses. Jake had never seen anything so erotic in his life. Impatiently he sat up and tugged off his shirt and he had to watch her lounging gloriously naked while his suddenly urgent and clumsy fingers dispensed with his boots and the buttons on his falls, but at her insistence he let her remove his breeches and she tortured him by duplicating the slow, sensuous disrobing he had subjected her to. Except this time, the fabric resisted and strained over his insistent, needy bulge. A bulge she was thoroughly exploring over the blasted fabric with the flat palm of her hand.

She grinned when Jake growled, drawing out the moment before slipping her hand inside and touching him properly. The inquisitive first explorations soon turned bold as she watched how she affected him. It was ecstasy. It was agony. But he endured it stoically by biting down on his lip and clenching his fists as she exposed him inch by inch.

'Is this your revenge?'

'I think you deserve a little punishment.'

'Haven't I suffered enough?'

Fliss pushed the fabric to the floor, her eyes fixed on the impressive sight of him in all his glory, and flicked him a wicked, passion-charged gaze. 'Oh, I think you need to suffer some more.' She had no real idea what she was doing and let her instincts guide her. Jake's magnificent body was an enigma which she burned to explore. Fortunately, that exploration was proving to be scandalously exciting for both of them. Brazenly she let her hands wander where they wanted—the broad expanse of his shoulders, the taut stomach, strong back, the delightfully compact and rounded bottom. Then her mouth, teeth and tongue followed and she learned that his hard, muscled body was as sensitive as her soft one. He shivered when her tongue traced his nipple and followed the dark dusting of hair as it arrowed down his abdomen. In fascination she traced the length and girth of his hardness, smiling as his jaw tightened or when he occasionally hissed out a strangled breath.

Every moan and sigh was accompanied by his heated gaze; deep blue eyes bright with mischief and love. To begin with Jake lay there passive, but soon he paid her back in kind. Every touch of hers which

tormented him was parried with a more thrilling intimacy from him, shocking yet unbearably pleasurable intrusions that made her grateful he had been a rake, yet none giving her the elusive fulfilment her newly awakened body seemed to crave.

Only when she was positively vibrating with need and he was breathing heavily did he position himself on top of her, staring straight into her eyes. His hardness cradled against her body. Her body wanting it inside her. That want, the significance of what they were about to do, made her suddenly nervous. She was the novice. He knew what he was doing. What if she didn't compare with the women before or meet his expectations?

'You're my first lover, Jake. Be patient with me.'

He brushed his nose against hers tenderly. 'And you'll be my last lover. That is just as significant. In fact, I fear it's you who needs to be patient with me.' Her mocking smile was met with pure seriousness. Jake laced his fingers with hers and brought her hand to rest snugly between them on his chest, holding it firmly in place. 'Do you feel that?' Beneath her palm his heart drummed steadily.

'I can feel your heart...'

'No, love, it's not my heart any more. It's yours. It always will be. Please be gentle with it because it bruises easily. And be patient with me, Fliss. Falling in love is the most terrifying thing I've ever done. I'm ill prepared for the adventure. So ill prepared I'm bound to make mistakes. I don't want tonight to be one of them. I've shared my body more often than I should have. I can't change that, but I've never *made love* to a woman before, nor wanted to. Making love

involves the heart and the body, and up until recently my poor heart was happily encased in cotton wool and robustly barricaded from the world. But as much as it scares me, as much as I fear all those messy and complicated emotions and responsibilities which walk alongside love, I know everything will be all right as long as you are beside me, too. This will be my first time and I don't want to make a hash of it.'

He kissed her softly and that part of him nudged at her entrance, while he nuzzled her neck. 'This is a huge responsibility. I need to show you how much I love you. How much I will always love you.' He gently eased inside, pausing to allow her to adjust to the intrusion. 'I need to make tonight truly special for you. I need to make sure you never look at another man some time in the future and wonder what if?' His expression became fierce and Fliss could feel the tension in his whole body as he held himself in check. There was a look of intense concentration on his handsome face as he came up against the barrier of her maidenhead. 'I don't want to hurt you, but know that I must to make you mine.' She sucked in a breath as he pushed passed it quickly and stilled as he kissed away the pain—only then did he fill her completely. 'I need you to believe that you are the one. My one and only. For always and for ever.'

As he began to move, the alien feeling of this new intimacy began to fade, replaced instead by a sense of complete rightness. Biology and fate. Two unpredictable factors which had made their love inevitable. She loved him so much, wanted him so much, it consumed her. Fliss happily succumbed to the building desire only Jake kindled. Each stroke reverberated

down her nerve endings, heating them, heating her and her wary heart. Every kiss fanned the flames. Every touch set her ablaze. With building need, she matched him thrust for thrust, revelling in the solid weight of him around her, shamelessly touching every part of him she could reach with her hands and clenching her internal muscles around the wonderful part of him she couldn't. All the while their eyes were locked. Now words were unnecessary because there were no words to convey how immersed in each other they were. Two bodies in perfect unison; two hearts beating in time with the other.

As the passion built, Fliss surrendered herself to every new sensation whole-heartedly, glorying in the effect their lovemaking was having on him, too. His eyes were so dark. His body so ardent. She had never felt so beautiful or alive. Special. So utterly adored and cherished. She remembered murmuring his name. Telling him she loved him, then the universe exploded in shimmering blue light as bright as his eyes and they dived into the sublime abyss together.

Chapter Nineteen

In the garden at Markham Manor

It had been a peculiar week. Idyllic, yet trying. A time of latent fear and of pure joy, noisy family camaraderie, quiet introspection and passionate intimacy. Jake was a creative and resourceful lover who had initiated her completely into the pleasures of the flesh. During the day, just as he had less than an hour ago, he found ways for them to steal a few minutes of privacy and utilised those scant minutes so fully and thoroughly her body tingled from the experience.

One minute she had been walking purposefully towards the Great Hall the Warriners used as a drawing room and the next she had been outrageously braced against the door inside the linen closet, her skirts around her waist, but her spectacles resolutely on her nose, because that was where Jake liked them when the mood struck, while he had his wicked way with her. Not that Fliss minded one bit. All those naughty wayward tendencies which she had always struggled to suppress happily came to the fore with

him and she always rejoiced in the frantic, breathless waylaying.

Late at night, when the house slept, the dynamic between them shifted. He would creep to her room and make slow, tender love to her and then she would drift off to sleep, feeling safe in his arms. In between times, they spent a great deal of time in one another's company, often with the others, but the Warriners and her incorrigible aunts were at great pains to leave them alone together frequently. It seemed everyone was equally keen to see them paired off, actively encouraging their deepening romance, and neither Jake nor Fliss made any attempt to slow things down. There was an inevitability to it all. Serendipity. As if they were destined to be together, so why bother fighting the mysterious forces which pulled them together?

Here, in his home, Fliss felt she was coming to truly know the real Jake. Of course he was charming, that characteristic was etched into his bones, and he shamelessly flirted with each of his brothers' wives and all of the female servants in his good-natured way, but she saw it for what it was and was not the least bit perturbed by it. She owned his heart. Lock, stock and barrel. His eyes told her so every single second they spent together.

But she also saw the other facets of his character which he hid behind his silver tongue. The enviable and unbreakable bond he had with his three brothers and their respective wives. The thoughtful man who took care to spend equal time with all his nieces and nephews in case he appeared to have a favourite. He really was a man who listened and paid attention, and not just to Fliss. He followed every thread of conver-

sation around the dinner table, remembered the tiny idiosyncrasies and details about people, whether that be Letty's latest embroidery project or the current state of little Jonathan's butterfly collection, and while he remembered all this, as well as the names of all of the servants' children as he frequently asked about them, he still tirelessly patrolled the grounds with Leatham and the Invisibles and kept a close eye on her security at all times. That attention to detail was beyond reassuring at a time when her nerves were often strung as taut as a bow.

It helped that Markham Manor was indeed a fortress as he had promised. Three-quarters of the sprawling parkland was surrounded by an enormous stone wall which appeared strong enough to withstand the force of a battering ram. Beyond it, several dense miles of Sherwood Forest cloaked the perimeter. Only one long lane led to the tall, forbidding locked gates. The remaining quarter used nature for protection. The River Idle provided the house with a wide barrier between them and the outside world, and in the dead of winter after all the rain the underlying current was apparently ferocious. The small but deadly battalion of the King's Elite closely monitored the vulnerable areas along the river bank, as well as the wall. While the sight of men wielding pistols constantly gave Fliss the shivers, she was supremely grateful they were there. Their presence allowed her to function relatively normally, or as normally as a displaced schoolmistress from a convent could be in the crammed house of her lover, waiting for evil to strike.

Jake was adamant she would remain here until he was satisfied the danger had passed. Danger he was

convinced still might be lurking despite the express they had received two days ago from Flint and Lord Fennimore, informing them that Sister Ursuline's had been attacked by a gang of men and, instead of them finding Fliss as they had anticipated, they walked into a deadly ambush of Excise Men. Of the twenty-six assassins sent to kill her, all but two were now quite thoroughly dead. Lord Fennimore was confident the danger was now passed and they had got their man in the skirmish. Any one of those men could have been the Londoner, but as only Fliss had ever seen him and there was nearly two hundred miles between her and those dead faces, Jake was not taking any chances. His efforts now concentrated on the two. Just in case, although how long his Majesty's government would continue to support her protection was still a mystery. As each new day passed uneventfully, it appeared less and less likely anyone was going to come for her—which in turn meant they were wasting valuable resources which were desperately needed elsewhere. Jake suspected that when Flint and Lord Fennimore arrived back from the north to meet them, then the rest of the King's Elite would leave with them.

She was trying not to think about that.

'Serena cheated!'

'I did not. You're just a sore loser!'

Fliss looked up from the book she wasn't reading at the sound of the two oldest Warriner children bickering again. The enforced proximity and near constant rainfall of the last couple of days had meant the poor dears had been cooped up in Markham Manor and were bored stiff. In desperation, Cassie and Letty had organised a lawn bowls tournament to be played on

the carpet. Letty's three boys formed one team, the eldest three of Cassie's girls the other. At the time it had seemed like a brilliant idea; within ten minutes it had descended into more arguing.

'Your cousin didn't cheat, Jonathan. She knocked your ball away fair and square. Play nice.' Fliss recognised the exasperated tone of her hostess and felt guilty for being the cause of it. Every Warriner's life had been disrupted because of her, but they were all being so nice and stoic about it as they fussed over her. It didn't sit right. 'It's your brother's turn.'

'We're still losing.' Jonathan said this to his youngest sibling with all the seriousness of an unimpressed seven-year-old and he clearly blamed him as the cause. 'Please try harder.'

Little James's tongue poked out in concentration, but his childish attempt rolled well shy of the jack, causing more eye rolls from his big brother. When Cassie's four-year-old stepped forward to take her turn, Aunt Daphne came behind her to help. 'Now remember what I told you, young lady, a nice smooth arm motion with a bit of oomph.'

The child eyed the jack with determination and threw it with all her might. It whizzed through the air and crashed into Jonathan's remaining bowl, sending it careening towards the wall as hers gently rolled to kiss the jack.

'I call foul!' Poor Jonathan was outraged. 'She was meant to roll the bowl, not throw it! Throwing is cheating. Isn't it? *Isn't it!*' Six angry children's voices jostled to be heard, while the two eldest cousins squared up to one another. Before outright war broke out, Fliss jumped up to intervene.

'Jonathan. Serena. Why don't we take a walk in the garden seeing as the rain has stopped?' As the two main protagonists, their swift removal and distraction would help to calm the situation. 'You can show me around as I have not seen barely any of it yet.'

Both children nodded, but their mothers both frowned. 'I'm not sure you should go outside, Fliss.'

'Every inch of the estate is guarded, Letty. What harm can it do? And these poor dears could do with some time outside to expel some of their pent-up energy.'

'Can I bring my ball, Auntie Fliss?' Little Jonathan, like the rest of the Warriner children, had already adopted her as one of the family. 'We could play catch.'

'I love catch,' Serena added with a wistful look. 'And can we show Auntie Fliss the stables? Would you like to meet Orange Blossom and Satan?' Pleading fingers tugged at Fliss's skirts.

'I suppose it wouldn't hurt to take them some carrots.' The frazzled Cassie had relented. 'The little ones do need a nap.'

Bella made the final decision. 'The men are all out there with Jake. I shall instruct Chivers to let them know we are taking some air. I for one could definitely use some.' She stood up and grinned, patting the tiny, growing bump lovingly. 'So could this little Warriner.'

In less than five minutes, they were all in heavy, warm winter coats and walking across the lawn. Daphne and Cressida had also jumped at the chance to leave the confines of the house along with Bella. All three happily watched the two children toss the

leather ball back and forth, laughing and giggling now that the ill feeling between them was now forgotten.

The crisp February air felt marvellous, as did the freedom. They set a brisk pace towards the stables, loitered a while to pet the horses, then took a circuitous route around the parkland, allowing Jonathan and Serena to guide them around places of interest. Typically, this meant visiting the very best part of the estate to play in: the wide-open meadow flanked by clumps of weeping willows. Bizarrely, watching those dark-haired cherubs running amok and climbing over everything reminded Fliss that life was much better when it was not shrouded in fear.

Every few minutes they passed one of Leatham's Invisibles, who emerged from their hiding places to offer them a reassuring smile and a wave as they continued on their way, reassuring her that this place *was* safe. It was a fortress filled with loyal brave knights and she was the princess they protected. It went a long way to lightening her mood until the laughing children made her forget the danger entirely and Fliss felt properly light again for the first time in weeks as she forced herself to believe the danger really might be past. Each day of peace surely proved it?

'I need to sit,' said Daphne without preamble as she placed her bottom on a log. 'All this walking is making me thirsty.'

'Now that you come to mention it, I am a bit parched.' Cressida sat beside her and produced a hip flask from her pocket. 'Fortunately, I filled this with some lemonade earlier.'

Lemonade which had doubtless been doctored with something from one of their host's crystal de-

canters. Fliss glanced at Bella and they shared a smile. The two old dears were incorrigible, but in a delightful way, and the way they embraced life and took everything thrown at them so completely in their stride was an inspiration. To look at them, nobody would know they had recently fled Mayfair for their lives or that the dark cloud of death still loomed on the horizon.

'Who wants to play catch?'

'Auntie Fliss, you can be in my team and Aunt Bella can be on Serena's.' Jonathan marched them to a spot of flat grass close to the trees and organised them to stand in a small square. 'Each time the ball is dropped equals a point for the opposing team.' When nobody dropped in several rounds, he declared the square too small and ordered everyone to take several paces back. Soon that became the game. As the ball hit the grass, the winning team crowed and everyone took another step backwards until poor Serena with her tiny arms could barely bridge the distance. Being plucky and stubborn, she used all her might to hurl it at Fliss, but misjudged it and sent it several feet to the left. The little leather ball bounced hard on the ground, then began to roll downhill towards the clump of trees behind them.

'Oh, Serena.' Jonathan shook his head and began to chase the ball, only to be swiftly halted by Bella.

'No further than the trees, young man. You know you are not allowed near the river in winter.'

Fliss hadn't realised they were that close. She certainly couldn't hear it, but visions of Letty's son tripping over and floundering in the cold water suddenly made her nervous, or perhaps her constant state of

nervousness made her imagination more vivid with nasty possibilities? Either way, Fliss was the only adult present neither aged nor pregnant entrusted with keeping him out of harm—Fliss and the two burly men posted at either end of their stretch of river—so retrieving the lost ball and restoring family harmony was her responsibility.

She spied it instantly, a little brown sphere poking out of some long grass near the waterfall of branches, and bent to retrieve it. As she stood, she saw it.

At first it appeared to be a log protruding from the overhanging branches of the largest willow less than five yards away, but as she turned the shadows changed. That log seemed to be wearing boots. Curious, she edged closer, then stopped dead in her tracks. One boot became two; they were attached to a man lying face down. Stood proud between his shoulder blades was the hilt of a knife.

Blind panic had her calling out a warning to the others, screaming at the top of her lungs to Bella and the children to run before she started up the steep incline herself.

'Oh, no, you don't.'

The voice behind Fliss chilled her blood a split second before an arm wrapped itself around her throat like a vice and dragged her choking back towards the trees. She fought and clawed, but the Londoner had strength, surprise and gravity on his side. The heels of her borrowed walking boots slipped on the wet grass, denying her any traction as he pulled her through the branches of the willow. The pressure on her windpipe was starving her of air, making her light-headed.

One meaty hand wove its way into her hair and shoved her down to her knees. 'Well, isn't this fortuitous? Miss Blunt, I presume? How lovely to finally make your acquaintance. You've caused me a bit of bother.'

Chapter Twenty

Under the ancient weeping willow

Denied the sight of his face as he growled close to her ear, Fliss's eyes darted around, searching for an escape route. They were shielded from the world by the ancient willow's cascade of branches. The sounds of the river were amplified in this cocoon, cold mist settling on her face suggesting it was close by. Another corpse lay on the soft mud within, his throat cut. She recognised him as one of the Invisibles and whimpered. He was dead because of her. Probably the other man, too. So many innocent people were now in extreme danger. Jake. His brothers. Their young families.

He forced her head back cruelly, making her look into his manic eyes. 'Were you the one spying on me?'

'I wasn't s-spying.'

'Liar.' The back of his hand slammed hard across her face. 'You took a hackney to the Albany while I was in your uncle's house. I know Jacob Warriner works for the Excise Men. I know they brought you here to hide and I know they set a trap for my men!'

His hand whipped across her cheek again, so hard her head snapped back and spun. He violently shook her out of the blackness. 'Was *he* with you that night? Has he seen my face?'

'No!' At least he referred to Jake in the present tense. Fliss forced herself to take some comfort in that.

'Who else has seen me?'

'N-nobody. Just me.' If she couldn't save herself, perhaps she could spare the others the fate of those poor men. 'I heard you telling my uncle you wanted my aunts murdered, too, so I dragged them with me. They know nothing. Only me. I'm the only one who has seen you.' Pride made her look him in the eye. Pure hatred made her brave. 'I'm your loose end.'

'Then come with me, my lovely, and you can tell that to the Boss. Let's hope he believes you, for both our sakes. He don't like loose ends.'

He was so strong, easily dragging her like a dead weight to the water's edge.

'You can get in the boat willingly or I'll drown you and deliver your body to the Boss. Your choice.' She hesitated and he smiled callously. 'I've got what I've come for. The quicker you move, the less chance there is of me killing someone else. Those wee ones or your fancy man, perhaps...'

Thinking fast, Fliss staggered to her feet and stepped into the small tethered rowing boat. Drowning right this minute served no purpose because Jake was coming. She knew that with the same certainty that she knew this monster before her was pure evil. At some point he would have to leave the sanctuary of this willow and sail in open water where he would

be vulnerable. Every man in the King's Elite had a pistol. Any one of them could take a decisive shot.

Before he pushed the boat off the muddy bank, the Londoner bound her hands roughly in her lap, the coarse rope so tight it made her fingers throb. Then he used the oars to dislodge the boat, his brawny arms holding one steady in the water to act as a rudder in the current. As they emerged from the branches, that underwater current proved to be too strong, sending the bouncing rowing boat drifting back towards the open meadow rather than in the direction her captor wanted it to go. His arms frantically dragged the oars, but the two opposing forces merely twisted them on the same spot. He'd misjudged things and was panicking. Fliss could see it in the wild darting of his eyes and the hard, determined set of his jaw.

As subtly as she could, she leaned towards the direction of the current to make his job harder and searched the horizon for help. While she was relieved to see no sign of Bella, the children or her aunts, the lack of anyone coming to her rescue was worrying. But the longer they sat here, completely exposed and floundering, the better. Jake would come and with him would come more men and guns. That certainty was like a soothing balm to her soul and gave her the calm she needed to think pragmatically.

The hard thud of a boot on her leg brought her sharply back to the moment. 'Sit up straight!'

Fliss complied roughly, purposely causing the boat to rock and freezing water to slosh in, soaking her feet. The more delays she created, the more chances she afforded Jake and his men. The Londoner's response was to kick her again, which only made the violent

rocking worse, and the boat listed and twisted, forcing him to use both oars and all his strength to calm it.

'They are going to kill you. You know that, don't you?' Her voice was sure and prim. Her Miss Blunt schoolmistress tone. Defiant. His eyes briefly narrowed.

'Not before I kill you first.'

Jake and Leatham had crept along the cover of the willows. The rest of the men were either on their way or already in position under cover. They weren't called the Invisibles for nothing. Somewhere, too, were his brothers, because Warriners always stuck together. Knowing that gave him some comfort, but did little to ease the clawing panic which consumed him. The sight of two good men murdered hadn't helped.

'Not before I kill you first.'

Both of them stilled at the gravelly sound of the Londoner and Seb silently gestured beyond the branches to pinpoint exactly where the voice had come from. Then he mouthed the word *Fobbing*. Jake understood instantly. He would confront the scoundrel, keep him occupied while his friend crept around and took the shot.

Taking a deep breath, Jake emerged from the curtain of the willow fronds, his pistol aimed. When he saw her, spinning in the river, bound and pale, his heart stopped and his arm wavered. The irony of the situation was not lost on him. Nor was the symbolism. Why did it have to be here? The exact same place...

He wouldn't fail this time.

'Put your hands in the air!'

Fliss turned then and her frightened eyes locked

with his in the same moment her captor placed the point of his pistol against her neck. 'Go ahead, Mr Warriner. Shoot me. I'll blow her pretty brains out before your bullet leaves the chamber.'

Jake didn't dare risk flicking a gaze left or right. Fliss's life depended on him trusting Leatham to do the job. 'And then you will also die. You're surrounded. All my men are armed. If you surrender yourself we will provide you protection from the Boss.' The man wouldn't live to step on the shore if Jake had anything to do with it, but now, the official lines might buy them some time if the bastard thought he could save his own sorry skin. 'Testify against him and I guarantee you won't hang.'

The chilling laughter echoed in the silence. 'I'd rather hang then spend the rest of my short life looking over my shoulder. I'm already a dead man walking. The Boss doesn't take well to failure.' He jabbed the pistol harder under Fliss's jaw. 'But you don't want *her* dead, do you, Warriner? So you'd best let us go.' His other hand groped for the oar and with Fliss clamped against him as a human shield, attempted to row away.

The tiny boat pitched again, and spun, then seemed to wedge itself against some underwater debris. The position was a bad one, denying Jake or Leatham a clean shot that wouldn't hit her as well.

Checkmate.

Jake stood rooted to the spot, his pistol raised in readiness none the less. 'Let. Her. Go.' The second he had a clear line of sight that monster would die.

'Urgh!'

The shout from the willow branches as Leatham launched himself out, pistol waving like an ancient

warrior, made the Londoner start. The smuggler's gun hand shifted.

Aimed.

Fired.

The bullet ripped through Jake's friend's body, throwing him backwards in a hideous spray of blood. Jake watched in horror as the Londoner briefly let go of Fliss to reach for another weapon. Like a dream, he saw her lurch to her feet in the boat. Watched her eyes widen and lock with his before they softened. Watched them harden to emeralds as she threw herself over the side and was instantly swept away in the current.

His guttural cry and the explosion from his pistol sliced through the air. Jake didn't care whether he'd hit his target. All he cared about was the woman in the water. Oblivious to everything else he charged in after her, first running, then swimming towards the tangled green skirts which floated on the surface like river weed.

As he got closer, he saw her bound hands had grabbed the willow fronds, but the current was winning. It was greedily flowing around her, each new surge ebbing higher and higher as she struggled to stay afloat. For one heart-stopping moment, her face disappeared under the surface, only to emerge again a few seconds later spluttering as she fought to stay afloat.

Jake battled to swim alongside, wrapping one arm tightly around her as he, too, grabbed the ancient willow, but her woollen winter skirts were like an anchor, sucking her down until he could barely hold her face free of the river. She gasped for air and swallowed a mouthful of river instead, her eyes staring helplessly

up at him from beneath the icy tomb. Terrified. She didn't want to die.

Yet he was losing her. He wasn't strong enough. She had trusted him to save her and he was failing, just as he always failed when people stupidly depended on him. He stared back at where his fingers gripped the branch. The irony wasn't lost on him. Fate's last cruel joke at his expense. He should just let go and let the angry river take them both. Selfishly he didn't want to live without her. Knew he wasn't strong enough to carry that burden. Knew his heart only beat for her.

'We've got you!' His eldest brother Jack's voice boomed through the despair. He was waist deep in the water, his other hand locked tightly in Joe's. Behind him was Jamie. Strong as an ox and braced round the same gnarled branch Jake had scrambled along all those years ago.

His brother grabbed his collar and pulled, freeing Jake to finally let go of the willow. He wrapped both his arms tightly around Fliss and kicked for all he was worth, until his feet scraped along the river bank and his lungs burned from the exertion. Together they dragged her to safety.

Except she wasn't safe.

She lay on the ground like a wet rag. Pale. Frozen. Deathly still. Jake stood back to allow Joe to do what he was trained to do, knowing in his unworthy heart it was futile.

'She's not breathing, is she?'

'There's water in her lungs.' His brother's face was grave. Joe turned Fliss's head and river water spewed out of her slack mouth. Then he turned her head upright again and pushed on her chest. When the trick-

ling stopped he bent and began to blow deeply into her mouth while Jake stood powerless and broken, the pain in his own chest so severe he wished he had let go of the branch so that he didn't have to face the future without her. Knowing he'd failed her when she had needed him the most.

His eldest brother's arms went around his shoulder. He didn't offer platitudes or false hope, simply his strength, and as he had all those years before Jake leaned on him and wondered how the hell he was supposed to cope with this. His heart was bleeding. His life now meaningless. Tight bands of pain corded around his body and he wished they'd strangle the life out of him and get it over with.

'This is all my fault.'

'No, it isn't. You did all you could.'

Which was never enough. It was all so hideously familiar. Damn fate and its twisted games! Damn it all to—

Her violent coughing and spluttering was the most beautiful sound Jake had ever heard and he dropped to his knees and wept. He didn't care who saw it or what they thought, he just scrambled towards her and gathered her close while she caught her breath, smoothing her wet hair from her chilled face and telling her how much he loved her.

Close by, Bella and Jamie were bent over Leatham, then Joe joined them, too. All Jake could do was pray for his friend because he couldn't let Fliss go. From somewhere, a dry greatcoat was placed around his shoulders and he used it swaddle her in. After several long minutes, her arms wrapped around his neck. 'Oh, Jake...' Her voice was so weak, hoarse from her or-

deal, but hearing it healed his broken heart instantly. They still had today and tomorrow and for ever.

'I thought I'd lost you.' She was going to be the death of him and the light of his life. A life he now couldn't wait to get started on. A new life with a wife and a home. Children perhaps. Love. Laughter. Light. 'What were you thinking, woman? Throwing yourself overboard...'

Her finger pressed against his lips softly, silencing him and she smiled. 'You do have an uncanny knack of being in exactly the right place at exactly the right time, Jacob Warriner. I trusted you implicitly to save me.' One frozen finger brushed a tear from his cheek. 'I knew you wouldn't disappoint me.'

Epilogue

Markham Manor—February 1830

'Jake. It's time.'

Although he'd been on tenterhooks waiting for those words for three long weeks, they still caught him by surprise. He quickly rolled to sit, but fell out of the bed instead.

'Right! Right! Don't panic!'

'I'm not panicking, darling. You are.' She was shaking her head and smiling at him as he stuffed his legs into his boots. Then laughed as he stalked to the door. 'Clothes, Jacob?'

He looked down at his body. Nude except for the Hessians he had jammed on the wrong feet, he smiled, too. 'You'd think I'd be more prepared fourth time around, wouldn't you?'

He tried to be calm as he dressed, tried to ignore the way her pretty face contorted with each contraction and kissed her softly as he went to raise the troops. Each of their three children had been born in Markham Manor. It had become a tradition and they

had travelled up from Mayfair a month ago to be with his family for the birth.

Flint was holding the fort in his stead at the King's Elite. Lord Fennimore had made Jake his successor when he had finally retired last year. In Jake's opinion, it should have been Leatham's job. His brave, selfless friend had always been the better spy. But Seb had been lured away by the Prime Minster himself and was helping to create an entire police force for London, so Jake now found himself with the responsibility of the ever-expanding secret service they had created together. To his greater surprise, he rather enjoyed it.

He paused briefly outside his brother's door, wondering if he should wake them at this ungodly hour, then realised Jack would have his guts for garters if he didn't. Jack had quite exacting standards and took his responsibilities very seriously. Those same morals now made him a well-respected magistrate. A man who judged men solely by their deeds rather than their reputations and understood what it meant to be poor.

He tapped lightly. 'Jack, Letty. It's time.'

A few seconds later his brother's dark head appeared, grey now just at the temples but still fiercely handsome. 'Have you sent for the others?'

'Footmen are winging their way to their houses as we speak.' Houses which all stood within the walls of the estate. 'They won't be long.' They never were.

Several hours later and three of them were pacing the floor of the Great Hall, while Joe was irritatingly calm and watching them with amusement as he polished his spectacles. Spectacles his scholarly eyes now needed all the time.

'I thought you said that this labour would be quick!' Snapping at him made Jake feel less helpless. He'd been banished from the birthing room by a very stern Bella some time around dawn, instructed in no uncertain terms to *leave this to the ladies* because he was getting in the way and all his pacing and hand wringing was stressing his poor wife. When the wives all ganged up together, there was no arguing with them.

'It's only been three hours.'

'It feels like three weeks! Why don't you go and write a paper or something!' While his practice was still loyally based in Retford, Joe was now one of the leading lights in the Royal College of Physicians and his words of wisdom were relentlessly hung on by medical students the length and breadth of the land. His calm brother merely grinned in response.

The distant newborn cry had Jake breaking into a run, but he was met at the door by Cassie and Letty. The two sentries took their guard duty very seriously. Their folded arms and firmly planted bodies wouldn't let him pass. 'You can't come in until Bella says so.'

'The hell I can't!'

'Oh, let the poor thing in.' Fliss's voice, strong and healthy, filled him with relief. The door opened and Jake practically floated in, mesmerised by the sight of the fuzzy dark-haired bundle in his exhausted wife's arms. She held out the baby and he took it. Cradling it close. Behind him he felt his brothers, all peering over his shoulder to see the latest addition to the growing Warriner brood. The baby's eyes opened and stared blurrily at him. Deep blue, not the usual blue of a newborn—Warriner blue.

'I told you so.' Joe grinned and held out his hand and Jack huffed before smacking a pound note into it.

'One of these days, one of us *has* to produce a child with their mother's colouring!' But alas, now all seventeen of their combined children were Wild Warriners through and through, thankfully the only thing they had inherited from their troublesome ancestors.

'Never mind the colouring. What is it?' Jamie limped forward, leaning on the incongruous floral cane his talented third daughter Thea had painted for him. Like Jack, he was greying slightly too, and just like Jack it only improved his appearance. He and Cassie still created magical children's books and remained perfectly content to spend every minute of every day in each other's company.

'A girl.'

'Two from two, then. Pay up.' Joe held out his hand again for Jamie to slap another pound in it, then flapped his winnings in the air. 'Never argue with science, boys. A girl was inevitable.'

Jake had no words. They all smiled as he staggered to sit still, cradling the precious bundle. Already, he loved his daughter unconditionally, just as he did the other three. But really! Fate seemed determined to give him an apoplexy with yet another cruel joke at his expense.

'I am the father of *four* daughters.' He was doomed.

Jamie grinned and patted him on the back. 'And I'm the father of five. Between us we have ensured that the little girls now outnumber the little boys.' Jack and Joe had four sons each. All carbon copies of their fathers. Competition between the two sexes was fierce as each child was stubbornly competitive—just like

their sires. 'I'm rather glad I lost that pound now. We have the bigger team.'

But Jamie didn't understand. He'd never been a rake like Jake and still slept the blissful, restful sleep of the ignorant. The man illustrated books, for pity's sake. He and Cassie had constructed a perfect, fairy-tale world in which good *always* triumphed over evil. But Jake lived in the real world. He'd played an active part in it. A very active part. He knew every single way a rake could waylay one of his precious daughters and worried about it constantly. He was already schooling the eldest two on what tricks to look out for. In a year or two, if he could keep it a secret from Fliss, he was going to teach them all how to shoot a gun and how to kill a man with their bare hands…

His wife squeezed his hand in understanding. She saw the way he tossed and turned at night when all the messy and complicated feelings intruded his dreams and his vivid imagination played with him. 'It will all be all right, Jake. You'll see. This one will be as feisty and fearless as her sisters.'

'And her mother.' He kissed her softly and they both gazed in adoration at the tiny miracle they had made. Yet another blessing in a life filled with them.

The lovely moment was interrupted by the heavy sound of an army stomping up the stairs as the children arrived back from the village. Jonathan and Serena had volunteered to take them all to the bakery to get them out from under the adults' feet, but the first Warriner to arrive was Edward, Joe's studious second son. His nose was bloodied and the wire rims of his spectacles were twisted out of shape.

He smiled at Bella, displaying the charming gap

from where he had recently lost his two front teeth. 'Chivers says we have a new cousin!'

'Oh, good gracious! What happened to you!' His mother began to fuss, then they all stared agog as the rest of their children filed in, in various states of dishevelment. Even the little ones clinging to Jonathan and Serena's near-adult hands sported scuffed knees and torn clothing. Sixteen battle-scarred next-generation Warriners with fire burning in their distinctive bright-blue eyes and steel in their spines.

'Have you all been fighting again?' Letty asked sternly. 'Could you not give it a rest on today of all days?'

Sixteen heads shook in consternation; all denying what they did noisily every single day.

'Not this time. That nasty blacksmith's son and his gang took Nick's toffee apple.' Edward grinned at his companions as he retrieved the sticky confection from his pocket and held it aloft in his grubby, grazed hand like a trophy. It was covered in twigs, leaves and enough grit to render it inedible. 'But *we* hunted them down and *we* got it back.'

'Of course we did.' Jonathan ruffled the younger boy's hair affectionately, as was his right as the leader of this new pack. The future. Their legacy. 'And that boy is an idiot as well as a bully. Surely every nodcock with half a brain knows by now? When you mess with one Warriner, you mess with us all.'

* * * * *

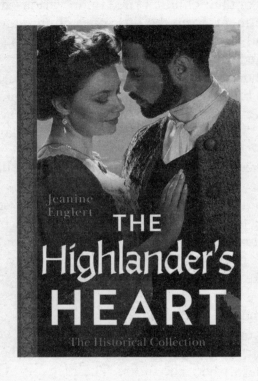